THE UNSEEN

JACOB DEVLIN

THE UNSEEN

ISBN print:: 978-1-945519-01-7
ISBN ebook: 978-1-945519-00-0

Copyright © 2017 Jacob Devlin
http://authorjakedevlin.com/

Library of Congress Control Number: 2017930018

Cover design by Michelle Johnson
https://www.facebook.com/BlueSkyOverBoston/?fref=ts

Blaze Publishing, LLC
64 Melvin Drive
Fredericksburg, VA 22406
Visit us at www.blazepub.com

First Edition: May 2017

FOR MY NIECE, KARINA VIVIANA.
MAY YOUR WORLDS ALWAYS BE FILLED WITH
WONDER AND LOVE.

"Everybody's youth is a dream, a form of chemical madness."

- F Scott Fitzgerald

CHAPTER ONE

THREE DAYS AGO - WONDERCITY

He stood on the top floor of the highest tower of the dark city, wondering if her presence would ever fully leave him.

Queen Avoria had disappeared only moments ago, stepping through the mirror on the wall as if it were a bowl of water, and just like that, the King of Hearts was alone again. Cornelius Redding had one empty throne beside him, though the beehive of his mind was full to bursting, no thanks to the powerful scent Avoria left behind. It was like a rose had been drowned in sweet vanilla and then tossed to wither away in a fiery dumpster.

The windows of the throne room offered a full view of Wonderland in every direction. Cornelius walked a full circle, surveying the land and wondering where Avoria was now. He wondered if he'd see her again, perhaps after she acquired all that she wanted in the New World. Of course she would succeed, as she'd brought Cornelius so close to conquering the World Between. His work was nearly done, but only a few steps remained.

With a snap of his fingers, Cornelius summoned a lanky guard and passed him a large key. "Chazk," the king said, "bring me the prisoners from cells L and C in chamber number seven."

The guard gave a dutiful nod and disappeared behind the elevator doors.

It had become something of a routine for Avoria to bring the old man and the little girl into this room, as was evidenced by the moonflowers that grew through the floor and the curious museum of woodwork that had bloomed around the throne room over the years.

Cornelius would have to do something about these damned statues. There were seven in total, four female and three male, none of which Cornelius recognized—except for the one that blocked his view of the plains.

She stood against the window, a smoothly carved woman of about thirty-five years old. Since the subject was a young girl, her face had grown a bit longer and had lost its childish naivety, but other than that, her features hadn't changed.

Cornelius stroked his chin with gloved fingers as he studied the wooden statue. Under his breath, he muttered, "I wonder how you got this way . . . Alice."

In a sudden fit of rage that caught even himself by surprise, Cornelius whirled around, scooping up the mace he kept by his seat, and brought the weapon's heavy head down on the carving with thunderous force. The statue he called Alice burst from head to toe in an explosion of dust and splinters, one of which pierced Cornelius's glove and bit into his thumb. His breath became forced and wheezy, and he almost didn't hear the guard's footsteps enter the room.

"Your Majesty." The guard's voice was lower than usual, which Cornelius instantly recognized as an attempt to keep the nerves in check.

The king turned to find his guard leading a frail old man and a young girl into the room. Whereas the guard stood tall and resolute, his escorts fell to their knees, the girl's messy blond hair masking her face in a thick mop.

"I've brought you your prisoners," Chazk said, his voice returning to its normal register. "Will there be anything else, Your Wondrous?"

Cornelius lowered his mace, took three steps and breathed, "Get out."

The guard turned on his heel. "Y-yes, sir."

"Not you, you blundering bandersnatch!" Cornelius barked.

Chazk planted his feet. As he lowered his chin in shame, the old man and the girl looked up, revealing their dirty, wide-eyed faces. Their mouths were both open, as if they hadn't dared to believe the king's words.

"I'm talking to you two," Cornelius said. "I want you out of my tower. Now."

The old man spoke first, his voice raspy from lack of use. Avoria had never given him permission to speak. "Sir? I don't understand."

"I said *get out*." Cornelius reached into the strap of his boot and plucked out an ivory knife, tossing it before the old man and causing him to jump. "I'm not jesting with you, Carver. Take the knife and that disgusting little girl with you."

The old man cleared his throat. His words rang more clearly. "But where are we to go? The Ivory Queen will never allow—"

"The realm of wonder is no longer Avoria's dominion. That privilege rests with me alone." *Or so it will.* Cornelius stole a glance at a colossal faraway structure, the centerpiece of a city that seemed to glitter in the darkness. *Once I wipe out the last remaining pieces.* "Believe it if you will, Geppetto, but it was Avoria's wish that I release you back into the wilderness of Wonderland. Of course, you're no better off out there than you are in chamber seven, but frankly, I care nothing of your well-being. You were Avoria's burden. I'm not going to feed you anymore."

A glimmer of light crept into Geppetto's pale-blue eyes. He straightened his back and exchanged a glance with the girl.

Cornelius scoffed, a wheezy breath escaping from his throat. "Run. Before I change my mind."

Geppetto swallowed and pulled himself to his feet, his ankles quavering so hard that he had to lean against the windows for support. He offered his free hand to the girl and hoisted her up with a few concentrated tugs. Cornelius doubted either of them weighed much anymore.

"Gretel," Geppetto whispered. "We're *free*."

"F-f-free?" the girl murmured as she looked up.

Cornelius grabbed the mace again and slammed it on the ground next to his former prisoners. "*Leave!*"

Geppetto took the girl's hand and broke into a run. "You heard him, youngling! *Go, Gretel, go! Run! Run!*"

Gretel and Geppetto disappeared behind the elevator doors, leaving Cornelius huffing again as the numbers ticked away their escape to the ground below. *Ninety-one, twelve, forty-two, seventy-six, ping!*

When his respiration returned to normal, Cornelius folded his hands in front of his waist and turned his attention back to the glittering city far away. *Mine,* he thought. Wonderland belonged to the Hearts. It wasn't for the Spades to share. There was a time when Cornelius had pondered the idea of a civil discussion with the city's leader, but Avoria, the queen of the Old World, had changed everything.

Avoria had a presence Cornelius would never fully understand. When she was condemned to Wonderland, he was simultaneously enraptured and terrified, intrigued and repulsed. He kept her in his sight but never much closer than arm's length. He offered her shelter; she offered him power. Every time he thought he had explored the full depths of her darkness, she revealed yet another layer until he had no choice but to fall into her trance. Before Avoria left to conquer new worlds and complete her ascent to power, the symbol of the Heart had grown to provoke fear and panic, something Cornelius had come to embrace. Plus, Avoria had given him an army. His ranks had grown by at least five hundred, and while he had no idea where they came from, he decided he would be foolish not to use his new soldiers. They would begin their assault of the Wondertown in roughly one week. With the Diamonds and the Clubs out of the picture, nothing would get in their way.

Nothing would ever threaten Cornelius's rule.

Nothing except for perhaps the soft blue light that suddenly opened in the skies directly above the plains.

It started as a pinprick in the clouds and then opened into a full column that beamed directly from the sky to the ground. Cornelius's gaze jumped from the city to the light, and his pulse accelerated as he watched three individuals fall from the sky. Avoria's orders rung through his memory: *The next poor souls to stumble into Wonderland . . . the children . . . break them, will you? Tear them apart and rattle their spirits. Pit them against each other. And then, unleash your new Hearts.*

"Chazk," Cornelius said softly. "Binoculars. Now."

The guard handed Cornelius a clunky device filled with many holes, and the king fitted it against his eyes, focusing on the three falling children, who all appeared to be sleeping: a blond spiky-haired boy, tall and lean; a shorter, goofy sort of boy with inky dark hair, and—

Her.

Cornelius adjusted the binoculars and looked again. Unmistakable. He'd seen that face before, albeit on slightly paler skin and underneath a blond head of hair instead of the silky dark mane that framed the new head. The daughter of Alice, live in the flesh.

When the children landed, it was as if Wonderland swallowed them up. The wicked, gloomy plantlife had grown so tall as to conceal their whereabouts, but Cornelius made a mental note before the blue light receded into the clouds and disappeared.

Avoria had expressly forbidden Cornelius from taking any of the children's lives, but really, what right did she have to rule a king? He had plans to break them, all right, but it was not Avoria's prerogative to specify how to do so. Anyone with ties to little Alice deserved to suffer for what she took from him, for beneath her golden hair and behind her once innocent face, there was a killer.

Alice killed the Queen of Hearts.

Cornelius didn't know how he knew, but he knew. Alice went to trial, and before she could be punished, somebody helped her escape. She fled the dark city. She fled the World Between. And it was thought that she would never be seen in the realm of wonder again.

But her daughter! Life has its poetry. Justice comes full circle.

"Here, have these." Cornelius shoved the binoculars back into his guard's hands, and at last he yanked the splinter from his thumb and crushed it under his boot. "Give me my cape."

"Of course, sir." Chazk wore a puzzled expression, brows angled and lips flat, but he had long been trained never to ask questions.

"I know you have queries, Chazk," Cornelius said. "If you must know, it's time for me to address my army. Some curious guests have arrived tonight. These ones are quite special, you know. Do you know what we do with special guests, Chazk?"

The guard tilted his head like a confused dog. "I—"

"Oh, I'm quite sure you know." Cornelius gestured to the mess of splinters and dust at his feet.

A few minutes later, the King of Hearts had five soldiers, including Chazk, in a straight line in front of him, and he addressed them outside of his tower. "You're looking for a girl of average height. Dark hair. Green eyes. Likely strong-headed, like her mother. Take her friends too if you must, but *she* is your priority. Understood?"

In response, the soldiers each stamped a foot, nodded, and slammed the tips of their spears on the ground.

"Good. Now go!" Cornelius roared.

As he watched his team disappear through the metropolis and toward the plains, the clouds darkened overhead, and their ghostly shadows loomed after the soldiers. Cornelius stalked back inside his tower, and when the doors thundered shut behind him, he smirked.

"Let the game begin, daughter of Alice."

CHAPTER TWO

Three stubborn thoughts plagued Alicia Trujillo's mind when the castle blossomed into view. One: *The last time I went inside a castle, a queen was about to eat my soul.* Two: *Why is this world so much darker than I remembered?* And three: *Rosana must truly hate me.*

Alicia was sure her friends still didn't believe her, especially Peter— or as he now preferred to be called, *Pietro*—but she knew where their children were. There would be a lot to explain if they ever saw their kids again. Alicia stole a glance at Carla as they approached the portcullis. Her dark hair frayed and her eyes bloodshot, the woman had barely spoken since they met three days ago. Poor thing. She was the only New World native in the group, probably still wrapping her mind around all she had recently learned about the *other* world.

According to Pietro, Rosana knew everything. She had journeyed with him, along with Pino's son, Crescenzo, looking for their families and trying to find a way into the Old World. Alicia still had trouble believing in the existence of different worlds, and she had even *lived* through everything: the man who kidnapped her from New York and imprisoned her in a ruby sleeping pod for half a year, the mad queen to which that same man sacrificed a part of her soul, and the fairy guardian who had been partially responsible for *everything*.

"Why do you think she summoned us?" Pietro wondered, cutting Alicia's thoughts short. Apparently he hadn't changed much since boyhood. Did he ever stop talking? "Doesn't Violet have more important things to do? Like, sprinkle fairy dust all over the Old World and fix it?"

"Don't *we* have more important things to do? Like *find our son?*" Wendy puckered her lips. "Oh, wait, I forgot. You don't care what happened to Zack."

"That's not fair, Wendy, and you know it. I'd appreciate it if—"

"Five minutes," Pino said calmly. "Hold it together for five minutes, my friends." He flexed his slender fingers. Lately he'd been fidgeting a lot, bending his elbows, and rolling his shoulders. He claimed that the New World hadn't treated his joints too well, and he relished his new flexibility. "This is Violet who asked for us. It must be important. We'd be wise to hear her out."

The group stopped in front of a marble fountain stained with blood and surrounded by uneven piles of dust. Four stone pillar stumps haunted the courtyard. Pietro folded his hands and rocked on the balls of his feet.

"What's on your mind?" Pino grasped Pietro's shoulder.

"Like, don't you even doubt her, just a little bit? After everything that's happened?" Pietro's gaze flashed between Alicia and Pino. "You ever think about the night we left this place? About Violet's request? Bring her the mirror so we could go to a new world and grow up?"

"I try not to think about that night."

"Well, think about this. How come Hansel grew up? How come Violet let us take the mirror, knowing it was gonna wake a queen she worked so hard to put to sleep?" Pietro crossed his arms and furrowed his brows. "Hmm?"

"She told us that growing up is funny in this place," Alicia said. "Some people peak as children and live forever. Some people just keep on aging."

Pino nodded. "And I suppose she cared so much about rescuing her father that she was willing to do whatever it took. We've seen what that looks like."

"I *know* what it's like," Wendy said. "Because we're going to do whatever it takes to get our kids back, right?"

"We'll get your kids back," a female voice cut in. The iron portcullis shot up, and there she stood: Violet, tall, winged, and glistening. Her lips were tight and her eyes were cold, quite unlike any expression Alicia had seen from the bubbly fairy. Alicia wondered if Violet had heard the entire conversation. "Please, everyone, follow."

Alicia and the group trailed Violet into the castle. Alicia took note of the suits of armor positioned around the foyer, along with the paintings centered about the walls. She rubbed the goose bumps off her arms. When she visited the Ivory Queen's dark castle twenty-five years ago, the paintings had been the first thing to catch her eye as well. She'd seen two of the portrait subjects before: Liam, the handsome man with the piercing blue eyes, and Snow, the jovial woman with the silky dark hair. The two were madly in love. Of course, their circumstances had roughed up their appearances a bit when Alicia last saw them. The woman barely left with her life, bandaged, bruised, and vengeful.

As for the man, he'd been standing stone still in the corner of the dining hall, polished to a sunny shine. Even in the fragile light of a tiny candle, the statue held a brilliant twinkle. Every inch of the prince's body was pure gold, and he held Alicia's attention even beyond the enormous table, at which eight people were already seated.

Alicia hadn't formally met him, but she was there for Prince Liam's last stand. He defied the Ivory Queen and stood up for the man who wronged him. He defended Hansel when she turned her venomous gaze to him, even managing to wound her twice before her skin closed up and healed like new. Avoria froze Liam with the heel of her hand, vowing that the worst was yet to come before she disappeared into thin air.

Alicia approached the gold statue, awestruck by the fact that such a handsome man was capable of such a wrathful expression. Unable to resist her wonder and curiosity, she ran a finger along the cold metal, gently grazing the prince's shoulder. *I'm sorry this happened to you,* she thought. Perhaps if Alicia had never asked Violet for a way into the

New World, Avoria never would have woken up, and Liam might be living happily ever after with—

"Don't you *touch* him!" A pale hand batted Alicia's wrist away. She spun around to find a long fingernail in her face, belonging to a woman whose beautiful features were strewn with distress. "Don't touch him now or ever."

Alicia massaged her wrist. "I'm so sorry! I didn't mean—"

"Everyone, this is Snow White," Violet said quickly. As Alicia stepped back, Violet flashed her an apologetic twitch of the lip. She waved to a group of short, stocky men at the table. "We are also joined this day by the seven dwarves—"

"Miners," one man corrected.

"Of the Woodlands," she went on. "Finn, Jinn, Chann, Bo, Garon, Wayde, and Zid. Two other individuals are expected to join us shortly."

At first, Alicia felt a swell of appreciation and calm sense of safety. She'd met the men long ago, and they defended her from a serpent longer than a football field. For that, she would always be grateful, but there was one other incident she needed to address. She approached one of the men and stood behind him with her arms crossed. The man tucked his chin into a raggedy shirt and squeezed his eyes shut, his rosy cheeks glistening with sweat.

"You took me away from my daughter," Alicia said. "I wanna know why."

The man tapped his thumbs together while his friends looked on. "I'm so sorry!" he wailed. "It wasn't my choice! Mister Hansel was going to kill—"

"'Twas not the fault of Mister Hansel, Wayde," another man interrupted.

"Garon is correct," Violet said. "We've nobody to blame for our hardships except for Avoria, the Ivory Queen of Florindale."

"What about you, Violet?" Wendy challenged. "You're the one who got us to wake her up, and for what? Your own selfish need to have your father back? Where *is* Mr. Bellamy, anyway? How has he supported us?"

Violet's wings sagged. "I made a mistake that day. But I don't regret it! Thus far, no true losses have occurred as a result of our actions that night, but we have many gains. You have children!"

"Children that we lost," Wendy said. "Don't forget that. And what about Gretel? She still hasn't come back, has she? *No true losses?*"

Pino cleared his throat. "Violet, do you have a plan?"

"Yes. Won't you please direct your attention to the center of the table?" Violet flicked a wrist and a purple cloud formed, expanding and crackling with tiny lightning bolts and glistening stars. A cluster of faces appeared as the cloud faded away, revealing four misty figures hovering in the air and rotating about the table: two men, a woman, and something like a scaly lion with horns.

"This is the Order of the Bell," Violet said. "They're my guardians. Merlin is the most powerful magician I know, and one who may know something about Liam's condition. Augustine Rose of the Woodlands may look small and sweet, but she's wondrous with poisons and firearms. Sir Jacob Isaac Holmes resides in Clocher de Pierre, and his strength and rhetoric are unrivaled. As for Captain James Hook, never have I known a man more clever or brave. We need the Order's help to defeat Queen Avoria, and I have not been successful in contacting them. They won't answer the bell ringer."

Pietro stroked his chin. "I was told they're all dead," he said matter-of-factly. "Mulan told me she's the only survivor."

Violet wove her fingers together, leaving the pointers touched together and pressed against her lips. "There was . . . a bit of an incident," she said, "and it left the Order out of commission. I, too, assumed that they had lost their lives. In truth, their fates were similar to your own. They lost a piece of their soul. But when Mulan and Crescenzo smashed the mirrors, the Order returned. They may not be the same as they once were, but they live, as do you. I have a suspicion that the thousand men and women who first battled Avoria have returned as well, but I have not been able to locate them."

"So what's our plan?" Pino asked.

Violet snapped her fingers, and the rotating faces vanished. "Unite," she said. "I want to expand the Order of the Bell. I want to reassemble my warriors, train you for battle, and bring down Avoria once and for all."

Wendy raised an eyebrow. "I'd like to point out that Violet still hasn't addressed how we're going to retrieve our kids. I'm sorry, Violet, but the last time we trusted you . . ." She waved her hand to Pietro, Pino, and Alicia. "I don't even know how to finish that sentence. Tell me why we should serve you now."

A silver tear appeared in the corner of Violet's eye. "Don't talk to me like I'm my stepmother! You do not serve me! You serve your realm. Your *children*. Your children are not here, and neither is Avoria. Consider that before you blindly reject me. If you help me, you can help them too. But there is much more at stake than seven precious souls this time. We're talking about an entire world, and all of those you care about, but we cannot succeed *alone*." Violet paused, surveying the faces in the room. "This brings me to my final instructions. Snow White, I have a separate task for you."

Snow White finally tore her gaze from the table and looked at Violet.

"I need you and a friend to go to the edge of the realm, where the Tower Nuprazel stands. At the top of that tower, a door has appeared. Someone needs to open it."

Snow raised an eyebrow. "I'm not doing a thing until I have Liam back."

"I know you grieve, dear," Violet said. "But if you can help me open that door, we can help you get your revenge on Avoria for separating you and Liam in the first place."

Alicia saw the gears whir to life in Snow's head, and for a moment, Alicia was afraid of her. Her eyes were so cold, stark with hate and resolve.

"If I may ask"—Garon thrust his burly arm in the air—"why is a door so important? What lies on the other side? If it is the New World, we are not ready to face Avoria."

Violet nodded. "A valid concern. Rest easy, Garon. It is not *the* door. I believe many of you are familiar with Esmeralda?"

There were a few nods.

"Long ago, Esmeralda made a prophecy for me. She told me that a door would appear in our hour of need. On the other side, there lies a resource of vital importance that will one day lead us in battle should we succeed with our tasks. Now I understand." Violet gestured to the gold statue in the room, running her thumb along the prince's shimmering knife. "Is this not our hour of need? Should we not do everything we can to reclaim what's lost?"

Silence fogged the room.

Snow nodded stiffly. "I'll go. Who must I accompany?"

Violet gestured across the room, and a man and a woman stepped through the doors. The woman was short and thin with subtly angled eyes and a full suit of crimson and gold armor. The man was much younger, though his eyes were weary above the thick scar on his cheek. The silence in the room grew thicker, pointed gazes like knives converging on the brown-eyed man.

"*Hansel!*" Snow shrieked. In a heartbeat, she was on her feet, her hands curled into tiny balls. She lunged for the man, but the new woman stepped between them and spread her arms.

"Stop," the woman ordered. "This man is not to be harmed."

"Step aside," Snow fired, to which the woman bore no reaction. "I can't have him in my home. In fact, I don't want any of you here. *Get out.* All of you. I'm going to kill Avoria myself."

"Snow, please. We are in this together," Violet said calmly. "You, and us, and all the people of the realm. Speaking of which, Mulan, what was the result of your mission? Have you any news to report?"

Mulan pulled up a seat while Snow paced back and forth, fuming and taking deep breaths. Hansel folded his hands at his waist and lowered his head.

"There is very little development," Mulan replied, removing a red gauntlet with gold swirls. "We were unable to locate the book of which you spoke."

Violet chewed a purple lip, nodding and staring off to the side. "And the Order?"

"I can't find them," Mulan said flatly. "Nobody has seen them. The people of Florindale won't help. They look the other way when I mention Avoria's name. They don't see her as their responsiblity."

Violet tapped her thumbs together. "I worried about this." She blew a long breath. "We'll just have to try harder to reach them."

"That's going to be extremely difficult now that our ultimate goal is against the law," Mulan said, drawing everyone's attention.

Mulan produced a yellowing sheet of parchment and held it in front of Violet. "Miss Violet, when did your father reassume the throne?"

Violet's brows crinkled. "He never really abandoned it. What's going on?"

Mulan passed the parchment along the table. "These notices are all over Florindale. I suggest we be discreet."

When Alicia intercepted the bone-dry parchment, her stomach dropped. She read the words over and over again, barely daring to believe them.

All persons attempting to leave
the Old World
shall be caught
and jailed effective immediately
by order of King Dominick Bellamy

CHAPTER THREE

THE OLD WORLD: SNOW WHITE'S CASTLE

Pino went so long without his wife's touch that every time he took her hand, his fingers tingled. He and Carla stood together on one of the castle balconies, their fingers laced like vines as they gazed toward the Woodlands. "Tell me what's been on your mind."

With her free hand, Carla massaged her eyelids and moved a strand of hair from her forehead. "It feels like just a week ago that I was sitting at home, reading some cozy mystery and thinking about what to make for dinner. Then all of a sudden, I wake up and three years have gone by. And I'm in fairytale land and my husband's Pinocchio and there's an evil queen and a fairy is giving me instructions and my son is gone and . . ." She drew a trembling breath and Pino squeezed her silky palm, which had begun to sweat. "I'm very overwhelmed right now. How are you so strong?"

"*Amore mio.*" *One of our wedding songs,* thought Pino. "I keep wanting to ask you the same thing. Most people's minds would snap like wood if they woke up in our shoes. But look at you. And look at us. I finally have you back, Carla! I *never* stopped believing that we would find each other again." He kissed his wife's wrist and clasped it in both hands. "That's why I'm strong."

Carla buried her head in Pino's chest. "I love you, Pino."

"Ohhh, man!" Pietro called from the doorway. "Wendy, let's go. Pino and Carla are getting too serious for me."

Pino turned his head. Pietro removed a hand from over his eyes and flashed a cheesy grin while Wendy leaned against the archway with a weary smile. "What's up, you two?" Pietro asked. "Am I interrupting? Good. I wanna talk to you." He plopped down on the ground and leaned forward with his elbows on his knees. "I just overheard Violet telling Mulan she wants to send me to Neverland."

Pino waited for the bad part, but Pietro stopped talking. "Is that not a good thing?"

"No!" Blowing a raspberry, Pietro rubbed his cheeks. "She was saying something about wanting to recruit the Lost Boys. My friends. But it's not gonna be the same! It's probably all *Tales from the Crypt* since Avoria woke up. Guys, I don't wanna know a dark Neverland. Virginia's my home now."

"Besides," Wendy said, "isn't that the first place one would think to look for Captain Hook?"

Pino finally understood why Pietro was so upset.

"Hook and I can't stand each other. Even if we're on the same side of the war now, if we spend too much time together, we're going to end up killing each other."

Pino's eyes rested somewhere on the horizon, where he observed two figures walking away from the castle. "Know who really might end up killing each other?" He aimed a callused finger at the screaming, traveling couple below. "Those two."

Pietro squinted and leaned over the balcony. "Snow White and Hansel. You know, I still don't get why Violet included *him* in all of this. Like, I wouldn't trust that man with a *napkin*."

"And she's just lost her love. There's nothing more dangerous than somebody with nothing to lose." Pino sighed.

Ten feet below, Alicia tiptoed out the castle doors, a burlap sack resting on her shoulders.

Alicia looked up at Pino and put a finger to her lips. "You didn't see me leave."

"What are you doing?" Wendy hissed. "We're supposed to wait for further instructions and leave *together*!"

"I'm going to get my daughter back."

"What? How?"

Alicia shrugged. "I'll find another rabbit hole, or I'll click my heels together three times. I don't know, but I'll do it. And I'll do it alone, the way I learned to do everything else."

"Alice, come on—"

"It's Alicia," she said sharply. "And unless you're coming with me, save your breath, because you're not going to stop me." Nobody moved. "That's what I thought. Good luck, guys." Alicia turned on her heel and marched away from the castle like a toy soldier.

By the droop in his friends' shoulders, Pino could tell nobody else felt right watching Alice walk away on her own, but in true fashion, Pietro broke the silence. "You know, you should meet her kid. If Zack, Rosana, and Enzo ever find themselves in front of the Ivory Queen . . ." Pietro let out a long whistle. "That lady's gonna have one big fight on her hands. I feel kinda bad, actually. Maybe they'll annoy her enough that she'll just turn *herself* into gold."

"The queen," Pino remembered. "You think the Order will really help us? Or that we'll even find them?"

Carla tugged on Pino's sleeve, her bright eyes fixed on a point below the castle. "Maybe we should focus on *that* first?"

Pino traced his wife's eye contact over the walls and beyond the forest, where a black, broken line moved into the trees. It took him a second to realize that the line was made up entirely of people on horseback, at least a hundred of them, and they were charging toward the castle at an alarming speed. His jaw dropped. The ground vibrated against his heels as he heard the hammering of hooves on dry ground.

"Who *are* those people?" Wendy asked.

Suddenly, Mulan charged onto the balcony, fully clad in her armor. She shoved Pino and Pietro out of the way and studied the horizon. "Oh, no."

Violet followed close behind, took one look, and conjured her wand. "We must leave at once."

Pino's pulse thundered so hard he almost missed his heartless wooden body. "Why?"

The hundred horsemen burst forth from the forest, and Violet aimed her wand at the squadron. "My father's here."

Pino barely had time to process the words before a flaming arrow sailed past his ear, leaving a thin ashy circle on the castle walls before igniting a broomstick on the floor.

On second thought, maybe it's better I'm not made of wood.

"Oh, sh—!" Pietro ducked just in time for a second flaming arrow to rocket over the balcony. "Violet, I don't think so highly of your pops."

Wendy screamed and threw herself over Pietro's crouching body. Pino and Carla seized each other's hands again.

Violet flicked her wrist and a geyser of water shot out of the tip of her wand, dousing the oncoming arrows and bringing several horsemen to the ground. When the arrows kept coming, Mulan produced a thin sword to deflect the artillery.

"Pino, Pietro, you all need to *leave*," Violet commanded.

"Why are they here?" Pino asked.

"If I know my father, he means to stop us from assembling the Order and combatting Avoria." Violet waved her wand back and forth, continuing to spew the stream of water. "He's deathly afraid of her. That much has never changed."

Pietro extended a hand to Carla. "I can fly us all out of here."

Carla swallowed hard and took Pietro's hand. Wendy held the other. "Pino, Mulan, you'll get my ankles," Pietro said. "Ready? Good luck, Miss Violet! We'll be back with the Order in no time! Up, up, and away!"

Arrows rained and the thundering horsemen drew closer than ever. A powerful rumble shook the castle from below, and Carla lost her balance. Pino stole a look over the wall. The army was in the courtyard. Two black boxes, each larger than his home in the New World, sat on a pair of carriages that required four horses to pull them along. At the head of the first carriage stood a tall, elderly man with a hooked nose and a red, glaring gaze that locked onto Pino's face.

Pino flinched. "Why aren't we flying?"

"Hurry!" Violet cried.

The group waited for Pietro to lift them off the ground. His eyes were scrunched shut in concentration, his nose aimed at the sky, but nothing happened. Their feet stayed planted.

"Why isn't anything happening?" Pietro wondered. "Why can't I fly? Miss Violet, I can't fly!"

Suddenly, Pino caught a chill and a mouthful of water as Violet's cascade rebounded and surged back over the balcony, knocking everyone to the floor. Stars exploded in front of him as he reached up to plug his nose. The water was a wrecking ball, simultaneously blinding him and cutting off his respiration. Instinctively, he rolled like a log and held his breath.

When Pino reached dry ground, he stood and shook the water out of his hair. He rubbed his eyes. All of his friends still lay unconscious. Violet's hair fanned out beneath her in wet clumps. Her wand fizzled out, and the geyser tapered to a lazy drip.

Thick footsteps stomped through the castle.

Pino took a knee and shook his friends. "Get up!"

Violet stirred.

"Come on, Violet! We need to leave!" Pino's heart raced as Pietro, Wendy, and Mulan shifted mechanically to their feet like wind-up toys.

Carla remained flat on her back, where a thin pool of blood diffused into a puddle of water. Her beautiful face looked disturbingly calm.

Oh no. "Carla!"

Pietro rushed to Carla's other side and pressed his fingertips to her wrist. "She's okay!" A crash sounded in the dining room below. "But we need to leave, Pino!"

"I won't leave my wife," Pino said. "Just go. Get Wendy out."

Instead, Pietro took Carla's arm and placed his other hand under her head. "Together?"

Without a word, Pino shoveled his hands under his wife's body and helped Pietro lift her. A scream echoed in the foyer, and Pino's blood curdled.

Violet.

"Go, go, go!" The two men moved as fast as they could with Carla between them. Pino stumbled over the corner of a rug and almost lost his grip on her.

When they made it to the staircase, Pino insisted on carrying Carla on his own.

At the bottom of the steps, Mulan and the seven miners had engaged a group of armored men in combat. Pietro took the steps two at a time. When he reached the bottom, he delivered a swift kick to an armored man's chest, driving him into the dining room table.

Bo narrowed his eyes at Pietro, tossing an apple up and down in the air. "Showoff. I could have taken him, manchild."

"*Where's* Wendy?" Pietro answered.

Mulan knocked a man to the ground, looked at Pietro, and shook her head sadly.

Pietro squinted. "What does that mean?"

"They took her." Garon pointed to one of the black boxes outside the castle doors. "She's in yonder cage with Violet, Finn, and Jinn. These vermin are taking us all away."

"No!" Pietro raced for the doors. Before he could reach them, a man in black armor seized him from behind and carried him out as if he were a doll. "Hey! Put me down, man! Let me go!"

After what seemed like an eternity, Pino reached the bottom of the steps, where Mulan continued her duel with three men at once. She ducked and spun and kicked with relative grace, but her brow glistened with sweat and her movements slowed.

When a fourth man entered the room, Pino knew the battle was over. The four warriors circled Mulan, and as Pino tried to rush past them, one spun around and lifted Carla effortlessly off his shoulders. Pino barely heard his own screams as the knight marched her out of the room and another pair of steel arms lifted Pino off the ground from behind. When Mulan turned to hit the armored man in the back of the neck, the remaining knights carried her away.

"No!" Pino shouted. He wasn't going to have the chance to save his son. He wasn't going to help Violet unite the Order. And somewhere out there, Avoria was going to get stronger and more terrible until Pino's second home would fall to darkness.

The man marched Pino away, leaving behind a room of broken china, splintered wood, torn fabric, and tiny drops of blood. The last thing to catch Pino's eye was the golden prince.

Liam had somehow gone untouched, which wasn't to say that he went undisturbed. Pino could've sworn the statue looked even angrier, as if wanting revenge on the men that stormed his home. A feral glint shined in the prince's eyes, his teeth ground together, and the dagger in his hand was poised for an action he'd never get to take.

Outside, the air was eerily still, laced only with the crunch of armor on dry ground as the man carried Pino to one of the enormous black boxes outside the castle. The warrior stopped by the carriage, lifted his visor, and spoke to the old man.

"This is the last one, my lord."

The old man known as Lord Bellamy wrinkled his nose. "Mm. You're certain there aren't more?"

"Quite certain, my lord."

Lord Bellamy scratched his head through a thick felt cap. "Curious. I could have sworn there would be at least three others."

"Shall I go back and check?"

"No, no, that won't be necessary. The others shall fall into our hands in due time." Lord Bellamy leaned forward, curling his bony fingers around the reins and piercing Pino with a crimson stare. "Don't worry,

Carver. You're all going to the same place . . . a place from which you or your people cannot prescribe ruin to my realm. Ever." He leaned closer, his greasy nose coming inches away from Pino's forehead. "And so it is ordained."

Lord Bellamy jerked his thumb behind his shoulder, and the knight marched Pino dutifully to the black box. A second knight opened a padlocked door and helped heave Pino into the container. Blackness pounced on Pino's vision, and the door slammed behind him.

Then came the snapping of a lock and the whipping of reins.

The ground lurched.

Pino's heart sank. He had failed Violet. Carla. Crescenzo.

For a while, all he heard was the drumming of hooves and the crackling of wagon wheels over cobblestones until a familiar voice took over. "Hey, Pin? That you?"

Pino's spirits lifted a little. "Pietro? Yeah, it's me."

"Wanna get off my leg, buddy?"

"Oh, sorry." Pino shifted, and faint shapes hovered in the dark. First there was Pietro's face. Then Mulan, her arms crossed and her expression hard. Wendy sat at Pietro's other side, her legs pulled tightly into her chest. Then there was Violet, her wings folded like wilted flowers.

Against an entire wall of the box, a few of the miners sat in a line.

"I don't suppose any of you brought some food, did you?" one of them whispered.

"Aw, shut up, Chann!"

"I'm only asking!"

Pino rubbed his eyes so hard little flashes of red and green swirled in his eyelids. "Is my wife in here?"

Pino was answered by a brand new voice he had never heard before: that of an elderly woman on the far side of the carriage. "I think she may be lying next to me, dear. Did she hit her head?"

Mulan gasped, and Pino faintly made out her widening eyes. "Who is that? Who just spoke?"

"Why, it's me! Augustine Rose! Really, Mulan, you don't recognize me? Merlin, I think you may need to work some magic on her memory, dear."

"Merlin's with you, too?"

"Aye!" a jolly voice answered. "We are all here, of course! Sir Holmes and Captain James are in the other carriage. Lady Fortune is rather temperamental this day."

"Hey, Violet," Pietro said, "I found the Order."

As Pino crawled in the old woman's direction to find Carla, Violet answered, "Such wonderful news! I only wish we'd found you in better circumstances." She sighed. "I'm never speaking to my father again."

"What can we do?" Wendy asked. "How do we get out?"

"It's hopeless," Violet moaned. "My father is a notoriously stubborn man. We're going to Florindale Prison, and we're likely going to be there for good. Our efforts have failed."

"So we're doomed?" Pietro asked. "We spend the rest of our lives rotting away and eating cat food in a box? Please say no."

"Isn't there *any* hope?" Garon chimed in. "How do we get out of a king's prison? What about the New World? The Ivory Queen?"

With another sigh, Violet stretched her legs, folded her wings beneath her, and lay on her back. "All we can do is wait, I'm afraid. If anyone can save us, they're a world away. Those who evade my father haven't much time to run. All I can say is, may the light be with us."

Pino curled up next to Carla, pulled her close, and hugged her. He had learned to count his blessings long ago, and having his wife beside him was one of the few he ever needed. Wherever they were going, they were going together. That was almost all that mattered, except for one thought that would continue to gnaw at his mind; *Crescenzo*, he thought. *My son, please be safe, wherever you are.*

CHAPTER FOUR

WONDERLAND: DARK PLAINS

"Somebody checked to make sure Enzo was still breathing, right? I'm really starting to worry about him."

"Relax, Rosana. He'll probably wake up any minute now."

"But earlier you said he usually snores. Why's he so quiet?"

At the sound of his name, consciousness trickled into Crescenzo's still body. When he recognized the voices, they spurred Crescenzo to life. He sat up and his eyelids popped open, his muscles protesting at the sudden movements.

Sure enough, Zack Volo stood there with his arms crossed and a brooding expression painted on his face, framed by the first traces of facial stubble. "Welcome back to life, Frankenstein. You had us pretty scared, buddy."

"Morning, sleepyhead." A warm, feminine laugh sounded behind Crescenzo. "I was beginning to think you'd never wake up."

Rosana flashed all her shiny teeth at Crescenzo. He wondered if she'd been a dream, a beacon of light in a twisted nightmare. He turned his head and took in the rest of his surroundings. Black, bulbous rose buds unfurled above him, and bees the size of horses circled around them until a Venus flytrap snapped one in its jaw-like leaves. A tangerine moon glistened in the sky. And he'd been sleeping on a bed-sized leaf. Maybe he was still dreaming.

"You've been out for a while," Rosana said. "You blacked out after we found out where we were."

All the weird memories slowly knitted themselves back together. Red carpets. Magic mirrors. Darkness. "Right. We're still in Wonderland?"

"Wondercountry, youngling." An old man in brown overalls and tattered shoes hobbled over to Crescenzo and laid his bony hands on his knees. "It's good to see you awake."

"Enzo, you remember meeting Geppetto?" Rosana asked. "Your grandfather?"

Crescenzo rubbed his face. His mind buzzed as if someone had conked him on the head with a soaring apple again.

Crescenzo shook Geppetto's hand. "It's nice to meet you, um"— *What do I call this guy?*—"Uh—"

"Geppetto."

"Geppetto," Crescenzo repeated. He stood and dusted off his jeans. His Converse had holes in them, and the Captain America shield had almost completely faded from one of his favorite shirts. "Did we find my parents? Pietro and Wendy? Rosana's ma?"

"It's just us," Rosana said. "I think, somehow, we went *through* the mirror when you smashed it. That might explain why Gretel's here."

"Gretel," Crescenzo repeated. "The little girl!"

"Yes. She's on Heart watch," Rosana said, as if that were supposed to make any sense to Crescenzo. "A little after you passed out, these ugly shadow things and armored people with spears attacked us. Geppetto says the shadows come from the Ivory Queen, but the soldiers are something else. We managed to get away, but we're on guard in case they come back. We take shifts watching for them."

"Shadow things?" Crescenzo said. "Like Zack's shadow?"

Zack sighed, twisting and peering at the ground. Crescenzo wondered if he was checking to make sure his shadow was still behaving, but it clung dutifully to his heel.

"I still don't get what you guys are talking about," Zack said.

"Your shadow flies," Crescenzo said. "Just like your dad's. *You* flew us to the magic mirror in the Old World."

Zack shrugged. "Whatever you say, buddy."

Crescenzo locked eyes with Rosana and tried to say everything with his face: *Did you tell him everything already?*

Zack picked up a rock and chucked it at Crescenzo's feet. "Stop trying to have secret face conversations. You and I have already been doing that since Kindergarten. Yes, Rosana told me everything. Mom and Pops are Peter Pan and Wendy. Your dad's Pinocchio. *Your* mom's Alice, and now we're in Wonderland."

Rosana put her hands on her hips. "You're pretty good at that face-reading thing. How did you do that? Second"—she swatted Crescenzo's shoulder—"now that you're awake, I suggest we start trying to find a way out of here. Enzo, Avoria was here in Wonderland, and she escaped before we got here. That means she's probably with our families, which means we still need to save them."

Crescenzo spun away and put his hands in his hair. "Avoria escaped from Wonderland?"

"She was a nightmare." Geppetto nodded, his hands clasped at his waist. "Look at all *this*." The old man gestured at their surroundings. Dark. Decaying. Malevolent.

Crescenzo watched in horror as a wolf spider the size of a house leapt from one rosebud to another, stringing a silver thread between the petals. He'd had ideas about what Wonderland would look like if it were real. He never imagined it would look so evil, like the ground itself wanted to swallow him up.

"Things weren't like this when I arrived. On the contrary, the land was actually quite beautiful. There was warm sunlight. There were puffy clouds. There was color, my boy! Scarlet and cerulean and honey and jade! The people were *happy*."

"How long have you been here?"

"Time is irrelevant here," Geppetto said, prompting Crescenzo to glance at his watch and see that the second hand had stopped. "I remember not when I arrived, but I arrived in a mineshaft. I had *just* told my boy to stay out of the mines, but I'd always find him playing there. So when Pinocchio didn't come home one day, I went looking for him, and I stumbled into this new life. That silly boy. Never once did he listen to me!"

"That's just so weird to think about," Crescenzo said.

"Is it not? My son being a father!"

"More like my dad being your son. You've been here all this time? Since that night?" The thought made him dizzy. For twenty-five years, Geppetto lingered here hoping to bring his son back home for supper, while Crescenzo *did* eat dinner with Pino every night and had what one would consider a perfectly normal life. Until Hansel abducted Crescenzo's parents and turned Crescenzo's world into a madhouse.

"I've seen it all since my arrival," Geppetto said. "Avoria brought the darkness with her. The land turned against itself. War wiped out the people Avoria left alive. This is important for you to know, my boy, because I imagine we'll be here a long time. Wonderland is not known for hospitality or unity. We currently stand in Wondercountry, once governed by the Diamonds. To the west, there's Wondertown. The Spades live there. Finally"—Geppetto pointed to a massive dark structure looming in the distance—"that's Wondercity, land of the Hearts. You need to stay away from them, no matter what. I've been there. Don't even cross into their territory."

A chill ran up Crescenzo's spine. "So, then, where are the Clubs?"

"They used to have the beaches, the forest, and the underground. And then they didn't anymore. Dear boy, the Clubs are gone, along with the Diamonds. Avoria got them." Pain flashed across Geppetto's eyes, and Crescenzo wondered if there was more that his grandfather wasn't saying before he cleared his throat and continued. "The Hearts and the Spades wrestle for control now. The Spades seem to favor a plan of unity, but the Hearts are far more hostile. Their king, Cornelius Redding, has been on a rampage ever since the Queen of Hearts was assassinated during the Jabberwocky Wars. And what's more: Somehow, their ranks have actually grown since Avoria left. Considerably."

Crescenzo couldn't believe what he was hearing. He focused on what he knew. Avoria was said to have killed half her people in the Old World and was sucked into a mirror once upon a time. Crescenzo had assumed the mirror was just a prison made of silver walls.

All along, the mirror was a portal to Wonderland, where the queen took out an entire population while she planned her escape.

"If Avoria escaped," Crescenzo said, "doesn't that mean—?"

"She took our parents' souls," Rosana finished, her eyes wide.

Crescenzo's heart sank. Violet. Mulan. Liam. Wayde. Mr. Bellamy. Were they still alive? Had Liam found Snow White? Had Hansel been defeated? Most pressing of all: Were Crescenzo's *parents* still alive?

Crescenzo sank to his knees, his heart assaulting his ribcage. His mind flashed to the last time he saw his dad. His father seemed to have gone stiff, paralyzed in his bed. Looking back on that day and knowing what Crescenzo learned a little over a week ago, he wondered if his father's condition had anything to do with his past as a wooden puppet. And he was going to ask Pietro to take him to the *hospital*. Would they have been able to do anything? In the end, it didn't matter. Hansel, under Avoria's influence, abducted Crescenzo's father first, just minutes after he had told Crescenzo, "*I love you.*" Crescenzo's reply echoed in his head. *Yeah, Dad. Don't strain yourself.* Were those really going to be his last words to his father? His last words to his mom were even more underwhelming. She said, "*See you when you get home?*" And he said, "*K.*"

"No!" Crescenzo screamed. The word came all the way from the bottom of his lungs, hung in his mouth, and quavered with sobs. His throat felt raw. "No!"

A warm pair of arms wrapped around Crescenzo's chest from behind. Rosana rested her head on Crescenzo's shoulder, her dark hair spilling onto his shirt.

"We didn't save them," he choked.

"They're not gone, Enzo," Rosana whispered.

"How do you know?"

"Because the proof is standing right in front of you." Rosana let go of Crescenzo and straightened her back. "Zack. Zack is proof that our families are okay."

Crescenzo wiped his eyes and approached Zack. His friend seemed to have grown taller while he slept for the past two years, standing about half a head over Crescenzo now. Zack's hoodie was slightly too small for him as well, exposing a bit of his arms beyond his bony wrists. Strangely, his spiky blond hair didn't seem to have grown at all, but a thin layer of stubble framed his face, making him look a lot like Pietro.

"You're really okay?" Crescenzo asked.

Zack gripped Crescenzo's shoulders. "I'm fine, Enzo." Zack paused and tilted his head. "I *know* I'm fine."

"Do you remember anything?" Rosana asked.

"I just remember going to take a nap. I did have some weird dreams, but I woke up and there you two were, along with that evil mirror. And here we are now. Maybe we're *still* having weird dreams."

"The point is that you're okay. That means they should all be okay," Rosana reasoned. "We just have to get back to them before Avoria makes another move." She fiddled with the strings on her red cloak. "Until then, I guess we're on Heart watch."

"No, dear girl." Geppetto shook his head. "It is my turn. You three stay and chat. Crescenzo gets the next shift. And watch out for that wolf spider!" The old man hobbled away, disappearing behind a thick black vine.

Zack clapped Crescenzo's shoulder and said, "You're related to that guy. I can't even imagine having Geppetto for a grandpa." After a quick pause, Zack said, "Wait. I don't even *know* my grandpa."

Crescenzo scoffed. "We're not *really* related. It's not like we share blood."

"Same family tree, though," Zack pointed out. Realizing that he'd made a joke, a smile spread slowly across his face. "Hey, get it? Tree? Because your dad was once made out of—"

"I got that. Thanks."

Rosana giggled.

Crescenzo's attention snapped away from Zack when a sharp, broken breath erupted somewhere behind him.

Zack craned his neck. "Aw. She's still crying."

"That poor thing!" Rosana shook her head. "I shouldn't have told her anything."

"Who?" Crescenzo asked.

He spun around and saw Gretel approach from behind a tree, her blue eyes angled to her small feet, which she dragged along the mud. She appeared no older than about twelve, which boggled Crescenzo's mind because, as he recalled from Violet's story, Avoria pulled Gretel into the mirror twenty-five years ago.

Tears cascaded down Gretel's face, but the strangest part was what happened when each tear fell from her chin. A creamy-white flower burst from the ground where the tear splattered, its petals blossoming into a delicate star shape. Crescenzo noticed that a long trail of flowers followed Gretel, and they gave off more radiance than anything Crescenzo could see in Wonderland.

"Moonflowers," Rosana said. "That's what she calls them."

Gretel approached the group and wiped her face with the back of her arm, finally making eye contact with Crescenzo. She smiled behind her tears. "You're the other boy. You're awake!"

"Um." Crescenzo wasn't quite sure what to say. During his last journey with Pietro, Crescenzo never really figured out how to greet fairytale characters. It felt a little awkward, having read or heard so much about their lives. It was like going to class and being partnered with a kid he'd never talked to but learned a million rumors about.

"Hi." *Your brother kidnapped my parents, and he's a horrible person.*

"I wanted to tell you that I'm sorry my brother was mean to you!"

Gretel might as well have read Crescenzo's mind. Her lip quivered violently. "It's my fault. I shouldn't have tried to help the witch. Now I'm here forever, and my brother is a . . ." Flowers sprouted in a circle around Gretel's feet as her tears rained on Wonderland.

Oh gosh. Gretel looked so sad that Crescenzo almost wanted to hug her, but there was another part deep down that felt she was right. Maybe it *was* partially her fault Hansel had turned to darkness and sacrificed innocent souls to a mad queen. Crescenzo crossed his arms and stuck his nose in the air. "Just be grateful your brother was willing to do so many terrible things for you."

Gretel wept even harder.

Zack rubbed the back of his neck, shaking his head at Crescenzo. *Not okay, man.*

"*Enzo!*" Rosana hissed. She pulled Gretel into her arms and made soft shushing sounds. "Gretel, have you seen the bunny anywhere? Or the kitten?"

Gretel sniffled. "I can't find them."

"Good," Zack muttered under his breath. He elbowed Crescenzo and said, "Whenever you see this so-called *kitten*, you'll think Rosana is crazy. I've seen kittens before. This thing is—"

"You'll know that I'm *what* now?" Rosana might as well have flown. One second, she had Gretel in a firm embrace. The next, she had a dagger of a fingernail in front of Zack's nose, her other hand curled tightly around his wrist.

Crescenzo smirked. He knew Zack's mistake. Rosana hated the word *crazy.*

"Nothing," Zack said quickly.

Rosana tightened her grip on Zack's wrist and leaned in so that their faces were about an inch apart. "*What did you call me?* Didn't we already talk about this?"

"I'm sorry! It just slipped out. That was my bad."

"Okay, people!" Crescenzo darted over to his friends, crushing several moonflowers in his path. He pried his hands between Zack and Rosana and shoved them apart, laughing nervously.

Zack crushed his lips together like he was trying not to laugh. He massaged his wrist while Rosana glared back. Gretel fidgeted with the edge of her dress, wrapping a small length of it around her finger.

"Great times joking around together, huh?" Crescenzo added.

"He wasn't joking," Rosana said. "We discussed that word while you were asleep. He was just trying to spite me."

Crescenzo turned to Zack. "You wouldn't do that. Right?"

Zack jammed his hands into his pockets. "Of course not! It's not like I'm trying to offend her. Look, I'm sorry. It was an honest mistake."

Crescenzo sighed. "Rosana, you can't take Zack too seriously. I mean, you know what a goof Pietro is. This is his son."

"Seriously, Enzo?" Rosana said. "You're taking his side? You feel like he's justified in calling me insane just because he's Pietro's son?"

"I'm not picking sides!"

"Well, you jumped in between us, so what's your verdict, Judge Judy?"

Crescenzo shifted his gaze back and forth. Zack. Rosana. Zack. Rosana.

Rosana shook her head. "The fact that you have to think about it means you already chose." She threw her red cloak around her back with a decisive twist and promptly vanished into thin air. Her voice receded along with the sound of footsteps. "Gretel, wanna come with me? These guys are jerks. I'll get us out of here myself."

Gretel wiped her cheeks, flashed Crescenzo an apologetic smile, and scurried after the sound of Rosana's voice. Crescenzo stood dumbfounded and angry, his nostrils flaring while Zack paced back and forth.

Rosana's voice quavered just a bit when she said, "Find your own way out of Wonderland."

CHAPTER FIVE

WONDERLAND: SOMEWHERE ON THE PLAINS

When the rain came down, Rosana regretted her decision to leave the boys and her shelter behind. The withered, car-sized leaves hadn't seemed like much of a roof before, but once she was soaking wet and out in the open, Rosana wanted them back.

"Where do we go?" Gretel asked.

Rosana resisted the urge to flop down on the ground and cry. "I don't know, Gretel. You have to know this place better than I do. Are there hotels here? Any kind of place to stay?"

She was heartbroken when Gretel shrugged.

"It's fine," Rosana managed. "I've done this before." *As if being homeless in Wonderland is anything like being homeless in New York.*

"Can we go back now?"

"No," Rosana said. "I don't want to talk to those boys right now."

Gretel grinned so widely that her eyes were almost closed.

"What?" Rosana asked.

"You like him!"

Rosana pulled the tail of her cloak over her head. "Who? Zack? No!"

"I mean the other boy!"

Rosana raised an eyebrow. "What are you talking about?"

"Enzo! You looked at him a lot when he was napping. And you got mad at him, and he just looked at you like this!" Gretel's expression contorted into a dumbfounded, goofy wide-eyed mask. She had to blink the rain out of her eyes a few times. "Like a puppy."

Rosana snickered. "You're silly. He looked at me like that because he was being stupid."

"Girls always call boys stupid when they're in love with them," Gretel countered. "And they fight with them, too. And look at them when they go to sleep because they're bored and they want them to wake up."

Rosana scoffed. "How do *you* know all this, Gretel? You're too young to know about love. And I don't love Crescenzo. I don't even like him like that. We've only known each other for . . ."

Rosana didn't know how long it had actually been. *Come to think of it, it feels like forever.*

Gretel made a sour face. "Do you think he wants to kiss you?"

"That's enough."

Gretel giggled.

In the short time she had known her, Rosana grew attached to Gretel. It warmed her heart, watching the girl play and listening to her make up stories—or recite memories, Rosana couldn't tell—and hearing her talk about her brother. The worst part was when she asked Rosana what happened to him. Rosana knew she couldn't lie. Perhaps she was too honest about his dance with darkness.

"I talked to him once," Gretel had explained. "I asked him to help me, and he promised."

"He tried to keep that promise," Rosana assured. "He just hurt a lot of people to do it. Do you think that was right?"

Gretel didn't have an answer.

"How did you talk to him?" Rosana pressed.

"Avoria made me stay in Wondercity with her. Sometimes she talked to my brother in a big mirror, and my brother answered. She never let me talk to him except for one time."

Rosana made a mental note: *Look for that mirror.* She shuddered. She'd never even seen Avoria, and it chilled her to the bone to think about Gretel spending all that time with the witch.

Gretel cried a lot when Hansel came up in conversation, and it made Rosana's heart sore. It wasn't hard to comfort Gretel because Rosana fully understood. She missed her mother. Then again, sometimes Rosana had even missed her mother when they still lived together. She was always something of a mystery. She was a friend, willingly taking her daughter out for pizzas or movies and providing homeschooling for her, but the rest of her was largely unseen. Rosana knew little about her mother's ambitions or previous jobs, her travels, and she knew even less about her father. She used to wonder how she could understand herself if she barely even knew her parents. How could she forge a future for herself without understanding where she'd come from?

Somehow, Rosana started to feel differently when Enzo waltzed into her life.

Ugh. Rosana shook her head, furious at herself for thinking of him. She didn't need Enzo. She didn't need the boys. But she needed Gretel, somebody Rosana could care for and protect from the harsh new realities she was discovering every day. Somebody like a little sister.

And that was why Rosana readied her fists when a dark shadow appeared on the horizon, humanoid and hovering above an ashy-looking tree with blood-red leaves. The shadow roughly possessed the figure of a tall and slender woman, but with some freakish variations. The shadow had fingers like snakes, tickling the ground and intertwining in haphazard patterns.

Behind the shadow, five pale men in crimson armor marched toward Rosana and Gretel, spears in hand.

"They're back!" Gretel cried.

Rosana spread her arms at her sides, her heart in her throat. "We can't outrun them this time," she breathed. "Get behind me. Under the cloak."

A stark, hot wind blew from the shadow's direction, mixing with the rain. The humidity suffocated Rosana's skin.

Gretel obeyed Rosana's order and hid under the cloak. Rosana threw her hood up and shut her eyes, concentrating on a blank space in her mind. *We can't be seen. We're not here. We don't exist to you. Pass by and be gone.*

The rain and the heat intensified, and with it, the shadow's presence grew . . . fixated on Rosana. She had been discovered.

The raspy voice pierced the air and echoed in Rosana's head. *"The daughter of Alice tries to hide in Wonderland. What a laughable idea. You cannot hide in Wonderland any better than the moon could hide amongst the stars."*

Rosana opened her eyes. The shadow hovered in front of her face, rippling like a flag in the wind. She could see right through it, just as she knew the shadow could see through her cloak. The five warriors lifted their weapons.

"You will face her fury, daughter of Alice, if only you live to see the world beyond wonder again."

Rosana suddenly wished she hadn't left the boys. Geppetto at least had a knife. All Rosana and Gretel had between the two of them was the cloak, but its defenses were useless.

The shadow curled its fingers and lunged, making a sweeping glide for Rosana's face. Rosana turned, wrapped Gretel in her arms, and dove to the ground, splattering both girls with mud. The shadow made a clean pass over Rosana's back.

"Gretel, run! Go back and get Geppetto and the boys!"

Gretel scrambled to her feet. A single moonflower shot up from the ground. "But—"

"*Go!*"

The shadow revolved in the air and spoke again. *"Don't leave me so soon."*

The rain poured even harder. The shadow ascended and began to spin, creating a sort of cyclone of water and darkness. The cyclone funneled from the clouds to the ground, growing with every rotation. Rosana clawed at the ground until she was back on her feet, ready to run with Gretel, but she was too late. Gretel had already been sucked off the ground, and she whirled in the air, her tears indistinguishable from the rain.

"*Gretel!*" With her mind blank and her reflexes in hyper drive, Rosana made an instinctive lunge for the twisting vortex. At the rate it was spinning, it was on the verge of becoming a full-blown tornado. But before Rosana could get any closer, something caught her elbow.

She turned and saw a man not much older than her but certainly much taller. Her gaze immediately flew to the man's eccentric straw top hat, adorned with a steel band and snugly seated on top of a head of dark, wavy hair.

"Let me go!" Rosana protested. "That's my friend!"

Gretel's wails grew louder, and then softer, and then louder again as she whirled in circles.

The wind caught the back of Rosana's cloak and tore her out of the stranger's grasp. She soared into the vortex at breakneck speed. She had gotten used to flying already, thanks to Pietro, but Rosana decided that being whipped around in a waterspout was nothing like flying. She screamed and took in a mouthful of rainwater. The world blurred before her as she soared higher and higher. Below, the stranger had engaged in combat with the five warriors, kicking and elbowing and twisting with impressive dexterity.

At the center of the cyclone, a face of soft indentations appeared on the shadow. It was like a black transparent jack-o-lantern, its mouth curved in a sinister, asymmetrical grin.

Every time Rosana opened her mouth to scream, water invaded. Even her nose was filling up. If the shadow thing wasn't about to eat her, liquefy her, toss her around in a tornado for all eternity, or whatever its intentions were, Rosana was surely going to drown.

But then she saw the top hat.

It left the man's head and appeared somewhere beside her, hovering upside down below the shadow. On the ground, the stranger was shouting and the five warriors were incapacitated at his feet. "By the power of the Spades, I hereby banish you from the realm of wonder! You are *not* welcome here!"

If Rosana hadn't seen what the man did next, she wouldn't have believed it. The top hat whirred like a Frisbee, faster and faster until it matched the cyclone's speed. A blinding light shot out from the opening, forcing Rosana's eyes shut.

The shadow produced the most horrible sound, as if gnawing on a chalkboard. But its volume decreased, the cyclone slowed, and the light softened until Rosana could open her eyes again. The hat was still whirring and shooting its piercing light, but it also seemed to be drawing the shadow *into* it. The creature stretched into a thin line, and then it fell into the top hat like a loose rope.

Without another sound, the hat stopped spinning, the rain ceased, and the light evaporated.

Rosana fell to the ground, landing much more softly than she'd expected, followed by Gretel. The top hat flittered back toward the ground like a feather. Its owner caught the hat with a gloved hand, a strange mix of brown leather and dark bits of metal like the rest of his outfit. "Whew!" the man huffed, shaking muddy droplets from his hat before securing it neatly to his head. "This world has gone mad!"

Rosana climbed to her feet and helped Gretel up, flicking water out of her hair. Catching her breath, Rosana wrung out her cloak, hugged the little girl, and then faced the stranger.

"You just saved our lives," Rosana said.

"Please. I merely did what any sane man would do." The stranger removed his hat again and scratched his head. "Maybe."

"Who are you?"

The man bowed so low he came back up with wet specks of dirt on his nose. "Matthew Hadinger, at your service. You may call me Matt. I belong to the court of Wondertown and was on a pleasant mission before that abomination showed up. His Majesty, the King of Spades, requests the presence of a one Miss Rosana Trujillo in his royal court this night. Are you she?"

Rosana's heart skipped a beat. *This has got to be a mistake.* How could she possibly have caught a king's attention already? She answered cautiously, "Why does the King of Spades request her presence?"

Matt dipped an arm into his mysterious hat, which was only about as tall as his hand was long, but he plunged elbow-deep without tearing, bulging, or otherwise affecting the hat in any way. He swirled his arm around, licking his lips and squinting in concentration. "I *know* it's in here somewhere. Nope, that's not it. Oh, there! Wait, nope, that is a candy wrapper."

Rosana smiled.

Finally, Matt produced a periwinkle scroll and unfurled it with a flick of his wrist. He replaced his hat, cleared his throat, and then read from the scroll. "*On this night, His Majesty, the King of Spades, would like to cordially invite the fair Miss Rosana Trujillo to attend an Evening of Wonder in the royal ballroom, where she shall then be entreated to tea and live entertainment, a seven-course meal, and a formal meet and greet with the king himself.*"

Rosana thought the cyclone must've rattled her mind. How could the King of Spades know who she was, and why would he invite her to eat a seven-course dinner with him? However, she had to admit that Matt had piqued her curiosity. She took a deep breath and said, "I am Rosana Trujillo."

Matt grinned, a bright, regal sort of smile that brought out a gold twinkle in his eyes. "Of course you are! Miss Rosana, do you formally accept His Majesty's invitation?"

Rosana bit her lip and looked down, her gaze resting on Matt's boots, which must have been at least a size fifteen. She didn't know this land. She and Gretel were alone. Avoria walked on these grounds. There was still so much to understand. "I . . . I don't know."

"I do understand your hesitation," Matt said. "But I believe you'll find the event most enlightening. I sincerely hope you'll join us for a spell. If you step through the doors and it doesn't feel right, you are most entitled to turn around. I would even escort you back here myself, should you prefer to brave these wicked grounds instead. You have my word."

Rosana sighed. It wasn't in her nature to trust strangers, but after all, Matt just saved her life and offered her genuine kindness. Could she really walk away from him after that? Would it hurt her to suspend her distrust for just one evening?

Gretel tugged on Rosana's cloak, and when Rosana looked down, Gretel nodded her approval.

"It does sound like fun." Rosana put a hand on Gretel's shoulder. "May I bring a guest?"

Matt squirmed a bit, his shoulders ruffling as if shaking off water. "Well, the invitation *was* rather specific." When the smile weakened on Gretel's face, Matt quickly added, "But I'm sure we can find a way to accommodate any guest of Rosana's at the Evening of Wonder!" He took a knee and extended his arm. "Who might you be, little miss?"

"My name's Gretel!" Gretel grabbed Matt's hand and gave it a confident shake.

To Rosana's amusement, Matt exaggerated the handshake, hopping around and flailing his arms as if Gretel had zapped him.

"Whoa, wow, gee!" he cried.

Gretel laughed so hard that tears came to her eyes, and Rosana couldn't suppress her smile any longer.

When Gretel let go, Matt shook out his wrists and dusted his knees. "That was quite a handshake, little miss, and you are *very* strong! Have you been eating from my gardens?"

Gretel rocked from side to side, tiny giggles sounding through her nose. "No, silly!"

Using his free hand to tousle Gretel's hair, Matt removed his cap once more.

"Let's see. I believe I may have something you'll enjoy." Matt reached into his hat, this time going all the way to his shoulder. He produced a colorful packet about as long as his forearm and held it out to Gretel. "These are my favorite. I do hope you like chocolate?"

Gretel squealed with delight and tore a corner off the candy wrapper. "Thanks, Mister!"

"Please, call me Matt! And, of course, I'm sure I'll find a little something for Rosana." Matt faced Rosana, winked, and reached into the hat. This time he pulled out a dozen fresh roses, all a deep, crisp shade of red that shimmered in the moonlight when he tilted them. They were even bundled together with a silver ribbon. "A token of our new friendship."

In truth, Rosana wasn't usually a big fan of flowers. They took space, time to maintain, and then they crumbled all too quickly. Who decided they should be a symbol of everlasting love? As an act of casual friendship, however, they were beautiful. Rosana took Matt's bundle and smiled, rubbing a silky petal between two fingers. "Thank you for these. That was very kind."

"Well, it's what any sane man would do." Matt bowed once more. "After all, we're going to be friends now! I can hardly wait for tonight's Evening of Wonder."

"Same." *Don't disappear. Don't disappear.* Rosana knew she was turning red. She eyed the fallen soldiers on the ground. "But . . . what about these guys?"

"We'll see to it that these broken Hearts have a proper burial." A sudden layer of pain deepened Matt's voice. He was silent for a minute, and then he spoke with new energy. "It is high time our factions cease our meaningless feud and catch Mr. Redding's attention! In the meantime, shall we proceed? I have much to show you!"

Matt offered his elbows to Rosana and Gretel. The girls accepted and hooked their arms into his.

"I think, my dear friends, that some surprises will await us in Wondertown tonight. Surprises of the grandest nature."

CHAPTER SIX

WONDERLAND: SOMEWHERE ON THE PLAINS

"I already told you: She's not my girlfriend."

"Don't lie." Zack jabbed Crescenzo's shoulder. "Your nose is kinda big to begin with."

Crescenzo pinched the bridge of his nose and ran his fingers down to his nostrils. "Hey! It's not *that* big."

"I'm just kidding," Zack said under his breath. "Don't be so sensitive. You're acting just like Rosana."

Crescenzo frowned. "That's kind of uncool."

Zack arched a brow. "How long have you known her?"

"How long have *you* known her?"

Zack paused for a second and then nodded as if to acknowledge Crescenzo had a point. "Touché. So, listen. Did my dad really jump off the Empire State Building?"

"You mean fly off?" Crescenzo scratched his head and then rubbed his arms. After the rain had cleared, a thin chill settled into Wonderland and raised tiny little bumps over his skin. "You know, I wasn't awake for that part, but yes. Your dad can fly. It's badass."

Zack crossed his legs pretzel-style and threw a wad of dry sticks into the small fire he had made. "I wish I could fly. Even though I'm afraid of heights and all, I wanna fly. More than anything."

"What kid doesn't have that wish?" Crescenzo asked. "I'd give just about anything. Especially knowing we have to fight Avoria one day.

I wish I had a *thing*, like how your shadow can fly and Rosana can disappear and Gretel does that thing with her tears. I need a thing. Help me come up with something."

Zack rubbed his chin. "Well, you can draw. You play drums."

"You think I should draw all over Avoria? Or drum on her head until she explodes? Come on, Zack, help me think."

"Well, what do you want me to say? I don't know how to fly or cry moonflowers. I think I know just what you need, though. Let's spar!"

"That's your thing, too," Crescenzo said.

"How do you know? For all you know, I could've lost my touch while I was sleeping. If nothing else, it'll be good for us to get some practice. We'll *both* get better. Come on. Grab a stick."

Crescenzo felt a sudden surge of affection toward his best friend and a slight burst of annoyance toward Rosana. Hadn't Zack tried to apologize to her for making an honest mistake? And yet Rosana remained too stubborn to see what a loyal friend she could have in Zack, who had never forgotten how to cheer Crescenzo up. Crescenzo was pretty sure that with or without a soul, Avoria could never change the fact that Zack had one of the best hearts anybody could ask for. He always knew what to say.

The two grabbed a pair of sticks and quickly fell into an easy rhythm of striking, blocking, and counterstriking, but it turned out that Zack hadn't lost his touch at all. In fact, it seemed he had grown stronger and quicker than Crescenzo remembered. Sparring was still Zack's specialty.

They quit when Crescenzo's stick broke and his stomach gave a heavy rumble.

"Hungry?" Zack asked, snapping his stick into manageable bits and throwing them into the fire.

"Starving. What do we eat here, anyway?"

Zack clawed into the trunk of a dark plant composed of black vines and bulbous, triangular leaves that towered over him. He peeled two vines apart, thrust his hand between them, and pulled out a green bean the size of his shoe. "Not much. Mostly these weird beans we have growing everywhere. There's also a river nearby. We can go out there soon if you want. Geppetto figured out how to filter the water so it's safe to drink. Wait 'til you see the fish. Some look like giant limes, and some look like oranges. They have tiny fins and huge eyes. They're the weirdest things I've ever seen, besides the aquamantulas."

Crescenzo's stomach dropped.

"It's what we call the water spiders. Picture an octopus, only here it's a spider."

"I don't think we need to go to the river," Crescenzo said as casually as he could. "So, fish and beans? Only thing is I'm allergic to fish, so, beans. Beans forever."

"Until we find a way out of here, that is. Which we will." Zack tossed his bean to Crescenzo and plucked another for himself. "For now, it's kinda cool if you think about it. You met your grandpa, we're in another world, we're hanging out and eating beans on a fire . . . I'm happy. How 'bout you?"

Crescenzo smiled. Zack was always the more optimistic one. "I'm wondering about our next move." Crescenzo tasted his strange wonderbean. To his surprise, it was amazingly filling and delicious, giving off an aftertaste of smoky bacon with a hint of lime. "How do you think we get out? Plant one of these and hope a beanstalk grows back to our world? Or should we be looking for another mirror?"

Zack swallowed a huge mouthful of bean. "You know what, Enzo?" He shook his head. "I really don't know. Maybe Rosana had the right idea. We won't find a way out if we stay put. Plus, those Heart soldiers are vicious. We have *got* to keep moving."

The boys didn't say anything through the rest of their dinner.

Geppetto appeared a few minutes later, swinging one of the lime fish by its tail. He threw it on a stick and sat by the fire.

"Where are the young ladies?" Geppetto asked.

Crescenzo and Zack looked at each other, each silently begging the other to answer.

"They ran away," Zack finally said.

Geppetto clucked his tongue. "I was a young boy like yourselves once. I know exactly what 'They ran away' means. You two *chased* the girls away."

Crescenzo tucked his knees into his chest.

"So, how did you do it?" Geppetto continued. "Did you pull their hair?"

Fess up, Zack, Crescenzo thought to himself. After all, Zack was the reason Rosana took off.

Zack stared back, his eyes pleading. *It's your turn to talk!* But it wasn't like Crescenzo could blurt out, "It's all Zack's fault!"

Unfortunately, that's exactly what came out of his mouth. As soon as it happened, Crescenzo winced and put a fist up to his forehead.

"Really? That's your side of the story?" Zack cut Crescenzo with a glare. "Because what I saw was Rosana storming off because she wanted to hear something specifically from *you*."

"You called her crazy."

"I told her I was sorry, and I meant it."

"Yeah but—"

"*Fine*," Zack snapped. "It's on *both* of us."

Geppetto cleared his throat and spoke through a mouthful of green fish. "I have a query." He peered at Crescenzo over his glasses. "Rosana got up and left because she was angry, no? And she took young Gretel with her?"

"Right," Crescenzo confirmed.

"So," Geppetto ripped another bite out of the fish, spraying lime juice into the air. "Did you not go after her?"

Crescenzo hung his head. Should he have gone after Rosana? He *had* thought about following her. He recognized that he should have worked harder to stick up for her—that much, he could admit. She didn't know that Zack was well-intentioned, and Zack didn't know much about Rosana, either.

But how could I have stopped her? Crescenzo thought. This was the same girl who tackled a dwarf in front of thousands of Hollywood red carpet guests. She knew it would be embarrassing, but she'd made up her mind, and her decisions were iron.

"Rosana's a big girl," Crescenzo said. "It wasn't my responsibility to stop her from walking away."

Geppetto raised an eyebrow. "She's your girlfriend. That makes it your responsibility, because she was clearly waiting for you stop her from—"

"She is *not my girlfriend!* Did everyone hear that loud and clear? I'm not going to correct either of you again, got it?" Crescenzo stood up and paced back and forth. "Besides, she won't be gone for long. After all, we're going to stop the Ivory Queen together. She'll come back once she cools down. Wait and see."

Geppetto set his fish down and folded his hands in his lap. His gaze became distant, drilling into the fire before him. "Those are the words you never want to speak, my boy. That is the assumption you never want to make. What you need right now is a good dose of honesty, and I'm going to give it to you. If you ask me, you're never going to see that girl again."

Zack winced. "Aren't *we* warm and fuzzy tonight?"

"*Stai zitto*, child!" Geppetto made a harsh zipping motion across his lips.

"Okay, I'll bite." Crescenzo scratched his head. "Why the pessimism?"

Geppetto shook a finger at Crescenzo. "I speak from experience. I speak of my son. Pinocchio was not yet ten years old when he ran away from home."

"Did he really run away from home?" Crescenzo interjected. "Or did you *chase* him?"

"Enzo!" Zack hissed.

"Just asking, not accusing." Crescenzo held both hands up.

Across the crackling fire, Crescenzo watched an intense glow trace his grandfather's eyes, which shined with tears. Finally, Geppetto blinked, straightened his back, and aimed a finger at Zack. "You. You're on Heart watch, now."

"Isn't it my turn?" Crescenzo asked. "I can go, too."

"No." Geppetto stood and tossed his fishbone into the flames. "I have a better idea for you. Come. Follow me to the river."

CHAPTER SEVEN

WONDERLAND: WONDERCITY TOWER

The king had watched the struggle from the top of his tower. When it was over, Cornelius Redding put his goblet through a window. It soared down eighty floors before it cracked the electric blue *S* on the neon marquee for the ocean-themed Wondershell Theatre.

It should have been so simple. Every element had been on his side: the shadows, the soldiers, Cornelius's personal guard, even the *weather*. So how in the world was the daughter of Alice still alive? And five of his soldiers were dead, including Chazk.

With a warm gust of wind, Cornelius's curtains burst open, and a tall, wicked woman with blood-red hair stared at him through the reflection of an enormous mirror. "Did you just try to kill the girl?" the woman asked. "After I *specifically instructed you—*"

"To break them!" Cornelius roared at the mirror. "That's what I'm doing, Avoria. Get out of my reflection. This is my show. Don't you have a world of your own to conquer?"

Avoria glared at Cornelius. "I've a few obstacles to overcome," she said curtly. "I'm on a property venture. But don't think my presence doesn't linger in the World Between, Cornelius. I'm watching you. I'm watching *all* of you. And I told you it was *my* prerogative to kill the daughter of Alice. If you take that away from me, I will peel your soul from your body."

"Silence, hag." Cornelius gripped two thick handfuls of curtain and swept the cover over the mirror, sealing Avoria's image away. A migraine pounded like a hammer at his skull. "Chazk, your life may have ended in failure, but I promise to avenge you." He turned to the empty seat beside his own throne and ran a finger against the grain of the velvet. "I'll avenge *both* of you."

Cornelius turned to the window, where a set of fireworks had just exploded over Wondertown, the land of the Spades.

A devious grin spread across Cornelius's lips.

That's where they're all going, he realized.

And since he couldn't count on his soldiers to work alone, he'd have to give them some personal support. He'd have to go after the children himself.

It was time to get out of his tower.

SOMEWHERE IN WONDERCOUNTRY

Soft snores and ominous growls filled the air as Crescenzo walked past toadstools in the dense forest. A pallet of colors littered the air, billowing from birds' mouths and changing hues with their intricate melodies. Sandpits hissed and popped, the acidic sand grazing Crescenzo's calf as he rushed to keep up with Geppetto. Memories of home filled Crescenzo's ears, from his mother's humming to his father's loving lectures. *You should be able to see the world, my boy.*

Crescenzo shook his head and looked at the sky. *Pretty sure this isn't the world you had in mind for me.*

While the memories of his family twisted his heart, Crescenzo stepped on a tree branch, and goose bumps shot up his arm when the wood started screaming at him. "*Ow! You horrible boy! Watch where you're stamping your dirty feet!*"

"*Hey!*" Geppetto spun around and pointed at the screaming tree branch. "I am Geppetto, renowned Carver of the Old World. I command you to be quiet and stop yelling at my grandson! Do you understand?"

Grandson. It was the first time Crescenzo heard Geppetto use the word. It didn't quite settle into Crescenzo's ears.

The tree branch mumbled something in protest, and Geppetto plunged his hand into his pocket and withdrew a slender object, bone-white with shimmering dark steel on one side.

My knife! Crescenzo thought. He reached into his own pocket and retrieved the knife that had come to him only days before when he crossed the threshold into the Old World.

Geppetto's knife could've been twins with Crescenzo's blade. When Geppetto aimed the blade at the shrieking branch, the branch went silent and he scooped it up.

Crescenzo looked at the wood as if it were a serpent. *Something is going to kill me out here.* "That branch just screamed at me."

"I should think that wouldn't surprise you after all you've seen already." Crescenzo frowned. Geppetto had a point.

"It just reminds me of the *Inferno*," Crescenzo said. "Don't the trees get mad when you break their branches? They're dead souls."

"Ah, you know your Dante!" Geppetto beamed. "Smart boy. *Nel mezzo del cammin' di nostra vita, mi ritrovai per una selv' oscura* . . . Don't worry. This isn't Hell, so far as I can tell. Close enough, though. Are you a good student, Crescenzo?"

"I guess. Solid Bs. I liked reading *Inferno*. Or the idea of it, at least."

"I remember your father being quite thrilled to start school. Too bad the interest didn't stick. Tell me, did he at least finish *liceo?* High school?"

"Yup," Crescenzo said. He gave Geppetto a thumbs up.

"What about that brat he used to play with? Percy? No, that's not right."

Crescenzo smiled. "Peter Pan. He goes by Pietro now. Yes, he finished high school. I think he even went to college in Arizona."

"That rascal is more educated than my own son," Geppetto muttered as he plopped down on the ground, still clutching the branch and knife. "Good for them, though." He fiddled with his knife, turning it slowly. "I wish I'd stayed in school. But there was only one thing I was good at when I was a boy, the only useful skill that stuck with me."

Crescenzo blinked and the tree branch was gone. Instead, Geppetto held a six-inch figure of Crescenzo. Knife resting dutifully on Geppetto's lap and smirking with obvious satisfaction, he offered the mini-Crescenzo to the real Crescenzo. "I learned to carve."

"*Whoa!*" Crescenzo traced his wooden counterpart with a fingertip. Spiky hair. Tattered Converse. Veiny hands. Soft dimples. "You did that in two seconds, and you didn't miss a detail!"

"Oh, I never do."

A crazy thought surfaced in Crescenzo's mind. "Do you think maybe you could teach *me* how to carve?"

"Why do you think I brought you out here? To fish?" Geppetto laughed, brushed a clod of dry grass from the ground, and ran his fingers along the dirt. He scrunched his eyebrows tight in concentration. Finally, he dug a small hole into the ground, plunged two bony fingers and a thumb inside, and uprooted a thick chunk of wood. With a clean *snap*, Geppetto broke off a hefty piece and tossed it to Crescenzo.

"Now carve it," Geppetto said simply.

Crescenzo stared down at the rough material. "How?"

"What do you mean *how*? Just carve it. You make one cut after another until you have a beautiful thing."

"Carve it," Crescenzo repeated. "That's the big lesson?"

"There's really nothing more to it, boy." Geppetto shrugged. "I suppose it's like drawing or playing with a yo-yo. You do it until you get better."

"*Hey*, both of those things are my hobbies, and there are some real techniques. I can tell you the real way to hold a yoyo, how to do breakaways and atom smashers, kwijibos and—"

"That's nice, Crescenzo," Geppetto interrupted. "*Allora*, look. Take the wood in one hand and your blade in the other. Close your eyes. Then, have at it."

"Close my eyes? Don't I need to see what I'm doing?"

"Not if you're a true Carver. *Feel* what you're doing." Geppetto grabbed a hunk of wood for himself, closing his eyes and letting his thumb linger over the corners and grooves. He reminded Crescenzo of a blind man studying a new texture or a face. "You have to let the wood tell you what's inside of it. What it wants to be." Geppetto picked up his knife and drew it across the wood like a pencil on paper. "Let the knife tell you where it wants to go."

Crescenzo rolled his eyes. "Cheesy!"

Geppetto's hands wove at the wood, tiny curls and a light rain of dust showering his pants, but he opened his eyes and cocked a brow at Crescenzo. "I'm teaching you what I know, young man. You'd do well to be receptive." He blew on his knife and continued. "Shall I tell you who one of the best known Carvers was, Crescenzo? You must have studied him in school by now."

"Probably not. We don't exactly study woodworkers in school."

"I was thinking of a man who worked with marble."

Crescenzo pulled his knees into his chest and leaned closer to Geppetto. "Marble?"

"Oh yes, boy, a true Carver can work with anything! Wood, marble, stone, diamonds, even the earth itself. Ask Michelangelo. By fortune, he came about a grand slab of marble one fateful day. It is said that he saw a man inside of it. He felt the marble's energy and became one with it. All he had to do was carve around that man and set him free." Geppetto paused, letting his knife rest on his lap. "I'll have you know that, today, that block of marble is known as *Davide.*"

Crescenzo's jaw fell. "Seriously? The naked guy?"

"And the first to slay a giant, you might remember," Geppetto added. "He lives on through Michelangelo's work. Some even say they've seen him breathe. You see, Enzo, Carvers are very special people. We feel the living souls of the world around us. We set them free, we tell their stories, and once in a while, we have the fortune of shaping the future. Would you like to know how your father came to be?"

A cool gust of wind ruffled Crescenzo's hair. This was a story he never thought he'd hear. He leaned closer. "Yes."

"Your father is the grand product of fortune and a rivalry I harbored with a fellow Carver in the Old World. His name was Master Cherry. If you saw his nose, you'd understand. Master Cherry and I were the best of friends for years, but, oh, how we could never get along! I wonder if we ever looked something like you and Mr. Volo? Your bond seems true, but surely life intervenes, yes?"

"Sometimes," Crescenzo admitted. "It's just that we get competitive sometimes. Mostly when we're sparring or playing *Halo* or something."

"I don't know this *Halo*, but I imagine you understand the relationship between Master Cherry and myself." Geppetto seized his handle and resumed carving, his eyelids lowering like curtains. "We were competitive. *I* was competitive." Geppetto's face darkened. "I knew I was good at what I'd come to learn. I carved a pair of shoes for a young orphan, and they were more detailed and beautiful than anything Master Cherry had done. I worked on the gargoyles on Clocher de Pierre. My work predicted the arrival of the chameleon wolf that terrorized Florindale and ate Tommaso Bugia. Master Cherry grew jealous of my abilities and set a challenge. Each of us was to carve the most fantastical, amazing creation of our dreams, given only one week and three cubic meters of the material of our choosing. The winner was to be deemed the Master Carver, which Cherry wanted more than *anything* in the world. The title? The status? It was everything to him. As for me, all I wanted was a son."

Something rustled the bushes with a violent shake, causing both Geppetto and Crescenzo to turn their heads. For a split second, Crescenzo thought he could make out a bulbous shape with many tiny humanoid arms in the shadows, but he blinked and the figure was gone. "Is something watching us?"

Geppetto craned his neck, squinted, and finally shrugged. "I'm sure we're fine. Just be on your guard. Now, where was I?"

"I think you were about to say you carved my father." Gaze wavering between Geppetto and the bushes for a minute, Crescenzo rubbed his arms to suppress the chill in the air.

"Yes. And so I carved my son, with care and with love and the promise to be the best father I could be. That meant getting proper sleep, setting a regimen, and tending to the needs of my work as I would tend to a living soul. *Cherry*, on the other hand, lost sight of this. He did not sleep. He did not take breaks. He threw and cursed his creation when things didn't go his way. The soul of the wood rebelled against Cherry. At the end of one week, Cherry had carved a table leg."

Despite Geppetto's serious tone, Crescenzo burst into laughter. "Ha! Some master! You carved a living being, and he carved a table leg! That's just really sad and hilarious. So you're the Master Carver, right?"

Geppetto shrugged, his grim expression unchanging. "Well, I suppose, but that wasn't important to me. All I cared was that my creation started to walk and talk and demonstrate signs of life. My son was a true being, despite remaining a mere puppet. But Cherry, overcome with the burden of failure, ceased carving forever. He was much more interested in what had come to pass with my creation. Life in a block of wood. He turned to other pursuits. Magic and its cousins, the sciences, as well as blacksmithing. Bounty hunting. I suspect he was looking for means to put souls in other objects." Geppetto's brows creased, and he sucked on the inside of his cheek. "And then he ceased to be a part of society. Even before I stumbled down here, I hadn't seen my friend in ages."

Silence passed, and Crescenzo simply stared at his grandfather, contemplating his strange story. Geppetto continued to grind at the wood, his eyes open but unseeing as he stared through a spot on the ground.

"Let that story reveal its lessons to you, young man," Geppetto continued. "First, you must care for your art and your hobbies. They are extensions of your very soul. Second, when you have a friend such as Mr. Zackary Volo, never allow him to belittle himself. And you,

Crescenzo, don't get cocky. Friends are to lift each other up and learn from one another. There is no master among friends." Geppetto raised an eyebrow and nodded as if to ask, *Do you understand?*

"Yeah. I get it." Crescenzo bobbed his head slowly. "Thanks, you know, for the story. It's neat to know where my father came from. I'm sure you love him like crazy." Crescenzo had the sudden urge to see the two men interact and resolved to bring them together.

"And he, you," Geppetto said. With a grandiose swipe, Geppetto flicked his blade across the wood one last time and pocketed the knife. He held his new creation up to his face and squinted before blowing a tiny tempest of dust away. "Love is most important, Crescenzo. In moments of darkness, when the shadows are out, don't forget that."

Crescenzo nodded again.

With that, Geppetto pressed a tiny figurine into Crescenzo's palm and wrapped his fingers tightly around his creation. "Put it away and keep it safe."

Crescenzo pocketed Geppetto's gift without looking at it, growing concerned when the old man started to laugh. It was a full, throat-and-belly laugh that shook him as he doubled over and began to clap his hands. "Oh, my boy!"

Crescenzo rubbed his cheeks and his nose, trying to figure out if he'd mutated or given Geppetto another reason to laugh. "Did I do something funny?"

"Oh, my boy!" Geppetto repeated. "You've done something, all right. I must say, you're a quick learner."

He pointed at Crescenzo's lap, where a bed of wood shavings peppered his jeans. Crescenzo's knife lay neatly at his side. His fingertips tingled like they'd been bathed in electricity. He flexed his hands and rubbed them together, getting rid of the excess dust on his palms. He didn't understand where the mess had come from, but his hands remembered, his knuckles feeling strong and limber. All the while, as Geppetto told his story, Crescenzo's hands had been working at the wood, grinding and weaving and tracing an invisible outline, until Crescenzo freed the figure trapped within: a tiny rabbit. It rested in his lap, seeming to stare up at its creator and listen with two long, unhearing ears.

An involuntary breath shot out of Crescenzo's lungs as he picked up his new figurine with trembling fingers. It barely stood two inches high, but the detail was magnificent. "I made this?"

"*You* made it," Geppetto confirmed. "You, my boy, are a Carver, and I am one spectacular *maestro!*"

Crescenzo blinked, expecting the rabbit to vanish from his palm, but it remained perched on hind legs, staring expectantly at its maker. For a second, Crescenzo could've sworn he saw the rabbit blink back, twitch its nose, even tap a foot. "*No way,*" he breathed. "Why did I make this?"

A flash of white zipped over the river, a tiny ghost over haunted waters. Crescenzo and Geppetto turned in the direction of the flash, and sure enough, there was a real, living rabbit peeking back at Crescenzo on top of a spotted, throbbing tree stump. It stood stone still when Crescenzo locked eyes with it, and Geppetto smirked. "Young man," he said, stretching his arms and flexing a knee. He looked like he was preparing to run a marathon. "Let's go find out."

In that instant, the rabbit bounded away, and Geppetto followed.

"We're chasing the rabbit?" For a second, Crescenzo couldn't believe what his grandfather was suggesting, but it quickly snapped into place. His life wasn't normal anymore. Whether he was grabbing hold of a flying shadow, carving detailed figurines that rivaled his own father's talent, or being asked to chase a rodent through Wonderland, Crescenzo understood that nothing should surprise him anymore. He threaded his knife through his belt loop, stood and pocketed his figurine, and took off after Geppetto, wondering what the rabbit could possibly have in store for them.

As focused as he was, and as determined as he was to keep up with

Geppetto and the rabbit, Crescenzo couldn't shake the strange and sudden feeling that somebody—or something was watching him run. The chill crawled down his spine again when he looked to the bushes. But even the sky seemed to have eyes. There was a vibration in the air, somewhere high above, and the one time Crescenzo allowed himself to stop and look behind him, he saw that two fat, slow-moving drones were coasting the sky like airborne whales. From each drone, a misty white searchlight frantically scanned the ground.

CHAPTER EIGHT

WONDERLAND: WONDERTOWN

There was a time when Rosana used to keep a diary, a little purple notebook she had covered with stickers shaped like pandas, superheroes, and cartoon characters. She started it when she was eleven, and by the time she turned twelve, her name in Sharpie had already faded from the cover. Somewhere in the middle, she started a list: *Places to visit!* It started with Saturn and ended with the Taj Mahal, with eighty-three other places in between.

Then she went on her walk with Gretel and Matthew Hadinger, and her new destination trumped every place she had ever written on her list. She wished she had a camera, and yet she knew no lens could ever do justice to Wondertown.

Matt proved to be wonderful company during the walk, both whimsically entertaining and delightfully charming. He pointed out all the most interesting features of Wonderland and all the strange elements to avoid, such as the bumblebees that were bigger than Rosana. Glee spread through Matt's face as they drew closer to Wondertown. When they finally approached the border, he came to a jumping stop, clapped his hands, and made a grand gesture to the scene before him. "My friends! I humbly welcome you"—he removed his hat and bowed to the ground—"to Wondertown."

Gretel's mouth fell open, barely containing a mouthful of chocolate.

Rosana wanted to pinch herself. *Is all of this real?* Wondercountry was amazing in its own terrifying way—towering rosebuds, jumping spiders, and weather that changed with the shadows—but Wondertown was something else entirely.

The ground was patterned in black and silver tiles that created interlocking spades straight out of a deck of cards, each one spangled with tiny stars Rosana suspected were made from fragments of diamond. In the orange moon, the effect was spectacular, casting mini-fireworks on the ground with every step. The road stretched as far as she could see, wide enough for a massive parade to march through. The buildings along the sides were made from the same shining substances that coated the ground, but there were also houses of vibrant red stucco interspersed throughout the street. As the road stretched forth, the buildings grew taller. The street attracted more people, and the ugly spidery plants of Wondercountry made room for towering crystal trees in which fireflies buzzed like jittery Christmas lights.

Rosana hadn't expected the residents of Wonderland to look so . . . well, normal. The only element that set them apart from the people of her world was the way they dressed. They were clad almost entirely in black, with their apparel ranging from sparkling dresses and pressed coats to black jeans and long-sleeved shirts. Some were dressed more eccentrically, with one woman looking like a black-and-white peacock and a man who seemed to have coated himself in tree bark, but none of them seemed particularly out of place or in the least bit frightening to Rosana. Her gaze wandered between the passersby and the large buildings, some of which had names like *WonderCuts! Premiere Hair, Eyebrow, and Tongue Stylists,* along with *Humpty Dumpty's Steak and Eggs, Tweedle Dee's Deelightful Deesserts,* and *Ace's Pet Store: Fully-Bred Dodos!* Strangest of all to Rosana was the red stucco building to the right, where a crowd of people had lined up outside the door.

"Is that a Starbucks?" Rosana asked. "Seriously?"

Matt pressed his gloved fingers to his mouth. "Rosana! I can hardly understand why you're surprised. Is there not a Starbucks on every corner in your world?"

True, Rosana thought. "How do you know that?"

"You'll need to check out our library while you're here." Matt gestured to the largest building on the left, and Rosana wanted to melt. *There must be millions of books in there!* He pointed straight ahead to the farthest point of the spangled road. A bejeweled castle sprouted from the end of the road, and above its turrets, Rosana was able to make out—

"A floating island!" Gretel exclaimed.

Rosana couldn't believe her eyes. Gretel was right. High up in the air, a crust of land hovered over the castle, powerfully green and full of life. From the ground, Rosana spotted an apple tree, a series of park benches, and a misty waterfall that spewed its shimmering liquids over the side of the island, though every droplet evaporated before it could touch the ground.

Whoosh!

Rosana lost her breath when two gold stars shot into the air from either side of the castle, rocketing above the floating island and leaving trails of smoke behind. *Boom!* The two stars exploded into fireworks, fanning out across the midnight sky. Several more streams of fireworks followed, bursting into electric blues and ruby reds.

"Hurrayyy!" the townspeople cried.

"Wow," Rosana said. "This place is incredible! Is all of this for the Evening of Wonder?" *It's too good to last.*

"Just keep watching," Matt said. "It gets better."

A series of enormous glass screens blossomed from the ground, and one descended from the bottom of the floating island. Rosana fixed her gaze on the nearest display, where a bright image of a four-paneled shield appeared. The crest bore the four symbols of a standard deck of playing cards: hearts, spades, diamonds, and clubs all linked by a silver cross. The shield revolved against a checkered background, underlined by the words *Please Stand By For an Important Message.*

"This is going to be spectacular." Matt removed his hat and the screens flashed, replacing the shield with an image of lush trees, crystal brooks, and flying horses. Solemn music filled the air, and a voiceover began in deep, soothing tones.

"*Once upon a time, the people of Wonderland were united.*" A black-gloved hand shook a red-gloved hand. "*The Hearts, kind and caring, the lifeblood of our nation.*" A woman in red silk smiled while serving a sky-colored soupy substance to a child in black. "The Clubs, innovative and logical, engineering our future." A dark-skinned boy in white armor tinkered with a set of colorful wires before flashing a thumbs up at the camera. "The Diamonds, illustrious and mystical, expanding the limits of art and magic for all." A plum-haired woman waved a conducting wand at a stage full of orchestra instruments, all of which played themselves without musicians. "And the Spades, bold and strong, the defenders of our wonder." Two armored men stood together by a castle door, armed with glimmering swords. The four-paneled shield flashed on the screen again. "Four factions, one people in the heart of Wonderland, working together toward a common goal: peace, prosperity, and wonder for all."

"*Peace, prosperity, and wonder for all!*" the crowds blurted. The outburst was so sudden and forceful that Rosana twitched in surprise.

"Today," the voice continued, "though Wonderland has stood divided since the first Dark Age, Wondertown remains the stronghold and capital of our yesterday, our tomorrow, and our yesterday's tomorrow! Wondertown, the official base of the Spades, welcomes guests and refugees, and we proudly invite all to celebrate in our streets and come together for our Evening of Wonder!"

The video panned over an image of a massive army, clad in red, white, silver, and black, standing in a block of thousands and facing a blooming tree. "It is time for our people to be one again," the voice boomed. "It is time for our people to be whole. The Second Dark Age has passed, and now we must rebuild. We must give thanks to the peoples who have liberitated us from ungoodness. We must honorify our heroines!"

"Peace, prosperity, and wonder for all!"

The crowd breathed the same phrase over and over, growing louder and more animated with every repetition until their fists were in the air and their chests puffed out with pride.

Rosana stood awkwardly with her arms at her sides, not really sure what to make of the scene before her. For Gretel, the novelty and excitement seemed to have worn off, for she was fully immersed in her candy bar again.

The image on the screen zoomed in on the united army of Wonderland, fireworks bursting behind their backs. "Happy day, Wonderlings, and may you thoroughly enjoyify tonight's Evening of Wonder!"

With a thunderous *boom,* a shower of fireworks rocketed over the town in every direction, igniting the skies in a blanket of red and white. Rosana shielded her eyes, squinting at the spots that stained her vision while smoke curled around the buildings.

Matt wrapped a gentle arm around Rosana's shoulder and leaned in to her ear. Rosana actually found his presence comforting and willed herself not to blush—or disappear—when his breath tickled her earlobe. "I know this doesn't make much sense to you yet, young one, but I promise I've brought you exactly where you're supposed to be." He paused, and Rosana could almost hear his smile. "There's a grand movement beginning, Rosana, and the King of Spades wants you at the center. You can make our world whole again. You, and you alone. After all, it's in your very soul. Your legacy."

Matt squeezed Rosana's shoulder and patted it twice before letting go. Rosana turned to him and smiled, mostly out of gratitude for trying to make her feel welcome. He was close to succeeding, and Rosana wanted nothing more than to trust him. They locked eyes for a brief moment before Matt pointed at the nearest screen, where the image was still zooming in on the army of Wonderland.

Before the screen faded to white, the image isolated a single figure in the center of the military block, adorned in all four colors of the Wonderland shield. An exquisite helmet covered the figure's head, bolder and heftier than all the other helmets in the block. A sword hung at the soldier's right side, a dutiful shield on the left. The music intensified as the helmet suddenly levitated off the figure's shoulders, revealing a tangled cascade of honeyed hair.

Rosana's heart rocketed faster with every inch the helmet receded, first unmasking a pair of lips that looked astonishingly like her own, and then two sea-green pools of light that she saw in the mirror almost every day. When the helmet came off, hovering inches above the warrior's head, Rosana clutched Matt's elbow for support. She feared she would pass out, for on the screen, staring out at Wondertown with burning, stark resolve on her face, was the mirror image of Rosana, betrayed only by the color of her hair.

The centerpiece of the army was her mother.

CHAPTER NINE

THE OLD WORLD

It was easy for Hansel to pretend he wasn't broken. He'd been pretending most of his life, from the day he last heard from his parents to the day he last heard from his sister, and even the day Snow White invited him to her wedding. Hansel knew better than to be surprised that after all he'd been through with Snow, she was still the hardest person to fool. By his guess, they'd been traveling together for about seven hours since Violet had sent them off, but because the moon didn't budge from the sky and nobody had seen the sun in weeks, he couldn't have been sure. All he knew was that the ground wobbled under his feet, and his eyes grew weary. He kept his complaints to himself.

"You're such a fake," Snow muttered, leaning against a boulder to catch her breath. Jagged rocks peppered dry ground for miles, even though Hansel was sure they should have already crossed several rivers. He wondered if Snow's mood altered his perception of time.

Hansel decided not to respond to Snow's comment. She'd gone too sour, and with good reason, he decided. It wasn't worth provoking her bitterness. The only way to get her to listen was to mention her husband.

"You know, for what it's worth," he said, "I think Liam should be the proper king of Florindale."

"What?" Snow snapped. "Hansel, you can keep lying to yourself about how you're fine and dandy. I don't care. But you can't lie to me about how you feel about Liam. It isn't hard to know how much you hated him, even before you started playing Avoria's game. I *always* knew."

Hansel clawed at his temples, both embarrassed and frustrated with Snow's coldness. "Okay, I've never been overly fond of your husband," he confessed. "But as of late, I do possess great respect for him."

"It's too late for *respect*." Snow put her arms out at her sides, stabbing him with her eyes. "It's too late for him to care, and it's too late for you to earn *my* respect. So you can stop trying, because I don't want your sympathies."

Hansel planted his feet. "You don't want my sympathy, and I don't want your respect. I don't want your love, and I don't even want your friendship. But you're going to let me escort you to the tower, Snow, because I owe this world a debt. Your husband fought for me when the queen returned, even though I nearly destroyed you. And now you're going to let me protect you, because I owe you. I owe Liam, and I owe the people. I'm going to fix this and protect you."

The wall of ice started to thaw in Snow's expression. "I don't get you," she said. "That's the past. What about now, Hansel? What do you need to protect me from? The queen isn't interested in us anymore. She's gone."

But her eyes are everywhere, dear. You made her stronger.

Hansel froze, his body tight and frigid with fear. There was no mistaking that shrill whisper in the air, disembodied and omnipresent. He seized Snow's wrist. "Did you hear that?"

Snow's face said everything. She had no idea what he was talking about.

"You think I'm crazy," Hansel said.

But of course she does. You've completely lost it, and she only continues to gain.

"What is the matter with you?" Snow asked.

Hansel put a finger to his lips and turned in a slow circle, trying to track the source of the chill in the air. "Stay," he commanded. "There's something evil here."

Snow had every intention of abandoning Hansel when he walked away, creeping like a fox to follow a disembodied voice that only he could hear. He was clearly out of his mind. He would only become a burden if they stuck together. Having made up her mind, Snow gathered her belongings and walked away, only to bump into the ugliest creature she'd ever seen.

Slimy, pink, and small, the creature appeared to be some sort of imp with decaying teeth and greasy hair. Snow leapt back in disgust when she bumped into it, but the imp only smiled.

"*Hallo*, Little Snow White. What a happy surprise!" the imp said in a squeaky voice.

"What are you?"

"I am the lord of deals and bargains! The fallen fairy of Florindale! Rumpelstiltskin is me name!"

Snow shook her head. She'd heard stories about this creature. "Get out of my way."

Rumpelstiltskin frowned, stroked his oily chin, and turned his lips into a grin. "I see what has occurred! Little Snow White went for a stroll, found the queen, and lost her soul! Little Snow White went down the hole, and now her heart's as black as coal!" Rumpelstiltskin clapped his hands in a series of short, quick staccatos. "That's why she's so mean now! She's lost her perfect little light and innocence. She doesn't know how to forgive, how to smile, or how to love. That's what will make this next part so easy!"

"I know how to love," Snow shot back. "I know more than you'll ever know about love."

The imp grinned. "Ooo! Little Snow White has a little white knight?"

"That's not your business."

"Then Rumpelstiltskin has something for you. A bargain!" His sharp yellow teeth were flecked with dark spots and holes, reminding Snow of an ear of corn every time his mouth opened. "My favorite thing! Does Little Snow White want to hear it?"

"Stop calling me that." Snow aimed her nail in the imp's face. "Tell me what you want."

"A book!" Rumpelstiltskin squealed. "A pretty book! A magic book! One with all the secrets of the worlds! Some call it a journal, a diary, a sketchpad . . . I calls it a book, and I want it. Rumpelstiltskin wants a book, to read and love and take a look! Rumpelstiltskin wants a book. Give it to me, not—!"

"Okay!" Snow rolled her eyes. "Frankenstein's book, you mean?" She shrugged. "You're not the only one, and you're probably out of luck. I don't think that book exists."

"But it does, pretty one! It really does! Will you bring it to me?"

"I told you, you're not the only one looking for it. The chances of *me* finding it are less than nothing. And I have more important things to look for. You couldn't offer me a great enough trade to abandon my quest and find your *diary*."

Rumpelstiltskin's grin grew even wider, seemingly spreading over the full lower half of his face. "I can help you get your soul back."

"No," Snow said, and she meant it. If her soul made her nice, she didn't want it. Her tenderness made her weak.

"I can save your prince."

The words were a sudden chemical in Snow's veins, sealing away the outside world so that all she saw was Rumpelstiltskin and the image of her husband that had been burned into her eyelids. Wide-eyed and heavy-hearted, she took a step closer to the imp. "Keep talking."

"I know all about your Liam and his strange new predicament. Our future king, frozen in time by Avoria!" Rumpelstiltskin trilled the woman's name like it was a treat for his tongue. "Such a shame, pretty one! But let's not forget: I am Rumpelstiltskin! I've been known to spin straw into gold for the right price. What makes you think I can't also *unmake* gold?" He dipped his grimy fingers into a tattered pocket and produced three gold coins, like miniature suns in the palm of his hands. He held his arm straight in front of him and dropped the coins one by one. *Clunk, clunk, clunk!* By the time each coin hit the ground, it turned to dull, smooth wood.

Snow found her heart picking up speed and she turned away, clawing her fingers into her hair in a moment of epiphany. It certainly made sense that somebody like Rumpelstiltskin could help her. She could feel his toothy grin blinding her from behind, his tiny feet padding back and forth on the forest ground. *It would be daft to refuse his offer. What if he's the only one who could ever help me?*

Then again, did she even have a chance of finding the coveted book? Perhaps more importantly, what could Rumpelstiltskin have wanted with it? What was so important that he chose this trade for Liam's freedom? Snow remembered that Violet had been after the book, too, potentially looking for the key to defeat Avoria and restore order to the realms. Somehow, Snow sensed that Rumpelstiltskin must have had entirely different motives than Violet and that the book was far from ordinary. In the right hands, maybe the worlds could be saved. In the wrong hands, what could happen?

What was worse than Avoria?

"The clock haunts you, my dear. What will Little Snow choose?"

Snow shut her eyes and Liam's ghost seized her senses, a gentle aroma of winter and cured leather teasing her nostrils. She imagined a pair of gloved hands wrapping her own in a snug hold and bringing them up to a pair of firm lips. When he lowered her hands again, he flashed that smile she knew so well.

"You swear you could bring him back to how he was?" Snow asked. "You promise with all of your being? I want your word."

"You bring me the book, and I restore your husband to his former sterling glory."

"Your *word*."

The imp made a show of extending his hand. "I, Rumpelstiltskin, promise to cure Prince Liam of his golden ailment and restore him to his former self, on the condition that Snow White bring me the book that hath belonged to Dr. Victor Frankenstein. Do we have a deal?"

Snow blew a deep breath and took Rumpelstiltskin's hand. It was like picking up a wet slug. When their palms connected, they made a squelching sound. "Deal. You better not break it."

"I would *never*!" Rumpelstiltskin said. "Oh, and one more thing: Snow White has three hours to complete her quest."

Snow jerked her hand away. "Three *hours*? But I don't know where to start! How do I even tell time when it's always dark these days?"

Rumpelstiltskin snapped his fingers, and the three wooden coins jumped back into his hand. *Click, click, click!* He pressed them together in his palms, one hand over the other. When he took his hands apart, the coins became one object, which he held out to Snow.

She took the strange new contraption and rotated it in her fingers. It was no bigger around than either of the coins, but it was thicker than all three put together and encased in thick glass. Two dials rotated on the inside. One reminded Snow of a clock, numbered only from zero to three. The other hand appeared to be a compass.

"Let that point the way," the imp said. "The compass knows what you want the most. As for the numbers, don't let them reach *null*!"

Snow raised a skeptical eyebrow. "Why didn't you just follow the compass?"

"Because the compass points you to what you want the most. And I want too many things! How will I ever have time to have them all? Unlike you, I have *forever*!"

Crack!

A crossbow fired.

A flying bolt soared.

Snow barely had time to process the noise and the blur that sailed in front of her. But within a second, the blur came to a stop, and Rumpelstiltskin fell lifeless onto the ground, a small glob of sticky blood pooling on his chest.

Snow spun around and found herself face to face with the crossbow's wielder.

"Close one," Hansel said, lowering the silver weapon to the ground. "I'm glad I didn't think to give this back to you right away. Are you all right?"

An eerie silence passed as the imp dissolved in a slow cloud of black dust and then billowed away, leaving nothing behind but a star-shaped imprint in the ground. Snow rounded on Hansel, her blood boiling.

"Am I *all right*? Hansel! You just killed my best chance of rescuing my husband! You just . . ." Before she could think about it, her fingers curled into a firm claw and seized Hansel's throat, a dagger of a nail digging into a thin bone in his neck. "You may as well have killed my husband, you horrible, wretched *beast*! What is wrong with you?" She clenched tighter, and Hansel's face began to turn a satisfying shade of red. She squeezed even harder, listening to the empty, failed gulps of air. "I should've done this long ago!"

"*Stop!*" a woman cried from behind. Without letting go, Snow shifted her gaze and saw the blond woman from the castle, lunging for Snow and sinking fingertips into her shoulders. The woman used one hand to pry Snow's fingers away from Hansel's throat, the other shoving Hansel away. "You're hurting him!"

Snow stumbled backward and caught her balance, massaging the color back into her knuckles. She shook her head as Hansel doubled over, clutching his stomach and taking generous gulps of air. "That was kind of the *point!*" she spat. "What are you doing out here alone, whatever-your-name-was?"

"It's Alicia." The woman paused for a moment and cleared her throat. "And I'm trying to find a way into Wonderland."

Snow scoffed. "Good luck." She tapped her finger against her thigh. "That's not what Violet asked you to do."

"With all due respect, I don't care."

Snow crossed her arms, still clutching the compass-clock in her hand. "I respect that. Wonderland, huh? Why don't you make a deal with Rumpelstiltskin to let you in? Oh, wait." She turned back to Hansel. "He just killed him!"

Hansel finished catching his breath and backed away, speaking unapologetically. "That creature was never going to help you. You can take my word for that."

"You don't know that!" Snow protested. "He was going to save my husband. He was going to fix everything. We had a deal."

"Yeah? I've had deals with him, too. He's dangerous, he's deceptive, and he's a liar. Trust me, he *wasn't going to help you.*" Hansel craned his neck and looked at the newcomer, a joyful smile spreading over his face. "Alice! It's been too long, old friend. How are you?"

Alicia aimed a palm at Hansel. "That's the first thing you're going to say to me after you had one of your henchmen kidnap me and trap me in a jewel? After you were directly responsible for the theft of my soul and the disappearance of my daughter?"

Hansel wrung his hands. "I suppose I deserve that," he said. "I haven't been the best man I can be. I caused a lot of pain . . . some wounds that may never close. But I want you to believe that I am a changed man. I want to be a hero. I turned to darkness to help me find things I've lost in my life, but I don't want to go down that road again. I want to make up for my mistakes. I can fix this. So, I'm sorry. Really."

Alicia sized Hansel up and kept her arms folded, evidently deep in thought as she processed his words. Finally, she nodded. "All right. That's all I needed to hear."

"You have got to be kidding me." Snow rolled her eyes as the two shook hands, Hansel spouting gratitude and sincerity.

Alicia shrugged. "Some people need their second chances. I need them, too."

"You know magic isn't all warm and fuzzy, right? Your daughter isn't just going to waltz into your life because you found forgiveness in your heart. People think good guys get rewarded in our world. True love's first kiss solves everything, and believers get what they want just for wishing hard enough." Snow threw her hands up. "Nope. Your newfound appreciation for this man who wronged you? It's misplaced. You'll get nothing."

"I'm not looking for anything from him."

"Well, then, good."

Hansel ignored Snow. "I've an idea," he said to Alicia. "I can help you look for Wonderland. To make up for all the trouble I've caused you and your daughter."

Alicia's face was a mix of compassion and surprise. "You'd do that?"

"Aye. It's the least I can do. I have no leads, no information that can help you, but I can protect you." He stole a glance at Snow. "*We* can protect you."

Snow mashed her lips together, staring down at the wooden contraption Rumpelstiltskin had given her. One of the spinning points decided to aim behind her, and Snow wondered if it was still pointing to Frankenstein's book. With the imp dead, was the book still worth looking for? *It has to be*, she thought. *Maybe there was something in it about undoing Liam's curse.* As for the door Violet told her to seek with Hansel, what good would a door do in fixing her husband? She'd felt this way all along . . . doors were useless against gold, and Snow didn't care what was behind Violet's door.

Snow had made up her mind. She was going after the book instead.

"Sorry, chums," Snow said, stealing one of Liam's favorite words. "I don't have time for Wonderland. If we're sticking together, we go my way."

Alice shrugged. "Guess we're not sticking together, then. It's okay, really. I'm fine on my own. You two go ahead."

Hansel's mouth twisted, and he squinted at Alice as if trying to see his future on her forehead. "Excuse me one second." He pulled Snow aside and said, "What is it that you're looking for exactly? You're not really going after this book, are you?"

"Yes," Snow said. "And by now you should know that it would be pretty stupid to try and stop me. You can't change my mind. You may have killed my only hope, but I can at least find out what he wanted." Snow narrowed her eyes. "I'm not going to pretend I want you to come with me. Go with *her*. She forgives you, whereas I despise you. Help her."

Snow hated the expression on Hansel's face, that dopey *you hurt my feelings* kind of look she'd seen too often. What happened to gruff, rebellious, devil-may-care Hansel? But the sadness quickly melted.

"And the door?"

"Go back for it later or something; I don't know. I never really cared about the door. Miss Violet's intentions are gray at best." She shrugged. "Good luck out there. It's getting awfully quiet around here with the king starting to round people up. Let's not meet again in a prison cell."

Snow returned her gaze to the wooden gadget, spinning away to follow the arrow wherever it decided to point her. The smaller arrow, however, which had previously been fixed on the roman numeral III, budged the slightest amount and slowly began to tick toward the number II, freezing Snow in her tracks. It seemed that even with Rumpelstiltskin dead, she was still on a deadline. She had to find the book. But even if she did, who would she give it to? And if she failed to find it in time, what would happen when the compass ran out?

CHAPTER TEN

THE OLD WORLD: FLORINDALE PRISON

"Light!"

Despite the determination in Violet's voice on the other side of the marble wall, damp, cold blackness filled Pietro's vision. Only a glimmer of pallid moonlight disturbed the darkness in Florindale Prison.

Pietro leaned back against the wall, wondering if the fairy could hear him on the other side. "You know, you keep saying that, but all I see is black, black, black, which raises an important question: Are we in your father's soul right now?"

Violet responded with a tinge of annoyance in her voice. "His soul was probably the blueprint. Is everyone okay, Peter? Who's with you?"

Pietro surveyed the hollow cube. With one fist, he rubbed the redness out of his eyes. He'd been sleeping off and on. There was simply nothing better to do, but he was glad to see that Wendy was okay. "My wife and two of the short dudes!"

One of the miners growled from the corner of the cell. "That's *Zid* and *Chann,* you know. Remember this, manboy."

"Right. I think it's the dragon guy and the one that eats a lot of food! Speaking of which, is your father going to feed us?"

On cue, the sound of boots on tile thumped somewhere beyond the iron bars of Pietro's door. He stood, pressed his face to the bars, and absorbed the sounds of his new reality. In addition to the footsteps, a tiny sizzle pierced his ears from the other side of the door, like eggs frying through cotton.

"What is that awful, annoying sound?" Wendy asked.

Pietro cocked his ear to the door and followed the sizzle until he identified its source: a padlock blacker than death, surrounded by a strange, glowing blue aura. It was about the size of Pietro's fist, and it fizzed gold sparks from the keyhole, which wasn't shaped for a key at all. Instead, the hole was a long black slit, as if somebody had poked a knife through it. It sputtered and popped like a dying car. When Pietro reached for it, Zid darted to his stubby feet and slapped his hand away.

Pietro winced, shaking the pain out of his wrist. "There's this thing called *basic manners*, you know. Please explain yourself, Munchkin."

Wendy gasped. "Peter!"

Beneath Zid's brows, his eyes looked like shiny little beetles in the dark. "You want to touch the lock, manboy? Then be my guest."

"I'll do it!" Pietro poked his hand through the iron bars. "I'll touch the lock. You think I won't?"

Chann raised his head from his arms and knees, unraveling from the ball he'd been curled in to for the last hour. He smirked at Pietro. "This I must see."

Pietro extended his arm until the pads of his fingers were an inch from the lock. "Wait, why are you so excited? I change my mind."

Zid uncrossed his arms and aimed a charred, disfigured palm at Pietro's face. "Wise decision, Pan."

"*Oh!*" Pietro withdrew his arm and leapt away from Zid's dark appendage strewn with red lines like lava seeping through ash. "Evil! What happened?"

Chann tossed a pebble through the bars. Pietro's jaw fell as the pebble burst into flame and crumbled to dust on contact with the lock. "That cursed lock will only open at the whims of very particular conditions. It may only be touched by a special object."

Pietro flopped his hand around like rubber. "What kind of object?"

"One we shall never possess. Our only hope of rescue is long gone. We left it behind the minute we let Mr. Bellamy snatch us up in that castle."

"So we're . . . ?"

"Doomed." The footsteps came to a halt outside the bars, and Lord Bellamy stood tall on the other side, armed with only a lantern and his piercing glare. "Are you comfortable, Pan? I hope you are, for you *all* are going to rot here for your attempted plot against the Old World."

Wendy scrambled to her feet and gripped the bars, having to tilt her head up to make eye contact with Lord Bellamy. "Conspiracy against the Old World? Straighten your story! We're trying to save everyone. Why can't you let us out?"

Lord Bellamy cringed. "Your insolence is a torch against my ears. No supper for this cell tonight."

"*What?*" Chann wailed. "No! Sir, that's not fair!"

"I am the king," Lord Bellamy said. "I decide what's fair now, and what's fair to the realm is that Avoria stays far away. If that means I must use force to put a halt to your meddling, so be it."

Pietro threw his arms in a V and pressed his forehead to the bars. "But your daughter! Your *own daughter*! You'd lock her up forever against her will?"

"Silence, Pan!" Bellamy sneered. "My daughter has a good life. Ever hear the tragedy of Rapunzel? Or Cinderella? *They* were locked up against their wills. Violet *chose* her fate, as did you and your simpletons. You, Peter Pan, and the rest of your friends, are *never* getting out of this prison."

Several floors above, Augustine Rose paced back and forth with her hands behind her back. "My dears, you know we're getting out of this prison, right?" She surveyed her cellmates:

Merlin, James Hook, and Jacob Isaac Holmes. "My soul didn't hang on to this world just to spend an eternity rotting at the whims of some—"

"Scoundrel?" James interrupted.

"Fish-head?" Merlin offered.

"Beast?" Jacob said.

"Miserable old man," Augustine decided. "We are the Order of the Bell. If we are to die together, we damn sure will not meet a humiliating end such as this cage built for—"

"Scallywags!"

"Miscreants!"

"Beasts!"

"Ms. Rose," James said, "are you suggesting that we break out of Florindale Prison?"

"Precisely, dear."

A slow, gold-toothed grin crept across James's face. "I like the sound of that."

Jacob heaved himself to his feet. "I'm afraid what you're suggesting is impossible. Nobody breaks out of here. It was built to resist the darkest of forces. Wraiths, sorceresses, dragons—"

Merlin chimed in, "And let us never forget that we are powerless now. I knew the moment I most recently woke up in Camelot that I was no longer whole. Our souls have been fractured, Augustine. Hansel, at the will of the Ivory Queen, took everything that made us powerful. Had that not been the case, I may have easily been able to overpower Lord Bellamy's army with my magic when they invaded Camelot. But that magic is no longer there. I am one simple peasant brought back to Earth by another."

Augustine pursed her lips. "So you're not even going to try?"

"Why should we?" Jacob raised a paw to indicate the walls around him. "We are no match for this structure. We aren't even a match for the king."

"Stop," Augustine ordered. "That man is not our king. He is a coward, and Avoria is still out there." She paused and looked out the window, barely big enough to squeeze three fingers through. "Can't you feel that? That's why we are here. Mr. Bellamy is trying to keep Avoria out of our world by keeping us in. If we won't stand up to him, what makes us worthy of standing up to *her?*"

Merlin cleared his throat. "Do you have your gun, Ms. Rose?"

"Of course not. It was confiscated when Bellamy tracked me in the Woodlands."

"Then we have nothing," Merlin said simply.

James dusted off his jacket with the curved groove of his iron hook. He breathed onto the metal and polished it with the other sleeve. "Well, we can sit and parlay for all eternity, or we can count our wins. We have no gun, no magic, no strength, but I do have a hook"—he eyed the fizzing black lock in the center of the barred door—"just thin enough for me to pick us out of this cursed trap."

Without thinking twice, James leaned into the bars, fed his arm through a small opening, and aimed the tip of his hook into the sputtering keyhole.

Pfft—crack!

Before the hook could meet the lock, a green flame erupted from the keyhole and singed the end of James's leather sleeve. A tiny crack of lightning shot out from the slit and zapped the hook, throwing James backward until he careened into Merlin, knocking him into slow slumber. The lock remained defiantly sealed, quietly fizzing in the darkness.

Pfft—crack!

Pino jerked awake, his muscles protesting against the cold, rough ground. Carla stirred at his side, while Mulan and one of the miners—Garon, Pino remembered—leaned against a wall with their knees tucked into their chest. When Carla opened her eyes, Pino's heart soared.

"Did you hear that?" she croaked. "Did Enzo try to microwave a DVD again?"

Mulan and Garon both smiled, while Pino grabbed his wife's hand and pulled her into a tight embrace, shutting his eyes and memorizing the warmth of her body. "Oh, thank you, Lady Fortune! You're awake! I thought I was going to lose you."

Carla sat unmoving in Pino's embrace. "What happened? Where are we?"

"Prison," Mulan answered tersely. "Bellamy caught us. There are still no signs of Crescenzo."

Pino watched the light fade from his wife's face as she remembered her strange, grim new reality.

"Crescenzo," a gruff voice boomed. Footsteps clocked their way down the hall, and Lord Bellamy appeared outside the prison cell, his hands folded in front of him and his head fixed with a thick, pointed crown. He leaned forward and locked his red glare on Pino's face. "You two should know the boy loved you. It was rather admirable, despite his persistent annoyance. However, you are highly unlikely to see him again."

"Why?" Pino asked. "Do you know something?"

"I suspect your boy got himself stuck in the World Between. You see, the laws of the mirrors were very specific. When one made a wish or orchestrated a plan such as Avoria's, they would release their captives, but they always demand a prisoner. Once upon a time, I was banished by my wife. When I was freed, they claimed her in return, and she dragged young Gretel with her. I saw Avoria escape with my own eyes, which means the mirrors demanded new prisoners. I can only assume they claimed your children. Only now, the mirrors are broken, and that means there is no return."

Pino's body went numb. His heart bellowed in his chest. "My son! There *has* to be another way."

Mulan rose to her feet and calmly approached the door. "You say you were there once? In this 'world between?'"

"That is correct."

"Are they going to be okay?"

Lord Bellamy stuck his chin in the air. "That, I cannot say. Now, it is your turn to supply information. I suggest you cooperate, as your friends' defiance has me in a particularly foul mood." Bellamy gripped the bars and squeezed them as if he was trying to get juice out of them. His bony fingers turned red, and his lips parted to reveal his yellowing teeth. "I want the ones that got away from me."

Pino leaned his head back against the wall. He had no desire to speak anymore. Lord Bellamy's news made his head feel heavy, and Carla seemed frozen in a state of utter shock.

"By my count, my daughter's plan should have involved three others," Bellamy continued. "Two women and Hansel. One of you is going to tell me where they are. Who shall it be?"

"What are you going to do with them?" Mulan asked.

"Simple. I require justice."

Mulan folded her arms, drumming her nails on her shoulder. "What if we don't know where they are? You may be out of luck, *sir*."

"Mmm. I was prepared for your resistance. All four of you, hear me loud and clear: I am going to find and imprison *everyone* involved in your plot to find this door to the New World."

"You sure are intent on stopping us from getting to Avoria," Garon said. "Mr. Bellamy, do you still love that witch? Afraid we might actually have a chance against her?"

"*Silence!*" the old man roared. "Any prisoner who raises the topic of my feelings toward that woman shall be executed, effective immediately. In the meantime, for every day that I do not find the three missing conspirators, somebody will go to the gallows. This is your last chance, fools. Where are they?"

"We don't know!" Pino protested. "You've had us in here for what feels like days already. We have no idea where the others could be. I'm still trying to understand what happened to my son. Can you leave us in peace?"

"Peace is a luxury we do not have in our age." Lord Bellamy's tone was astonishingly calm when he spoke the words. But as if he'd flipped a switch, his face grew cold and stern, and he wagged a finger somewhere beyond Pino's line of sight. "Lancelot! Bring forth the dwarf."

Metallic footsteps clanked along the hallway until two people appeared: the knight that carried Pino out of the castle, and one of the seven miners bound in shackles. When Pino first saw the miner many years ago in a fight against a terrible serpent, he was neat and tidy, with shiny boots and a trimmed beard and hands that looked like they'd never seen dirt before. Standing beside Lancelot, Pino realized that was no longer the case. The miner was covered in dust, and his fingernails were black.

"Lancelot," Bellamy said, "we will take Finn to the gallows and execute him immediately. You will then return to the castle and burn it to the ground. Tomorrow, we resume our search."

The knight bowed stiffly. "Yes, my king."

Garon sprung to his feet and shook the bars. "No! Finn! Mr. Bellamy, don't do this! Send me to the gallows instead! I beg you!"

"Your turn may come, Garon," Lord Bellamy said. "Your deaths will be small casualties compared to the genocide we would see in Avoria's presence."

"No!" Garon sobbed, tears streaking his beard. "Finn, don't let them take you! This isn't right!"

Finn raised his gaze from the ground and locked eyes with Garon. "My friend," Finn said, his voice admirably steady and calm, "if I am to die today, make sure it counts."

Garon said nothing, only soft sobs choking this throat.

"Promise me, Garon."

"I . . . I promise."

Lord Bellamy scowled. "Take him away."

Pino's heart broke as the knight marched Finn away, metal ringing through the hall as armor clanked and shackles jittered, all drowned out by the sound of Garon weeping. Pino's own eyes filled with tears when he heard Finn mutter something before he marched out of earshot. "For Snow."

CHAPTER ELEVEN

WONDERLAND: THE PLAINS

Zack had fallen into a nasty habit when he was on Heart watch: He fell asleep when he got bored.

He never used to be obsessed with napping, but he valued productivity and action in his life. His mom had grounded him once for hiding a bad report card from her, and he thought he was going to die of boredom that week. Heart watch—sitting on a black toadstool with nothing to do except watch the horizon—gave him a similar feeling. He missed having a phone or a basketball to keep him occupied. And so, without really intending to, he napped.

But no nap had ever been as strange as the one he took after Rosana's disappearance.

He dreamed he was sitting at a round table inside a purple tent. As with all dreams, he didn't remember how he got there or why. He was conscious of the cool weather, though, along with the fact that he was alone until the cloth ruffled behind him and a dark woman entered.

The woman wore a red cloth in a band around her forehead, and her wrists jittered with heavy bangles when she folded her hands at her waist and smiled warmly at Zack.

"Son of Peter Pan," she said dreamily. "Madame Esme knew you'd come see her." The woman pulled up the seat across from Zack and studied him with intense curiosity. "I, too, had been most interested in visiting you. Perhaps we've met somewhere in between." She looked around the tent, and then at her hands, and then she traced a swirly pattern on her tablecloth. "Ah, the realm of dreams."

Zack wrinkled his brows. "Who are you? Why have I come to see you? I don't even know you."

"You wouldn't know of Madame Esme. But she certainly knows of you. Lady Fortune keeps painting your name in the cosmos. It would appear there is an important role for you in the journeys of Pinocchio's son."

"Enzo," Zack said quietly.

"Yes." A chill rippled through the air, and Madame Esme cast a wary gaze around the tent. "Now, Madame Esme has very limited time to speak to you. Please listen carefully." She lowered her voice, reached across the table, and then seized Zack's elbow. "I have predicted the death of one of your own . . . the son of Pinocchio. Madame Esme cannot be sure of the circumstances, but it is to take place soon in the realm of wonder."

Zack yanked his elbow out of Madame Esme's grip. "What are you saying? Why would you tell me something like that, even if it were true? That's . . . an evil thing to say."

The woman edged forward, impossibly calm given the horrible news she delivered. "Madame Esme is never wrong, Son of Pan. Oh, how often she wishes she were! Avoria arrived seven days ago, and what a mess we have become! The lands of Roma are falling to ruins once more. The Grand Canyon crumbles to dust as we speak. Avoria seeks a territory in which to build her citadel, and nothing will ever be the same. But the son of Pinocchio is destined to lead us all to battle. Thus, we need you, Son of Pan. We need you all to dethrone Avoria and restore peace. But if The Carver dies, hope dies with him."

Zack swallowed hard, his throat drying up. He lowered the shield. "Again, why would you tell me this? Why not just tell Enzo himself?"

"The knowledge would only hasten his demise. Madame Esme can only share certain blueprints with the subjects they depict. He must never know." Madame Esme stood and squeezed Zack's shoulders.

"You are his greatest companion, Son of Pan. You *may* prevent his death, even if Lady Fortune works against you. Madame Esme knows you can protect him. It is the highest honor you can serve in your story."

Zack's blood turned cold. He didn't want to believe Madame Esme, but he knew she believed her own words with every fiber of her being. He decided it was better to believe her and find out she was wrong than to discredit her and learn that she was correct. "Why is all of this happening to us, Madame Esme? Why do we have all this responsibility?"

Madame Esme smiled sadly. "Peace is the responsibility of *all* beings, dear," she whispered. "But when tomorrow isn't certain, the young fight the hardest to protect it. The mark of the young is to fight for tomorrow. The mark of the elderly is to learn from yesterday. Son of Pan, guardian of youth, please defend our tomorrows. Do not let The Carver die."

Another chill, much stronger than the first, jolted the air, rattling the tent. Madame Esme's eyes widened in alarm.

"She's coming," Madame Esme whispered. "You must leave, Son of Pan. Go back to the realm of wonder. And lastly . . ." A beam of light shot out of Esme's phone and fanned out into a hologram of a tall, white-bearded man cloaked in crimson. "Beware the King of Hearts."

Zack awoke with a jolt, sitting straight up on a black toadstool that had been trying to pull his feet into its cap. His respiration was heavy, and he'd never been more confused or afraid. Had the dream been real? It felt too real to discount. He mopped some sweat off his forehead and collected his breath.

Enzo, he thought. *Enzo's in trouble.*

Zack bashed the mushroom cap until it released his feet, and then he bounded off and ran back to the spot where he'd last seen Crescenzo.

The river. Geppetto took him to the river.

Zack sprinted, pondering his dream and silently praying that nothing had happened to Crescenzo already. *What did Madame Esme mean? Beware the King of Hearts?*

When Zack got to the river, he was disheartened to find that his friend was nowhere to be seen. There was no trace of Zack or Geppetto except for a mess of wood shavings and dust along the riverbank.

"Enzo!" Zack shouted, tipping his head back and cupping his mouth. "*Enzo!* Where are you?"

"Shhh!"

Zack jumped when the hiss sounded behind him.

"Stop screaming! You'll wake the shadows!"

Zack spun around and almost willed himself to die when he confronted the largest, ugliest caterpillar he'd ever seen. It had a lime fish in two of its many arms, which seemed to be made of ethereal tendrils of darkness. Every inch of the ten-foot creature seemed to be oozing shadows and smoke. Its face looked vaguely feminine and strangely humanoid, with a pointed nose and dark-painted lips that smacked together as the caterpillar chewed its fish.

Before he could stop himself, Zack twisted his face into an expression of pure disgust.

The caterpillar spat a bone fragment out of its mouth and wrinkled its bushy brow. "What are you staring at? I'm not this *Enzo* you're screaming for. Go away and let me eat in peace!"

Zack forced his lips into a flat line and blinked a few times. "Sorry. I've just never talked to a caterpillar before. It's a little strange for me; that's all."

"*You're* weird. I don't even know what you are. You almost remind me of that Humpty thing, but you're less . . . rotund. Don't get me started about your hair, though." The caterpillar raised a number of her left arms in a sassy manner.

Zack found it pretty confounding to have his hair insulted by a creature that was almost entirely covered in hair and shadowy mist. He decided to ignore the caterpillar's comment. "Um, why are you a *shadow*?"

"Because the shadows are on the move, and us caterpillars aren't equipped to evade them. They caught me. They swallowed me. Their darkness affects everybody different. For me . . ." The caterpillar shifted her gaze in a faraway expression. She blinked, and black smoke poured off her enormous eyelashes. "I can never transform."

"Transform?"

"Into what I'm meant to become. I will never be any more than what I am today. Forever *Cat*. Never a butterfly." The caterpillar sighed, and her posture wilted so that she was nearly bent in half.

"Is that really such a bad thing, though?" Zack frowned. He found himself feeling sorry for the caterpillar. "They say my father wanted to stay young forever. Sometimes I do, too. I wouldn't mind if I were always, you know, like this."

"True as it may be, I've always wanted to *fly*. Now, the darkness anchors me to the ground." After a thoughtful pause, Cat pointed into the distance with all of her legs. "Your Enzo followed the shadows to Wondertown. I watched it leave with an older, wrinklier Enzo. Perhaps you still have time to save yours."

A glimmer of hope soared through Zack's heart, but a feeling of dread weighed it down just as quickly. Enzo was okay, but he was still in danger. Zack nodded at the creature. "Thank you," he said. "What's the *fastest* way there? I need to make sure my friends are okay."

"Have the shadow cat take you," the caterpillar said simply, as if Zack was supposed to understand.

"The what?"

"*Him*." The caterpillar pointed in the other direction. "He'll take you to Wondertown. Won't you, Chester?"

A cat, ten feet long and taller than Zack, bounded out of the dark beanstalks, dropped a colossal bone from its mouth, and started panting like a dog.

Great. It's the cat again. Zack hated this thing. Gretel loved the beast, which appeared at odd times in the day carrying the same bone in its mouth each time, but Zack couldn't stand it. As soon as he spotted the creature, a tickle invaded his nostrils, and he drew in a sharp, involuntary breath.

Atchoo! Zack sneezed so hard he was pretty sure something popped in his shoulder.

"Oh, *no!*" the cat said, its deep voice quavering with distress. "I can't give this one a ride! He's allergic to dogs!"

"For the last time, Chester," the caterpillar said, rolling her eyes, "you're not a dog! You are a cat, only you've been touched by the shadows like me, so now you *think* you're a dog."

Zack's gaze darted back and forth from one creature to the other. So the caterpillar's name was Cat, and Chester was a cat who thought he was a dog. *This explains a lot,* Zack thought to himself. Gretel often liked to play fetch with Chester, and Zack had never known a cat to be so amused by *anything.* He had also never heard Chester speak until now, which was quite a feat to understand on its own.

Chester stretched out and laid his head on his front legs, growling so that all his pointed teeth were on display. "I am *too* a dog!" he protested. "And I'm a *good* dog, too! You're barking mad!"

Atchoo! The second sneeze knocked Zack onto his back. A dull pain punched through his nerves, but he was more embarrassed and frustrated than anything.

Cat contorted her body, wiggled onto the ground, and picked up Chester's bone. She passed it from her bottom legs to her top legs, and then she launched it into the fields. "Fetch!" When Chester sped after the bone, Cat helped Zack get back on his feet and mumbled, "Quick. Eat one of the beans before he gets back here. It should help with your cat allergy. Why am I always playing Miss Nurse around here?"

Zack rubbed a sore spot on his neck and then clawed into one of the black beanstalks until a bean fell into his hand. He took a bite, noting that this one had a bit of kick like a chili pepper, and his throat immediately opened up. The tickle released its hold on his nose, and he no longer had the irresistible urge to rub his own eyeballs out of their sockets.

"Better?" the caterpillar asked.

Zack swallowed then took a deep breath of fresh air. "Much. Thanks."

"Good. Chester!" Cat put two fuzzy arms in her mouth and whistled. "Take this thing to Wondertown. It's lost its Enzo somewhere."

Chester leapt out of the fields, gnawing on his bone. Zack started to question what the full skeleton must have looked like and where the bone came from. "*Uhn-er-hown?*" Chester spat out the bone and tilted his head to indicate the glittering structure on the horizon. "That's where you're going?"

"Uh, I guess so?"

"I'll give you a ride!" Chester exclaimed, his bulbous orange eyes acquiring a childlike enthusiasm. "Two rules, though. First, no kicking. I'm a dog, not a horse." He raised a front paw and scratched behind his ears. "Second, hold on. You won't be able to see me once I'm in motion, and I don't want you screaming that you've lost control."

"What do you mean I won't be able to see—?"

Before Zack could finish his sentence, Chester bent down and gently closed his teeth around Zack's waist. His nerves suddenly kicked into hyperdrive, but thankfully, rather than swallowing him whole, Chester turned and set Zack on the nape of his neck. Despite Chester's assertion that he wasn't a horse, Zack immediately recalled some of the horseback lessons he took with his dad. *You're the master, dude. You wanna be the horse's friend, but you also wanna show that you're in charge. Take the reins, buddy!*

"Are you seated?" Chester asked. "Are you comfortable?"

"Seated, yes," Zack answered. He squirmed around a bit, trying to find a tolerable position on the cat's bony back. "Comfortable, not entirely."

Cat shook her head and scoffed. "I'd say Chester's the uncomfortable one. You can't be very light, as tall as you are."

Zack narrowed his eyes at the caterpillar.

"I'm only saying." Cat picked up Chester's bone. "Are you ready to run, Chester?"

"Yeah! Yeah! Yeah!" the cat exclaimed. "Oh, boy! A bone!"

"That's right, dull creature." Cat wound her arms back like a baseball pitcher, and she smirked at Zack as if to say, *I hope you're ready for this.* "All right, Chester! Ready? Set? *Fetch!*"

The caterpillar launched the bone farther than any baseball player could have managed, and the bone rocketed toward the glittering horizon of Wondertown. Chester sprang into action and bounded after his treasured object, leaving Zack clinging for dear life as the cat ran at an unnatural speed.

The cat hadn't been running for ten seconds when Zack looked down and saw that the beast had disappeared. Its backbone still pressed against Zack's body, but all Zack could see was the ground ten feet below.

Despite Chester's warnings to hold on, Zack put his arms in the air and grinned. It wasn't quite like flying, but it was the closest he ever thought he would come. And it was enough to make him feel invincible until a fat, airborne drone shined a spotlight on him, screamed like a firetruck, and followed.

CHAPTER TWELVE

Rosana could barely believe the words on her own tongue. "My mother was a war hero."

Matt gripped her shoulder in that firm way she was coming to appreciate. "Rosana, your mother *is* a war hero. She helped us defeat the jabberwockies. She united us all, and what a glorious unity it was until the Queen of Hearts was assassinated."

"The Queen of Hearts. Right. What happened to her?"

Matt sighed. "People still argue to this day. Who killed the Queen of Hearts? What happened to her? You can see the documentaries and news reports in the library, and every faction pointing fingers and trying to play detective. All that's known is that she was poisoned. They poisoned the tarts she loved so much. And, well, the Hearts believed it was your mother."

Rosana gasped. "No! Why would they think such a thing?"

"The queen was after her head. She was not a good person, to be sure. She detested your mother. The King of Hearts accused her, brought her in for trial, and held her captive in Wondercity. This was back when I was still their servant. Gratefully, we both escaped, but how I miss your mother so! She could've helped us when Avoria came here." Matt dabbed some sweat from his forehead with his sleeve, suddenly looking weary and distressed. "As you can see, she ruined us. The Diamonds and Clubs are no more. Few lucky survivors fled to

Wondertown and we took them in, but most of them are gone, and the Hearts have darkened beyond recognition." A glint of nostalgia crossed Matt's face, locking his gaze somewhere in the distance, until he blinked a few times as if waking up from a trance. "Honestly, my dear friend, we're about one incident away from going completely mad."

The way his voice trembled and his eyes widened when he finished his sentence, Rosana had the sudden urge to wrap him in a firm hug. Gretel beat her to it, however, burying a cheek in Matt's hip and closing her tiny arms around his waist. When Gretel shuddered, Rosana realized the girl was crying quietly into Matt's jacket. A single tear spilled onto his shoe, bursting into a hundred little spheres and rolling onto the tiled ground. The tear sunk into the tile as if the surface drank it, and a creamy white moonflower popped out of the ground.

Rosana knelt and plucked the flower out, roots and all. She offered it to Matt, twirling the stem between her fingers until its star shape became a circular blur. "You know, I think it's awesome, what this town is doing to try and unite the realm again. And I understand how you feel, being one small poke away from crumbling. But sometimes in those same moments, one beautiful thing can build us back up again."

With a trembling hand, Matt picked the moonflower out of Rosana's fingers and held it really close to his face, nearly going cross-eyed studying the little filaments that tickled the air. Lively color inked into his cheeks as the life returned to his eyes, his gaze shifting between Rosana and the flower.

"One beautiful thing."

Rosana was pretty sure the color was swimming in her own cheeks as well.

"Those are great words, Rosana. Very wonderful, very *beautiful* words. Thank you." Matt threaded the flower into his hat and took Rosana's hand, his other arm still tight around Gretel. "Do you believe in destiny?"

Rosana sucked in her lower lip. She barely believed the story about her mother, a prisoner in Wondercity and a potential assassin. "I don't know. So much has happened to me in such a short time that I'm not really sure what's safe to believe in anymore."

"There is no belief without at least a little risk," Matt said. "What do you *want* to believe?"

Rosana thought about her adventures with Crescenzo and Pietro. She thought about her mother and what played out on the video screens of Wondertown. "I guess I try to believe that, sometimes, we end up right where we're supposed to be."

Matt nodded slowly. "Do you believe we have any control over our futures? That sometimes we decide how things are supposed to be?"

Rosana found it harder and harder to maintain eye contact with Matt. It wasn't that he was hard to talk to or to look in the face. It was just that she wasn't normally the kind of person to answer such loaded, thought-provoking questions. It was part of the reason why she was so glad to be homeschooled. Public school icebreakers made her tense up right around the point where the teacher made her think about what flavor ice cream she'd be or what color her personality was. *Just answer the question, Rosana.* "I didn't decide to drop into Wonderland. There was no control over any of this."

Matt's grip tightened in a gentle way—a fitting way—like a boot closing around an ankle. "What if you can control everything that happens here from this point forward? You can make Wonderland's destiny."

Rosana shook her head. "I'm not sure what you're getting at here."

"Oh, you're more sure than you think," Matt said. "You said it yourself. These people of Wonderland just need *one beautiful thing.*"

Rosana's heart sped up. "I'm sorry, I'm still not quite following y—"

Whoosh! A flash of white streaked from one corner of Rosana's vision to the other, catching her off guard. She jerked her hands out of Matt's grip and snapped her head from side to side, not even sure what to be looking for. Wondertown continued to buzz normally, or at least at the local definition of normally.

"What was that?" she asked.

Gretel turned in a full circle, evidently having seen the flash of white as well.

Matt, unfazed by the flash, pulled out a shimmering gold pocket watch, clicked it open, and gasped. "We're late! Listen," he said, cupping Rosana's elbows. "Tonight is incredibly important, Rosana. I need you and young Gretel to head straight into the capital. That castle over there. You should have no problems, but just in case, tell them you're with me."

"Where are *you* going?" Rosana asked.

"Why, I'm part of the show, of course! We'll see each other in there. It's going to be a jabberwocking blast! A spectacular show, a feast, a meeting with the King, a dance . . . which reminds me!" Matt reached up and lifted the very top of his hat as if he were opening a can. He plunged a hand into the opening and swirled his wrist around, looking like he was only scratching his head, but he fished out two silky bunches of cloth. He handed one to Gretel and one to Rosana. After Rosana shook it open, she realized the shining navy bundle in her hands was a dress, and it was the most beautiful item of clothing she'd ever beheld. She had the chance to raid Hua Mulan's closet before a venture to the red carpet in Hollywood, and she'd found some spectacular clothes there, but the dress Matt pulled out of his hat made Mulan's closet look like a thrift shop. Every angle Rosana held it at, stars blinked in the material like cameras flashing at the Emmy's. There were no frills, bows, or lacy embellishments that Rosana tended to hate anyway—only a soft, flowing curtain of shiny material. "Matt."

"Put that on before you go inside," Matt said. "My gift to you. Oh, and do me a favor." He took a knee and tilted his head forward. "Reach in and grab your shoes? Gretel's, too."

Rosana dipped a skeptical arm into the dark, cavernous hole in the top of Matt's hat, dumbfounded that she was already elbow deep and hadn't even grazed his hair. Suddenly, her fingers scraped something smooth and hard. She pinched and pulled out a pair of navy pumps. Amazed, she plunged the other hand in and pulled out a small pair of white flats for Gretel.

"That's it!" Matt snapped his hat shut and grinned. "What a surprise! I hope you like your gifts."

"They're lovely, Matt," Rosana said. "Thank you."

"Thank you!" Gretel said, hugging Matt again.

"You're welcome." Matt put two fingers in his mouth and blew. "Oh, Jub-Jub!" he cried.

Within seconds, a large shadow blanketed the ground and a black and white bird the size of a cow descended from the skies, rubbing its head along Matt's shoulder. With about as much effort as it takes to blink, Matt hopped up, swung a leg over the bird's back, and mounted it like a horse. He patted the bird's head and spoke to it like a toddler. "Good Jub-Jub."

Rosana couldn't believe her vision when the bird nodded.

Matt flashed one more grin at Rosana and Gretel, gently wrapping his arms around the bird's neck. "Okay, I'll see you two at the Evening of Wonder! Remember, you're with me!"

Matt jerked his heel and the bird cawed, ruffled its feathers, and soared high into the air. Rosana and Gretel stood side by side, watching the spectacular man fly toward the castle.

CHAPTER THIRTEEN

WONDERLAND

Crescenzo was out of breath, and it seemed that the white rabbit had only picked up pace since he and Geppetto started chasing it. *Rabbits suck.* There was no telling how long they'd been running after the animal, but Crescenzo was starting to perceive changes in the environment. Less trees. Less mushrooms and giant bees. More huts and more humidity, coating Crescenzo in a film of moisture.

He stole a quick glance behind him and stumbled on a stray root sticking out of the ground. "You doing all right, Grandpa?"

"It's Geppetto." His grandfather moved with impressive speed and stamina, almost putting Crescenzo to shame for part of the way. "Don't let him lose us! Keep going!"

The strangest part was that when Crescenzo fell behind, it seemed as though the rabbit paused and waited for him. Crescenzo would catch up and find it standing on two legs. After making direct eye contact, the rabbit would bound away again.

"Do you think he wants to be followed?" Crescenzo asked between breaths.

"I think he *needs* to be followed," Geppetto insisted.

And so they followed the rabbit all the way to a glistening town of red, black, and white, strangely empty and quiet for a landscape with so much potential for activity. Crescenzo was particularly impressed and surprised by the Starbucks on the edge of the town, which slowed him down considerably as he tore his gaze away from the rabbit.

"A *Starbucks?*" Crescenzo marveled. *Pietro would freak.*

Geppetto sprinted past Crescenzo and trailed the rabbit. "Now is not the time, boy."

"But this place is so amazing!" Crescenzo let his eyes wander around the buildings, the sky, and even the ground itself. There was a brilliant castle, a floating island, and several enormous screens that seemed to descend from nowhere. When Crescenzo saw the young girl featured on the screens, the rabbit escaped his mind completely. "Where are we, Geppetto? And who's *she?*"

With an irritated groan, Geppetto slowed to a stop, laid his hands on his knees, and caught his breath. With a thick sleeve, he brushed his forehead before turning around and approaching Crescenzo again. "We're going to lose the rabbit," Geppetto said. "Are you proud?"

Crescenzo ignored his grandfather's voice, staring up at the screen that had come down from the floating island. "I need to know who that girl is. She looks so much like . . ." Everything clicked before Crescenzo could utter a name. "That's Alice. That's Rosana's mom! Why is she on the screens right now?"

Geppetto clawed at Crescenzo's shoulders. "You're not understanding me right now, *ragazzo.* You have so many questions, such a tiny attention span, and yet it is incredibly important that we continue to follow the rabbit. Have you understood nothing in your adventures? You must always follow the signs of The Carver. If you stray from their path, you risk everything."

Crescenzo gently pried Geppetto's hands off his shoulders. "I feel like you're being a little dramatic. It's a bunny."

Geppetto pressed his grip back onto Crescenzo's shoulders. "And I feel that *you* don't comprehend the fact that you're not at home anymore. You are not in a world bound by logic anymore. The minute Hansel invaded your realm and swiped your mother, everything changed for you. You cannot tell me that I'm being *dramatic* and expect my sympathy when something goes wrong. I'm telling you the rules of our world. Please acknowledge them."

Crescenzo caught a flicker of white out of the corner of his eye, and he watched the rabbit dart through the spangled city until it approached the castle doors.

From the distance of about three football fields, Crescenzo watched two husky guards in overalls step in front of the doors. Their faces were turned at downward angles and their spears rested upright in their pudgy hands, whereas the rabbit stood on hind legs before them and tilted its head up, its ears swiveling back and forth between the two guards. Finally, the guards clicked their spears on the ground, stepped apart, and the doors swung open. Silver light washed the air from within the castle and a faint bass drum sounded from within, like the castle had a heartbeat.

Perfectly in sync with one another and with one of the drumbeats, the twin guards bowed and the rabbit hopped into the light. The doors clicked shut behind it.

"Um, wow," Crescenzo said. "The guards just let that rabbit into the castle."

"It would appear that they *invited* the rabbit into the castle," Geppetto corrected.

"And now I'm guessing you want us to go in there."

Geppetto was already making his way down the lane, paying no mind to the girl on the floating screens or the massive island in the air.

As Crescenzo followed his grandfather, he didn't take his eyes off the screen ahead of him. It was ridiculous how much Alice looked like Rosana. All one had to do was darken her hair and adjust her skin tone just a bit. But those eyes, the facial structure, that stance she took as her cape billowed behind her armor and her irises pierced the air, and her lips in a flat line . . . Crescenzo had seen that exact face before.

"Did you know her?" Crescenzo asked Geppetto.

"Did I know Alice?" Geppetto repeated. "Yes."

Crescenzo waited for more, but Geppetto didn't offer any elaboration. His leather soles slapped the glistening ground, casting tiny echoes into the empty streets. *Clop, clop, clop, clop.* He seemed to be studying the castle and the two guards in front of the doors.

"And?" Crescenzo pried.

"And she was just another bad influence on my boy. She wanted to know about every little thing, always poking her nose around places where kids shouldn't go. If you ask me, it was she who found those mines and started playing in them. She and Peter Pan. And she kept getting lost, you know. My son would come home so distressed because she would vanish for days at a time. Little did I know she was playing war in another kingdom."

"Wow," Crescenzo said. "Sounds like you didn't like her much."

"I never said I didn't like little Alice. She was also fiercely loyal to my son, and she was *smart*. I can only begin to imagine what a clever woman she grew up to be. So different from that rascal Peter Pan."

Crescenzo furrowed his brows. "Peter Pan's a great man." He paused, realizing that was the first time he'd referred to Pietro using his *other* name. "But yeah, he is kind of a goof, too. Also, do you want to explain to me how you plan to get into that castle? Those are guards, and it's not like we're anybody important."

Geppetto didn't answer, to Crescenzo's dismay. Crescenzo was mostly concerned because they were closer than ever to the castle, and they had already attracted the guards' attention. Big, bald, and squinty-eyed, they appeared to be twins, and there was no questioning why somebody would choose them to guard a pair of castle doors. Crescenzo took one look at their arms, the size of cannons, and knew there was no way he was going to get past them if they didn't want him to. They muttered unintelligible blubberings to each other, tapping their spears against the ground, and studied Crescenzo as he approached.

Crescenzo glared at his grandfather and spoke in a hushed tone. "If you have a plan, you'd better say something right now!"

Geppetto flashed Crescenzo a wink and stopped ten feet in front of the guards. "Hello."

The guards nodded in unison. "Sir."

"My grandson and I would like your permission to pass. May we enter?"

"Enter. All are welcome." The guards slid to the side, their boots scraping the ground with a loud squeak. "Enjoy."

The doors swung open.

Boom! Boom *boom*, clack! The sounds of drums jittered Crescenzo's veins and penetrated his senses. It was a wonder he didn't go deaf. There must have been at least a hundred men and women on a stage against the far wall, banging on barrel-shaped drums ranging from the size of a soda can to the size of an elephant. The drummers' arms moved like windmills, swinging high above their heads and slamming their mallets down with ground-shaking force. Their rhythm stayed the same until the doors shut behind Crescenzo, when the drummers picked up speed and the beat became more complex.

Facing the drummers, there had to be at least a thousand people, not one of which Crescenzo recognized. He certainly didn't see any runaway bunnies in the crowd, either. And all the castle's guests were clad in dresses, suits, tuxes, and strange patchwork outfits that looked more like thrifty Halloween costumes. Even so, Crescenzo knew that he and Geppetto were out of place.

"We're not supposed to be here," Crescenzo said to Geppetto, but the drums masked his words and swallowed all other sounds in the room. Nobody even took heed of the doors.

Geppetto cupped his ear and leaned toward Crescenzo. *What?* The old man mouthed.

"We shouldn't be here! We weren't invited."

But if all are welcome . . . is she *here?*

Rosana was having the time of her life. Nothing had ever come close to the joy, excitement, and sheer awe she experienced with every passing moment of the Evening of Wonder.

For one thing, she hadn't eaten so fully in over six months. It was strange to think that not so long ago, she was living off of scraps and the kindness of strangers in underground New York. She never exactly went hungry. Petrelli's Pizza always had fresh veggie scraps left over at the end of the night, and the occasional cheese slice. A local cinema threw out bags of popcorn early every morning before the concessions crew left. Some people would bring her salads or half a sandwich or an apple they picked up at the neighborhood market. Other times, Rosana resorted to pickpocketing. She wasn't proud.

She did well on her own, but she never exactly got to feast like she did in Wondertown, and she worried that nothing would ever compare again. The mashed potatoes! So fluffy and so light with just the right amount of butter, salt, and pepper. How did the cream of mushroom soup get so rich and thick, especially when all the mushrooms Rosana had seen in Wondercountry were black and shriveled? She decided not to think about that. *Magic.*

There was also a Jell-O bar complete with every flavor Rosana had ever known, and many she had never tasted before. Each flavor was piled into a mountain at least as high as the Christmas tree she used to visit with her mom in Rockefeller Center. Next to each Jell-O mountain, there was a barrel of whipped cream, which she had to tell Gretel not to stick her hands into.

A wave of nostalgia crashed over Rosana when one of the servers offered fried macaroni and cheese on a stick. She ate two and thought of Pietro.

As she and Gretel ate and sipped chocolate root beer, music and festivities played through the night. Colorful dancers did the Charleston. Acrobats whipped around the ballroom and glided through the air, seemingly without wires, swings, or support of any kind. They were also skilled contortionists, winding themselves into tight, backward circles and perfect Zs as they sailed above Rosana's head. The magic show toyed with her mind. Wonderland's standards of magic were much higher than her world's. She expected card tricks, trap doors, and gimmicked wands, but the mysterious masked woman on stage created sunlight from tea leaves, projected clouds above their heads, made a moonflower sprout legs and grow ten feet tall and dance around the room, and she even seemed to have a mysterious effect on some people's ages. An old woman volunteered for one of her acts, and she regressed to a comfortable youth as the dinner went on. Similarly, a baby sprouted into a toddler in the time it took Rosana to eat a mac-and-cheese triangle.

Rosana's rational mind protested against everything she had seen, but her heart rejected nothing, and her grin only grew with every bite, every minute, and every exciting feat of the evening. There was only one real question on her mind as the night went on: *Where's Matt?*

She got her answer when a portly man in a sparkling bow tie took the stage, cleared his throat, and announced the next act. "And now, ladies and gentlemen of Wondertown, the moment you've all been waiting for! I'm happy to introduce his illustrious majesty, Mr. Matthew Hadinger, the King of Spades!"

Zack wasn't sure how long he'd been riding toward Wondertown on Chester's back, but as long as his allergies weren't acting up, he probably could've ridden forever and basked in the simulated feeling of flying. He found himself wishing his dad were around to demonstrate what he could do. But when Zack thought of his strange dream about the fortuneteller, he wished for his mom to give him assurance that everything would be okay. And then he wondered if *they* were okay.

Zack shook his head and cleared his parents from his thoughts, remembering that he was on a mission.

"Wondertown, dead ahead!" Chester announced. *"Oh boy! I see the bone. I see the bone!"*

Atchoo! Zack sneezed so hard he accidently drove his heels into the cat's sides.

"Hey! What'd I say 'bout kicking?" Chester scolded.

"Sorry," Zack muttered. "You can let me off here if you want."

Chester blinked into view again, skidded to a stop, and bent down to snatch up his bone. He used his tail to scoop Zack up and set him back down on the ground.

Zack caught his breath and raised an eyebrow. With his arms folded, he studied the world before him. "Wondertown, eh? Do you think my friend went in that castle?"

"I think the shadows are in that castle. Be careful," Chester warned. "Tonight feels rather . . . strange. I should enjoy another game of fetch with you if you live."

Without another sound, Chester vanished, and Zack started toward the castle with his head up high, doing his best to look braver than he felt.

After a brief conversation with the guards, Zack quietly slipped through the castle doors and pressed his back against the walls.

There were no shadows to be seen.

This. Is. Amazing. For a second, Zack almost forgot he was there to look for Crescenzo and Rosana. The atmosphere was sensory overload. The scent of baked desserts and salted meats ensnared his nostrils. The whirlwind of color entranced his vision. The laughs of the merry crowd captivated his ears. He wanted to join them. He wanted to join them with his friends.

Enzo. Where are you?

Zack stood on his toes, sweeping his gaze from left to right. He looked for any sign of inky dark hair, a red cloak, a small girl with braids, or an elderly man. However, there were hundreds of people in the castle, and all the guests had cast their attention on one: A man in a sparkling bow tie who had taken the stage.

"And now, ladies and gentlemen of Wondertown, the moment you've all been waiting for! I'm happy to introduce his illustrious majesty, Mr. Matthew Hadinger, the King of Spades!"

People stood, clapped, whistled, and applauded as if a rock star were about to enter the room. "*Matt! Matt! Matt!*" they chanted.

The King of Spades—or Matt, as the crowd continued to chant— appeared in the form of a lone man on stage with a plum-colored tux and a dark-felt top hat. When he strode out to address the crowd, the ballroom went wild. *Wow,* Zack thought. *People really love this guy.* With his cheerful charisma, quirky and easy confidence, and movie star looks, it wasn't hard to see why.

As the audience continued to cheer, Matt removed his top hat, showed the opening to the crowd, and gave the lid a heavy swat. A seemingly endless stream of balloons spewed out of the hat and tumbled into the ballroom. As Matt rotated the hat, intricate balloon animals galloped out from the opening and pranced about the room, while simple helium globes bubbled and soared up to the ceiling. His guests reached for them and clapped and hooted, and it was one of the happiest moments Zack had ever seen. *Nothing will ever excite me again,* he thought as a six-foot balloon penguin waddled up to him and bowed.

"Tonight," Matt cried, instantly commanding the crowd's attention, "we celebrate an important legacy. We honor an important history: that of Alice the Brave!"

"Alice!" the crowd cheered.

"Alice the Brave!" Matt repeated, fixing his hat back on his head. "She gave us hope of a Wonderland united and a vision of a perfect world. After all we've been through, my friends, do we not deserve this vision? Is it not time that we bring Alice's hope to life?"

"It is time!"

There was a comfortable pause while Matt let the atmosphere sink in. "Alice should have been our queen after the fall of the jabberwockies. She was a ruler we could trust and pour our hearts into! It is a real shame that she disappeared from our lives." Matt paused again. "But let's not be broken anymore. Let's be the world that Alice wanted to see. I can think of no better reason to come together than the fact that Alice's own daughter is in our presence tonight."

Excited whispers lit up the room. Guests tapped each other's shoulders and speculated. "Is she *really*?" "Where is she?" "What is he talking about?" But one feather-haired woman pointed a red-gloved finger across the room, and Zack traced its trail.

"He's looking at *her*!" the woman said.

Rosana! At last, Zack saw her standing next to a balloon giraffe, her face red with embarrassment, and his heart smiled. *She's okay.* He'd been so worried that their argument had driven her toward the dark city, or that something might have snatched her up after she'd separated from the group. But if there was one thing he'd learned from the short time he'd spent with her, she was a survivor. Not only that, but according to Wonderland, she was a hero.

So where's Crescenzo? Of course he had to have followed Rosana to the party. Zack scanned the room.

"Miss Rosana," Matt continued, "as our guest of honor tonight, would you like to come up and say a few—?"

Boom!

A colossal sound interrupted Matt's speech and thundered through the room, causing all of Matt's balloons to burst at once and spill onto the ground in tiny little knots of latex. Zack doubled over and covered his ears, desperately hoping for the persistent ringing to go away. When he straightened his back again, the room was deathly silent, and he noticed all the partygoers had turned toward a single point behind him and in front of the castle doors. Nobody was smiling anymore.

Zack followed the crowd's gaze to a bearded man of about seven feet, robed in red garments. He wore a black crown on top of his head, and Zack had never seen such cold eyes before, like marbles rolled in powder and encased in ice. It didn't take long for Zack to decide he didn't like the stranger at all.

The man surveyed the curious crowd with an eerie calmness, his head turning almost robotically, and then he fixed his gaze on Matt and roared in the most aggressive voice Zack had ever heard, "*Matthew Hadinger!*"

Matt drew his brows together. "Cornelius? Have I sent you an invitation?"

"I'm hardly here to party, you bandersnatch," Cornelius spat. "Residents and guests, allow me to introduce myself." Cornelius bowed, and when he came up, his stare was even colder. "Cornelius Redding, the King of Hearts at your service."

The hairs prickled on Zack's neck. *Beware the King of Hearts.*

The dream was real.

"Hadinger, you're hiding somebody I want," the king continued. "Might you consider revealing her to me? I should very much enjoy the opportunity to welcome her to the World Between."

Zack's gaze tore between the two men. The tension was overbearing. It reminded him of an old western he watched with his dad, where the sheriff and the outlaw finally tromped into the desert, spurs jangling and bootheels drumming, and prepared to duel.

"I hardly know what you're talking about," Matt said. "Look around, Cornelius. I invited hundreds of merry men and women to the Evening of Wonder in *my* city. If they're hiding, they've chosen some questionable places to—"

"Don't. Play. Stupid with me. I refer, of course, to the daughter of Alice. I know she's here. I heard them *cheering* for her before I entered." The king broke into a series of long, slow strides, pacing around the room and swiveling about the crowd, fixing his intense, glassy gaze on unsuspecting guests. "And I surmise she's hiding amongst us. She has a gift for this, does she not?"

Zack's heart dropped. He scanned the room for his friends. Rosana was in danger, and so was Enzo. Who was this man, and what did he want with Rosana? Was he also the one responsible for Enzo's future death? *I've got to warn them,* Zack thought. *I need to save them from this man.*

"If you were to reveal her to me, Matthew, then perhaps Wondertown would enjoy a period of peace. We can come to an agreement over the rule of this realm."

"I'm sorry, Cornelius." Matt shook his head. "I can't do that."

"What's that, you said?" There was a collective gasp from the attendees when the king produced a long, bejeweled mace and brandished it with a smug, threatening curl of the mouth. "You'd like to know how this mace works?"

Matt sighed and spoke in soft, even tones as if undisturbed by the threat. "I think I'd like you to leave."

"Because I *can* show you how this mace works," the king continued. "And I *will* show you if the daughter of Alice doesn't come forward. *Right. Now.*"

Zack's blood turned ice cold when a bundle of crimson flashed through the air and coiled onto the ground, revealing Rosana on the other side of the ballroom. She stood meek and pale next to the tall man, her eyes wide and her lips quivering. An icy pang of guilt shot through Zack's body when he saw the fear on her face. Maybe if he hadn't upset her, they never would've gotten separated, and she wouldn't be standing right here under the threat of a mad man.

The King of Hearts put away his mace, smiled impishly, and took another step forward. "Aha! There you are!" He spread his arms, and his grin widened with them. "Good girl. I admire your bravery. Why not take it a step further? Come and kneel before me. Come here, Rosana."

Beware the King of Hearts.

Rosana took a small step.

"*Nooo!*" Zack heard himself scream, and before he knew it, everybody had turned to stare at him, including the venomous king.

"*Zack?*" Rosana took a step back.

"I don't like this!" Zack declared. "Don't take another step, Rosana!"

"Ah! The second child emerges." The king pivoted and advanced toward Zack. "Pleased to meet you, Mr. Volo! And where might the third child be hiding?"

A small eternity of thick silence passed, and then Crescenzo shot his hand up by the banister, igniting both relief and terror in Zack's chest. "I'm right—"

"It's time for you to leave!" Matt shouted. "Get out of my castle!"

"Not without claiming a party favor. I came for the daughter of Alice," Cornelius replied. He did a half-turn, reached out, and stroked Zack's chin, sending shivers down his spine.

"You shall not touch her!" Matt roared.

He let go of his hat, and it hovered in the air. Zack watched in awe as the hat soared in front of Rosana's chest. A soft pink rectangle of light appeared in front of it, guarding Rosana like a plastic shield.

Keep your cool, Zack, he told himself. *Be brave. Find your opportunity to run.*

But the opportunity didn't come, for the king took a grand, sweeping step and placed the crook of his elbow around Zack's neck. Cornelius elicited a shrewd, deep laugh, and said, "That's quite all right for now, Hadinger. I didn't expect you to cooperate, of course. But for the time being"—Cornelius tightened his hold with such intensity that Zack could almost feel his face turn blue—"*this* one will suffice!"

Dizziness clouded Zack's mind as his lungs tightened. Screams from all directions poured into his ears. He clenched his teeth and reached up, clawing at the enormous man's arms in an attempt to free himself, but with every scratch, the king only pressed his arm tighter against Zack's throat. To his horror, the ballroom was filling up with new people. Soldiers in red armor materialized out of nowhere, just as Rosana had when she removed her cloak. They blinked into existence in every part of the room, some brandishing swords while many carried a bow and a quiver of arrows.

"Release the boy!" Matt cried.

Rosana attempted to run in Zack's direction, but the top hat and the pink rectangle followed her and blocked her movements. Matt waved his arm as if commanding the hat's actions.

"*Zack!*" Crescenzo broke into a run, but he was quickly stopped by a pair of soldiers barring his path by crossing their swords. Every time somebody moved in Zack's direction with the intent to help him, another Heart appeared.

"Please welcome the main event of the night!" Cornelius used his free hand to indicate his soldiers. "I trust they'll hold your attention for the rest of the evening." Cornelius popped a yellow grape into his mouth. Juice burst through his lips, and without wiping it away, he took a step back toward the doors and dragged Zack with him. The doors swung open with a loud creak. "I thank you for your hospitality tonight. Rosana, I'll see you soon."

"*Stop!*" Matt ordered. The hat returned to his hands, and he smacked the brim. A bird the size of an airplane burst from the opening and soared over the crowd. "Jub Jub! Go!"

The bird let out a shrill screech, spread its wings, and rocketed toward Zack and his captor.

For a terrible second, Zack thought the bird was going to bite his head off, but Cornelius dragged Zack outside while the ballroom spiraled into chaos.

Before the bird could reach him, the doors thundered shut and sealed him away from the castle.

He was alone with the king.

CHAPTER FOURTEEN

THE OLD WORLD

"So the thing about Wonderland is that there are several entrances. At least, that's my theory. The first time I went there, I fell down a rabbit hole, and I swear it was *right here*." Alicia beat her hands together, letting a glob of mud fall away in a pile by her side. She picked up a large, jagged stick and drove it into the ground like a shovel.

Hansel dug his bootheel into a patch of dirt. Grass and pebbles from the riverbank caked his knees. "You're sure it was here?"

"I couldn't be more positive. I was sitting against that tree, and I remember that rock because it reminded me of a face, and this river used to be crystal clear. Not this nasty pea-green stuff. Yuck."

"Maybe this land will return to its natural beauty one day," Hansel said. He put his hands on his hips and stared at the horizon. "Alice, I'm inclined to believe your rabbit hole isn't here anymore."

Alice didn't have the heart to say it out loud, but she agreed.

"How did you get to Wonderland the second time?" Hansel asked.

"Through a mirror."

Hansel cringed at the word.

"But that's not going to work again. I tried to tell my father where I had been when I came back through. He was furious. He told me to stop lying, stop reading so many fantasy books, and get my head out of the clouds. He sold the mirror the next day."

Hansel's jaw dropped. "He sold your mirror? And yet you don't find this significant? To whom did he sell it?"

Alicia tossed her stick on the ground and leaned back against the tree. "Some woodcarver. Why would it be significant? I highly doubt it was the same mirror I stole from Queen Avoria all those years ago. Even if it were, it's broken. We're not getting back through it. We're going to have to find another way."

"I'm surprised, Alice. We've been digging all day, and you haven't thought to at least go looking for that mirror? Who was the woodcarver? Surely it wasn't—?"

"Not Pinocchio or his father," Alicia said. "Some guy named Cherry."

Hansel rubbed his chin. "You never thought to go looking for this *Cherry*? To get the mirror back?"

"I'm telling you it would be a lost cause. I don't even know where Cherry lived. I don't know how I'd find him, and even if I did, what would I tell him?"

"How about the truth? Stranger things have happened in this world. Wouldn't it be worth a try if you had a chance to save your daughter?"

"Well, yeah, but—"

"But nothing. Let's find out where Cherry lived. It'll be no more of a waste of time than"—Hansel brushed some dirt off his sleeves—"digging."

Alicia crossed her arms and studied Hansel. "Why is it so important for you to help me?"

Hansel heaved a slow, deep sigh and tilted his head back. "Because I want to be a good man, and helping you is what any good man would do right now." He paused and swallowed, his Adam's apple sinking a full inch before it rose again. "I suggest we start in Florindale. We can ask the townspeople what they know and survey the crowd. Hopefully somebody knows who you're talking about, and we'll learn everything we can about Cherry."

For a brief moment, Alicia saw her childhood friend in Hansel, innocent and good-hearted. She smiled, shook some mud off her feet, and massaged her knuckles, a dry film of shiny mud seeping into her skin. "Okay," she said, "we can go to Florindale together. And thank you, Hansel."

Snow was furious. She'd been following the compass ever since she separated from Hansel, but she determined it was leading her in circles through the Woodlands. What was more: Her time was already halfway up. The clock, compass, or whatever it was that Rumpelstiltskin had given her, ticked relentlessly with no regard for her effort. She'd passed the same little house three times already, and still she felt like she was no closer to Dr. Frankenstein's book, to Violet's door, or to any cure for her husband.

Snow had lived in the Woodlands for a great deal of time. She knew them inside and out, and she couldn't imagine there was a single place where an old book of research notes would be hiding. Dr. Frankenstein most certainly didn't live nearby.

She walked around and around, even peering into a few houses to see if anybody was home. The compass needle would swing south. Snow would turn around, and the compass would spin north again. She looked up into the trees, electing to climb the tallest one, and peered down at the Woodlands from her bird's-eye view. She saw nothing more than rocks, patches of dead grass, and abandoned houses. When a small boy, likely no older than twelve years old, emerged from a cottage, Snow's heart fluttered and she scrambled down the tree to catch up with him.

"Hey! You there, boy, please wait! I need to ask you a question!"

The boy spun around and regarded Snow with round amber eyes. In his hands, he protected a half-eaten fruit pastry like an injured bird. He didn't speak a word when Snow caught up to him with her heart in her throat.

"Boy," she breathed, "what's your name?"

The boy took a careful step back, pocketing the pastry in a small pouch at his side. "Thomas," he said. "If you please, ma'am, who are you?"

"I'm Snow White. I need to ask—"

The boy's eyes widened, and he took three more steps back. "S-Snow W-W-White? Everybody says you're dead!"

What? "No, no, Thomas. I'm alive." Snow inched forward and held out her hand.

Tom stepped back again, this time tripping over a rogue tree branch and toppling onto the ground. "Stay back!" Thomas cautioned. "Don't come any closer to me. You're a ghost!"

"I'm not a ghost. I'm real," Snow said, her voice low, steady, and careful. She picked up an apple and tossed it up in the air a few times. "See? Nothing goes through me."

Thomas hopped to his feet. "That doesn't mean anything to me! They said you died in battle and that your blood stains the courtyard. If you're alive, then where's the Prince? Tell me or I'm going to the king!"

"No, don't go to King Bellamy! I promise you, I'm alive. Liam, he's . . ." Snow sighed. "He's also alive. Sort of. I need your help, though. The Ivory Queen turned him to gold."

"You're lying," Thomas decided. "You're telling lies, and you want me to trust you so I can be like *you*. I won't let you take my soul!"

Snow covered her mouth, hurt by the accusation. "Thomas, I wouldn't—"

"Help!" the boy yelled, turning and running into the woods. "Help me, there's a ghost!"

"Wait!" Snow called after him. "Please, I'm trying to find an old book! Do you know where Dr. Frankenstein used to live?"

But Thomas was long gone, his cries and footsteps fading into silence.

Snow collapsed onto the ground with defeat in her heart and an hour remaining on her timer. Her trials had hardened her so much that she couldn't bring herself to cry.

Snow decided that it ultimately didn't matter what would happen if the timer reached zero. Maybe she would drift into eternal sleep when the time ran out. Maybe the Ivory Queen would return to the Old World and turn *her* to gold, or kill her with a swift cut to black. Any of the above would be an act of mercy. Nothing in the world would be worse than losing her husband forever.

So Snow gave up. If the timer was going to run out, she was going to be by Liam's side when it happened, and she was going to say her goodbyes, regardless of whether or not he could actually hear her in his new form.

She trudged back to the White Road and made her way back to her castle, wishing that she really *were* a ghost.

CHAPTER FIFTEEN

WONDERLAND: WONDERTOWN CASTLE

Crescenzo heard the screams and saw the arrows fly, but he hadn't fully processed everything he just witnessed until his grandfather tackled him.

The walking balloon animals, magic tricks, and dancing moonflowers were of little importance. Instead, his mind was fixed on the people around him.

Matt, the King of Spades who commanded his people's attention with such poise and gentility.

Rosana, who looked absolutely stunning in her dress. Who was apparently the guest of honor at this extravagant celebration.

Cornelius Redding, the King of Hearts. Crescenzo couldn't remember feeling such terror in his life when the man started yelling.

Zack, who Crescenzo had left sitting on a mushroom to chase a white rabbit, who had appeared in the ballroom for but a minute to stick up for Rosana, who had instantly been abducted by the terrible king.

Chaos. The king had taken Zack and left an army in the ballroom.

"Zack!" Crescenzo screamed over the chaos. "Geppetto! We have to go after him. We have to follow and save my—"

"Crescenzo it's not safe!" Geppetto fired in a quick breath. "What makes you think you can do that alone? It would be *suicidio*!"

"Zack would do it for me! We're best friends!"

"Don't be thick. Think, my boy!"

Crescenzo scowled. *Everyone always tells me I need to act. You're telling me to think. I'm so confused.*

"*Get down!*" Geppetto shouted.

Stars exploded in Crescenzo's vision, and his skull collided with the ground. Geppetto's elbows hammered into Crescenzo's back.

Whoosh! Tik!

Screams rang through the hall, and thousands of shuffling feet stampeded in every direction.

"Don't stand until I tell you," Geppetto ordered, "unless you see the rabbit. If you find him, follow him. Don't wait."

Crescenzo swiveled his head, unsure what to make of the chaos. His pulse thundered in his temples. "What's going on?"

"It would appear our kings are at war. And one of them wants your heads."

Crescenzo winced as a heavyset man kicked him in the back of the neck and promptly tripped onto the floor. The six-piece band scattered off the stage. Two thoughts came to his mind. "I have to find Rosana. We have to get her out of here."

And find Zack.

A red-tipped arrow speared the ground, inches away from Crescenzo's nose. His eyes widened and he rolled over, pushing Geppetto off. "We gotta go!"

Geppetto stumbled to his feet. "Run! Head for the exit!"

Boom! The castle doors locked, sealing the outside world away from the frightened guests. A large group of patrons banded together and tried to make a sort of human battering ram, heaving their bodies against the doors as they seemed to have been locked from the outside. Crescenzo thought of the two pudgy guards and wondered if they were inside trying to fight off the ambushers. Had they fought the King of Hearts when he escaped with Zack?

What does he want? Crescenzo wondered. He ran toward the doors and collided with a thick, bearded man with a scar above his brow. The man was clad entirely in red velvet-coated armor. The man sneered at Crescenzo, swatted his cheek with the back of his hand, and raised a dark bow, aiming an arrow between his eyes.

"*Duck, boy!*" Geppetto cried.

Crescenzo heeded the order just in time. The archer's arrow whizzed over his head, fluttering his hair in its trajectory. Instinctually, Crescenzo dove for the archer's legs and tried to knock him off balance, but the man was too steady. The archer grabbed another arrow.

Swish!

Crescenzo looked up and saw Geppetto's knife glimmering in the light, and the string of the archer's bow had been divided in two.

"Get away from my grandson," Geppetto growled. The old man gave the archer a right hook and knocked him to the ground.

Whoa, my grandpa is a badass! Crescenzo's excitement was short-lived. A bald woman in red armor came up behind Geppetto and unsheathed a crimson scimitar. She bared her teeth and made an ugly cackling sound as she positioned her blade for attack.

Crack!

A crystal sphere fell from the second story of the castle and burst over the woman's head, bringing her instantly to her knees. The walking moonflower was upstairs tossing fragile items down at the intruders.

But what terrified Crescenzo the most wasn't the army causing chaos in the ballroom. It was the bird that had flown out of Matt's cap and started terrorizing the Hearts. The bird reminded Crescenzo more of a pterodactyl than anything. Its wings created wild gusts of wind that toyed with Crescenzo's hair. Every few seconds, the creature would screech, swoop down, and catch one of the soldiers in its talons. Without a care in the world, it would zoom around, fly up to the highest point of the room, and drop its captive.

Other Hearts weren't so lucky. Some of them were swallowed whole.

Crescenzo sprang back to his feet, silently praying that the bird wasn't going to develop a taste for innocent teenagers. He grabbed

Geppetto's elbow, pulling him away from the bald woman and from any trace of red armor he could see. Arrows whizzed past his ears and sailed from nearly every direction. *We're trapped.* Meanwhile, guests were falling everywhere, trampling each other and walking directly into the line of fire. Small handfuls managed to fight back, but most were untrained to handle the assorted men and women in the red armor.

Crescenzo tried to distract himself from his fear. "Where did you learn to do that?"

"Do what?" Geppetto asked.

Crescenzo dodged an arrow coming at him from an angle. "I'm pretty sure that archer guy teared up when you punched him. It was *awesome.*"

"Look, just because you think I'm *old*, doesn't mean I'm incapable of—"

"*Enzo!*"

The anger flushed from Crescenzo's face. Rosana was running toward him.

"Enzo, I've been so worried!"

"Rosana, you're okay!"

Rosana threw her arms around Crescenzo, and Matt and Gretel dashed along behind her. Crescenzo eyed the man's top hat and then shut his eyes and returned Rosana's hug. They didn't hold the pose for long.

"Matt," Rosana said, "do you have a plan? How do we get to safety?"

"I need to get you underground." It was admirable how he'd managed to speak in warm tones and keep his composure, showing little sign of nervousness besides a compulsive twiddling of the thumbs. He studied Crescenzo and then Geppetto. "Are you chums of hers?"

"Yes," Rosana said quickly. "They're friends of mine."

Matt beckoned the four guests to a nook behind one of the staircases, where Crescenzo noticed a rectangular patch in the wall that looked about half a shade lighter than the rest of the area.

"There's not enough room to save everybody." Matt frowned and cast a sad gaze around the ballroom. "But I can save *you* all if we hurry. I'll hide you, and then I'm coming back out here. I cannot let this madness endure." He twisted a torch in the wall, and the rectangle slid open. "Please stay very close behind me. Especially you, Miss Rosana. I have reason to believe you're in the most danger."

CHAPTER SIXTEEN

WONDERLAND: WONDERTOWN CASTLE

Everything's a mess.

Rosana's thoughts seemed to be the loudest thing in the room, even as she hugged Gretel and made soft shushing sounds. The young girl hadn't exactly been crying, but it was clear by her vacant expression that she was in a state of shock over what she'd just seen in the ballroom. "It's okay, Gretel. Everything's okay."

Everything's a mess.

Matt had led them into a dimly lit stone cellar stocked with the barest of commodities before he sealed them underground and returned to the ballroom to continue fighting off the Hearts. A part of Rosana felt irresponsible and guilty letting him hide the group. But she found herself wondering what sort of power she possessed. What could she possibly do to aid Matt in his battle?

"We should be going after Zack." Crescenzo slumped down against the wall and buried his face in his hands, sweat plastering his hair to his face.

A cold pang of sadness and anger crept into Rosana's stomach. *Zack.* She was annoyed with him. She was grateful to him for sticking up for her. She was horrified at having witnessed his abduction.

Who *was* that man? What did he want with her?

"We should be saving him from . . . from whoever that was." Crescenzo's voice was deep and raw with emotion.

"I told you," Geppetto growled. "It's *not safe*. Be grateful we have this moment of reprieve." He rested his hands on his knees, slumped down next to Crescenzo, shut his eyes, and took a deep breath. "I'm going to take a nap and rest my bones."

Rosana got on her knees and took Gretel's face in her palms. "Do you wanna go to sleep?"

The girl nodded silently.

Rosana untied her cloak and handed it to Gretel. "You can use this as a blanket, okay? Or a pillow."

With almost catatonic motions, Gretel accepted the cloak and crawled into a corner, bunching Rosana's cloak into a thin mediocre pillow.

With that, Rosana sat down next to Enzo and hesitantly reached for his hand. When their skin touched, she pressed more boldly and gathered his fingers in her grip. "Enzo," she said, her voice barely above a whisper, "talk to me."

Crescenzo lifted his head and locked eyes with Rosana. "You're not upset with me anymore? After everything that happened on the plains?"

"No, no, it's fine." Rosana sighed. "What happened after I left?"

"Zack and I got separated. I kind of, uh, left him behind. I shouldn't have done that. My grandfather and I arrived here together."

Rosana looked down at her hands, kneading her thumbs together. "I should have guessed you'd go looking for me when I ran off like that." She managed a wan smile. "You're so stubborn. You know that, right?"

"So I've been told."

"I appreciate you." Rosana squeezed Crescenzo's palm, smooth and firm between her fingers. "How did you know to come here, though? Did you get an invitation?"

"No." Crescenzo rubbed his forehead, his grim expression transitioning into one of deep thought. His eyebrows drew together, and he took a deep breath. "It's kind of a weird story, actually."

Geppetto had fallen into a light slumber, his chin dropping and his head rocking back and forth. Every few seconds, he'd lean too far in one direction, catch himself, and straighten his back, only to start tilting in the other direction. Heavy breaths tumbled out of his open mouth.

Rosana forced herself to grin, which was much easier to do when she looked at the snoozing Geppetto. She took a deep breath, determined to distract herself from the night's horrors. "What's weird is hearing you talk about a grandfather."

To Rosana's delight, Crescenzo laughed. "You're telling *me*. For most of my life, nobody even mentioned a grandfather. I mean, there's my Grandpa Weston on my mom's side, but I never got to meet him, and nobody ever talked about Geppetto. He's interesting, though. He started teaching me how to carve. Wanna see what I made?"

"*Do* I wanna see what you made? It's not a carving of me at the red carpet, is it?"

"Nope. Check this out!"

Crescenzo took a wooden rabbit from his pocket and pressed it into Rosana's palm. She rolled it around in her fingers, parted her lips, and studied it with childlike wonder. She studied the texture of the rabbit's fur, the angles of its ears, and the way it even seemed to wiggle its nose with its lifelike beauty.

"You did *not* make this today," Rosana finally decided. "It's too perfect."

"No, really!" Crescenzo said. "Geppetto was telling me a story, and I kind of, well, made it without thinking about it. It's even better than anything I've ever *drawn* before. It's like, in my mind's eye, I saw it somehow without really seeing it. And then there it was in my hands, you know?"

At that moment, a panel in the wall slid open and Matt stumbled into the dim room, his hat askew and his coat tattered. Outside the door, the ballroom was eerily silent compared to the symphony of terror that had been ringing through Wondertown earlier.

"The Hearts . . . have fled," Matt said between heavy breaths. He adjusted his tie and hat. "We will be safe for the time being. Miss

Rosana, how are you feeling? Are you hurt? Are you frightened?"

Rosana tucked a lock of hair behind her ear and rubbed her neck. "I'm confused," she said. "Why did you bring me here? Who was that man? What's going on in this place? And why didn't you tell me you were the *King of Spades?*"

Matt blew a raspberry and collapsed purposefully onto the floor, crossing his legs and pulling his knees up to his chest. "Miss Rosana, as the daughter of Alice the Brave, you are entitled to all these answers and more. You are the daughter of my dearest friend, who was a gentle soul for which I cared tremendously. When I knew that you had come to Wonderland, I wanted nothing more than to meet you, not only to see you but . . . I had rather hoped that I could play a role in your protection."

Rosana thought her heart was about to come unspooled. Here was an old acquaintance of her mother's, simply reaching out as an act of friendship. Rosana couldn't have imagined kinder words, even if they raised a burning question.

"Why does she need protecting?" Crescenzo asked. His tone was flat, and Rosana could tell he had reservations about Matt. She couldn't tell if they stemmed from skepticism or jealousy, but she found Crescenzo's stance endearing, and it pulled at her emotions even further.

Matt raised one eyebrow and leaned forward. "You *all* need protecting. Especially Rosana."

"From the King of Hearts," Crescenzo guessed. "That Cornelius guy."

"*Hearts,*" Geppetto growled, stirring in his sleep before settling back into deep, slow breaths.

Matt folded his hands. "Cornelius Redding is a dangerous man. Wrathful. Greedy. He wants this realm for himself, and Wondertown is the only place left that he doesn't control. So he taunts *me*, the rightful king of Spades. I'm sorry I didn't come clean straight away, Rosana. When I met you in the plains, I had hoped to first have your trust *without* my royal title. And, I *live* for grand surprises."

Rosana nodded, considering Matt's explanation.

"You should know that Cornelius has become even more dangerous since he met Avoria. After all, she lived with him during her stay in Wonderland. And even if she didn't, the King of Hearts also had a vendetta against Alice the Brave."

"Because he thinks she assassinated the Queen of Hearts," Rosana realized. "And if he hurts me, he'll feel like he's even."

She shuddered. Her mom *was* innocent, right? If Rosana could prove it, could she evade the King's wrath? Would it even matter now that he was in league with Avoria?

"If that's all he wanted, though, why did he take Zack?" Crescenzo asked.

"Because Zack stood up for her. He showed that he cares," Matt said. "I must assume that he's bait to lure Rosana into the Wondercity."

Rosana's gaze fell to the ground. *Zack showed that he cares. And now he's in trouble. My existence got him in trouble.*

"So you think he'll keep Zack alive?" Crescenzo asked.

"I'm almost certain of it. Whether that's a *good* thing is a bigger question. Cornelius knows you two will try to save your friend. And when you do, he'll break you. So it's most wonderful that you're not going to try."

"But—"

"You *will not* try," Matt pressed. "Your lives are precious, and without you in the picture, Cornelius will most certainly take Wondertown for himself. And I shiver to think of what Avoria will do to your world without you." Matt rubbed his elbows, his boots quavering as he spoke the Ivory Queen's name.

"I *hate* Avoria," Crescenzo muttered. "I've never even met her, but I hate her. She's caused too much pain for my family and friends. I want to get Zack back."

"Splendid bravery," Matt commended. "But you must think about how you're going to do so. I will not let you leave this town without a plan and proper training. You'll stay here with me and each receive a bed, food, clothing . . . the castle walls aren't impenetrable, but they're the safest I know."

Rosana stood up. "You invited me all this way just so you could protect me?"

"Miss Rosana," Matt replied, a bit of a twinkle in his eye, "it's what any sane man would do."

With that, Rosana took a step forward and embraced the man, whose skinny arms fit perfectly around her and warmed her to the core. She could feel Crescenzo staring, which made her gently pull away. "Thank you, then," she whispered.

"Of course," Matt said. "By the way, Mister Enzo, is that a model of my mapmaker you're holding?"

Wrinkling his brows, Crescenzo held up his wooden figurine. Rosana still couldn't believe he had carved the rabbit himself. Just looking at it made her proud of him.

"*This?*" Crescenzo asked. "This is a model of the rabbit we followed here. My grandfather's idea."

"Then I'll have you know, sir, that the rabbit is my personal mapmaker," Matt said. "His sole job is to run along and map the layout of this realm for me. However, since Avoria left, it seems he only runs circles around the land. I may have to let him go someday . . . My friends, I am going to prepare your bedrooms and check that the castle is secure. Please sit tight."

Matt swept out of the room, and to put a dam on the emotions that were trickling from her heart, Rosana looked at Crescenzo's figurine. He'd been rolling it around in his palm, and when he saw her studying it, he tipped it into her hand.

"This is so amazing," Rosana breathed. "Maybe you can carve me something!"

Crescenzo nodded. "I really do want to practice. I want to get good at this."

Biting his lip and squinting his eyes, Crescenzo leaned over and reached into the pocket of Geppetto's overalls, where a thin strip of wood had been poking out of the opening. Crescenzo pulled it millimeter by millimeter, careful not to wake his grandfather. Then Crescenzo wiped his forehead and took a breath, picking his knife out from his pocket.

Rosana's respiration hung mid-breath as she watched to see what her friend would do. Crescenzo closed his eyes, and then his fingers began to move.

His hands grinded and scratched and peeled with almost mechanical movements. At no point did they hesitate, twitch, or slip.

Within minutes, a figure took shape. At first, she could've been anybody. But familiarity bloomed from the wood when Crescenzo sculpted the figure's hair. And then the jacket. And the legs. And the warm face. The whole time, his eyes were shut tight.

When Crescenzo's eyes snapped open, he beheld what Rosana had already been entranced with: a small replica of a woman she knew.

Rosana covered her mouth, and her eyes watered.

Crescenzo swatted the wood shavings off his knees. "Rosana," he said, "is this—?"

"Mom. That's my mom." Rosana tearfully accepted the figurine from Crescenzo and traced it with her thumb. "It's beautiful, Enzo."

Crescenzo pocketed his knife and slumped back against the wall, looking as though the carving drained him. He must've been concentrating for no more than two minutes, but the fatigue in his eyes made him look as though he'd just run a marathon. When Rosana thought about it, she felt the exact same way. Today had been one of the longest days of her life.

Rosana crawled over to Crescenzo and hugged him tightly, noticing for the first time that he smelled like rain, cedar, and a spearmint gum wrapper all at the same time. She didn't really want to let go any time soon. "Thank you."

Crescenzo patted Rosana's back. "I-I *saw* her, right now, almost as clear as looking out a window at her. She was walking up to this bell tower, and it's *amazing*. Tall. Magical. Gargoyles at the top, and there was a man looking down at her. The last thing I saw was her raising her fist to knock on the door," he said. "I bet she's looking for you."

CHAPTER SEVENTEEN

THE OLD WORLD

Welcome to Florindale!
Population: ~~1~~,823
Clocher de Pierre–12 baruqs
Goldilocks Falls–217 baruqs
Grimm's Hollow–525 baruqs
The Woodlands–984 baruqs
Have a magical stay!

Alicia stared at the rickety sign, her attention hovering over the population and a chill crawling over her spine. "Isn't that because of Queen Avoria?"

Hansel folded his arms and returned a single firm nod. "It is said that she took a thousand souls at once here, in the center of the square. They all marched out to defy her, and she didn't spare a single soul. One got away on her own, though."

"So technically she only took nine-hundred and ninety-nine souls, right?"

Hansel shrugged. "Debatable. I'd venture to say Hua Mulan never really had one in the first place." He smirked to himself and then shook it off. "Sorry, that was in poor taste."

Alicia pursed her lips. "Yes, it was. Come on, let's go find Cherry."

Hansel slumped his shoulders apologetically and continued ahead of Alicia. That was one thing she'd come to appreciate about him during their travel. He was eager to lead the way, throw himself in front of Alicia when he sensed danger, and offer unhesitant protection. Alicia was grateful, even if she wasn't one to follow somebody's lead. She wasn't going to play the damsel in distress if danger did arise. So when Hansel walked ahead of her, she increased her strides to catch up and walk beside him.

When they passed the sign, something caught Alicia's eye.

Population: 1,825

Alicia rubbed her eyelids and tapped Hansel's elbow. "Did you see that?"

"What?"

"The number changed. It was eight hundred twenty-three and now it's eight hundred twenty-five. We changed it by walking into Florindale!"

Hansel squinted at the sign, rubbing his chin. "No we didn't."

"Yes, we did," Alicia said firmly. "I distinctly remember it was eight hundred twenty-three because my daughter's birthday is on August twenty-third. Eight-two-three. Now it's eight hundred twenty-five. I promise you, it's different now."

Hansel shook his head. "Then why hasn't the _1_ returned? If we increased the population, the thousand souls should have done that, too. They should all be back. _You're_ back."

Alicia frowned. He had a point. "Well, maybe they didn't come back to Florindale."

Hansel kept walking, ignoring the sign. "I think you're tired. The number is the same."

Alicia rolled her eyes. _Whatever._

They reached Florindale Square a few minutes later, where they were pleasantly surprised to hear the low bustle of civilization. The dirt beneath their feet slowly transitioned to mossy cracked brick reflecting the soft light of the lanterns overhead. Midas's Pub hummed with light conversation and the clinks of glass, though it wasn't the lively hangout that used to spark with energy and merry clapping and singing. A weary old man hobbled about the public gardens, exhausting great effort to heave an oily, thorny shrub out of the ground. Just ahead, the brick road pulsed with the clopping of heels as a lone, silver-haired witch carried a mug of coffee to a picnic bench. As she crossed, she made brief eye contact with Alicia and nodded politely.

"Hello," the woman said.

"Hi," Alicia said. "That coffee smells good."

The witch took a deep sip, grimaced a bit, and then set her mug down. "Never did acquire the taste for it." She gestured to the picnic bench, inviting Alicia and Hansel to sit down. "I'm only trying to stay awake in case I ever have to make a run for it."

Hansel tilted his head to the side. "I beg your pardon, but why would you need to run?"

The witch leaned in, beckoning for Alicia and Hansel to do the same. She lowered her voice and made intense eye contact with Alicia, green eyes pleading and burning. "You're not spies for Mr. Bellamy, are you?"

Alicia shook her head, regarding the witch with a mix of compassion and wonder. "I'm sorry, Miss—?"

"Yuna," the witch answered. "I always knew Florindale and its surrounding provinces couldn't be all there was. I knew about the other realms before Bellamy issued his decree. I want to see them all. I'm trying to get out of here, by any means necessary. I fear that Mr. Bellamy will discover my efforts, for you see, he's been taking people away when he suspects they're trying to leave. He's even started *hanging* folks who cannot prove their innocence."

Alicia swallowed a bubble in her throat. She wanted to tell Yuna that she was trying to get out of the Old World, too. A small part of her wondered if the witch was a spy for Bellamy, trying to lure people into confessions. "Miss Yuna, I wish you all the best of luck. I hope you're able to get out of here and see what you want to see."

Yuna nodded. "As do I." Her gaze shifted between Alicia and Hansel. "And what is your story? Your faces are new to me."

"Just looking for an old friend," Hansel said. "You wouldn't happen to know anything about the old Carver who lives around here, would you?"

Yuna swirled her mug around, staring into the dark depths of her coffee. "Geppetto? Why, nobody's seen Geppetto in years. He and his boy—"

"Actually, we're looking for another Carver," Alicia said. "We all called him Cherry. Is he still around here? Do you know him?"

"Cherry." Yuna stared far away, struggling to steady her hands, and her eyes became glassy. After a long silence, she blinked, crossed her legs, and continued to drink. "No. I can't say that I know."

Alicia's spirits deflated like old tires. She was sure the old woman was hiding something, but Alicia had been taught to respect her elders and to remain polite to strangers. "Okay," she forced herself to say. "Would anybody else know?"

Yuna raised an arm and pointed to the bell tower in the center of the square. Alicia followed Yuna's finger all the way to the top, where a gargoyle hovered over the town and the bell swayed ever-so-slightly, barely a little dot from Alicia's point of view. The tower reminded her of the buildings of New York. "The man in that tower . . . he sees everything. If you need information in Florindale, you need to talk to the bell ringer."

"Quasimodo," Hansel said. His tone was sad, like he spoke the name of a friend he lost long ago. "He's always there, isn't he?"

Yuna folded her hands. "Always. Now, in exchange for what I have told you, I'd like to make a request."

Alicia nodded once.

"I know you're trying to get out of here, too," Yuna said. "Your eyes betray you. If you find him, or if you find a way out of here, you will take me with you. When you get to where you're going, I will leave you in peace and you will never see me again."

Alicia hesitated. "Well—"

"Yes," Hansel interjected. "We'll tell you if we learn anything. You have my word."

Yuna smiled wide enough to expose her imperfect front teeth. "Your word will suffice. You'll find me near Grimm's Hollow when you're ready."

"Grimm's Hollow," Hansel repeated. "Thanks for the information, Yuna. Good luck to you."

"And to you." Alicia turned her attention back to the bell tower, an unexpected pit of sadness bubbling within her as Yuna sipped coffee alone.

When Alicia pushed the door open at Clocher de Pierre, it was like breaking a dam over her eyelids and her heart. The tears came slowly at first, and then all at once like rivers of sorrow. She couldn't pinpoint what exactly she felt or why it made her cry, but she knew it grew heavier and heavier on her shoulders as she made her way up the steps with an equally distraught Hansel behind her.

In fact, it seemed to be too much for Hansel, and about thirty steps up from the ground level, he looked at his feet, rubbed his face, and leaned against the wall. "Go on without me, please."

Alicia turned. "What?"

"I cannot face the bell ringer. His pain is . . . too much. This tower is too much. It's overbearing, Alice. If I go up to the top with you, it will crack what's left of me."

"What? Why?" Alicia crinkled her eyebrows.

Hansel scoffed and jammed his hands into his pockets, turning on his heel. "I'll meet you at the bottom."

"Okay, fine." Alicia shrugged and continued up, dabbing at

her cheeks with a sleeve as she climbed. Her curiosity over Hansel's reaction was short-lived, because with every step she took, she thought more about Rosana. About Liam and Snow White and all the trials they must've endured together. She thought about Rosana's father. If she hadn't trusted him so much—if she hadn't told him the truth about where she came from—would he have stuck around for her? For Rosana?

It's my fault, Alicia thought. *It's my fault she doesn't have her father.* She hadn't told herself that since Rosana was about five years old. Alicia had learned to stop blaming herself long ago, but the tower reached into her brain and pulled those thoughts back to the surface. With every step, the thought looped in her head. *It's my fault.*

"Excuse me, miss?"

The voice startled Alicia out of her loop. She blinked and a man appeared in front of her, his back curved like a crescent moon and his face scrunched really tight. An enormous bell hung above her. A neatly made bed sat in the corner, and a pail of water rested against the foot of it. "Oh! I'm so sorry, I didn't mean to intrude—"

"Please." The man held up a hand. "It's quite all right. May I know your name?"

Alicia swallowed, wiped her tears, and did her best to collect herself. "I'm Alicia Trujillo. I used to go by Alice once. I lived over there when I was a little girl." She approached the balcony and pointed to a small, cozy neighborhood beyond Goldilocks Falls. "Are you Quasimodo?"

"Yes. Pleased to meet you, Alice." Quasimodo looked like he was trying to bow, but the gesture was little more than an arm across his belly and his gaze on the ground. "I know all about you, Alice. I watched you battle the serpent king. I watched you and your friends cross the land with Avoria's mirror. The New World appears to have been good to you."

Alicia took a step closer. Quasimodo's tone of voice was softer than butter, and the light in his eyes undercut his grotesque features. Alicia thought she might've been intimidated because he was so nice. Like she wasn't worthy of talking to him.

"So, you never leave this tower? Even when you see somebody in danger?" She immediately wished she'd found a less accusatory way to phrase her words. "I'm sorry, I didn't mean . . ."

Quasimodo waved her off. "No. I do not leave the tower. My place is up here, away from the rest of the world. It's my sworn and sacred duty to ring this bell at the designated times, and I feel it is also my duty to remain hidden." He passed his palm over his face in a tight circle. "The world doesn't need to see this. *I* wouldn't want to see my face."

Alicia took a step toward Quasimodo and thought about hugging him, but she wondered if she'd be overstepping her bounds. She was also a little angry with him for being so cynical. "That's a horrible way to treat yourself, you know. You are a good person, and the world is *not* so horrible as to cast someone away without getting to know the real you."

Quasimodo rested his hand on Alicia's back. "You don't seem sure of that."

Alicia looked at her feet. He saw right through her. Memories of high school surfaced, along with her last interactions with Rosana's father. *You're crazy, woman. You truly belong in the psych ward. I hope our kid—your kid—doesn't turn out like you.*

Quasimodo continued, his soothing voice only feeding Alicia's tears. "I'd rather live alone than in bad company. I take joy in watching over these people, without the burden of having to watch them react to my appearance."

"What if you found someone who could love you?"

"I did. She's gone." Quasimodo sat on his bed, folded his hands, and watched Alicia from the other side of the room. It embarrassed her that he was the one comforting her after explaining his situation. She could hardly meet his gaze. "And now, I'm quite sure that your presence means something for our realm. You were one of Violet's chosen ones. You were among the seven fated to lose their souls in the Cavern of Ombra. And yet here you are in front of me, days after

Avoria returned from her prison. Please. Tell me how I can help you."

Alicia dabbed her face. "Cherry," she said simply. "I'm looking for Master Cherry."

Quasimodo stood and nodded, his expression steeped in recognition.

"You see," Alicia continued, "I need to get my daughter out of Wonderland. But the mirror that can take me there was sold to Master Cherry. Do you know where I might find him?"

Quasimodo smoothed the wrinkles that appeared on his bed. "I feel obligated to tell you that if you go looking for Master Cherry, you may find more than you're prepared for. But if you so wish, I will tell you where I last saw him."

Alicia found her hands shaking. She was so close. "Please."

Quasimodo raised an arm and pointed to the horizon. "In Grimm's Hollow, there is a hole in the ground. The man you call Master Cherry disappeared into that hole not so long ago. He spends most of his time underground, and of course the mines and tunnels under this world are all interconnected."

Alicia's heart sank. *The Cavern of Ombra.*

Quasimodo continued, "If you want to find him, I suggest heading underground now. The quickest way is underneath this tower."

Alicia leaned against the balcony for support, unable to find her next words. All she could do was nod in acknowledgment of Quasimodo's advice.

"Please," he said, prying a large stone out of the wall. Quasimodo reached inside the hole he'd created, plucking out a clean loaf of bread. "Take some bread with you. I'm told that in the underground terrain, one can get lost for days and go hungry without proper care."

Alicia accepted the bread and tucked it under her arm. "Thank you, Quasimodo."

"Don't thank me until you find your daughter and eliminate the Ivory Queen. Then we can celebrate! Florindale Square holds the best festivals."

"I'm sure." Alicia smiled. "I'll look forward to that."

"Yes. And one more thing before you go?"

"Of course."

"Tell Hansel to be strong. I've seen his pain from afar. I know who he's looking for. In some ways, we are kindred spirits." Quasimodo sighed. "I hope he finds his sister again. Just as I hope I'll see my Esmeralda again."

CHAPTER EIGHTEEN

WONDERLAND

They'd been in Wondertown a full week by Crescenzo's count. Time, as the citizens kept reminding him, was irrelevant, but he'd been through seven full sleep cycles in the castle, thanks to Matt and his generosity toward the visitors.

With every passing day, Crescenzo's spirits darkened a bit. He would close his eyes and see his parents imprisoned in rubies. He'd see Zack in a chokehold. He'd imagine his home being soaked in the same darkness as Wonderland.

Some nights, Enzo would sit on his bed with his knees tucked into his chest, staring out the window and silently resolving to correct everything that had gone wrong in his life. He would get his friend back. He would take Rosana, Gretel, and Geppetto and get out of Wonderland. And then, he would find his parents and go home.

In what seemed like it would be the darkest time of his life, Crescenzo was glad to have Rosana, Geppetto, and Gretel around. He was also glad to have his new carving skill to keep him occupied. Working with his hands helped him clear his head, and it always helped to improve his mood when he finished a new project.

Some days, it was hard for him to concentrate on his woodwork. Crescenzo would go into a sort of trance, open his eyes, and find nothing but dust or a gnarled piece of wood in his hands. Other times, his work was impeccable, and he'd nurture tiny replicas of a bell tower, a pirate's hook, or at one point, *himself*. It was the most shocking of all the carvings he'd made so far, especially because out of all those made in his family, it was the only figure he'd ever seen with its eyes closed.

None of his carvings made sense to him. It wasn't like the rabbit, which appeared to him immediately after he'd completed his work. Crescenzo took his figures and asked around the castle, wondering if the people of Wondertown would understand what he'd created.

"A bell tower? We don't have any bell towers in Wonderland," Matt said. "Curious!"

"A hook?" one of the guards said of Enzo's second carving. "Only place I've ever seen one of those is at the meat market, which I don't recommend going to."

Crescenzo wrinkled his nose, his lips puckered.

He brought his third carving to the dinner table. "But why would I carve myself sleeping, though?" he questioned. "I don't like it."

Rosana and Geppetto dismissed it as a pointless, unimportant mystery. "Maybe you just blinked," Rosana suggested. "Like if you were taking a picture with a flash."

Geppetto shrugged. "You're still learning, *ragazzo*. You have a lot of practice to do."

The next day, Matt made a proposition during dinner. "Come play mini golf with me!" With that, the king pulled a lime-green flamingo out of his hat and swung it by its feet. The bird blinked at Crescenzo a few times but didn't protest or show any signs of discomfort. Matt smiled brightly. "I'll even teach you how to use *these*."

"No thank you," Crescenzo said. "I'm sorry. Mini golf's just not my thing. I wanna keep working on my carving."

Rosana looked down. Her lips fluttered as she swallowed her soup. "You don't think maybe you should take a break from that? You seem really stressed out lately, Enzo."

"Naw!" Crescenzo exclaimed more loudly than he intended. "You think so?"

A hush descended on the group.

Rosana's spoon clattered against her bowl. "Enzo, please. I'm just trying to look out for—"

"I know. I know you are. I'm sorry."

Matt tucked a napkin into his shirt. "Is there something the matter?"

Crescenzo wanted nothing more than to exclaim that Matt was half of the problem, insisting on keeping the group inside the castle when Zack was probably suffering at the hands of a madman. Matt had been so gracious to protect everybody, feed them, entertain them, and give them shelter, but Crescenzo couldn't sit around eating lavish meals and playing flamingo golf when his best friend was missing. "I'm *fine*," he finally said, standing to push in his chair. "I just need some space. Here, want the rest of my soup, Gretel?"

"Yes, please!" Gretel banged her spoon against the table. Her face lit up as Crescenzo pushed his bowl over to her.

"I think I'll be excused, too," Rosana said, tossing her napkin over her bowl.

To Crescenzo's surprise, Rosana didn't try to follow but stormed away in the opposite direction, sweeping her sleeve across her cheek before pointing her chin in the air.

"Wait for me, Crescenzo! We have, a—uh—carving lesson, no?" Geppetto wiped his mouth, stood, and followed Crescenzo. "Young Gretel, Your Majesty, I bid you good evening. Don't be too hard on those flamingos, now."

Before Crescenzo could protest, Geppetto pressed a palm on Crescenzo's back and steered him toward the front door.

"Umm," Crescenzo said, "my carving stuff is in my room."

"Don't need it." Geppetto pushed the door open and guided Crescenzo outside.

"But—"

"You don't need it. We're not going to carve today."

"Then what are we doing?"

"Look here. I know why you're so upset, and I don't blame you. You want to fight for your friend? Then I want to help you. The stars only know I wouldn't try to stop you after I've come all this way to look for my son. But we need a *plan*. We need training." Geppetto smirked and drew two wooden swords out of his sleeves. He looked like a magician pulling flowers out of thin air. "While you've been carving bell towers and sleeping Enzos, I've been working on these. And now, we're going to do some sword training." He tossed Crescenzo a sword. "We both know those Hearts are not going down easy. We could use the practice."

"*Yes!*" Crescenzo cheered. He fit his fingers around the handle, surprised at the sword's lightness. "Time to level up! Enemies, beware the son of Pinocchio!"

With a smug smile, Geppetto took a long stride forward and swung his sword. *Thump!* Crescenzo's knee protested in pain.

"Ow!" Crescenzo rubbed his knee, scowling at his grandfather.

"Now hit me back," Geppetto dared. "Show me how much you want to learn."

"Well, I don't want to fight *you*. Aren't we using practice dummies or something?" The more Crescenzo looked at Geppetto, the more his enthusiasm receded. "I don't want to hit an old man."

"Hit me back. Are you worried I'm going to win?"

"No. I just don't really wanna hit my grandfather."

"Hit me back," Geppetto insisted. "Pretend I'm not your grandfather. Pretend I'm the Ivory Queen."

For a hilarious second, Crescenzo had a mental glimpse of Geppetto in a white dress and dark red wig and chuckled to himself. "You're *not* Avoria."

"I promise you're not going to hurt me. Come now. Take a swing."

"Okaaay, but remember you insisted!" Crescenzo blew out a long breath and shook out his wrists, bouncing on the balls of his feet to get his blood flowing. *Maybe this will make some good bonding time.*

When his joints felt nice and loose, Crescenzo lunged for Geppetto with his sword in the air. "*Ahhh!*"

Thwack!

With a smirk, Geppetto raised his sword above his head and parallel to the ground so that the two swords met perpendicularly. Man and boy held the pose for a minute, a triumphant gleam in Geppetto's eye. Finally, he lowered his sword and brought Crescenzo's arm back down. "Great! So you can move! You don't need strings! Again. Pretend I'm the King of Hearts. I have your buddy, and I'm coming for Rosana."

Crescenzo dug his toe into the ground. "Really? You have to bring Rosana into this?"

"My boy, Rosana has *been in this* with you since before you even met. Consider that," Geppetto mused, pacing from side to side. "Try to hit me again, Crescenzo. And this time, don't give yourself away. Breathe first. Clear the mind. And for every minute that you don't hit me, the Ivory Queen gets closer to winning. Wonderland gets closer to destruction. And you and Rosana will *never* go home and see your parents again."

Thwack!

Geppetto clucked his tongue. "I told you not to be obvious. Let's try that again."

Crescenzo gripped the sword tighter and spun into his next swing. *Thwack!*

"Better, but you're still giving yourself away. You don't need to spin like that. Again."

Crescenzo nodded, pretended to lower his guard, and his next attack came quicker and harder.

Geppetto blocked the sword with ease, knocking it back down to Crescenzo's side. "You'll have to do a little better."

"I'm just getting warmed up!" *Thwack!*

"We're doing this for your friend," Geppetto insisted. "I hardly think his captor is going to give you much warmup time. Avoria can probably get us before we even know she's near us. Should we continue? Or should we just play the funeral march now?"

Crescenzo scoffed. "Look, I appreciate the training. I really do. But I didn't ask for you to come out here and taunt me." He scowled. He should've been doing this with Zack. Where was he? Was he even still alive? "I didn't ask for any of this!"

"Well, you got it. What are you going to do about it? Start by getting your head out of the clouds. I know you're not this slow, Crescenzo. You're *distracted*. I get it! Your buddy's missing. You miss your parents. You're falling in love—"

"*Shut up!*" Crescenzo bellowed. "Geez! You know what? I finally get it now. I finally see it."

Geppetto arched an eyebrow. "Enlighten me. What do you see?"

Crescenzo exhaled sharply, his jaw tight with defiance. "Why my dad ran away from you."

It was the meanest thing Crescenzo had ever said, and he immediately regretted it.

Geppetto suddenly looked older than ever before, his posture wilting in about seven different places from the curve in his shoulders to the corners of his eyes and mouth. His elbow fell to his side, and the sword slipped from his fingers. "Well," he said softly, "I suppose we're done here, then. I'll leave you alone."

"Wait." Crescenzo shook his head. "I didn't mean that."

"*Lascia stare.*" Geppetto turned away and waved his hand in a *forget it* sort of gesture. "I suppose I should be grateful that he taught you the value of honesty. When you see him again, tell him I'm proud."

A hefty sigh anchored Crescenzo's heart to the ground as Geppetto walked farther away. "Fine!" Crescenzo called. "Walk away from me, then! I told you I was sorry, but—"

A flash of metal cut Crescenzo's words short.

Two Heart soldiers appeared in Geppetto's path.

"His Wondrous, the King of Hearts sends his regards, particularly to Hadinger's incompetent sentinels," one of them sneered, snapping a spear handle on his kneecap. "We're here for the boy."

"Throw me my sword, Crescenzo!" Geppetto spread his arms apart, bracing for a catch.

One of the soldiers ran for Geppetto's wooden sword. In a storm of adrenaline, Crescenzo skidded along the ground, swiping the weapon before one of the Heart soldiers could reach it. "Catch!"

"Get ready to fight, boy!" Geppetto caught the sword and narrowed his eyes. "Take a breath. Focus, relax your grip, and *swing behind you at ten o'clock!*"

As Geppetto broke into a duel with one of the Hearts, Crescenzo whirled to his left and brought the wooden sword over his shoulder. The blunt handle connected with the bridge of a crooked nose, and Crescenzo winced at the sound of bone cracking.

He hit the other gaunt-faced Heart soldier whose dagger came inches away from breaking the skin on Crescenzo's neck. The soldier sneered, a bit of blood trickling onto his lip, and he seized Crescenzo's wrist with a thick-gloved hand. "That wasn't so nice, little boy!"

Crescenzo raised a knee and drove his weight against the soldier's stomach. The soldier was heavily armored, though, and all Crescenzo managed to do was mess up the soldier's balance and bring both of them to the ground. "Geppetto! Some help here?"

"Busy! Fight, Crescenzo!"

Crescenzo heard a similar struggle occur behind him, but his attention quickly fell away from it, and all he knew was his immediate danger.

The Heart solider growled and fumbled for his dagger. "We're going to carve your heart out, boy-o. And then we're going to make the old man eat it."

Crescenzo didn't answer. He was putting all his mental stamina into breaking his hand free from the soldier's stone grip. Blood poured freely from the Heart's nose, like the sweat on the back of Crescenzo's neck.

"And then," the Heart continued, "we're going after the girl." A broken, throaty laugh rattled his body. "Perhaps her mother will even come back to witness her death. We'll throw her off the floating island and watch her tumble. We'll make the other boy watch. Maybe by then he'll be such a lost boy, he might even *participate*."

At last, Crescenzo wrestled his hand out of the evil man's grip and seized the Heart's dagger. Overcome by instinct, he hammered the heavy handle as hard as he could against the Heart's forehead and then struck him twice more on each temple. "You talk too much, man."

Crescenzo couldn't bring himself to stab the soldier, but the man had gone limp enough that Crescenzo knew he'd succeeded in knocking him out.

Feeling quite proud, Crescenzo pushed himself back to his feet. But before he could turn to help his grandfather, a blunt force struck the back of his head, and he fell again. Stars skipped in front of Enzo's eyes, his muscles went limp, and the breath rolled out of his lungs. He was losing consciousness fast. Anger trickled through his veins. He had beaten one of the Hearts. It wasn't fair that he was about to pass out.

There was a blurry moment somewhere between dream and reality before Crescenzo lost consciousness. He wasn't sure what was real, but he would always remember two things.

First, though he appeared to have struggled greatly, Geppetto overcame the second soldier by feigning terror and pretending that the enormous bird had appeared in the sky, then stabbing the Heart when he turned away.

Second, a gargantuan cat padded into view, used its tail to scoop Crescenzo and Geppetto onto its back, and told them to hang on.

After the cat sped away, there was only black for a very long time.

CHAPTER NINETEEN

THE OLD WORLD: UNDERGROUND

When Hansel lit the torch, Alicia saw the fear in his eyes. "This is the last place I ever wanted to come back to," he said. "The best day of my life will be the day this mine caves in on itself and destroys every lingering memory inside of it."

Alicia put a finger to her lips. "Don't jinx us, now." But deep down, she felt the same way. She never wanted to return to the Cavern of Ombra, and she would be glad if all those little rocks and minerals toppled and sealed away every hope of letting somebody walk around inside of it again. She only preferred that it didn't happen while she was down there. "So, will you lead the way?"

"Me?" Hansel asked. "Why me?"

"You practically lived down here while you were . . ." Alicia meant to go on and say "kidnapping us," but she stopped herself and let her voice trail off before she could offend Hansel. "Anyway, you should know your way around here, shouldn't you?"

"Would you like to know something, Alice?" Hansel raised an eyebrow. "I don't think there's a single living soul who knows the full layout of this place. The dwarves drew me a map once, and they told me they were still expanding it. I even learned they didn't include everything they knew on it. There were pathways to the New World, for example, that they kept secret from me. If they knew Master Cherry lived down here, they certainly didn't tell me about that, either."

Alicia's heart jumped. "Pathways to the New World?"

"Yes," Hansel affirmed. "But they were all destroyed. So far as I know."

Alicia took one small step and then the gurgle in her belly reminded her of something. She pulled the loaf of bread out of the pouch in her jacket. "Bread."

"Food." Hansel clutched his stomach and shook his head. "We can't eat that."

"Why not? This place is really big. What if we get lost down here and we can't find our way back to the surface? We could be stuck down here for weeks. We could starve. We could *die*," she whispered. The thought of death itself didn't frighten Alicia as much as the idea of leaving the world behind without a chance to see her daughter again, without telling Rosana that she was loved so fully. Alicia looked at Hansel and saw him work through the same thought process.

"Listen." Hansel rubbed his face with two hands, clawing at the rough stubble that had been thickening around his jaw. "I have a little bit of bread in my pocket as well. I took it from Snow's castle before we left." He handed Alicia the torch and pulled the bread out of his vest, once whole but now a bit mushy and crumbled like a deteriorating sponge.

"That's kind of gross." Alicia winced. "I'm not eating anything that was in your pocket."

"Eating isn't exactly what I had in mind." He scraped off a crumb with his thumbnail and tossed it on the ground. "This is an old trick my sister came up with a long time ago."

Alicia smirked. "Wasting food?"

"I call it using my resources." Hansel took ten long strides and dropped another crumb. "Here, we'll use yours for eating and mine for leaving a trail in case we need to backtrack. It's not the fanciest method of mapmaking, but it should do, no?"

Alicia clapped a palm to her forehead. "In my world, a lot of people would be getting mad at you right now. There are—"

"Starving children in Florindale, I know. When we beat Avoria, I'm going to take an apprenticeship with the Muffin Man, and we'll bake enough bread and pies and sweets to feed all the worlds between us!"

Alicia summoned her resolve and followed Hansel along the cavern walls, stepping around the breadcrumbs so she wouldn't grind them into invisible particles of yeast. "Is that so?" she asked. "You want to be a baker?"

Hansel shrugged. "I don't think so hard about it, but if our worlds are safe again, why not? I always enjoyed food. You know my mother swore my love for food would undo me, three days before I found the candy house? Lady Fortune can be so cruel sometimes." Hansel smiled and turned into a dark corridor, throwing bits of bread at his feet. "What about you? What will you do if we survive all this?"

Alicia pressed her lips together. "I guess I haven't planned that far ahead. Part of me doesn't expect to survive, if I'm being really honest. The other part of me is going to fight like hell, if only so I can go back to the life I know."

"To which life do you refer?" Hansel wondered. "This life? The way you remember when you were a little girl? Or the life you wished upon yourself?"

"The life I made," Alicia said. "The life I had in New York, with my daughter. Although, I'd really like to do better from now on. Yeah. If there's one thing I want to do after Avoria's out of our hair, I'd like to do *better*."

"Here's to that," Hansel said. "But I'm curious. You imply that you aren't happy with the way you've lived. Why?"

Alicia sighed. "Because I haven't been there for my daughter nearly as much as I'd like to be. I even homeschool her, and I'm never there. I'm always traveling with the airline I work for, taking off, zoning out, and trying to find those thrills I once had when I would go to Wonderland. I'm a compulsive wanderer, Hansel. I can't stay put, and I never even thought about how that might be affecting Rosana. On top of that, I didn't give her a father who would stick around. I didn't give her anybody. Not even a *dog*. She must be so lonely."

Hansel was silent as he ripped another crumb off the bread loaf. They approached a strange, circular hub that branched out into seven other corridors. "Well," Hansel said, surveying the options in front of him, "here's to choosing a new path."

By the fourth time they'd returned to the hub to choose a new path, Hansel's calves were wailing. *Was this maze always this damned impossible to navigate?* He was especially mad about the first path, which went entirely uphill the first way, only to lead to nothing. Alicia climbed behind him, and if her legs were hurting half as much as his were, she was doing a fantastic job of hiding it.

The second path grew narrower and narrower until Hansel and Alicia had to walk sideways to keep from getting their shoulders stuck between the walls, which were lined with a sort of maroon metal Hansel had never seen before. When they discovered that it had led them in a circle right back to the central hub, Hansel kicked the wall.

"That leaves a few more," Alicia said, "and we're running out of bread, so what do you want to do?"

Hansel squatted, unable to keep his face straight while his calf muscles burned, and he clawed at his hair. "I don't know," he said. "I really don't know."

Alicia rolled her eyes and pulled Hansel back to his feet. "We pick another one. Let's go that way." She haphazardly aimed her finger and started down the next corridor, Hansel scattering crumbs behind her as she waved her torch around. "I'm gonna start eating this loaf," she said. "Want some?"

"No," Hansel breathed. "You need your strength more than I do."

Alicia ripped the bread in half and jammed a piece of it in Hansel's pocket. "*We* need our strength. Just eat it."

"Thanks," Hansel muttered. "I'll save it for when we get out of here." His foot landed in something wet, seeping through his boot and soaking his sock. Wet socks were one of his least favorite sensations in the world.

Alicia took five steps ahead of Hansel and shined her torch just below her waist. She was knee deep in dark water, which was creeping through the fabrics of her clothes. Additionally, the cavern ceiling was getting lower, so that in a few more steps, they would have to crawl. No, they would have to *swim*. The water gathered in a pool that extended farther than Hansel could see. Alicia shoved the torch into Hansel's hand and rolled up her sleeves. "Can you swim?"

Hansel shined the light into the water, looking for eels and piranhas and anything else that might slither around him. "I'm not overly fond of the water, but I suppose we keep going."

"We can always turn around and pick another path," Alicia said, although her tone hinted that she would blame him if he agreed to it. "Here, eat your bread, drop the last of our crumbs here, and let's swim."

Hansel's palms started to sweat. "And our torch?"

Alicia grabbed the torch and dipped it in the water, extinguishing the flame with a thin *tssss* sound. Suddenly they were drowning in blackness. "Looks like we don't have one anymore."

"So we're swimming in the dark, under a really low ceiling." Hansel gulped. "Okay."

"I'm going under," Alicia said. "Try and stay close to me. I hope this pool isn't very big!"

"Yeah me too." Hansel crammed the rest of his bread into his mouth.

The moments that followed made him realize that his biggest fear was not candy houses and the witches who lived in them. It wasn't enchanted mirrors. It wasn't even Queen Avoria. His biggest fear was cramped spaces, particularly those that were dark and filled with water. When he submerged into that hollow space beneath the low ceiling, with his clothes stuck to his body and his hair stuck to his forehead, he became hyper-conscious of his nose pumping frigid water into his lungs. When he plugged his nose, his mouth opened. When his mouth closed, his eyes opened and burned despite their inability to process anything around him. The dark was overwhelming, like a liquid winter night. Hansel couldn't find Alicia's silhouette. He couldn't find walls. He couldn't find his hand in front of his face. Despite his instinct to move slowly and carefully, his sore legs pumped like motors behind him and propelled him through the darkness until his head hit a wall and he forced himself to swim in the direction he thought must have been upward.

To Hansel's great relief, his face broke the cool surface of the water, and he drew a sharp intake of breath before he opened his eyes. When his eyelids popped open, a soft blue light tickled his vision. The ceiling was much higher, with all its rocky nooks exposed, and Hansel could hear a faint buzz from somewhere down the corridor, reminding him distinctly of an electric eel. He clawed himself out of the water and back onto solid ground.

"Alicia?" The cavern distorted Hansel's speech and threw it back at him three times. *Alicia? Licia? Icia?* After the echo slipped away, silence pervaded, and Hansel's heart pounded. Where was she?

Please don't make me go back in there to get you.

When Alicia burst through the water, gasping and coughing before she pulled herself up, Hansel collapsed onto his knees. "Oh, thank you, Lady Fortune!"

He reached out and grabbed her hand, helping her back onto the rocky path.

They sat for a minute, shaking water out of their hair and letting their muscles relax before Alicia surveyed their surroundings. "Blue light."

"We must be close," Hansel said. "Maybe Cherry's down here?" He stumbled to his feet and started toward the light. The path forked three directions, though Hansel was relieved and confused to see that there were signs posted. The middle path was the only one without a sign, but it was clearly the source of the cavern light. The left had a wooden sign that said, *The White Road.* To the right, *Florindale Square, Midas's Pub.*

"Convenient," Hansel remarked. "So glad we came all this way when we could have just—"

"Let's go." Alicia started toward the blue light. "Look for that mirror. Or that Carver."

Hansel followed, wringing out his clothes and running his fingers through his hair. His socks were still wet, to his great annoyance, but he looked forward to accomplishing their mission and getting back to the surface of Florindale.

When they passed under the archway, the source of the light was immediately apparent. A metal contraption bigger than a cow spewed blue lightning bolts between a collection of wires and springs, its energies crackling and fizzing through the air. It took up quite a bit of space in the new cavern they had entered, but the area seemed to be at least twice as big as the Cavern of Ombra. Though there was nobody else in sight, it was apparent somebody lived there. A rusty old cot rested against one of the walls, and a careful pile of chopped wood sat on top of the smoky gray sheets.

Opposite from the cot, there was a black desk cluttered with all sorts of random objects. A quill and inkbottle. A knife with an ivory handle. A bronze bow.

Wait a minute.

Hansel rushed to the desk and picked up the bow. "I know this bow! This belongs to—"

"Master Cherry has definitely been here," Alicia interrupted. "That knife, the wood, and look at all these strange figurines! If only I could find that mirror!"

"I don't think Cherry lives here," Hansel said. "This bow belonged to my old employer." He ruffled through a chest of drawers and pulled out a green tunic. "Robin Hood."

Alicia picked up the knife and Hansel picked up the bow, and the two stared at each other with wonder in their faces. Hansel knew he was right, but how could Alicia be wrong?

Alicia shook her head. "But—"

Hansel's gaze wandered back to the desk, where a single leather book collected dust in the caverns. Its pages were impossibly tattered and its cover was charred, but its title was still legible. *Research Notes.* Behind him, the strange machine continued to pulse. *Zzzt. Zt zt. Zzzzt.*

Alicia lowered her voice to a whisper. "What is this place?"

Zzzt. Zt zt.

Zzzzzzzt crack boom!

The lightning machine exploded in a ball of flame, and Hansel threw himself on top of Alicia. His ears suddenly felt like cotton, and his vision was obscured by smoke and fire. The ground rumbled and the ceiling shook, small bits of rocky ceiling raining down on him.

What the devil just happened?

Alicia stirred underneath him, and Hansel leaned closer to her ear. He could barely hear his own voice over the high-pitched ringing in his head when he shouted, "Are you okay?"

"I'm okay," Alicia said. She said something else, but all Hansel understood was wump wuff wumpuh.

Hansel pulled himself to his feet and steadied against the wall for balance. The bed and several lumps of wood spewed smoke into the air, while the metal contraption looked more like plane wreckage. Scrap metal was strewn everywhere.

Hansel's vision and hearing cleared bit by bit and Alicia managed to stand as well, but he hadn't recovered his balance for long when a man in wet, black armor stepped into his field of view and swung a sword at his neck. *Whoosh!* Drops of water speckled Hansel's face. He ducked just in time, and the newcomer's sword sliced through the wall like butter. Alicia tumbled away from the man and raised her fists.

The knight straightened his posture and leveled his sword. He raised his visor and spoke with a sneer. "The peasant and the war princess, together! Lord Bellamy will be quite happy to know that I've eliminated you just before my next stop! My, my, His Majesty is having a wonderful day."

"Tell the *king* we don't answer to cowards," Alicia said. "We're not going with you."

"Who said I'm taking you with me?" the knight said. "His Majesty's orders were specific: termination. This cavern will implode at any second. If I have to die with it, so be it."

Alicia narrowed her eyes. "You'd die for a king who won't even make his own moves?"

"On the contrary, the king is quite actively preparing for a public execution in Florindale Square right this moment, for two lowly beings who have done far less to spite him. He sends me for the high priority targets, because I never fail. Notice how efficiently I tracked you in this maze. Your bread trail took out most of my labor."

Boom!

A section of the ceiling imploded, nearly crushing Hansel's head. On instinct, he threw his arms over himself and rolled to the side.

"Grab that book!" he yelled to Alicia.

On the other side of the cavern, the knight regained his balance, knocked a falling rock away with his sword, and started toward Hansel.

Hansel grasped Alicia's wrist and looked into her eyes, suddenly much dimmer with fatigue. "Listen, we're going to split up, okay? I'll go to the White Road, and you go back to Florindale Square. The guard will go after me instead of you. I'd be a greater threat to Bellamy in his eyes. I want you to *run*, Alice, and don't stop until you know you're far away from this man. I'm sorry we didn't find your mirror down here, but get somewhere secure and read the book. See what you can learn. If I get caught, you keep yourself safe because you might be our very last hope."

Alicia shook her head. "Stop it. You don't have to be a hero right now, Hansel."

Hansel seized Alicia's shoulder. "I want to redeem myself for the mistakes I've made. If I get caught, you go ahead. You go find help so that everyone else can be protected. That's freedom for me. I'm not giving you a choice in this, Alice. Take the book and get to the surface *now*."

Alicia stared back at him for a second and nodded. "If I don't get a chance to say this later—"

Boom! Another implosion. Moonlight streaked into the cavern. Alicia covered her face and snatched the leather book off the desk. The knight whipped his blade around and spun at Alicia like a helicopter. She leapt away and stole one last glance at Hansel before disappearing into the *Florindale Square* corridor.

"The bell ringer says to be strong. Oh, and thanks for jinxing us earlier."

CHAPTER TWENTY

WONDERLAND

"Hey."

The voice was female, raspy, and heavy with something like fatigue. Perhaps it was sadness? Or maybe it was the kind of rough wall that sometimes went up around a person who had been tired for too long.

"Hey! Boy!"

Each time the girl spoke, her voice was a rock against the coccoon of sleep, chipping away at Zack Volo's slumber until his eyelids slid open and he began to process the world around him. A nauseating feeling gnawed at his stomach. A dark aura clouded his vision, and the smell of mildew assaulted his senses. His head throbbed from within as if his own brain had been swinging a hammer at his bones, desparate to break loose from the confines of his skull.

Similarly, Zack found that he was confined to a dark cell flooded with moonflowers that had sprouted from iron, concrete, and marble.

"Get *up* already!"

Zack sat up and beheld a tall, red-haired girl in crimson armor on the other side of the bars. A red patch covered her left eye, and sewn on the patch was a black heart. She wore a silver chain around her neck, from which a pointed tooth hung. She brandished a spear while she stared at him.

"Finally!" she said. "I really didn't wanna have to use this stick on you, but you wouldn't move your lazy bum. Starting to wonder why the king is so interested in you."

With the heel of his palm against his forehead, Zack winced. *The king. Beware the King of Hearts.* What happened? The last thing he remembered was being dragged out of Wondertown with a huge bearded man who had put him in a chokehold. He must have blacked out since then. "Where the hell am I?"

"Wondercity Tower," the girl said, each syllable a biting staccato, "where the king lives. I'm supposed to take you up to him right now, so"—she raised her spear and pointed the tip at Zack's face—"stand up."

Zack crawled back away from the spear and raised his arms. "Whoa!" he exclaimed. "Put that down. And you can do whatever you want, but I am *not* going up to see the king with you."

"Get *up!*" The soldier made a jabbing motion and clenched her teeth. Her gaze flickered to the side, and she cast a fleeting glance over her shoulder. "I'm serious! Do you want him to take off both our heads? Because I've seen him do it before, and I will not lose my chance at getting out of here because of a stubborn, lazy little pretty boy like *you!*" She made another jab, this time coming nearly an inch away from skewering Zack's eye.

Zack's heart rate picked up as he stared at the tip of the spear. The letters *T* and *R* had been carved into the metal, along with a hastily carved flower.

"I'm gonna count to three," the soldier said. "If I have to proceed to four, I get a new eye. One . . . two . . ." She drew back her elbow like she was about to shoot a cue ball on a billiards table.

"Okay! Okay!" Zack wiped his forehead and climbed to his cold bare feet, feeling slow and clumsy like a mountain of wet clay. "Okay. I'm standing. I'll come with you."

The soldier relaxed her posture and heaved a thick sigh. "Good. That means we're not enemies yet." She drove the tip of her spear into a heavy lock on the cage and twisted. The cage sprung open, and she beckoned Zack to follow her. "Come on. He's waiting."

Zack shuffled out of the cell and into the girl's path. "What does he want from me?"

"That's not my business."

Zack raised a brow. "Well, he obviously threatened to do something to you if you couldn't make me cooperate. So it kind of *is* your business." His voice came out husky and gruff. His throat tingled. "Anything about this feel wrong to you, whatever-your-name-is?" His gaze flashed to the spear again. "Rose?"

"Tahlia," she growled, poking Zack's neck so he would start moving. "*Tahlia* Rose."

"Tahlia," Zack repeated. "I'm—"

"Zack, the son of Peter Pan. I know already."

"We could run, you know. I have friends out there trying to find a way out of this place. They're trying to get out of Wonderland."

Tahlia shook her head. "They won't."

"Then they'll find *me*," Zack said. "I'd hate to be the king when they do."

The soldier used her spear tip to press the button of a large elevator. She didn't respond to Zack's latest statement, but he could see her thinking in the elevator doors' reflection. She sighed, and her one-eyed gaze was fixed somewhere on the ceiling.

"I don't know what he wants," Zack continued, "but we can make a stand."

"Word of advice, *Zack*," Tahlia growled. "When you get up there, don't take that tone with him. And when he makes his offer, do not fight him. This is one battle you cannot win."

Ping! The elevator doors erupted open, and Tahlia swept out her arm and shoved Zack into the cart. The doors slammed shut and he rocketed upward, watching the ground recede through a grimy window. Wondertown's castle sat on the horizon like a tiny dollhouse, while neon signs whispered a soft aura into the darkness directly below, barely illuminating the murky skyscrapers and black streets of a dim metropolis. *Ping!*

When the doors opened again, Zack was in a sort of penthouse apartment, where two big empty chairs sat at the far side of the room. A red curtain covered the wall behind it, while the ceiling and the two walls at either side of them were entirely made of glass. Six life-sized wooden statues were positioned about the room, each feeding Zack's nausea. It wasn't that the statues were ugly or scary; in fact, they were beautiful and magnificently life-like. If he hadn't recognized the subtle intricacies of Geppetto's handiwork, Zack would have sworn that they were the living, breathing people he loved.

Mr. DiLegno, Enzo's father, hands in his jean pockets as he stared back at Zack in paternal contemplation.

And Mrs. DiLegno, arms folded and flashing that loving school teacher smile.

A beautiful raven-haired stranger, one hand on her hip while the other stared thoughtfully at a shiny red apple in her hand.

The next three statues set his pulse racing: a honey-haired woman with a book in her hand, a tall and lanky man with a goofy, childlike smile, and . . . *that's me!* All three of the Volos stood side-by-side, the fake Zack cradling a basketball under his arm.

Wait a minute. We're six of the people who . . . Zack's thoughts unspooled haphazardly from his brain and tied themselves back into knots. *But where's . . . ?*

When Zack found the pile of splinters and dust gathered around a pair of feminine wooden legs, he doubled over and vomited at last, narrowly missing his bare feet.

"I hope you're going to clean that up."

Zack finished retching, turned around, and there was the king who had abducted him, tall, cotton-bearded, and murky-eyed. With dry, cracked lips, Zack forced himself to say, "Why am I here?"

"Zackary James Maxwell Volo," the king said. "I never properly welcomed you to Wonderland." He picked up a silver goblet and filled it with a fizzing orange drink. After a deep sip, he smacked his lips and let out an airy "*ahhhh*." He gestured to the wooden statue of Zack's father. "The old man is a rather gifted Carver, isn't he? They look so . . . alive."

Every word the king spoke was like an ice cube sliding down the back of Zack's shirt. He stood up as straight as he could, trying to look brave. "What are these?"

"I watched Geppetto make these with his bare hands. The mirror, of course, told him what to do. Avoria would take it from there and communicate with her *huntsman*. Now you're here, of course, and what a fortune that is for *me*. I could use you, you know."

"What do you want?" Zack snapped.

The king took another drink. "Perhaps you are aware that my realm is at war?"

"I may have picked up on that when you crashed the Spades' castle, yeah."

"It's madness, dear boy. So much resistance from the Spades in a land where the Hearts already *have* control. We are the past, present, and future of Wonderland, made even more powerful since the arrival of Queen Avoria some time ago." The king folded his hands at his waist and stared out the window. "Notice how my city stands stronger than ever. Avoria granted me a gift far beyond my greatest imagination. She made me twice the leader I once was. She helped me conquer the Diamonds and the Clubs. The Hearts are now under my unwavering, unquestionable command."

Zack closed his hands in a fist to steady his twitching fingers. "And yet I feel like you're upset about something."

"Observant! I admire that in a warrior. Please sit."

Zack scoffed, refusing the king's command. "Warrior? You have the wrong guy."

"But you are," the king insisted. He sat in one of the large thrones and gestured to the one beside him. "Take note of the seat beside me, Mr. Volo. What do you notice?"

Zack swallowed. *Do I run? Can I make it out of here in time? Do I have any chance?*

"It's *vacant*," the king continued. "Do you know why? Because the queen who once filled it is *dead*. She was assassinated." The king's eyes shifted from a stormy shade of gray to a cold, milky blue coated in a film of frost. The pupils contracted into tiny pinpricks of darkness that drilled into Zack's face.

Zack started to sweat, his stomach churning as though he were going to be sick again.

"While I am a merciful and forgiving man, the assassination of my queen is an act I cannot allow to go unpunished any longer. That's where *you* come in."

"*What?* You don't think *I* killed your queen?"

The king waved a hand as if swatting a fly away. "No, boy, don't be dense. I know the one responsible for the vile act of which I speak. She evaded us long ago, before the age of Avoria. *She* killed my wife. Nobody else in Wonderland will confirm this, so potent is the terror that she struck into our collective hearts. I speak of the woman whose offspring has come to corrupt Wonderland once more. I speak, of course, of the girl who has come to finish what her mother started and acquire my realm."

A horrific realization burrowed deep into Zack's heart.

"Alice, the bold and terrible," the king continued. He stood and advanced toward Zack with slow, calculated steps. "Zack, I'll see to it that you have your heart's deepest desires. After all, I specialize in the heart." The king tapped Zack's chest with a thick finger and drew an imaginary circle around his heart. "The heart houses the soul, and I see that you, too, are missing something vital in the center. In many ways, you've been a shell. Your soul lacks a nucleus, and with it, everything that makes you special. I can fill that shell with everything you need and so much more. You could ascend to the heights of Wonderland history. You could *fly!*"

"Look," Zack said, "I'm not looking to make any deals, especially with you. Soon my friends and I are going to reunite and find a way out of this place. And we owe you nothing."

The king's brows crinkled. "*We*? You, plural, have no obligation to me whatsoever. As for you, it's quite simple, Mr. Volo. I can get you out of here and back to your family. All you have to do is agree to one thing." The king's eyes grew even colder, and Zack thought that little hollow spot in his own heart would freeze over when the monarch continued. "The King of Spades is very protective of his city and especially of the daughter of Alice. That's why I want *you* to terminate her and then bring me her head."

CHAPTER TWENTY-ONE

WONDERTOWN

Crescenzo had been asleep for days, and even in the warm presence of Matthew Hadinger and Gretel, Rosana had never felt lonelier.

She didn't think she'd ever forget Crescenzo's dormant face when he showed up at Matt's doorstep, draped over the neck of the huge cat Gretel liked to play with. Matt and Geppetto helped Crescenzo off the cat's body and into a bed. A Spade nurse checked his vitals while Geppetto told them what happened—how the Hearts had attacked yet again—and Rosana watched with lead in her heart and a frown on her face as the nurse hooked him to various tubes and monitors.

"He'll be okay," the nurse assured. "But this can't happen again. When he wakes up, keep him in bed. His safety comes first."

"I was to protect you all," Matt said, a note of pain producing a subtle quaver in his voice. He produced an assortment of gifts from his hat and placed them around Crescenzo's bed: chocolates, a pre-signed card, a yo-yo, a pair of drumsticks, a shiny pencil. "I've failed. Miss Rosana, you must never step outside this castle without me. Can you promise me this?"

Rosana's heart was torn. On one hand, she *never* wanted to leave as long as Crescenzo was asleep. She wanted to stay at his side and read him books and hope that if she thought good thoughts, he'd dream good dreams.

On the other hand, Rosana was wholly unwilling to yield to the mercy of a pair of warring kings. The King of Hearts wanted to scare her into surrendering her life, but the King of Spades wanted to scare her into being someone she wasn't: a damsel in distress. A passive princess. Someone who would idly sit by and live in fear.

Does he know what Crescenzo and I have been through? she asked herself. *We dropped everything and took a chance on the love of our families. I left home at the suggestion of a fortuneteller and a flying man-child to find my mom.* So why should Rosana stay put when a terrible king had just kidnapped a friend and broken another?

"I'll stay in the castle on one condition," Rosana said. "You teach me how to fight. He wants your city. He wants *me.*"

Matt bit his bottom lip.

"I want to know how to defend myself. I trust you to protect me, and I appreciate all you've done for me, but I want to know my potential. Teach me."

With a warm, paternal smile, Matt nodded. "Very well."

And that's when Rosana's sword training started. She'd wake up each day, eat a small breakfast loaded with oats and assorted berries she'd never seen before, and then she'd work with Matt until her muscles were sore and he made her take a break. Sometimes, he'd keep the swords locked up and suggest the two go for a run instead and work on their speed. Gretel would tag along some days, only to get distracted by mice and rabbits and other fuzzy creatures.

But Rosana couldn't deny that training gave her a rush. It gave her a sort of confidence and strength she hadn't fully realized before, and she wondered what her mother would say if she saw what Rosana could do. By no means did her skills come easy, but she knew they could come in handy someday.

When she wasn't training, she would visit Crescenzo. She hovered over him, checking back between meals and rest periods to see if he'd healed up even a little. She wanted to lift his shoulders and check the knot on the back of his head, but she worried about disturbing his healing. She found herself analyzing every inch of his face. *Has his nose always been a little crooked? Has he always had that tiny scar above his lip?*

Seeing Crescenzo asleep like that, Rosana started thinking of her favorite fairytales. A lot of the main characters seemed to drift off into long bouts of sleep at some point, but usually some dashing hero would come along to wake them up. It occurred to her that if she were in a fairytale, it was completely backward. Crescenzo was the closest thing she had to a dashing hero, and here he was, battered and limp and snoozing without a care. And how was he to wake up?

It's always true love's first kiss, Rosana thought. Her face turned red for even thinking about it. *What if?* What if she were the hero this time and she had to save the boy? Did she have that kind of power? Did she owe it to him to find out?

She thought about something Liam told her on the plane ride from Maryland to California after they first met. She had asked him about Snow White and the moment they fell in love, and she was disappointed when Liam told her it was a story for another day. He followed up with a question of his own.

"Have you ever been in love before?"

"Love? Please," Rosana had scoffed. There had been boys and there had been feelings, but there hadn't been love.

Liam smiled knowingly, a sly sort of twinkle in his eye. "Just you wait, fair lady. You're young, you're pretty, and you seem intelligent. A gallant lad will sweep you off your feet when you least expect it."

Crescenzo had also been sleeping during that conversation, and as soon as Liam said that, Crescenzo rolled over and kicked the mini fridge. Rosana rolled her eyes. "I think I'd rather stay on the ground."

"I'm afraid love and Lady Fortune don't give you much choice." Liam crossed his legs pretzel-style and grinned. "Love doesn't knock on the door and await your answer. It kicks the door off its archway and saunters in unannounced, and it stays as long as it shall please. Treat it as your guest, or ignore it, but whatever you choose, consequences arise. When the love bug strikes you, remember this talk, fair lady."

As Crescenzo lay in his deep sleep in Wondertown, Liam's words played on a loop in Rosana's head and she stared thoughtfully at Crescenzo's face. Specifically her gaze hovered over his lips as she thought about the fairytales she'd heard as a child.

I can save him, she thought. *I can try.*

Rosana's heart sped up a bit, and she looked to the doorway to make sure nobody was coming. *Just one quick kiss, only to see if it works.* She stood up and drew closer, swallowing a dry mouthful of air as she leaned over the bed.

Here goes.

Rosana pushed her lips forward and bowed, lowering her head down, down, down . . .

And Crescenzo shifted in his sleep, his shoulders squirming before he turned his head to the side. Before Rosana could get any closer, she jerked away and covered her mouth, fearing that his eyelids might pop open. She flushed with embarrassment. *Well, at least he doesn't need me to wake up. That's that.*

She chuckled to herself, thinking it had been stupid to remember Liam's words at such a ridiculous time. *Love doesn't knock on the door and await your answer. Good,* Rosana thought. *Maybe it won't knock on my door at all. It's easier that way.* No, she didn't love Crescenzo. He was someone to protect and to care for like a sibling. Someone to laugh with and hug and lean on and—

Sensing that she was getting distracted again, she poked Crescenzo's arm before she turned around to walk away. "Keep resting up, Sleeping Beauty."

When she was halfway out the door, Crescenzo mumbled in his sleep. *"Stop throwing those at me."*

He stirred a little more, and finally, his eyes opened.

Rosana's heart soared higher than she ever imagined possible.

"*Enzo*! You're awake!" She dashed over to him and squeezed his hands. Impulsively, she bent down and kissed his cheek. She half expected him to wipe the kiss away or grimace, but to her relief, he smiled, his face turning a light shade of pink. "Oh my goodness! How are you feeling?"

"Awesome," Enzo said slowly. He stared up at the ceiling, his eyes acquiring a dreamy gaze. "The Hearts attacked me and Geppetto, Rosana. And I took one of them down! All by myself!"

He seemed so excited, Rosana couldn't bring herself to point out that there were hundreds of Hearts in Wonderland. She couldn't bring herself to point out that even though he defeated one, the other one had been quick to render Crescenzo unconscious. All Rosana could do was smile. She liked seeing Enzo in a good mood.

"I wish I could've been there to help," she said.

"I wish you could've been there to watch!" Crescenzo pantomimed a punch. "I've never done anything like that before." He paused for a second. "I've never really had to."

Rosana fidgeted with the strings of her cloak. "Let's hope we don't have to get used to it."

Crescenzo shrugged. "I could. I feel awesome."

"You were unconscious for *days*, Enzo. Do you understand how worried I was? Thinking you were never going to wake up?" She was surprised to feel her lower lip quivering. When was the last time she'd cried? "I could never get used to that. You will never scare me like that again, got it? Promise me."

When the first tear spilled down her face, Crescenzo's goofy demeanor changed. Suddenly he looked confused, his mouth agape and his eyebrows in an arc. "Are you crying?"

"Yes, but only because I'm mad at you for getting hurt!" Rosana said, her defenses flying up like a shield. "I'm waiting for your promise."

Crescenzo stared back for a minute. "I'm surprised to hear this coming from you, Rosana. Are we opposites right now? Because I distinctly remember sitting with you on Violet's beach and you lecturing me about how I needed to start being proactive and taking ownership of our quest. I just did that. Our lives aren't *normal* right now, Rosana. Who knows if they ever will be again? The new reality is that we're targets. As long as we're in this Wonderhell, we have a king after us. We're going to be attacked. I *got* attacked, and you're mad at me for it?"

"You didn't defend yourself hard enough!" Rosana argued. "You're in a bed, and there's a knot on the back of your head!"

"I feel nothing," Crescenzo said. "In fact, I'm ready to get up again. Give me my sword. I want to get back to training. I'm gonna march on over to the Wondercity and take them *all* down!"

"Don't you get up!" Rosana warned. "You're about to do something stupid."

"It's a free country."

"It's *Wonderland*. They have kings here, not constitutions."

"Give me my sword, Rosana."

"Lie back down!"

"Rosana . . ."

"Enzo!"

"You take me too seriously." Crescenzo smirked, his tongue hanging out of the side of his mouth. "Of *course* I don't want to go looking for a fight. I just had my butt kicked! All I'm saying is that I'm proud of myself for beating one. If I train harder, I'll be able to defend myself from *two*. And then three. And then Avoria. Right now, yes, I wanna lie down."

A hot breath shot out of Rosana's nostrils. "I swear . . ."

"You took me seriously," Crescenzo repeated. "It's 'cause you care, huh?"

Rosana scoffed. "No." Her gaze wavered from Crescenzo, and she sighed. "Yes. Maybe."

Crescenzo's smile acquired a genuine warmness. "I'm sorry I scared you."

"I suppose you shouldn't have to apologize. You're right. This is our new reality. It's a strange one, huh?"

"Strangest ever."

"Well, let's make a promise so it won't be so scary. Whatever happens, Enzo, we're in this together." Rosana stuck out her pinky.

Crescenzo extended an arm and locked his own little finger around Rosana's. "Always."

"Plus, I have to admit that there's something I kinda like about this confident new Enzo."

A comfortable silence blanketed the two for a bit, and then Crescenzo asked, "Where's Geppetto, by the way? Is he okay?"

"Oh, Enzo, I wish I knew," Rosana said. "When the cat carried you back, Geppetto only stayed long enough to make sure you got to safety. Then he took off. He said something about it being his fault you got hurt. He said he didn't want to hang around and bother you anymore."

"Oh." All the jovial life in Crescenzo's face melted away again. "And Zack? Any updates yet?"

Rosana shook her head. "Not a clue."

At that moment, Matt poked his head in the door, and his face lit up like Christmas when his gaze fell on Crescenzo. "Mister Enzo!" Matt took three enormous strides to Crescenzo's bedside and shook the boy's hand. "You live! You're conscious! Thank the stars you're okay."

Crescenzo reached for one of the chocolate bars Matt had set there a few days ago. "Is this for me?" Crescenzo grinned. "Shucks, man, you shouldn't have."

"It's *all* for you!" Matt exclaimed. "I'm happily, wonderfully, astoundingly bewildered that you're okay. In fact, this calls for celebration. I think preparations are in order for a tea party!"

CHAPTER TWENTY-TWO

THE OLD WORLD

The mines and underground caverns stood no more. Hansel was sure of it by the time he clawed his way back to the surface. It was almost as if he were the fire. With every step he took, the walls and ceilings crumbled behind him in a mound of dirt, metals, and flames.

He wondered how he could be faster than Bellamy's knight when his legs were sore to the bone, but Hansel managed to outrun him and emerge on the White Road just before the underground dissolved completely. He recognized the lichen-coated boulder in the middle of the road, which reminded him strangely of a green apple. The turrets of Snow White's castle towered over a dry stretch of trees.

The Cavern of Ombra, the miners' work, that infernal pool of dark water, all gone. The relief was exhilarating. Hansel slumped against a dead oak and tilted his head back, closing his eyes. *If I could just rest for a minute . . .*

He hadn't been resting for five minutes before a sharp click sounded in his ear, jolting him out of his meditation. It both warmed him and petrified him to gaze upon Snow White's face again, even if it was on the other side of her silver crossbow.

"Wow, this looks familiar," Hansel said, closing his eyes again and tilting his head back. "Snow, if you're going to make a routine of pointing that thing in my face, get on with it and shoot me already. I haven't the energy to beg for my life anymore."

Snow smiled smugly and tossed the crossbow to the ground. "That's too bad. Threatening you is my only pleasure these days. Is there anything else you'd like to take away from me?"

Hansel rolled his eyes.

"Want this amulet?" She jiggled the little ruby half-moon on her necklace. "How about my home? Want my castle?"

Hansel put a hand up to silence his old friend. "Snow."

"My land? My cows? All the water out of my well?"

A bubble of anger swelled in Hansel's throat. He took a deep breath in the hopes of forcing it down. "Snow—"

Snow took a step forward and rubbed her belly. "How about my first-born child? It'll be a few years, but Liam and I had some names picked out—"

"*Snow*! I'm done with this silly game you're playing with me!" Hansel spun around and struck the oak tree with his fist. "Done! I've been silent because I thought I deserved your wrath, but I'm *trying* to atone for what I've done. I just went through hell itself to find a way to save us. The Cavern of Ombra has been destroyed. I don't deserve your friendship, that's to be sure, but I damn sure don't deserve your hatred anymore. So show me some *respect*!" Hansel's voice rattled through the trees, shocking a flock of birds into flight.

Snow put her hands on her hips, her expression unchanged. She and Hansel stared at each other in the middle of the road while the wind picked up and the animals fled and the atmosphere changed. Hansel could've pierced the tension with one of the bolts from Snow's crossbow. Finally, she broke eye contact and glanced down at a small wooden object in her hand.

"My time is up," she said cryptically.

Hansel's stomach dropped. "What are you talking about?"

Snow laughed. "My time is up! I had three hours to find the book, and I couldn't do it. My time's up."

"The book?" Hansel said. "Alice has the book. She's gone back to

Florindale with it. We found it underground, right beneath your feet."

A fiery glow appeared in Snow's pupils, melting the blue tint around them and coloring her face with hate.

It was only when she screamed that Hansel turned around and realized the turrets of her castle had erupted into flame.

"Liam," she choked.

After her feeble plea, there was a thunderous explosion in the distance. The castle was gone, replaced only by dark smoke and empty memories. A hailstorm of marble, limestone, and ash showered down on them.

"Duck!" Hansel yelled, throwing his arms over his face and arching his back over his distraught friend.

"Liam! No! *Liam!*" Snow wailed with such force that her face turned red and Hansel thought her throat would shatter. On instinct, he wrapped his arms around her. In his shock and exhaustion, his attempts to comfort her seemed more aggressive than he intended.

"Snow!" Hansel pleaded. "Snow, you need to stop screaming!"

Snow wriggled out of Hansel's embrace and ran for the dark smoke behind the trees. The cloud and the swelling orange firelight swallowed the horizon. "I need to go get Liam!"

"You can't go back there!" Hansel protested. "Isn't it obvious who destroyed your castle? You can't run in there! Look, I'm sorry about Liam but . . ." It wasn't until Hansel said his name that stark reality set in. One moment, Snow White's castle stood whole and proud in the background, and the next, it had been blown to dust. And that meant bad tidings for Prince Liam, the man of metal whom Hansel had hated for so many years. Hansel imagined Liam melting into liquid gold, he and his dagger boiling together and seeping into a billion little cracks in the ground. There was a time when such a thought would have given Hansel immense pleasure, but things had changed. Hansel had changed. He owed Liam his life. In fact, it should have been Hansel to suffer the Ivory Queen's wrath before she fled to the New World. Hansel never had the chance to redeem himself. He failed Liam, and by consequence he failed Snow. He didn't even know if Alice escaped.

Most importantly, there was *still* no sign of his sister.

And the thought brought him to his knees while Snow ran screaming into the burning ashy cloud, screaming her husband's name until her throat was raw.

When the horsemen emerged from the smoke a few minutes later with Snow White in a dark cage, Hansel had no more will to fight. He knelt passively and went silently when the knight bound his wrists together and threw him in a box, and he didn't say a word as the horses rode through the night.

Alicia had been too late.

She made it to the surface of Florindale Square, having lost a shoe and severely tattered her jacket while she tried to outrun the crumbling caverns, but when she emerged and saw the crowd outside Midas's Pub, she knew she was too late. She just didn't know what for.

Tucking the leather book into her jacket, Alicia stopped to catch her breath and craned her neck to investigate the crowd's motives. There must have been hundreds of people packed into Florindale Square—men, women, and children—all with their attention converged on a single focal point that Alicia couldn't see. The sight gave her chills. She imagined it to be eerily reminiscent of the day Avoria took so many souls in battle. One thousand people gathered for one objective, only to be extinguished without transition.

Alicia thought about those thousand people and the sign outside Florindale Square. Where were all those people, and why had she been able to come back?

She took several careful steps around the corner and crept up behind a man in a pointed wizard hat, standing on her tiptoes.

Everyone seemed to be focused on a large stage that had been set up outside the bell tower, where five people stood together and faced the crowd. A wooden post was hung above their heads, and two of the five were clad in black armor. The fingers of their gauntlets were curled around a rusty lever. Alicia was so far away, she could barely make out any faces, but after squinting hard enough, she identified the other three people, starting with Lord Bellamy on the far left. He addressed the crowd:

"For their defiance against my decree—my rule—the two individuals you see before you shall pay the ultimate price. They have jeopardized my security and yours by conspiring with persons who would expose you to Queen Avoria. Does this make you happy, ladies and gentlemen?"

"*No!*" The crowd's volume, intensity, and enthusiasm made Alicia jump. Fists went into the air, and blood-red wine sloshed out of silver goblets.

"Do you take pity on these creatures?" Lord Bellamy scowled.

"*No!*"

"And would you have me spare their lives?"

"*No, no, no!*"

Alicia's heart dropped when she understood what was happening. The men in armor were Bellamy's guards, and the two others—Yuna and one of the dwarves who once saved Alicia's life—were about to be hung, and nobody was protesting.

A pang of guilt bubbled in Alicia's stomach when she thought about Yuna's request. *Take me with you.* Alicia had been so suspicious of her, thinking she was a spy for the king. Now, the woman was about to lose her life. Alicia felt even worse for the little miner who helped her fight Kaa so many years ago. She'd never really had a chance to repay him. To thank him.

Bellamy continued, "Then I hereby sentence these two to be hung until death, as you are all my witnesses! Let it be known that I do this in your best interest, that I serve the people of the Old World, and as long as I am your King, you shall never have to lose sleep. My rule may be strict, citizens, but I know how to keep you safe from the Ivory Queen, and it starts with *order*. Lady Yuna of Florindale and Sir Finn, have you any final words?"

Somebody has to stop this, Alicia thought. *This can't be happening.*

Yuna stared into the crowd, defiantly accepting of her fate. "I will only say that Queen Avoria is a very real danger, and she will come back here with or without being let in. She will finish what she started. She will destroy this dark land . . . and *I hope she takes you first.*"

Lord Bellamy snapped his fingers, and his left guard pulled the lever. Yuna dropped through the trap door and out of Alicia's sight.

While the crowd was busy cheering, Alicia turned away, squeezing her eyes shut and covering her sobs. She'd never felt so helpless or useless. If she had the cloak Violet gave her, she could go invisible and set them free. Instead, she was in the open, and if she wanted to save them, she'd have to do it loudly.

A cloud of anger rose through Alicia's throat and she turned around, summoning her courage to protest the hangings before the second guard could hang the dwarf. Her mouth was open and her words were about to spill out when a black-gloved hand pressed over her face and sealed her cries inside her lungs. Another hand pressed against her belly and pulled her back until she found herself in the arms of a hooded stranger, completely shrouded in shadow and at least two heads taller than her. She tilted her head back and tried to catch a glimpse of the stranger's face, but she could see nothing inside the hood. The stranger lifted a finger and pressed it right about to where his mouth should be. *"Shhh."* With that, he pulled her away from the crowd and back into Clocher de Pierre, closing the door behind them.

When they were alone, the stranger let go and stood in front of Alicia with arms folded across his thick chest. Alicia wondered if there was anybody inside the cloak. The figure appeared as a long hooded trench coat, almost sweeping the ground and concealing a pair of dusty black boots. Alicia backed up against the door.

The figure spoke, its voice deep and powerful without being loud. "I have seen what comes to pass if you intervene with fate today, Alice. All these people turn to dust. The New World withers to smoke. Wonderland crumbles to ash. Avoria wins, the lone victor in the war of worlds, all because the cowardly king captures you. Lady Yuna and Finn are but small sacrifices to preserve your fighting chance."

The figure's words made Alicia dizzy. She thought she would be sick at any moment and looked for a safe place to throw up just in case. "Who are you?"

The figure folded his hands behind his back. "I am your ally, though I have made many mistakes up to this point. I tried to be too many things, and now I am paying for all of them."

Alicia shook her head, frustrated by the answer. "Just tell me your name!"

"I'm known by many names. Some have called me the Prince of Thieves. Some know me as one who bestows life, as a wielder of both science and magic. But you, Alice, may have known me as someone else entirely."

The figure lowered his head, threw his hood back, and revealed a head of graying hair. Alicia's jaw dropped when she saw the man's red nose. "Cherry."

The old man under the hood stared back without responding. His eyes, once a gentle brown, glowed a harsh shade of orange with flecks of green in them, reminding Alicia of tiny jack-o-lanterns. "I haven't used that name in ages, but I must acknowledge that it is a part of me. As is Robin Hood. As is Victor Frankenstein. Call me what you will."

Alicia's fear melted as she processed the familiar face. She decided to waste no time asking her question. "The mirror my father sold you long ago. Do you still have it?"

"Ah," Cherry said. "The mirror that helped inspire my research. A portal between worlds. No, silly girl. That mirror no longer exists, for you see, I gifted it to Miss Violet on her two-hundredth birthday, and your daughter was among those who recently destroyed it."

Alicia wanted to crumble to her knees. *So it* was *the same mirror.* She couldn't believe she missed it before. "My daughter's in there. She's *in* Wonderland. How am I supposed to get her out if that portal doesn't work anymore? Weren't there only two mirrors?"

Cherry's expression remained firm. "I expect many have existed and will continue to exist throughout the ages. But I'm afraid time is not on your side, Alice. People will continue to lose their lives, and the queen grows ever so strong beyond our borders. You need another way into Wonderland, and it just so happens that I have one."

Cherry aimed a palm at Alicia, and something bulky stirred inside her jacket. When Cherry jerked his arm back, the old leather book flew out of Alicia's jacket and into his fingers. He opened the book and ran his gloves along the fraying edges. "Yes. Everything we need is in here."

Alicia swallowed, her breath returning to normal before Cherry threw his hood back over his head, concealing his face once more.

"My home, my lab, everything I know has been destroyed by Bellamy's forces. But for saving my life's work, I grant you a small gift of aid." Master Cherry reached into his dark coat and produced three red-tipped darts, holding them up to the light before tossing them in Alice's direction. "Yes, these should do the trick. They are the last of their kind. Do not burn your only chance at salvation. At *our* salvation."

Alice caught the darts and rolled them in her fingers. They were heavier than they looked, and the points reminded her of syringes. "What are they?"

"Opportunities. When you're ready, stick one in your neck. Go and find the little girl. Then get yourselves out."

"A little girl?" Alice repeated. "Who? Where? You don't mean . . . my daughter?"

"I don't," Cherry confirmed.

"But I have to get her out!" Alice said, a bit more frantically than she intended. "Please. This is the very reason I wanted to see you in the first place! My daughter is my first priority. Can't you please spare any more? Enough to save her, too?"

"I told you. They're the last of their kind. It is in your daughter's best interest for you to save the girl. If you yield to your greed, you will cause more harm than your daughter can endure." Even though Cherry's face was covered, his intensity was unavoidable, pulling Alicia's gaze into his hood like a dark abyss. "I've offered you this one lifeline, Alice. Do not make me sorry that I've done so."

Alicia looked down at her hands, her throat suddenly feeling heavy and tight.

"I must resume my research," Cherry continued. "Ages of knowledge are bound in this book, and there's much to learn about how to save our worlds. I'm particularly interested in the effects of the moonflower. Good luck to you, Alice, and may we stand together at the fated place for the final battle."

Before Alicia could stop him, Cherry clapped his hands and a puff of shadow carried him through the door. He was gone, and she was alone, feeling like she had come full circle with no new leads except a handful of sharp objects.

What little girl?

She sighed, shook her head, and plunged one of the darts into her neck. She had forgotten what it was like to disappear.

CHAPTER TWENTY-THREE

Zack waited in thick silence for any indication that the King of Hearts had been joking, but it never came. It was the longest pause of his life.

"Why?" he finally asked. "Why would I help you kill a friend? Why would anybody help you take a life?"

The king stood, laced his fingers together, and began pacing around the room. "Before I answer that, let me make myself quite clear. Do not linger under the mistaken impression that I am giving you a choice in this matter, for you *will* kill the daughter of Alice. Now, you have my sympathies in wondering why it has to be you, but as you will see, there is no better choice for this unfortunate necessity. Why you, Mr. Volo? Why don't you gaze upon my mirror?"

Whoosh!

The red curtain fell from the wall behind the king, and Zack's stomach broiled from within.

I should've known. I really should've known.

A mirror. The entire wall was a mirror.

Zack thought of the freak mirror he had seen when he woke up in the Old World. The way it whispered to him, the way it glowed blue, the way it took an enchanted blade to make the tiniest scratch on the surface . . . And then Enzo smashed it, and they were a world away. Zack never wanted to see another mirror again. A mirror interrupted his easy, happy life as a regular kid. It was because of a mirror that Zack was no longer the school stud with the basketball as Geppetto had portrayed him, but a shoeless nobody in Wonderland land.

A land where his parents couldn't reach him.

A land where his friends were probably in great danger looking for him and—

"*I think preparations are in order for a tea party!*"

The King of Spades, Matthew Hadinger, appeared in the mirror image, followed by Rosana, Crescenzo, and Gretel. The four were laughing, smiling, and sharing a bar of chocolate.

"This," Cornelius said, "is what your friends are doing right now. *Celebrating*. Eating chocolate. Bonding. Without you."

Zack, who had been standing as tall as he could, felt his chest deflate and his shoulders sag involuntarily. Why weren't they looking for him?

"When I abducted you," Cornelius continued, "you would have been correct in assuming that you were collateral. I was fully prepared to negotiate a trade for your safety, if only the daughter of Alice and the son of Pinocchio would have come looking for you as I expected. As you can see, they haven't done so. They're hardly conscious of your existence at all. I've either underestimated her bravery or overestimated her loyalty."

Taking a deep breath, Zack fought down the pange of disappointment that chewed at his stomach. "Well, maybe you've just underestimated her *intelligence*. Neither of them are stupid enough to come knocking on your door for me." He looked away from the mirror and down at his knees. "I'm glad for that."

"But are you?" the king pressed. "You aren't concerned the daughter of Alice has taken your place in the other boy's life? Thicker than thieves they're becoming. I wonder where that leaves you." He pointed to the mirror with his thumb. "Obviously, in no position of importance."

"That doesn't mean I'm going to *murder* somebody!" Zack yelled.

"I won't do it. I'll never be you."

The king's lips turned down, and he made a clucking sound. "What a shame, for you should know that I had such high hopes for you. But if you insist on mediocrity, I suppose I can't convince you. I'd like you to see just one more thing. After that, you may leave."

The mirror flashed, a bright light momentarily flooding the room.

Zack squeezed his eyes shut and turned away from the mirror, shielding his face. He could beat this.

"Mr. Volo, open your eyes."

"I won't!"

"Mr. Volo."

"No!"

"*Zackary Volo.*" This time, it wasn't the king. It was like a talking mountain, rattling Zack's bones and knocking him onto the ground. When his elbow smacked the floor, he opened his eyes.

The king grinned and stepped aside, and Zack beheld something he couldn't have been prepared for.

Himself.

He flinched and scooted backward, startled by what he saw in his reflection. He was just a shadow, hovering a few feet over the ground with an evil, terrifying grin. In his hands, he spun a black knife through his fingers, casting little needles of light all over the room.

"*Hello, Zack.*" The shadow grew closer.

"Shut up," Zack said, backing up even more as his reflection stared him down. "You have no right to talk to me."

"*You know you're only talking to yourself, right? Just FYI. You look crazy.*"

"Crazy is not a nice word to use. A friend taught me that."

"*But I can't think of a better word. You aren't sane. You aren't normal. We aren't normal. Why else would you be seeing me?*"

Zack flared his nostrils, curling his fingers at his sides. *It's a trick of the light. The king is causing this. It isn't me.*

The shadow scoffed. *"Don't flatter yourself. Everyone knows it! You're a rogue. You're a grenade. You're less than your father."*

As angry as Zack felt, he couldn't stop staring. His dark form was one of those disturbing sights he couldn't peel his eyes away from, like a fiery car accident or one of those disgusting surgery shows on TV. He wanted it to disappear, but he also didn't want to look away.

"You know why I can talk to you, Zack? Because Crescenzo failed you and you don't have a soul anymore. He was too late, too busy dawdling around with Rosana, his new best friend. I can fill all that empty space inside of you, you know. We can be whole!"

"Get out of my head!" Zack snapped. "Crescenzo did the best he could, and I'm *fine*. Whatever that stupid witch took away from me, I don't need it." He bared his teeth and his fingers shook, feeling as though the blood was boiling inside them. "And I don't need *you!*" Impulsively, Zack reached beside him and wrapped his arms around the king's mace. He hoisted it over his head and heaved it at the mirror, throwing all his weight into the weapon.

Truthfully, he hadn't been expecting anything to happen. He thought it would just be another freak mirror and the mace would bounce off the surface and roll away. He was wrong. The mace hit its target, and a web of cracks spread through the image like frost on a window. Zack's shadow laughed. If a volcano could laugh as its lava exploded into the world, that's what the shadow's laugh would have sounded like. It seemed to have twelve eyes with all the different glass shards spidering through the mirror.

Zack's heart raced into overdrive. He sprung to his feet and turned to run away, not sure where he would go.

The king stepped in front of him and barred his path. "You made your choice, Mr. Volo. You let your impulses dictate your decision. Now, you shall forever be one of my own."

The room sunk into darkness when the mirror burst into a thousand pieces and crumbled to the floor. Cold wind filled the room like a frosty hurricane. Zack began to shiver, rubbing his arms for warmth and comfort. He could hear the king and the shadow both laughing somewhere in the room as the cold seeped into his skin.

Beware the King of Hearts. Madame Esme blossomed into his mind, seeming to reach for Zack from across her table, begging him to take her hand, but her face only faded away with the sound of her voice. The chill in the air buried every other thought.

"Do not resist this, Zack. This will only take a moment."

So . . . cold . . .

He imagined he would be able to see his breath if the lights came back on. Something swirled around him like a funnel, and then the wind pried his mouth open and poured into his lungs. As hard as he tried, he couldn't close his mouth again.

What the hell is happening to me?

"I'm making us whole again! Not only whole, but better. Stronger."

Zack's heels peeled off the ground as if lifted by a magnet, and his toes followed suit. He felt lighter than air.

He was flying.

The cold funneled into his mouth until there was no more left to swallow, and Zack's mouth clapped shut like a Venus flytrap. His arms hovered at his sides, feeling as though they were on strings.

The lights snapped on, and the red curtain returned to its wall. There was no glass on the floor. There were no shadows in the air.

Except for Zack.

He looked down at his heels, floating a full yard above the ground. His once bare feet were adorned in black boots, oozing dark mist like the rest of his body, like his new tactical pants and his armored gloves and the bulletproof shirt that stretched over his arms . . . like his nose. He could see the black smoke steaming off his chin and dissolving into nothing.

And somehow, it felt good.

I'm weightless! I'm flying. I'm . . . amazing.

The king stood below Zack, hands folded behind his back as he surveyed Zack from head to toe. "Impressive. Quite magnificent, I must say. You exceed my expectations."

Zack said nothing. Felt nothing. Did nothing.

"You're under my control now, boy. You're my *puppet.* As my top soldier, I shall grant you a gift."

The king withdrew a dagger from his back pocket and pressed the handle into Zack's palm. The blade weighed nothing. It didn't feel like anything.

"With this, you shall perform the deed I have asked of you," the king explained. "You do remember what I ask?"

The words tumbled involuntarily from Zack's lips. "Yes, Your Majesty."

"Very good, Mr. Volo. Kill the daughter of Alice and anyone else who stands in your way." The king grinned, his irises reflecting a mix of both pride and hatred. "Either you stop her heart, or I take yours."

CHAPTER TWENTY-FOUR

THE NEW WORLD

Her own words must've echoed several hundred times before the haze finally cleared.

Don't let The Carver die. Don't let The Carver die. Don't let The Carver die.

The phrase looped in Madame Esme's mind as she sat at her fortune table, eyes sealed and chin down with her palms clasped together in her lap. Her breathing was slow, steady, and calculated, still dialed to the exact rate that she needed to relay her message to the son of Peter Pan.

Gradually, the warning faded from her mind, the words growing softer with each loop, and Madame Esme became aware of her surroundings again. First she registered the tingling in her toes, and then the snapping of her tent curtains. Frigid wind bit her ears and tore at the jade crystals dangling from her lobes. This was nothing like the weather in Wonderland.

Madame Esme's eyelids popped open, and she rattled her palms against her elbows, frantically seeking warmth. Tarot cards blustered around her booth, folding Death inside a wrinkle in her dress. She shivered, still chilled by her vision of the future. Besides, there was something about the wind that Madame Esme couldn't quite register. When she had drifted into her trance, the humidity plastered her tarot cards to the table. Her forehead had been sweating. All the other cast members at Ye Olde Renaissance Faire had rolled up their sleeves. The sudden change of weather unsettled her.

I need to leave, Madame Esme thought.

She leapt to her feet and jammed her arms into a light denim coat, tearing at her pockets for her gloves. When she realized she'd left them at home, she knelt and started snatching her tarot cards off the ground, grimacing every time a gust of wind would whip the card into the air before her fingers could touch it. After she'd failed to retrieve the Shadow, Madame Esme froze. A thick layer of silver frost had crept under her tent and blanketed the grass at her feet in a matter of seconds. The cold stabbed through her soles, and she abandoned the task of picking up her cards.

She grabbed a small iron box under her table and threw in the cards she'd managed to retrieve, sealing them inside with her stones, her wallet, and her phone charger.

Madame Esme tucked the box under her jacket and started toward the opening of her tent. She had only taken one quick step when her satin tablecloth tore into the air and smacked her in the face, the ends ruffling behind her back as she struggled to peel it off. The wind had such a tight hold on the cloth that she thought the satin was going to suffocate her. She ripped at it with both hands in a panic, causing her to drop her iron box and spill her tarot cards onto the ground again.

"A thousand curses!" Madame Esme shouted.

She untangled herself, tossed the tablecloth behind her, and picked up the box again, making a run for it.

The wind picked up the entire tent and flung it into the air. Madame Esme let out an involuntary cry of surprise. She was standing alone in the open, surrounded by the darkness of dusk and the bite of fresh snow.

"Hello, Esmeralda."

Esme's limbs turned to jelly. Four disfigured shadows squirmed in front of her, writhing in the darkness like gobs of black ink on a chalkboard. The worst part was that the shadows weren't the source of the greeting. The voice had come from behind her, with a tone like an icicle.

Slowly, Madame Esme forced herself to turn around and confront the woman.

"Avoria," she whispered.

The woman bowed. Snowflakes clung to her blood-red hair, which fell past her shoulders in a cascade smoother than velvet. Her eyes seemed to stab Madame Esme's heart, and there was no mistaking the arrogant curve in her fake, crimson smile.

"Is that how you address a queen?" Avoria droned. "Really, Esmeralda, I'd assumed better of you. Has your exile taught you nothing?"

Esme straightened her shoulders. She wasn't going to show fear to this creature. Fear implied respect. The woman in front of her deserved neither. "Madame Esme knows all," Esme said. "And I know you are not a queen. You bear no crown."

Avoria made a sound in her throat, like she was coughing out a laugh. "We'll get to that, my dear, once I've made some . . . adjustments to this realm. It's still a little bright for my taste, and somehow, I do not yet exhume the power I was promised." Avoria took three slow steps forward, her heels crushing the frosted blades of grass beneath her.

Madame Esme swallowed, willing herself not to be the one to break eye contact.

"This is a problem," Avoria continued. "I had originally been promised that if I reaped seven souls of the fierce guardians of light, the strongest lovers and truest believers, I would be granted life eternal and immediate power." Avoria's gaze trailed off, and a dreamy glint appeared in the centers as she stared at a falling snowflake billowing into her palm. "People would bow without my request. They would bend to my will like puppets on strings, and this world would be my ever-shifting stage, a dynamic theater limited only by the boundaries of my brilliant mind! Imagine! The gift of The Carver not only at my fingertips but in my blood. My gaze, my breath, my very core! I was promised all of this, and do you know what I have now, Esmeralda?"

Esme smirked.

"*Nothing!*" Avoria screamed. "I still have nothing!" Spit flew across her bottom lip and froze in a thin film. She reached into her sleeve and drew out a crumpled piece of yellowed paper. The smirk melted off Esme's face. "But I have a solution, Esmeralda. I've learned the wrinkle in my plan. I was off by one tiny little detail, and such a simple one at that."

She unfolded the piece of paper and jammed it in Esme's hands. Avoria's hands were like sandpaper. Esme flinched when they made skin contact. She brushed it off and let her gaze fall to the paper.

Avoria clasped her hands behind her back and began to pace back and forth. "You hold in your hands the missing page of Dr. Victor Frankenstein's research. One of my shadows was kind enough to snatch it for me on our way out of our ghastly home. It is the most important page as you may guess, and if you'll read it carefully, you'll notice that I was on the right track all along. But the design remains incomplete. That's where you come in, my dear."

Madame Esme's eyes hovered over the scribbled text and the strange drawings, her heart pounding with every morsel of ink she took in. Avoria was never supposed to see this. Madame Esme's fingers trembled, and her pulse hammered her skin. "Madame Esme shall not help you!"

"But you shall!" Avoria snatched the page from Madame Esme and folded it into eight uneven rectangles, jamming it into her sleeve again. "You will do this for me, or you will risk the lives of everybody who comes barging through that door when the time comes. I'm not dense, stupid woman. I know it's unavoidable. The Carver, the man-child, my stepdaughter, and *all* their spineless friends are going to come after me someday. Maybe even a certain bell ringer will join their ranks?"

Madame Esme turned away and closed her eyes, pressing her jaws together to keep her teeth from chattering too heavily.

"Have I touched a nerve?" Avoria said. "I don't need *your* gift to know that I have."

Tears welled up behind Esme's eyelids. *You shall not let her see them,* she told herself.

The shadows wriggled over to Avoria's side as the witch took one more step and put her icy fingers on Esme's chin. "Your choices are simple. Come now and I'll give you some time to think about them. Defy me and prolong the suffering of everyone you care about. Or, you may save yourself and the bell ringer to join me in eternal paradise. I'm merciful, Esmeralda, and you know that I will grant you this . . . *if* you reveal to me the whereabouts of the eighth and final core soul."

CHAPTER TWENTY-FIVE

WONDERLAND: WONDERTOWN SQUARE

"We are to be brave."

Crescenzo, Rosana, and Gretel stood together and watched the giant screens of Wondertown, where Matthew Hadinger was broadcasting a speech for his people.

"Cornelius Redding would have us crawl into our hats and cower, but we are to be brave. As long as I am the King of Spades, then I, Matthew Hadinger, am not going to yield to the volition of a madman. And neither are you. *That* is why our traditional tea party will continue! Won't you join me?"

Most people on the ground cheered and clapped, while some whispered to one another that the tea party wasn't a good idea.

"It's too high profile," Crescenzo heard an elderly man whisper. "The Hearts will attack us again, and how are we to defend ourselves with teabags?"

The woman next to him shrugged. "I like tea parties."

"Some of you may question the idea of having a tea party when we remain under the threat of the Hearts," Matt continued. "Let me assure you that security in Wondertown will increase twenty-fold. Should we come under attack again, we will have every measure in place to defend ourselves. Our army will be prepared. I will be prepared. *We* will be prepared. There will be no kidnappings. There will be no casualties. There will only be victory, and then, we shall go retrieve Cornelius's hostage!"

Crescenzo breathed a smile of relief. It was good to know that Matt hadn't forgotten about Zack. Rosana and Crescenzo made casual references to him every day, hinting that they wanted an action plan, but Matt would usually pull ice cream cones from his hat and insist that they didn't need to worry. Every time he did that, Crescenzo only worried more. So to know that Matt cared and had a plan in place, Crescenzo felt a great swell of appreciation for the man.

Crescenzo only wished he knew where Geppetto ran off to.

Things were a bit of a mess, but Crescenzo forced himself to keep his cool. Rosana helped him do that. He couldn't stop thinking about what she said after he woke up, about how she liked *the confident new Enzo.* And truth be told, she had grown in fascinating ways as well. He loved watching her interact with Gretel, inspiring her to eat her vegetables and reading her books when she got bored. He thought Rosana must have had a wonderful mother to model her behavior after.

He just wondered how the heck she got out of Wonderland.

Crescenzo woke up late the day of the tea party, and at the foot of his bed he found a note:

Sir Enzo, the tea party will take place tonight on the floating island in the center of Wondertown. Listen for the bell, and take the elevator at the end of the hall. Put on your best! – M.H.

He also found a red suit with a black button down and some formal shoes, and he couldn't help but groan. He hated dressing formally . . . the pinch of cap-toed shoes, the heavy sweat-inducing fabric of a suit jacket, and the way neckties felt like a polyester noose around his throat. After a long, toe-crackling stretch, he crawled out of bed and showered.

The shower didn't do much to wake him up. His eyelids hovered between open and shut, and he wanted nothing more than to go back to sleep. He wanted to sleep through the entire day and wake up back in his bed at home.

After he got dressed, he put a handful of his wooden figurines in his inner jacket pocket, including the miniature that his grandfather made on the day Crescenzo learned to carve. He'd kept it in his pocket everywhere he went, along with his knife.

The strangest thing about that morning was that Crescenzo was so groggy he had the idea of walking to Starbucks. He hated coffee, but soda wasn't a thing in Wonderland, and he needed the caffeine boost before he could get his hands on some tea.

When he shuffled out of the castle, he heard some of Pietro's words in his head: *Coffee is life, kid. When you grow up, you're gonna love the stuff, I swear!*

Crescenzo shook his head and smirked. *Whatever, Pietro.*

Before he could get far, two spears barred Crescenzo's path, and the husky guard clones stepped in front of him. Their usual stripes and shorts were replaced with heavy armor, bearing the insignia of Wonderland. "And where oh where are you going, Sir Enzo?"

"Look, uh, Mister Dum?"

"It's Dee."

"Okay. May I pass and go get a coffee?"

Dee leaned over and consulted with Dum, the two frantically whispering to each other with their gazes fixed on Crescenzo. Finally, Dee straightened his back and cleared his throat. "Do you need a bodyguard?"

Crescenzo was a little irritated at the question, but he was gradually getting used to the fragile treatment ever since the Hearts knocked him out. "No, no, I'm good. Thanks though."

"You may pass." The guards slid to the side. "Happy Tea Day!"

"Yeah, thanks," Crescenzo muttered.

He started down the road, his hard leather soles making obnoxious taps against the ground. All around, people scurried about from place to place, ducking into formalwear shops, strolling by the florist stands, and popping in and out of bakeries. The giant screens had also been lowered from wherever they came from, and they all projected the same thing: the words *Merry Tea Day, Wondertownians!* dancing around the screen in curly letters.

Crescenzo glanced up at the floating island. Bells and ribbons swirled around it, and floating LED lights made the waterfall flash between white, gold, and silver.

But for each element of excitement and levity, there was a guard poised on a building somewhere, each armed with a bow. Riflemen were on one knee, each taking position behind a cooling unit or some sort of camouflaging station they'd set up on their own. The other marksmen were in plain sight, walking back and forth with one hand hovering over a pouch full of arrows.

Then there was Gretel, just a few feet away from the Starbucks and toddling around with ringlets in her hair and a bouncy ball in her hands.

"Enzo!" She waved.

Crescenzo smiled and jammed his hands in his pockets, making a beeline for the girl. "Hey, kid. How's it go—?"

Boom!

There was a sound like a gun, and something hit Crescenzo in the stomach with a painful force that knocked him off his feet and sent him flying high into the air. It was like somebody clubbed him with one of those carnival mallets meant for testing your strength. It was like a cannonball to the belly. When Crescenzo looked down, a cannonball didn't seem like a bad guess. A dark, transparent sphere had latched onto him and carried him into the sky. As the ground peeled away, all the residents of Wondertown gasped and pointed upward like little ants. Crescenzo wondered if his spirit had left his body as a terrified scream poured from his throat.

As quickly as he had left the ground, Crescenzo landed again, back-first into something large, soft, and springy. He looked around, heart galloping with fear, and realized he was lying in the center of some sort of white fabric suspended in the air. He sank into it, stretching the fabric, until it ripped beneath his back and he fell again. This time, Crescenzo didn't fall very far. He hit the ground less than a full second later, staring up at a person-shaped hole in the cloth above him. It was a canopy set up for the tea party. The sound of rushing water filled his ears. Flickers of warm gold and cool silver light danced in his peripheral vision. An enormous waterfall careened into a river that burst into mist before it could drip onto the people of Wonderland.

He was on the floating island.

Crescenzo massaged his temples and looked down at his torso. The black sphere was gone, but a pulsing pain lingered while his back throbbed as well. He was grateful he at least had the canopy to break his fall, because if he had missed, he would have careened into a long, jagged table covered in teapots, silver plates, and a hot fountain of sweet molten chocolate.

But what the hell just sent me up here?

"Hey, tough guy."

A misty shadow materialized in front of Crescenzo, and when the full body appeared, Crescenzo had to squint to be sure he perceived it correctly. It had the right shape and height, the right spiky hair, but everything else was wrong: a foggy black shape clad in leather that seemed to be evaporating without really disappearing; a knife that looked a thousand times sharper than his own, like it could rip the clouds apart; irises cloudy like a block of marble veiled in cobwebs. Just by looking at the shadow, Crescenzo's blood went ice cold.

The figure hovered in front of him with the knife in one hand and the other flexing its fingers as if tickling the air. It locked eyes with Crescenzo and smirked.

Crescenzo choked out his friend's name. *"Zack?"*

When the figure spoke, there was a hollow octave underneath the voice Crescenzo recognized, like Zack had swallowed a robot. "What?"

"You're not you." Crescenzo shook his head, as if the act could erase what he saw. "What happened to you?"

Zack hovered forward, prompting Crescenzo to scramble to his feet. "I became everything I always wanted to be, Enzo." Zack swiped at the air with his dagger. "Probably everything *you* should be, too."

Crescenzo gasped when a hole opened in the air, dark and jagged, and he watched in awe as the space repaired itself, like an invisible hand drawing a zipper shut. "Dude!"

"You look scared," Zack said, his voice stripped of emotion. "What's the matter? Afraid of what a little magic can do?"

"I'm afraid of what that much *power* can do!" Crescenzo's heart picked up with every word. "Where did you get that knife?"

With a smirk, Zack spun the dagger handle effortlessly through his fingers, creating a portable shining windmill in his hand. "It was a gift."

"From who?"

"From the King of Hearts!" Zack raised his arms in a grand gesture. "And he sent me here with one goal in mind. But I need to take care of you first."

Crescenzo had a feeling Zack wasn't referring to taking care in the same way his mother might've used the phrase. *Something is definitely wrong.* He took a step back and his hand crept to his jacket pocket, where The Carver's knife rested in a thick leather sheath.

Zack's lips parted in an eerie smile. "Remember when we used to spar, Crescenzo? We'd use those flimsy little sticks your dad made, and my dad would show us how to use them with one hand tied behind his back?"

"Like I'd ever forget," Crescenzo said.

"Remember who always won?" Zack flicked the dagger again and tore another hole in the air. Crescenzo's throat grew tight. "I wonder if you've gotten any better? Or have you been too busy with your girlfriend?"

A hot breath flared out of Crescenzo's nostrils. "Just tell me what this is about!"

"This is about you, Enzo, and how you failed us. You failed my mom and dad and me, and your family, and Rosana's mom. We're all ruined because of you, and Rosana's next. I have orders to make sure of that. I know you don't really want to see her get hurt. Don't worry, Enzo. I've got your back. You don't have to see anything that's about to happen to her."

Crescenzo froze in his place, determined not to take another step back. He spread his feet and made a fist. "Let's not do this!"

"But we used to have so much fun. Are you not having fun anymore?" Another slash at the air. The holes in space looked like globs of blackberry jelly. "Don't get brave, Crescenzo. You've never won a single fight by yourself. The best you can do is delay your pain. And because we're best friends, I'm here for *you* before I take Rosana. No man should have to watch his girlfriend suffer."

Crescenzo shifted his shoulders and felt a pop in his back. He was already in pain, but he wasn't going to show it. *He's just trying to mess with you. Zack can't really hurt you.* His fingers closed over his knife. It tingled on his palm. He whipped the blade out of its sheath and pointed it in front of him, suddenly feeling braver than he'd ever felt before. "Stop this right now, and bring back the *real* Zack."

"You want me to stop this?" Zack sneered and hovered upward, approaching the hole in the canopy. "Fine, I'll make this quick!"

Zack flickered in and out of the air like a strobe light, rocketing closer to Crescenzo with each flicker. His face was in a terrible grin, and his blade was poised to strike. Crescenzo clutched his knife and wondered how he was going to counter the attack, his heart pounding faster and harder as the shadow grew closer.

Really should've practiced more with Geppetto! Crescenzo sprung out of the way and braced himself for death.

When a flash of scarlet ripped through the air, Crescenzo was certain it was blood. After he took cover behind one of the canopy's poles, he realized it was a scarlet cloak that had dripped onto the ground. A *clang* vibrated through the air, and Crescenzo's jaw fell open.

Rosana appeared, cocooned in black, red, and silver armor. She bore a jade scimitar, hoisted high over her head and perpendicular against Zack's dagger.

For a second, their blades remained locked together, their metallic ring echoing through the air. Without a word, Rosana made a sort of push with her elbows, and Zack lowered his arm to his side. A sideways grin spread across his lips. Rosana's expression, however, was bone cold. They held each other's gazes with intense persistence.

Rosana spread her arms out, pointing the scimitar at Zack before she spoke. "Don't you touch him."

CHAPTER TWENTY-SIX

WONDERLAND: THE SKY ISLAND

Once Rosana managed to steady her trembling arms, strength flowed through her veins like medicine. She'd been furious when Gretel told her that something had taken Crescenzo away—that something had hurt him again—and she snuck into one of the armories and grabbed the first things she laid her eyes on. She'd also noticed her cloak had been stashed away nearby, and she used it to sneak onto the Jub Jub bird and up to the floating island. That's when she saw Zack making a dive for Crescenzo, and rage lit up inside her like dynamite.

"I don't know what happened to you," she said, eyeing the shadowy figure, "but you need to leave."

"Ah, Rosana." The shadow grinned. "Just the person I came here for!"

Crescenzo sprung back to his feet. "You shouldn't be here, Rosana."

Rosana scowled. "Shut up, Enzo. Remember our promise? We're in this together."

"See?" Zack sneered. "Crescenzo can never fight his battles alone. Do you really need a girl to do the fighting for you? Especially the girl I was sent here to kill?"

Crescenzo nudged Rosana, looking as though he might be ill. "Go. I have this."

"I know you do," Rosana said. "But remember our promise. You protect me, and I protect you."

Crescenzo nodded. "Together?"

In a flash, Crescenzo and Rosana pivoted and stood back-to-back, each poised with a blade.

"Together," Rosana said. "You look great in that suit, by the way."

"Thanks!" Crescenzo said. "You look pretty badass in all that armor."

Zack blinked out of sight, and Rosana tensed up. *Where did he go?* The shadow was nowhere to be seen, and the sounds of the waterfall masked any rustling under the canopy. The stillness chilled her bones. She tilted her scimitar to the side and held the pose, ready to defend herself. "Crescenzo," she whispered. "I want you to get under my hood and hide."

"Fat chance," Crescenzo said. "I'm not leaving you."

Shing! Zack popped into the air inches away from Rosana's face and swung his dagger. Rosana raised her blade with perfect timing and blocked the dagger, but she wasn't prepared for the dark rift that had opened in front of her. A pool of black spilled in the air, and for a minute, Rosana saw stars and moons and swirling clusters of gas all contained within a hole in space no taller than Gretel. It captivated and frightened Rosana, and it wasn't until it was too late that she realized the space was pulling on her scimitar. The handle fought her grip like a magnet, and she tightened her hold with both hands, gritting her teeth and burying her heels into the ground. Meanwhile, Crescenzo spun around and broke formation, taking a swing at Zack's backside.

The shadow burst out of sight again, and as Crescenzo recovered his footing, Rosana lost the blade. The dark space wrestled it out of her hands and sent it tumbling into the dark depths of, well, whatever Zack had opened up in the air. Her mind whirled, and her heart sank as she watched her scimitar fall at a million miles an hour until it was no bigger than a speck of dust, and then the rift in the air closed again. Rosana was defenseless. Instinctively, she seized a teapot and prepared to throw it overhand.

Zack reappeared on the other side of the canopy and laughed. "Is this worth it for you, crazy woman?" he taunted. "Are you willing to give up your life for this place?"

Rosana launched the teapot in the air and charged for the shadow in a wrathful sprint, not knowing what she was going to do when she caught it. All the while, Zack hovered in the air, taunting and laughing. She saw him spinning his knife in front of his chest, but she didn't stop running.

Crescenzo gained speed behind her, leapt forward, and pushed Rosana aside. "No!"

Rosana careened to the ground, angry at *two* boys now as Crescenzo raced ahead with his knife at his side.

Cling! Clang! Clack! Cling!

Crescenzo and Zack danced across the island like pirates, crossing their blades without managing to land a single blow. Rosana found the sight rather impressive, the way Crescenzo managed to maneuver throughout the fight. "Get him, Enzo!"

"Don't distract me!" *Clang!*

"Right. Sorry."

But a cacophony far more distracting had begun far below, where the sounds of marching feet and synchronized chants carried up to the island. Rosana peered over the edge to see what had changed, and she watched the army of red march in from the east.

The archers and riflemen on the buildings took aim.

A clash of spears on tile sounded below, and an army of black moved forward. *Left right left right left right.*

No, Rosana thought. The war had begun. She turned around and found Crescenzo and Zack continuing to jab at each other, slashing and parrying. Zack taunted Crescenzo from high above and then swooped down in a low-hanging arc while Crescenzo rolled out of the way.

"Come, Enzo!" Zack said. "You can do better than this!"

"I don't wanna fight you, man! Give it up already!"

"Ha! Pathetic. Try saying that to the woman who took my soul. Ask her to give up and let you win."

Enzo crouched down and caught his breath. "I'm sorry, okay? I'm sorry I didn't make it in time to save you all! I tried. I really tried, and I hate myself every day for letting the queen out. But you're supposed to help me stop her! You can still help me get your soul back! I can't do it all alone."

Zack clucked his tongue. "If you can't do it alone, you can't do it at *all*. You haven't even touched me with that puny little knife of yours."

Crescenzo straightened his back and wiped his forehead with his sleeve. "Then fly back down here and see what I can do."

"Fine." In a flash, Zack blinked out of the sky and appeared behind Crescenzo's back, and there was an awful flash of red in the air as a moan poured out of Crescenzo's lips.

Blood. Crescenzo's blood poured on the ground, and he fell to his knees with a long slash in his jacket.

Rosana screamed. "*No!*" She ran under the canopy and knelt by his side. "Enzo! Talk to me!"

Crescenzo winced.

Zack crossed his arms and smirked with a triumphant gleam in his eye. "I told you I always win. You should've practiced more."

"Shut up!" Rosana barked. She grabbed Crescenzo's hand and studied the wound on his back. "Can you move?"

Crescenzo shook his head. "I . . . I can move."

A pair of light, quick footsteps scurried under the canopy, and Rosana felt a tiny hand on her shoulder. "Rosana? What happened to Enzo?"

Rosana whirled around and saw Gretel in a beige dress, her eyes wide with fear. "Gretel! You shouldn't be here. Go back down to the castle! No, run and get Matt for me!"

Gretel stared back with her mouth agape.

Rosana snapped her fingers. "Gretel, I said go! Run!"

Gretel nodded slowly. "Enzo?"

Crescenzo pointed behind Rosana's shoulder, giving Rosana just enough time to duck and move when she whirled around to find Zack cleaving at the air behind her. In the time it took her to evade the shadow, Gretel seized a teapot from one of the broken tables and hurled it at the back of Zack's head. It sailed straight through him and burst into a tiny bomb of broken china and orange brew. Zack turned and slashed his dagger in Gretel's direction, opening another rift in the air. When Gretel screamed and ran back to the elevator in the waterfall, Zack doubled over in laughter. "Kids."

Rosana pried Enzo's knife out of his hands. "Let me fight for you now."

"Isn't that sweet?" Zack said. "Looks a lot like love to me. But of course, it can't be love, can it?"

Rosana stood and swatted the dust off her knees, memorizing the weight and feel of the knife in her hands. "Zack," she said, "you talk too much."

Clack! Cling! She attacked.

Out of the corner of her eye, she watched Crescenzo quietly shift onto his knees and crawl over to her cloak, which had drifted onto the ground beside him. He gathered a handful of silk and pulled the hood over his body. He disappeared immediately.

"Love isn't real, by the way," Zack said. "It can't do anything. Can it buy you power? Can you trade it for a house? Can it save you from *this*?"

Zack lunged forward with his dagger. Rosana parried the blow and attempted her own jab. To her surprise and satisfaction, she nicked his calf muscle.

"Ooh! That tickled a little bit. Ten points if you hit the same spot again!"

Rosana slashed. Zack blinked out of the way and appeared in the air again.

"Love *is* real," Rosana said. "And it can do a lot of things."

"Too bad it couldn't save Enzo."

Rosana shook her head. "He's gonna be okay. Don't believe me? Where is he? He got away!"

Rosana watched Zack's expression, waiting for the arrogance to melt away and the defeat to take over. She wanted to spite him. She wanted him to be upset that he'd failed. Instead, he grinned, blinked in and out a couple times, and appeared by one of the canopy poles. He wasn't floating anymore. He leaned back against it with one foot crossed over the other and his arms folded. "Look here, Rosana," he said, "there's a big difference between things that aren't real and things that aren't seen. Wanna know how I know this?"

Rosana's expression flattened, unsure what Zack was getting at.

"*Because I know where you're hiding, Crescenzo!*" Zack zipped to the spot where Crescenzo had pulled the cloak over himself, and Rosana's heart stopped.

"*No!*"

With a sneer, the shadow bent over, raised the dagger over his head, and pulled a handful of red cloth from the air. The cloak slid through his fingers and fell in a messy pile at his feet, but to Rosana's bewilderment, there was nothing else to look at. Zack's gaze darted from side to side. He turned in a circle. He picked up the cloak and shook it again, but he didn't find what he was looking for.

There was nothing under the hood. Crescenzo was gone.

CHAPTER TWENTY-SEVEN

WONDERLAND: THE SKY ISLAND

Nobody's going to rough me up today. Crescenzo squeezed his eyes shut. He wasn't about to get another slash in his body, which stung more than he could put into words. He resolved never to endure this from Hansel or Avoria, and certainly not from his best friend, who was screaming somewhere above him. *Other note to self: Don't look down.*

The first glance off the top of the island had nearly scrambled Crescenzo's brain, but once he was under the crimson cloak, he realized what had to be done. *All I need is one minute.* While Zack and Rosana went back and forth, Crescenzo scooted his way to the edge of the island, careful to ensure that not a single inch of his body poked out from under the hood. With a deep breath, he swung his legs over the ledge and willed himself to be brave as he looked down for a safe spot to drop down to and slip out of the cloak. Just a small protrusion in the land was all he needed to buy some time.

And here he was, clinging to the floating island like a spider on the wall while the cloak remained in a pile six feet above and dirt rolled off the back of his heels. Sweat gathered on Crescenzo's fingertips, and his heart thundered as he realized that with any misstep he could slip from the island and plummet to his doom. But somehow, that would seem like a more honorable death than being pummeled by his best friend's shadow.

Think, Crescenzo, think. How do we win this?

Above, Zack's voice sounded like a cannon. *"Because I know where you're hiding, Crescenzo!"*

I'm done for. Crescenzo braced for an attack, and a flash of scarlet rippled above him as Zack shook open the cloak. Silence hammered the air.

He still thinks I'm under the cloak?

"What did you do?" Zack asked. "Where is he?"

A sigh of relief escaped Crescenzo's lungs. He stifled it, gritted his teeth, and started shuffling sideways. Terrible memories of the rock climbing wall in seventh grade gym bubbled to his mind. *If seventh grade me could see what I'm doing now . . . Don't look down.* It was only a matter of time before Zack would think to look over the side of the island, so Crescenzo would have to keep moving.

"Where is he?"

"What do you care?" Rosana shouted back. "It's me you really want, isn't it? Is that what this all comes down to? Me versus you?"

"Silly girl, you're missing just a couple of variables. Nothing is ever so simple. But if that's what you make of this, then fine. *Long live the King of Hearts, the shadows of Wonderland, and the Ivory Queen!"*

Crescenzo secured his foot on a jagged protrusion in the side of the island, and then he froze. Zack's cry had chilled Crescenzo to the bone. Where did everything go so wrong? It was exhausting enough worrying about Avoria's return, wondering what happened to their parents, and trying to find a way back to them. His best friends were at war, along with the entire world they'd fallen into.

Above, metal scraped metal, and Rosana's angry, determined grunts filled the air again.

Crescenzo couldn't let her fight alone. He couldn't let any of this go on anymore. If they got out of Wonderland, they were never going to stand a chance against Avoria with so much conflict between them. According to Mulan, even a thousand souls united couldn't defeat The Ivory Queen. They'd tried before in their hour of need. Years later, the hour of need was circling back on Crescenzo.

Love is most important. In your hour of need, remember this always.

Geppetto's words echoed in Crescenzo's mind. There was a lot to mend, but for starters, Crescenzo needed Zack back. The real Zack. He needed the shadow to remember who he really was. What he should really be fighting for. Crescenzo had an idea, but he needed the right moment to come along.

Rosana's grunts grew more desperate as metal clanked above Crescenzo.

"*Give up yet?*" Zack taunted.

"*Gah!*"

While Rosana and Zack were busy locked in combat, Crescenzo decided to climb up and risk a glance at them. His left foot hovered above his right knee until it found a steady hold, and then Crescenzo put all of his weight on the ball of his foot and pushed himself upward. *Don't. Look. Down.* He brought his ankles together, gripped the edge of the island, and raised himself until his nose was at ground level.

Rosana and Zack shuffled about in the center of the island, crossing daggers and waving arms from shoulder to finger.

Get him closer to the edge, Crescenzo silently pleaded. All he needed was one moment of opportunity.

The two spun so that Rosana's back faced Crescenzo, and Crescenzo dipped his head behind the island ledge so he wouldn't be within Zack's sight. *Bring him closer and turn him around again.*

The metallic clanks grew louder and closer.

Crescenzo's fingers screamed. He couldn't hold his own weight much longer.

"Heh, I didn't think you'd last this long, daughter of Alice." *Cling!* "I should commend you."

Clang! "I'm a survivor."

Cling! Clang! Clack!

"*Uh!*" Something thudded on the ground, and Rosana cried out in frustration and pain.

"A survivor, huh?" Zack droned. "I suppose you're proud of your ability to pick yourself up when you fall."

Crescenzo pulled himself up again, and his stomach dropped when he saw that Rosana was flat on her back, the knife just out of her reach. And Zack had her pinned to the ground with his knees on her chest, his fingers clamping her wrists at her sides, and his back pointed at Crescenzo.

No.

"But I have orders, Rosana," Zack continued. "I have to bring your head to the king. I'm not so sure you'll be able to stand after that. I'm sorry. I know it sucks. First I thought you were crazy, but now you're about to completely lose your head!"

Rosana said nothing.

As quietly and as quickly as he could, Crescenzo climbed back up to the ground, relief coursing into his fingers and toes. He straightened his back and flexed his fingers, summoning all his strength.

Zack reached beside him and plucked the ivory carving knife off the ground, crossing it with his black dagger and holding both weapons like an X, impervious to Rosana beating against his chest once her hands were free. "You know," Zack said, "I'm really going to miss arguing with you. But my heart breaks for Crescenzo. Don't worry. When I find him, I'll deaden his pain. He'll barely feel a thing."

Crescenzo narrowed his eyes.

Zack raised the two blades over his head. "Do you have any final words? Something you'd like me to tell Crescenzo?"

Rosana smirked. "Long live The Carver."

Crescenzo broke into a mad dash, the wind cutting against his cheeks, and made a flying leap for Zack, screaming with rage as his knees connected with Zack's shoulder blades. Crescenzo clamped his fingers around Zack's wrists. The two tumbled off Rosana, twisted, and rolled three times until Crescenzo's back lay flat on the ground.

He pulled Zack face-up on top of him. Crescenzo swung his legs and drove his ankles into Zack's shins as Rosana sprang to her feet.

Zack writhed like a worm. *"What is this? Enzo, I swear—"*

"Enzo!" Rosana cried.

"Grab him and hold him down for me," Crescenzo commanded.

Rosana seized the two blades from Zack's fingers, jammed them in her armor, and then grabbed Zack and wrestled until Crescenzo had squirmed away and Rosana was sitting on top of Zack's chest. Gritting her teeth, she jabbed the dark knife through his sleeve and plunged it into the grass, pinning the shadow's arm to the ground. She took the carving knife and did the same to his other arm. *"Hold still and shut up!"*

"I'm here!" Matt cried from behind Crescenzo. Footsteps pounded across the island. "I'm here to protect you!"

When Crescenzo turned around, Matt had removed his hat and was pointing the opening toward Zack. Gretel hid behind the King of Spades.

"Shadow," Matt declared, "by the power of the Spades, I hereby banish you from the realm of wonder! You are *not* welcome here!"

The hat started making a sucking motion like a vacuum cleaner, and as Crescenzo's hair flipped wildly in the wind, Zack began to stretch as if he were made of Play-Doh. The shadow's cry was agonizing, and it would haunt Crescenzo forever.

"No!" Crescenzo cried. "Matt, stop! You're gonna kill him!"

"Precisely. And then you'll be safe."

"This is my friend! Matt!"

Sensing the king wasn't about to stop, Crescenzo leapt up and swatted the hat out of Matt's hands.

Time seemed to stop for a moment as Matt watched his hat skitter away from him, his mouth agape and the twinkle fading from his eyes. He blinked in an almost robotic manner, pointed at Crescenzo, and grimaced. "You have no right—"

"I'm sorry," Crescenzo snapped. "There are better ways to do this." He knelt again and pressed his knee on Zack's chest.

Zack continued to squirm and writhe. "I hate you two! You were gonna leave me out of your friendship from the start. It was always gonna turn into you two against me!"

"That's *not* what this is about," Crescenzo argued. "Get a hold of yourself, Zack. This isn't who you are."

"What would you know about who I am anymore? I only have half a soul, Enzo! You don't know what I am anymore!"

"But I know where you came from!" Crescenzo took a step so that he could stand directly over Zack's face, which was pulled into a sinister grimace. "I know all about your home and the people who want to see you again. The *real* you!"

"Please enlighten me, then, o high and mighty son of Pinocchio!"

"Enlighten *yourself*," Crescenzo shot back. He reached into the pocket inside his jacket and closed his fingers around a single figurine. One he'd been saving for just the right moment. Geppetto had told Crescenzo about this moment . . . Geppetto carved the figurine himself and told Crescenzo to be ready. *Love is most* important, Geppetto had said. Crescenzo drew the figure out of his pocket and held it over Zack's head.

Rosana gasped. "Wow."

The sneer on Zack's face gradually receded into a flat line on his lips.

"Recognize these people?" Crescenzo asked, turning the figurine in his thumb to show off every angle. "You should. That's your mom. And your dad. And they're *looking* for you! Your dad and I left home together to look for *you*. Do you know why? Because that's what friends do, Zack. That's what *family* does. We look for each other, and *this* is your family. See? Your mom, your dad, and right in the middle there, that's you. That means you're going to find each other, and even if they find you like *this*, they're still going to love you. They are always going to love you. Like your friends do! Like . . . like I do."

There was a long pause as Rosana, Gretel, Matt, and Zack just stared, and Crescenzo continued to twirl the figurine, rotating the miniature but mighty Volo family in his fingers. It was a simple carving, like a three-dimensional family photo. In the figurine, Zack stood at the front with his arms crossed, while his parents stood just behind him with one arm around the other's shoulder and the other resting on Zack's. And their smiles could've powered the moon.

"You're loved," Crescenzo said. "I just hope you know that." He lowered the figurine until it was about a foot in front of Zack's face, and Crescenzo was surprised to see the shadow's eyes had filled with dark tears the color and consistency of car oil. Some stray drops spilled out of the corners of Zack's eyes and splattered the ground, burning single blades of grass in their path.

Crescenzo nodded at Rosana, and she gently removed one of the daggers from the ground, freeing Zack's sleeve. Crescenzo reached down, moving slowly and cautiously, and he pressed the figurine into Zack's icy palm.

Rosana had to spring to her feet and step aside when, in the blink of an eye, Zack's shadow returned to the tip of his toe while the darkness fled, spewing like smoke from every pore and rocketing back toward Wondercity. When it was gone, the real Zack lay stunned on the ground, his fingers loosely wrapped around the figurine. After a few hard blinks, he turned his head and smiled weakly at Crescenzo.

CHAPTER TWENTY-EIGHT

WONDERLAND: THE SKY ISLAND

Rosana had a million questions and concerns after the fight on the floating island, but she was too exhausted to articulate most of them. By the lack of color in Zack's face and the redness in Crescenzo's eyes, it was clear they were exhausted, too. They had barely moved, instead taking a seat on the ground and sitting in silence for what seemed like hours.

Zack broke the silence with a long sigh, clutching the figurine he'd received from Crescenzo. "What. Just. Happened to me?"

Rosana buried her head in her hands. "You almost killed us. You were *trying* to kill us. Not to mention how you said some pretty awful stuff. I'm not sure how I'm ever going to trust you."

"But it wasn't *me*. It was like . . ."

"What do you remember, Zack?" Crescenzo asked.

"There was a girl in the tower. She woke me up and took me out of a cell to see the king. I remember a giant mirror and him talking to me about wanting Rosana's head. And then everything sort of went dark. I could see everything that was happening, but it was like I was a prisoner in my own body. It's not like I ever would've *wanted* to hurt you two. All this time I've been paranoid that something else was going to hurt you, because . . ."

Rosana narrowed her eyes. "Because what?"

"Because I dreamed of Madame Esme. She told me Crescenzo was going to die. And that I had to save him. 'Beware the King of

Hearts,' she told me."

Rosana gasped, clapping her hands over her mouth.

"And all this time she was talking about *me*," Zack continued. "I was the one you had to be saved from. She specifically told me not to tell you because you'd stumble into the prophecy faster if you tried to prevent it. And in the end, *I* stumbled into it by trying to save you. The king used me."

Rosana shook her head, biting her lip so hard she almost drew blood. "Madame Esme's *never* wrong."

"Well, she was wrong today," Crescenzo said confidently. He stood and made a fist. "I want the king to know I'm alive. We're all alive, and we're getting out of Wonderland alive one way or another." He took a deep breath and bellowed, *"Do you hear me? I'm alive!"*

Rosana smiled to herself. Crescenzo constantly surprised her with his increasing depths of bravery, slowly developing from a passive savior to a take-charge hero with a Superman complex. For a short second, she started to pity Avoria and any other witch who ever tried to break his spirit. He was too stubborn to break, and Rosana wanted to be there when he triumphed. But when she thought about what happened to Zack, a weight dropped in her heart as she remembered all the other worries she still had. "Do you guys think that what happened to Zack is also what happened to Hansel?"

"Hansel?"

Rosana knew the voice was Gretel's before they all turned their heads. The girl had approached them from behind, and Matthew Hadinger was sitting on his knees, brushing grass and dirt from his hat.

After Matt fixed the hat back on his head, he shook a finger at Crescenzo, and the king's tone was unlike anything Rosana had ever heard: hard, dark, and even threatening. "Never. Touch. My hat. Again."

"You were going to hurt my friend," Crescenzo said. "I'll do whatever I *need* to do, thanks."

"He injured you!" Matt cried. "He meant to kill Miss Rosana! Are you blind?" He grabbed Zack's chin and tilted his head back. "Whoever you are, explain the meaning of your actions."

"The King of Hearts," Rosana answered. "He used Zack to attack me." She hated seeing this side of Matt.

"Let go of his face," Crescenzo ordered. "He's *fine* now. Aren't you, Zack?"

Matt gritted his teeth and pulled away from Zack's chin. "Cornelius Redding is a dangerous man. Vengeful. Disturbed. Mad. And mark my words. Knowing that Zack failed to kill you, the king will come back to finish the job. *Today.*"

Rosana wasn't sure if Crescenzo scoffed next to her or if she just imagined it. "I hate this. I just want to go home," she confessed. "I want things to be like they used to be. I want a *normal* life and a normal home . . . I want to be with my mom again."

When Rosana looked up, she saw a peculiar wrinkle in space, like the air around her was made of plastic wrap and somebody had just walked into it. Rosana stared at it, squinting with her head tilted to the side, until there was a loud *pop* and a flash of light so bright she had to shield her eyes.

When it all cleared away, a woman stood on the other side of the island, enveloped by the waterfall's mists so that she almost looked like a ghost.

When the figure stepped out of the mist, she stared down at her hands and rubbed her arms as if testing to see if she were real. Rosana wasn't so sure the woman was real either.

Gretel looked up, and a spark of faint recognition gleamed in her eyes.

Zack lifted his head and leaned forward, as if trying to recognize the woman who was walking toward them. Crescenzo smirked as if he already knew.

Rosana pulled herself up and stood frozen until the words escaped from her throat and she broke into a sprint, bounding over the moonflowers, the rocks, and the withered shrubs along the island. "*Mom!*" she screamed. "Mom, it's really you! It's really you!"

She caught the woman in a powerful embrace, nearly knocking her over with her zeal.

Matt dropped his hat, and it rolled far away from him in a gust of wind.

Rosana's heart nearly soared out of her chest when the woman returned the hug. "Rosana! Oh, my goodness, I've finally found you! How are you? How are you doing—oh, no, you've gotten so skinny! Are you even eating?" Rosana's mother peered around her and stared at the scene under the canopy. "What's happened to this place?"

Rosana pulled back and grabbed her mother's elbow, leading her back to the canopy. Rosana walked slow, knowing her mother was young and healthy and perfectly capable of walking faster, but she looked like she'd had a rough couple of days. Her fine blond hair was in tangles. Her leather jacket was in tatters. Her knees were coated in mud, which faintly streaked her face and her palms. "I'm fine, Mom. I'm really okay. What about you? What are you doing here?"

Rosana's mom shook her head. "I don't have much time to explain, Rose. I wish I did. We're all in big trouble if I don't get back soon, so I'll give you the short version. Do you know Lord Bellamy?"

How could Rosana forget? "Of course."

"He's retaken the throne of Florindale, and he's using his power to throw everyone in prison and stop them from getting to Avoria. He's already executed some of us. I've been working with Hansel to get you back and to evade Bellamy, but things got complicated. A man named Cherry intervened and set me on a different course. He told me that if we were all to survive, I would need to collect somebody, and he sent me here for her. For . . ."

Rosana watched her mom stop and process the group around her. "For who?"

"Are you Crescenzo?" Rosana's mom smiled.

Crescenzo stepped forward, his hands clasped behind his back. He stood face to face with Rosana's mom and grinned. "Hi, Mrs. T. It's good to meet you."

Rosana's mom grasped Crescenzo's shoulder. "*Wow*. You look so much like him. It's stunning. I dreamed of you when we were all sleeping, you know." She turned to Zack and took a few steps toward him. "And I saw you. You looked so peaceful standing next to your mother. And your dad's . . . something."

Zack laughed, and some of the color oozed back into his face.

"So they're all okay?" Crescenzo asked. "My mom and dad? What about Mulan? Prince Liam? Violet and Wayde?"

"They will be."

Rosana studied her mom's face, trying to decipher whether or not she thought she believed what she had just said.

"Gosh, there's so much that isn't being said between us right now. The last time I saw you, Rose, we had just had a slice of pizza together. It's equally strange to think about the last time I saw *you*." Rosana's mom rounded on Matt. "Hello, Matthew."

Matt took a cautious step toward the woman. "Alice." His voice was heavy with emotion. "But I thought I would never see you again. Have you . . . have you come back to stay?"

Rosana's mom shook her head. "I can't."

"But what about us?" Matt asked. "We need help, too, Alice. King Redding has gained too much power since you left. He's commanding the Hearts, and so many of them have lost their souls! He wants all of Wonderland, and he'll stop at nothing until the rest of us crumble. He even used Zack with the hopes of killing your daughter. And I imagine there will be casualties tonight unless we prevail. And now that *you're* here . . ."

"I can't stay, Matthew. I've missed you, but I only came here because there's something I need. My home is in trouble, and our resources are drying fast. The only ones left who can help are Hansel and me. And

I don't even know that Hansel is still alive. He risked his life so that I could evade capture by Bellamy's forces."

"Wait a minute," Crescenzo said. "*Hansel* risked his life for you?"

"That's right. Would you believe he's really a *good* man? Who would do anything for his sister?" Rosana's mom turned once more and approached Gretel. She took a knee and gently moved a lock of hair on her old friend's head. Her fingers trembled slightly. "Gretel. You look exactly the same."

Gretel looked up, a single tear spilling onto the ground.

"Do you remember me?" Rosana's mom continued.

Gretel stared back the way a little kid stares at fireworks the first time she sees them. "Alice?"

"It's me." Rosana's mom plucked the flower out of the ground and twirled it between her fingers. She smelled it and brushed it against her cheek. "I never forgot how you used to make these flowers. So pretty. Are you sad?"

Gretel nodded once. "I miss my brother. But I'm also happy. I thought I'd never see you again!"

"For a very long time, Gretel," Rosana's mom said, "I thought the exact same thing."

"So then." Rosana couldn't help the grin that spread across her face. She was finally going to get out of Wonderland. "When do we leave, Mom?"

CHAPTER TWENTY-NINE

WONDERLAND: THE SKY ISLAND

Nothing had ever hurt worse than the joy in Rosana's voice when she asked Alicia when they were leaving Wonderland.

Master Cherry's words looped endlessly in Alicia's head as she twisted one of Gretel's flowers in her fingers. *"I'm most interested in the effects of the moonflower. Go and find the little girl. Get yourselves out."*

Of course. It's supposed to be Gretel.

Alicia sighed, wishing the breath would also release this new pain from her heart. She wrapped her arm around Rosana's shoulder. "Come sit with me."

Those four words diminished the joy from Rosana's face. The hopeful gleam remained in her eyes, but her lips closed and hid her beautiful teeth. They walked together, far enough to where Crescenzo, Zack, and the others wouldn't hear their conversation, and they sat crossed-legged in the grass.

Now where do I begin? Alicia shut her eyes, willing herself not to cry. "I just went through Hell itself to find you, baby. I can't even imagine what it took for you to find me in my old world, only for us to be ripped apart by things we couldn't control." The dam broke. A tear spilled from the corner of Alicia's eye. "And it's not fair, Rosana. It's not fair because now I have a choice. I *can* control what's about to happen, and the right one is going to rip us apart again."

"What do you mean?"

"Master Cherry didn't give me enough resources to get all of us out of here. All I have are these." Alica rolled the two darts around in her palm. "Two darts meant for me and another. Unless . . ." An idea came to Alicia.

Rosana took Alicia's hand, and Alicia saw a pained expression of understanding in her daughter's eyes. "You can't send me," Rosana said. "If that's not meant for me, I'll find another way."

"But I can't let you stay here," Alicia said. "I can send you and Gretel. This place is at war, Rosana. I don't like to think about you in the middle."

If you yield to your greed, you will cause more harm than your daughter can endure.

Cherry's words were like sandpaper against Alicia's thoughts. She kept recalling his voice, his request scraping against her instincts. Was he even on her side? How much did he really know?

"Would I really be safer alone in the Old World?" Rosana asked. "With Bellamy locking people away?"

And starting to execute them one-by-one.

"I made a promise to Enzo," she continued. "I don't want to leave without him. And Zack. We're in this together." Rosana turned to face Gretel, who was chasing a butterfly. "And Gretel's special, Mom. She shouldn't be caught in all this anymore. She should go see her brother again. She deserves to know him." Rosana lowered her head, looking deep in thought. "Did he really risk his life for you?"

"Yes, he did," Alicia said, standing up and helping her daughter back to her feet. They began to walk back to the group. "I suppose I should thank him for that. But I don't have much more time, Rose. I don't know how I'm going to do it, but I need to get everyone out of that prison *right now*. When I left, Bellamy was starting to execute people one by one."

Crescenzo balled his hands into fists. "I *knew* I hated that guy! Ugh, when we go back and kick his—"

"Alice," Matt interrupted. Alicia had forgotten about him for a while. Quiet, sweet Matthew Hadinger, who had been like a guide to Alicia the first time she ended up in Wonderland. And he hadn't aged a day. "You cannot leave us. You *must* stay."

Alicia held up a hand to quiet him. "Matt, you're going to be *fine*. I promise."

"But you just got back! You just got back, and you came back right in the nick of time. The Hearts are marching toward us this very moment, and I cannot defend this place without you. Plus, you were my friend! You were supposed to stay with me and—"

"I didn't belong here," Alicia said softly. "I stumbled down here on accident one day, and you dragged me into all this conflict that I didn't want to be a part of, you know? And I'm sorry to be like this because I was happy to help you as much as I could, but when I started getting *framed* for killing a queen and everything started going wrong around here, I just knew that it wasn't my place. I have my own battles to fight."

"But look at this!" Matt seized Alicia's elbow and dragged her to the edge of the island. Below, the sea of red closed in on the city from every direction. "You can fix this, Alice! You can end this war and save us all again! You were *born* to save us!"

"Don't put this on me." Alicia wriggled out of Matt's grip. "This isn't my war anymore. I'm sorry." She turned on her heel and walked back toward her daughter.

Matt pouted at the ground, fiddling with a loose string that hung off one of his gloves. He started to mutter unintelligible nothings from the corners of his lips.

"Rosana," Alicia said, "it's time." She shut her eyes again. "I wish I could tell you how to get out of here, but the exits are always moving. Promise me you'll be okay? I need you, Rosana, and so does everyone else. Do everything you can to get yourself out of here, and fight like hell. Do you understand?"

Rosana pursed her lips and blinked a tear out of her eye. "I understand, Mom."

Alicia leaned forward and kissed her daughter's forehead. "I just love you so much. You're growing right before my eyes. I'm sorry you had to be a part of this, but I'm proud to call you my daughter. These worlds could not be in better hands. When I was out there looking for you, I made a promise to myself. I made a promise that when we come together again, I'm going to do *better*. I'm going to be there for you and never let you out of my sight again, do you understand?" She pulled her daughter into a deep, tight hug. "This is the *last* time we say goodbye."

"Mom, can I give you something before you leave?"

"What's that?"

Rosana pointed to the red cloak on the ground, gathered in a bunch near Crescenzo's feet. "That's yours. I don't feel like I need it anymore. Not right now, at least."

Alicia picked up the cloak and ran it through her fingers. She thought of its dizzying history and everything it must have been through since she first wore it to hide from Kaa. "Are you sure?"

"I'm sure," Rosana said. "And Mom? Go and kick Mr. Bellamy's ass for us, please."

Alicia narrowed her eyes and laced the cloak around her back. It was remarkable how the fit didn't seem to change even though she'd grown a good two feet since the last time she wore it. "Remind me to talk to you about your language when we find each other again. And you, boys?" She pointed to Zack and Crescenzo. "Stay safe. We need you. When you're ready to go back, we'll be waiting for you on the other side. We'll meet up. We'll train together. We'll make a plan, and we'll go get Avoria and end all of this once and for all."

Crescenzo, Zack, and Rosana stood side by side, nodding proudly.

"See you soon, Mrs. T," Crescenzo said.

Alicia gave her daughter one last kiss on the forehead and knelt beside Gretel.

"Hey, Gretel." Alicia pulled the two darts out of her jacket pocket and rolled them around in her palm. In the other palm, she took

Gretel's hand, and for a second, Alicia almost changed her mind. She was still thinking of Rosana and how her hand used to be the same size. "How would you like to see your brother again?"

CHAPTER THIRTY

THE OLD WORLD: FLORINDALE PRISON

"I understand if you never want to see me again. I'm sorry things worked out this way."

Hansel wasn't looking for an answer. Even though Snow shared the prison cell with him since they arrived, he might as well have been talking to the walls. They sat with their backs in opposite corners and their knees folded into their chests. Hansel's feet were bent neatly in front of him, and he rested his chin on his arms. Snow's gaze had barely moved from a spot on the floor.

"Look," Hansel continued, "I'll make you this promise right now. You don't have to answer me or do anything for me again. When—if— we ever get out of here, Snow, you will not see me again. I won't try to protect you. I won't try to bother you. I won't leave a footprint in your life. I'll go far, far way, should I even choose to continue my life." Hansel swallowed a mouthful of dry air. *Where* would *I go?* "You can go back to the cottage. I'll remove all my belongings. I'll erase all traces that I ever—"

"Stop." The syllable was barely above a whisper, yet it was powerful enough to derail Hansel's words. It was the first word Snow had spoken in hours. The only word she spoke on the way to the prison was Liam, over and over again until her voice was cold and raw.

"I'm sorry."

Snow responded with twice the volume but half the substance. It was a harsh whisper, lifeless and drained of all passion. "Stop feeling sorry for yourself already."

Hansel frowned. "I—"

"We're not going to get out of here, we're not going to survive, and we're not going to have the opportunity to start over. Didn't you see the *malice* in the grooves of Lord Bellamy's face? This has one of two outcomes, Hansel, and frankly, I don't care about either one of them. Everything I care about ended when that castle burned to the ground." Snow rubbed her red, swollen eyes and shifted her gaze to Hansel's face. "You can stop feeling sorry for yourself because I don't feel that it was your fault. You've nothing to atone for."

"Frankly, there's no grief you can give me that I haven't already given myself. For everything. I'm a monster." Hansel's shoulders twitched as he reconsidered Snow's words. "Wait. Have I understood you correctly?"

"What have you understood?"

"That you"—Hansel stretched out his legs, still on fire after all the time he spent wandering the underground caverns—"you forgive me?"

Snow's head rocked slightly from side to side. "That's not what I said."

"Oh." Hansel wanted to kick himself for thinking out loud. "I see."

Snow sighed and continued on. "But I suppose I do. It wasn't you who destroyed my castle. I hadn't intended to leave it. I intended to spend my last hours with Liam, and I strayed too far and lost my opportunity. You came all this way to help me. You threw yourself over me and tried to shield me from all that falling rock, all the smoke and debris. I never would've thanked you for that because that smoke has been clouding me for eons now. The day you first took Liam away from me, you left a *graveyard* of debris at the bottom of my heart."

Hansel's shoulders sank. *Just when I was starting to feel better.*

"And now that he's really gone," Snow said, "I need him to live inside of me until I decide not to go on anymore. I need him"—Snow made a fist and pressed her wrist against her chest—"in here. And I just don't have enough room for him to be there if I let all that smoke and debris stay there. So I'm pushing it out, Hansel. I'm done resenting you." Snow pushed herself up to her feet and paced around the room, only able to take about four steps in each direction. Tears rolled down her cheeks, but for the first time in ages, she smiled through them. Snow finally managed to grin again. "If these are to be my final days, I want to live them the way Liam lived every day. Peacefully. Happily. Without hate."

Hearing Snow's forgiveness was too much for Hansel. A small dam of tears broke through and spilled onto his chin, soaking through the rough stubble that patched his face. He stood and met Snow in the middle of the room, gently squeezing her palms. "Then I suppose I should like to die the same way."

Snow pulled her palms away, rubbed her face, and hugged Hansel. The warmth spread through his body like a hot toddy on a winter evening, a powerful current awakening his veins. His friend was back, and she had forgiven him. He was so shocked by the hug that he didn't do anything with his arms for a minute. "And you don't have to stay far away from me," she said. "You can just be there and be a friend, the way you were when we were young."

Hansel thought of the young girl who would weave through the meadows and gather flowers for her hair. "Yes, just like when we were young. That's what I'll do then." He returned the hug at last. "Thank you."

At that moment, Hansel's vision went blank. White. Whiter than white. For a frightening moment, he worried that he'd gone blind, but he soon realized that it was all light. Pure, unfiltered, unbridled light that could put the sun to shame. It wasn't a hot light, but Hansel thought it might boil his eyeballs and fry him from the outside. He let go of Snow and threw his palms over his face, squeezing his eyelids shut, but it still wasn't enough to keep the light away.

Like a black rose, a vision bloomed in Hansel's mind. A dark silhouette took shape in front of him, blissfully carving a hole in the light. Hansel was grateful until he got a better look and understood who the silhouette belonged to.

The light peeled away like lifting fog, and Hansel saw a slender woman in a bone-white dress, blood-red hair falling to her shoulders, and her milky-white hands moved across her stomach. She appeared to be standing in some sort of cathedral, stone gray with flat slabs of rock all around and pointed archways that seemed to lead to infinity. The look of horror on the woman's face was enough to give him nightmares for life, just in case her name didn't do the trick.

Avoria.

Hansel shivered as if a cold nail scratched his spine. Avoria looked much more emaciated than the last time he'd seen her. Her cheekbones could cut glass, and her chin could probably do the same. She rubbed her hands around and stared down at her toes, her mouth stretched into a tall oval.

"One of them is gone," she wheezed. "One of my precious seven souls is *gone!*" Her breathing became short and heavy as she scrambled around the cathedral, turning over tables and chairs and several modern objects Hansel didn't recognize. "Who took their soul back? *Who? Who did it?*"

The scene swirled around, and Hansel observed a dark-skinned woman in the corner, her hands bound together by a thin silver substance, her eyes in an expression of defeat like little brown commas. Avoria strode over to the woman and tilted her chin up. When she did, Hansel recognized her immediately. *Esmeralda.*

"You," Avoria sneered, "how much do you know?"

Esmeralda glared back. "Madame Esme knows you're not invincible. The Order is growing, and they're going to stop you. The movement has already begun."

Avoria slapped Esme so hard Hansel winced, but the gypsy was incredibly resilient. She turned her head back and stared with more defiance.

"Show me the future," Avoria commanded.

Esmeralda spat in Avoria's face.

Slap! Avoria reached into Esmeralda's pocket and pulled out a cell phone. Esmeralda slapped it out of Avoria's hand and crushed it beneath a thin stiletto heel.

Avoria slapped Esmeralda a third time. "Lest you forget, Esmeralda, that if you wear out your usefulness to me, there will be no reason for me to keep you alive. Now tell me what you know."

Esmeralda smiled smugly. "The Order is coming, and the wicked witch can do nothing to prepare."

"Is that so? I can do *this*." Avoria snapped her fingers, and five hundred men and women marched into the cathedral in a block formation. They all wore black hoods and carried silver hammers across their laps. "Tear down this building!" Avoria commanded. "With your bare hands! Then rebuild it! Make it taller! Make it inpenetrable! Make it glorious! And, somebody, *get me that soul back*. I require two to fulfill my destiny! Your training begins *tonight!*"

The vision faded away, and Hansel confronted the blinding light again. This time, though, it faded, funneling away into one focal point until it all went away and Hansel was left standing with Snow White again, blinking away everything he'd just seen. But something had changed since the light came. Snow looked more complete somehow. More alive. More radiant. The way she used to look before she lost her soul.

Across the hall, someone called out, "Hey! Who just turned up the lights all crazy and turned them off again? Where did you find a switch? Because I really need to know."

"Who cares, Peter? Look what the light did to the lock! It's not all black and fizzy anymore!"

"Whoa, do you think that means we can touch it now?"

"I volunteer you to be the one to try this time."

Listening to the conversation on the other side of the hall, Hansel noticed it, too: the dark padlock that had been sputtering and flaring since he arrived had cooled to a silent steam, and the black had faded to a soft gold. He'd been afraid to touch it before, but suddenly he was tempted. He cast a glance at Snow, wondering what had occurred. Had she made that light by forgiving Hansel? Was her light connected to his vision of Avoria losing one of her souls?

"Yep, it's dead. The lock died, people! We can touch it again!" Peter shouted from his cage.

"All right, then, enough talking. Start picking and rattling and jamming stuff in there. We're getting out of here!"

CHAPTER THIRTY-ONE

WONDERLAND: THE SKY ISLAND

"Rosana," Zack said, "I know I have a lot to apologize for, but can I start by saying that your mom is one of the coolest people I've ever met? Seriously, the way she—"

Rosana cleared her throat and tugged on Zack's sleeve. She guided Zack and Crescenzo to the edge of the island, where a massive army was gathering from all sides. "As grateful as I am for the love toward my mom, I'd like to point out that we're still here, and *they* are down *there*." The troop of Hearts was enormous, and there was also the added unease from the fact that some of the Hearts could blend into shadows. There had to be *at least* a thousand of them with spears and arrows and slingshots at the ready. "What do we do?"

"Well," Crescenzo said, "I guess at this point we just try to stay alive long enough to get out of here."

Zack lowered his voice and leaned in so close to his friends that Rosana could smell the leather on him, no longer dripping or evaporating darkness. "Except that we seem to have a more immediate problem," he whispered. "Look at Matt."

In the excitement of seeing her mother again, Rosana had forgotten all about Matt. She whirled around and observed him sitting on a black rock near the blinking waterfall, staring into the water with his back pointed toward Rosana and the boys. He seemed to be rocking back and forth a bit, and strangest of all, his hat was steaming between all the layers of straw. While the smoke coiled in the air, a knot formed in Rosana's chest.

"Wait here," she commanded, holding up a palm to Crescenzo and Zack. She spun on her heel and strode across the island, taking care not to look at the blood on the ground or any other traces of the battle with Zack and his shadow. *Only look up,* she said. *That's what we're going to do from now on.* She imagined her mother as a girl in the Old World, putting her foot down and making the decision to leave and grow up. Did that woman ever look back or down at her feet? She usually walked with her gaze skyward, tracing the skyscrapers as if daring the world to knock her chin down.

Rosana made heavy footfalls on her way to speak to Matt. She wanted to catch his attention without startling him or sneaking up on him. She hated when people snuck up on her. "Matt," she said as she got close enough to see his reflection in the water. She waved her arms over her head. "*Matt.*"

Matt continued to rock back and forth, mumbling to himself. "Miss Rosana, have you any idea why a raven is like a writing desk?"

Rosana gently brushed a hand against Matt's shoulder. "Matt . . ."

"Matt," he repeated. "That hardly sounds like an answer at all."

"Talk to me. What's going on?"

Finally, the rocking stopped. Matt turned and gripped Rosana's hand. "Hello, my dear," Matt said softly, "would you be so kind as to fetch your mother for me?"

Uh-oh. Rosana squeezed Matt's fingers and sat down next to him. "About that, I need to tell you something."

"Great! Why don't you get your mother and let her tell me."

Rosana sighed and wrapped her arm around him. "That's the thing. My mother just left. She took Gretel and went back to save her world, like she told you she was going to do. She's not here anymore. I thought you saw that happen."

The black mist swelled until it looked like a mushroom cloud foaming from Matt's hat. He furrowed his eyebrows, looking at Rosana like he didn't even recognize her. She might as well have been a newspaper to him, the way he studied her with such calculated thoughts. Finally he grinned and shook his head. "Nonsense, my dear. She took her magic cloak, and she's hiding somewhere. Why don't you go and get her for me? Thanks."

"That's what I'm trying to tell you," Rosana said in a soothing whisper. "She's not here anymore."

"Yes, she is," Matt said. Every syllable was hard and assertive with an empty space in between. "Please cease your frippery and retrieve her at once."

Rosana swallowed, her heart rate escalating with the clouds fuming from Matt's head. "But don't you see? I can help you, too. I thought that's what we agreed on. You protect us, and—"

"No!" Matt cried.

Despite her sudden fear, Rosana held her ground. "What do you mean *no*?"

"It's supposed to be Alice. She's alive, so it's supposed to be her!" Matt's face grew red, his breaths forced and rapid. "*No!* She can't leave! Bring her back!"

"I can't. When my mom makes up her mind to go somewhere, she goes." She paused, feeling an unexpected knot in her throat. She quickly forced it down and continued. "I'm sorry, but you're stuck with me or with whatever you choose to do with this place. Because nobody else can help you, but I'm offering to help you. Do you want to beat the King of Hearts?"

Matt was silent, and the only thing that could be heard over the sounds of the waterfall was a pair of footsteps scrambling across the island. Rosana didn't have to turn around to know that Crescenzo and Zack had followed her.

"What's going on?" Crescenzo asked.

"You!" Matt growled. "*You made Alice go away.*"

"No, we didn't," Zack said. "She did what she had to do. On her own."

"You made her go away! *Didn't you?*"

Crescenzo raised his hands. "Calm down. Tell us what you need, and *we'll* help you."

There was a *pop* like a gunshot and Matt's hat bounced on top of his head. Mist and smoke oozed from every inch of its surface. Matt went cross-eyed for a split second when the pop sounded, and when he shook off the expression, he glared at Crescenzo, Rosana, and Zack. "I should drown you in this waterfall for taking away our chance at salvation. I should throw you all off this island and let the Hearts have you. I should never have let you sons and daughter of a jabberwocky into *my* castle!"

Zack took a stride backward. "The hat man's gone mad."

Rosana lowered her voice and gave Crescenzo and Zack the side-eye. "We need to get away from him. He's not himself right now."

"Don't walk away from me, Rosana!" Matt bellowed. "After all I've done for you? After all this, you would let your mother escape, and you would take everything away from me!"

"But you didn't even know she was *coming!*" Rosana protested. "None of us did!"

Matt's hat leapt off his head and a wall of wind burst from the opening, knocking Rosana, Crescenzo, and Zack onto their backs.

Rosana rolled onto her knees and flexed out a kink in her shoulders. *Okay, now I'm mad.*

Matt stepped over Crescenzo with a long stride, hat floating close behind, and plucked the black dagger out of the ground. He studied his reflection in the blade's surface before pushing it into his pocket.

Boom!

Something struck the ground behind Rosana, shaking the island and spraying the waterfall in haphazard directions. She whipped around and watched a cannonball explode before her eyes. "Matt! Come to your senses! They're attacking the island now!"

"Let them!" Matt snarled. "A world without Alice is not a world worth saving."

Rosana sprang to her feet and made a fist. "I won't let you give up this way. Not when you've held up hope for so long! Look at all those people down there, ready to help you defend this place!"

"Those people can't think for themselves, believe for themselves, do anything for themselves," Matt said. "Most of them haven't even got a soul!"

"Hey. I don't have a soul, either," Zack said, his tone even and cool, "but I can still decide that you're being an idiot."

"Decide what you will," Matt replied, "but when the King of Hearts finds you again or when Avoria comes back, you won't have a say. You'll be no better than puppets! Only a champion like Alice could have broken that spell, and you ripped her away from me. You ripped this world away from me! You want to see this land spill? Then you'll fall with it!"

The hat shot out another massive gust of wind, and this time, there was no resisting it. The canopy soared off the island and far into the air, and Rosana, Crescenzo, and Zack flew off the ground as well. Cannonballs and arrows exploded all around them, narrowly missing Rosana several times. She tumbled head over heels until she was upside down with no point of reference, and as she screamed, she looked for Crescenzo.

"Rosana!" she heard him shout, but she couldn't spot him anywhere. Zack turned up right above her, his arms flailing and his feet kicking through the fall. She flipped in the air again.

From upside down, Rosana watched Wonderland spring into combat. Hearts charged the borders. Spades remained firm on their buildings and in their archery posts, until the first building crumbled on the edge of Wondertown, swallowing the archer in its rubble before it could hit the ground.

A line of black armor rippled through the red crowd. A sea of red charged against the black.

So this is the last thing I'll ever see, Rosana thought. *A thousand people marching to their deaths.*

Meanwhile, the ground hurtled toward her, and it was going to crush her any second. Rosana closed her eyes and braced for impact.

CHAPTER THIRTY-TWO

THE OLD WORLD: THE WHITE ROAD

Alicia assumed that the darts would send her and Gretel to the exact point in the Old World from which she'd left. She was wrong.

Traveling by dart was a terrible sensation, and she hoped never to do it again. The actual dart was like getting a shot and having peanut butter pushed into her veins. The travel was fatiguing. Despite the fact that it happened in the blink of an eye, she arrived in the Old World and felt as if she'd run the whole way. It wasn't much of a problem traveling from the Old World to Wonderland, but the way back had been much more taxing, probably because she felt the weight on her daughter's shoulders as well. Alicia collapsed immediately on a bed of fragmented marble and stone, and Gretel appeared in Alicia's arms a second later.

Smoke billowed in the air, masking the stars and weaving into dead tree branches. The ground glowed warm against Alicia's back. Wherever she was, it hadn't burned to the ground long ago. Alicia coughed and waved away some of the ash haunting the air.

"Gretel," she croaked, "are you okay?"

The young girl nodded through a heavy yawn, winding her arms behind her head.

"Can you stand?"

Gretel pushed herself off Alicia's knees and rose to her feet.

Alicia followed suit. She pulled the top of her shirt over her nose to cloak the smoke and peered around the rubble. Very little remained intact. A charred feather flapped in a shimmering puddle Alicia assumed was once a birdcage, or maybe a suit of armor. A man's leather boot lay crushed under a pile of blackened marble. A roasted apple core steamed nearby. There were also some heavily contorted swords, a useless saddle, and a pearl necklace severed into a mess of scattered beads.

And not too far away, a fountain spouted crystal waters, defiantly intact and unscathed from whatever had harmed the surrounding territory. Alicia picked up one of the pearls. "This used to be Snow White's castle."

She trudged around the rubble, not quite sure what she was looking for, and Gretel didn't stray too far behind.

"Be careful." As Alicia walked, she began piecing together what must've happened. The White Road was covered in hoof marks. Alicia knew they must've belonged to Lord Bellamy's forces. They'd been through here, and they must've been the ones who burned the castle.

Which meant Alicia had to assume the worst for Snow White. She must've been taken. Dragged to Florindale Prison. Possibly hung like Yuna and Finn. Who else had suffered since Alicia had been gone? *What if I'm all that's left?*

A crow squawked and pierced Alicia's thoughts before it flew away, disappearing in the smoke. Alicia looked back at Gretel and saw her hunched over something on the ground. She had a long stick in her hand and swirled it through a hole in the rubble, poking at whatever she was looking at. *What is she supposed to do?* Alicia thought. *Why did I need to bring her back?*

A knot rose in Alicia's throat when she stepped closer and saw what Gretel was poking at.

A pool of gold lay flat at the bottom of the hole, lifeless and dull.

"This used to be a prince." Alicia's eyes welled up. "I can't believe he's gone."

Gretel stared into her reflection. "A prince? Was he nice? Did he fight dragons?"

"Honestly," Alicia said, "I didn't know much about him. But from what I saw, he was very brave, and he loved his princess more than anything in the world. He seemed like the kind of man I hope my daughter will find someday. Or *you'll* find." Alicia turned away, overcome with emotion. *When did things get so bad around here?*

Gretel crossed her legs and stared up at Alicia with curious eyes. "Tell me a story about the prince."

Alicia swallowed her tears. "His name was Liam. All I know about him was that he married Snow White and helped my daughter try to save me." She tucked a lock of hair behind her ear and closed her eyes, trying to remember those dizzying moments when she woke up in the Cavern of Ombra. "I came to in a dark cave, feeling like I'd lost a part of myself. I saw my old friends Pinocchio and Peter Pan clearly feeling the same way, and the Ivory Queen stood in the center of the cavern, smirking at us all like she'd just thought of some hilarious joke. It was terrifying, Gretel. You can't imagine how scary that woman is."

Gretel looked at her feet, pouting with a faint tremble. "Yes I can. She dragged me into Wonderland."

"Then you know how just one look from her seems to boil your blood. She took my soul. Or part of it at least. I don't feel at all the way I should. I woke up feeling cold, vulnerable, and exposed. Like I could never escape my fears. And then I saw Liam fight the queen. He defied her against *all* the odds. She was going to hurt the man who kidnapped us. The same man she used to return to power."

"My brother?" Gretel asked.

Alicia nodded, feeling her heart twist and bleed for the girl. "I'm sorry about that, Gretel. But Liam believed that there was still some good in Hansel. The queen was about to hurt your brother, and Liam got in the way. He paid the price for all of us, really." Alicia pawed at the ground with her foot. "And I just can't think of anything braver."

A single tear rolled down Gretel's cheek, spilled onto the charred earth, and a tiny drop splattered the golden pond. She sniffed. "I hope my brother's okay."

Two more drops fell from the girl's face, and this time they sparkled when they splattered the gold. Ripples ricocheted to both edges of the molten metal, bouncing back in great circles and converging in the center. Where the ripples crossed, a thick, shimmering bubble swelled on the surface, burst with a light pop, and rippled again.

"Gretel," Alicia breathed. "What are you doing?"

Another drop. *Splish.* "I don't know! I'm sorry!"

Alicia's eyes widened when a dull shape protruded from the pool. Five small humps.

Fingers. They were slightly bent when the hand emerged, as if ready to spike a volleyball. They wiggled a bit, receded back into the earth, and two full hands came back out. This time, one of them was curled around a black dagger, which was completely unchanged by the gold. The two hands stretched into forearms, planted themselves on the ground, and pushed.

Alicia gasped while Gretel took a cautious step back, drying her face.

The golden hands pressed down and heaved until a head burst through the gold, with short, straight hair rustled from battle, and eyes and lips sculpted into a terrifying grimace. A pair of slender, muscular shoulders emerged next, followed by a lean torso dripping with ruffled gold.

"Liam," Alicia breathed. The statue was knitting itself back together, with the arms returning to the original threatening stance Alicia had remembered before it melted. It was a fascinating process to watch, like rewinding a video of a melting wax statue. Alicia imagined an invisible hand from above, pulling the prince out of the puddle.

Liam's face froze in his livid expression. Gretel couldn't take her gaze away as the prince's knees and ankles took shape, the last drops of the gold puddle oozing into the toes of his boots.

For a long minute, nothing happened. Alicia and Gretel stood dumbfounded at what they had just seen, and drops of moonlight bounced off the newly reformed statue. The black dagger especially drew Alicia's curiosity, from the glimmering tip to the ruby-encrusted handle.

"Gretel, I think this was you!" Alicia said. "Your tears!"

Gretel said nothing. She simply raised an arm and pointed at the statue.

The statue blinked. Once. Twice. Three times. Before Alicia could question her sanity, the grimace melted and Liam flexed his jaw, wiggling it from side to side. The gold started to fade from his skin, and Alicia watched Liam's natural hue return to his handsome face.

Slow as Jell-O, the prince lowered his dagger and slipped it into his belt. He rolled his shoulders, massaged his jaw, and pushed himself out of the hole in the rubble. He locked his clear blue eyes on Gretel. She promptly fell to one knee, gesturing for Alicia to follow suit. Alicia was too dumbfounded to do so.

"Your Majesty," Alicia whispered.

Liam inspected his gloved hands. "Stars," he said softly. "Melting is a most unpleasant sensation."

CHAPTER THIRTY-THREE

THE OLD WORLD: THE WHITE ROAD

Liam sat cross-legged with his back against a dark willow and his fingers clawed into his hair. His body felt stiff and heavy, like his bones were made of lead and his joints had rusted together. The woman and the girl sat at either side of him, silent and dreary-eyed after finishing their story.

"Should I have understood you," Liam began, "the Ivory Queen is in the New World, Snow and the others have been locked away by that loony old man, and the young heroes are stuck in a World Between. Have I missed anything?"

Alicia shook her head. "No, Your Majesty."

"I prefer you call me Liam." Liam moved his palms from his hair to his face, covering his eyes. "You'll understand if I'm not feeling so princely this day."

There were a million things Liam wanted to say, like how he felt like he'd failed Snow, not once but twice, or perhaps even three times. He'd failed to quell Hansel's madness when the Queen began to take over his mind, and it was this madness that had caused Hansel to send Liam to the New World. Liam felt like he'd abandoned his wife then, doomed to a strange life throwing knives at a Renaissance faire.

Secondly, he hadn't made it back to the Old World in time to save Snow from Hansel's ritual. Snow, along with six other individuals, lost a part of herself, and Liam wondered what she would be like without that part.

Third, he'd let the Ivory Queen turn him to gold somehow, which meant he was entirely powerless to save Snow yet again when Lord Bellamy locked her away. He was powerless to save the worlds from the Queen. He was powerless to do anything but stand and watch his realms crumble to dust, including his own home. Hua Mulan had told him so many times that the world would require his bold action one day. He'd rejected his master's words for years, refusing to resort to violence or to accept the Queen's danger, and just when he was finally ready to act, he was powerless.

Liam sighed and shook his head, hating the heavy kinks in his neck that still felt like gold. "I've failed everyone. I'm worthy of nothing. I'm unworthy of Snow, of my master's training, of my nobility . . . of this cursed *dagger*!"

"Stop it." Alicia aimed a finger at Liam's nose. "If you feel like any of this is your fault, then that means I should feel about this tall." She pinched the air and made a claw with two fingers. "If I hadn't asked Violet for help with growing up, the Ivory Queen might still be sleeping. We wouldn't be in this situation. But do I regret anything? Not one bit. I have my daughter now. You have an opportunity."

Liam picked up his head. "Opportunity?"

Alicia shrugged. "You're practically back from the dead, Your Majesty. Half an hour ago you were a *puddle of solid gold* on the ground. Now you're here again, thanks to Gretel. Do you believe in fate, sir? Destiny?"

"Lady Fortune?"

"Sure."

"You believe Lady Fortune wants me to live?"

"I guess I just think that if you're given a second chance, why not take it?" Alicia tucked her knees into her chest. "Things are looking pretty grim right now. But we haven't failed yet, right? Snow's alive, my daughter is alive, and the queen hasn't won over the New World yet. At least, I don't think she has."

Liam pulled himself up to his feet and paced back and forth, suddenly looking a bit brighter. "How is Miss Rosana?"

Alicia sighed. "I'm worried."

"Rosana is an intelligent young lady," Liam said. "Wonderland is in fantastic hands. Furthermore, if young Master Enzo is alive and well, then Rosana is in capable company, the way those two *clearly* fancy each other. Surely you knew?"

Gretel grinned and giggled, covering her lips with a small hand. As for Alicia, a hint of a smile spread across her face.

Liam took a knee. "And you. I owe you my life. How shall I repay you?"

Gretel rocked on her heels, avoiding Liam's gaze.

"If I may," Alicia said, "there's really only one thing you need to do now, and we can do it together. We need to break into Florindale Prison and rescue our friends. You and I both know that our best chance at beating Avoria is by doing it together. We can't leave a single person behind. And then, when my daughter and her friends come back safely from Wonderland, we go get Avoria."

"Stars, take it one step at a time, please! I agree with you wholeheartedly, but I'm not sure any of us are going to be ready to fight Avoria so soon. We're laughably unprepared. Might I suggest we train before we go any further?"

"You can suggest whatever you want when we have our friends back," Alicia said. "And I think I know just what to do. You see, you have a blade and I have a cloak that will keep us hidden as long as we concentrate hard enough. Breaking into the prison should be simple. Fighting Bellamy's army *wouldn't* be."

"What about me?" Gretel asked. "I want to see my brother! What can I do?"

Alicia frowned. "I'm sorry, sweetie, but I can't let you get hurt in there. We'll send you to the bell tower and let you keep an eye on things until we get out."

Gretel shook her head. "No. I want to see Hansel."

"*Gretel,*" Alicia said in her mom voice. "If you go in that prison with us, you will not be safe. If anything happens to you, I won't forgive myself. We don't even know if he's in there for sure! Maybe he got away!"

Gretel didn't look convinced.

"Look, I'm *not* letting you come, okay? It's too dangerous."

Liam raised a hand. "I know this is hardly my place, but I owe this young lady a favor. I feel that if she wants to come, she deserves the chance to accompany us."

"And if she gets hurt?" Alicia challenged. "What then? I'll blame you."

"Let's not forget that this *little girl* has lived as long as you have," Liam pointed out. "She's technically old enough to make her own decisions."

Gretel flashed Alicia a cheesy, toothy grin.

"We'll protect you, fair one," Liam continued. "And I suppose . . . I suppose we'll release your brother." The thought made Liam cringe. Hansel had been responsible for more pain than Liam could have described. Not to mention, there were Hansel's romantic feelings toward Snow. Could Liam ever learn to be Hansel's friend, or at least his ally? *Do we really have a choice?*

Gretel hugged the prince. "Thank you, Mister Liam."

Alicia shot him a *you better know what you're doing* sort of look.

"Of course," Liam said. "Now, I suggest we find a pair of horses, gain their trust, and *eat.* I also need a good stretch. Tonight, we ride into Florindale."

CHAPTER THIRTY-FOUR

WONDERLAND: WONDERTOWN SQUARE

Zack thought falling would be a pretty ironic way for him to die. He saw the biography in his head as he plummeted toward the ground: *You Can Fly!: How the Son of Peter Pan Went Splat.* Could there be a crueler death?

Just when he uttered what he thought would be his final words—*no fair*—he landed on something firm and bony, and then he popped up in the air again.

Braaack!

The only thing scarier than falling was landing on a giant bird that could fit an entire soldier in its mouth. The infernal beast caught Zack, soared ten feet into the air, and hovered around the skies.

Wind whooshed all around, flapping Zack's cheeks and framing his entire body. The short locks of his hair whipped around like wheat in a sandstorm. For a terrifying minute, his heart jackhammered while he tried steadying himself and finding balance on the bird's bony back. Luckily, it was about twice his size. He could've easily decided to lie down on a single wing, stretch his toes, and make a snow angel with his arms.

When the bird got into a steady flight pattern, Zack swung his legs around and nestled them up to its sides. He leaned forward and wrapped his arms around its neck, careful not to choke it out of the sky. Finally, he looked down.

Bad idea.

For a boy who always wanted to fly, Zack was terrified of heights. His eyes nearly popped out of their sockets when he saw all those people down below. It was like watching ants climb all over each other.

"Spade Brigade, halt!"

"Heart Squadron Four! Fire!"

A sea of orange illuminated the air as a mass of arrows, cannonballs, and streams of fire shot over the armies' heads. Much of the assault was aimed directly at Zack and the bird. Zack threw his hands over his face and squeezed his thighs together to maintain balance. The bird swerved away from the artillery, making a series of dives, zigzags, and upward maneuvers that almost made Zack sick.

Braaack!

The bird leveled when they flew past the top floor of a skyscraper, which exploded almost the moment Zack looked at one of the windows. A cannonball hurtled into the corner and burst into flame, immediately swallowing the archer on the roof. It was the first time Zack had ever seen somebody die.

No!

A knot squirmed in Zack's stomach, and he covered his mouth with his fist.

Boom!

This time, the cannonball clipped the edge of the bird's left wing, causing it to caw with rage and pick up speed. Suddenly, it was coughing up spheres of fire the size of disco balls. Each one hurtled toward a group of Hearts with lightning speed, occasionally colliding with a cannonball and bursting like a firework in the air. Zack looked up in the sky. *If I don't fall, get shot by an arrow, or have a heart attack, I'm definitely going to blow up tonight.*

The bird kept spitting fire, annihilating Hearts here and there, and Zack hated it. He didn't want the animal to keep killing. He didn't want any more people to die. He wanted to put an end to all of it. But how? How would anything end when he was a hundred feet in the air, everyone below him pelting each other with spears and arrows, and the beast under his rear shooting fireballs at the ground?

His panic doubled when he saw people he recognized on the ground.

Rosana, thankfully, had landed safely. At first it seemed she landed in some sort of invisible net, and then Chester appeared beneath them . . . the giant cat who faded in and out of the shadows. Zack shook his head. *Stupid, ridiculous luck.* Rosana swung her legs over Chester's back and whispered something in his ear, and then the two charged back toward the castle. *Now where's Enzo?* A pang of guilt speared his heart. *I can still protect him. I'll protect all of us.*

One of the Hearts caught Zack's eye when a sad scream pierced the air. It was the scream of a girl in pain and distress . . . a girl who clearly didn't want to fight. It was Tahlia Rose, the guard who had let him out of his cell in the king's tower. She was rocking back and forth on the ground while one of her comrades lay motionless at her side.

"Stop!" she screamed. "I don't want to fight anymore! I want to go home and see my grandmother!"

The bird continued circling the skies, coughing up fire and dodging arrows. There was something strangely familiar about the warriors below. It wasn't the kind of familiarity that made Zack think, *Hey, I went to school with you!* It was a deeper, more innate kind of familiarity, like the first time he picked up a wooden sword and knew it belonged in his hand.

These people.

Zack fixed his gaze on a Heart whose skin was tinged a very light blue beneath his helmet, like the little crystals in a piece of chewing gum. His face seemed to be sculpted into an ice-cold glare.

Boom! The bird spun a full 360 degrees to avoid a cannonball, ripping Zack's gaze away from the blue man. He tightened his grip on the bird and gritted his teeth. *It's just a roller coaster. It's a big, loopy roller coaster, and I definitely don't have my seatbelt on.*

He steadied his nerves when the bird turned right side up again. Zack thought he made eye contact with a woman on the ground, a Heart armed with one of the biggest bows he'd ever seen. She had dark skin and wavy black hair that spilled out of her helmet, and despite her standard red armor, one element of her outfit set her apart from everybody else in the army: her shoes. While everybody else wore knee-high greaves and heavy boots, the archer woman wore boots that gleamed as though they were made of thin glass.

Zack cringed. What if the glass broke beneath her?

Wait, Zack thought. *Didn't I hear a story once that made me feel this way? A woman who ran around with glass on her feet?*

Nah.

Zack had to duck when the glass-shoed woman shot a flaming arrow directly at his head, pretty sure the tip singed a hair. When the bird opened its beak to retaliate, Zack tapped its neck and started to plead. "No, bird, no! Don't shoot!"

Brack! the bird protested.

"Don't you do it! This doesn't feel right!" *But why?*

Zack's eyes made another quick pass over the fighting crowd below. It was disturbing how many Spades and Hearts he saw on the road that used to shine in the moonlight. He doubted there was any room to walk over the lifeless suits of armor.

A third soldier caught Zack's attention, and this time it was because he picked up on an impossibly delicious scent. *Nothing should smell good on a battlefield. Nothing.*

Apparently, the bird also noticed the tart, fruity smell in the air, because it jerked to the right and descended like an airplane. Zack squeezed his eyes shut. He didn't particularly want to stay in the air, but then again, he didn't feel much safer on the ground, either.

A thin wisp of steam rose from a single point near one of the bakeries, and Zack followed it to the hands of a tall, burly man with red hair and a bushy mustache. He looked decidedly out of place in his apron and white pants, but nobody seemed to turn their suspicions toward him. Nobody pointed an arrow, cannon, or spear at him. Instead, the nearby crowd of Spades dropped their weapons and shuffled greedily over to the red-haired man, drool gathering at the corners of their lips. The man held a tray big enough to bake a pizza for twenty people, but instead of a pizza, it was loaded with fresh muffins.

And the aroma was intoxicating. Zack decided he wanted a muffin almost more than he wanted to live.

The man's eyes gleamed as he turned to the bird and raised the tray in the air with one hand. Zack's stomach did flips as he imagined how amazing it would feel to stop eating those beans and all the weird Wonderland food and to start eating warm, spongy pastries filled with all the best fruits man could grow.

Zack watched the muffins go one by one as the Spades grabbed them from the tray, took a giant whiff, and bit into them.

"Come," the baker said. "These are fresh out of the oven just for you."

Zack heaved himself off the bird's neck and caught his breath. He extended his hand, grabbed a muffin filled with oranges and cranberries, and brought it to his lips.

Before he could sink his teeth into the muffin, thirty men crumbled to the ground, convulsed, and went stiff. Thirty paper muffin wrappers also fluttered to the ground.

Zack dropped the muffin in horror. "No!" he exclaimed, pointing at the baker. "You're a terrible man!"

"I am?" the baker replied. He threw his head back in a fit of laughter and pushed the tray toward Zack. "Silly boy, you hardly know me!"

That's when it clicked. Tahlia. The pale blue man. The woman in the glass boots. The warrior baker. There was a reason why many of the Hearts were all so familiar.

Why so many of them returned to Wonderland when Avoria left, probably around the same time Zack returned to his own body in Violet's den.

We have to stop fighting, Zack thought.

At the same time the light bulb went off in his head, Chester galloped over the lifeless Spades and knocked the baker onto his side, spilling fruity death muffins all over the ground. Rosana sat on top of the huge cat and extended a hand. "Need a lift?"

"Rosana!" Zack exclaimed. "We need to make them stop fighting. These people are—"

Atchoo! Oh no. Not this again.

"I know," Rosana said. "I know who these people are, and we can't let them keep fighting, but we have an even bigger problem, Zack. Enzo went back inside the castle."

Zack waited for the problem part. "And?"

"And, the King of Hearts is in there, too. Enzo followed him." She patted the spot behind her on Chester's back. "Jump on. Let's get Enzo back and end this."

CHAPTER THIRTY-FIVE

WONDERLAND: WONDERTOWN SQUARE

Rosana spurred Chester into action with Zack close behind.

"Ow!" Chester growled. "You don't have to kick so hard, you know. You can just say go. I'm not a horse."

"He thinks he's a dog," Zack muttered.

"Really?" Rosana whispered. More loudly, she said, "Go!"

"I don't know that I'm a fan of the attitude," Chester said, but he sped through the crowds and back toward the castle, barking and growling the whole time.

"Rosana, do you have a plan?" Zack asked.

"No," Rosana said, the word a short, crisp bite on her tongue. "Beat the king. That's my plan."

"We don't stand a chance," Zack said, his gaze falling to his feet. "But I'm *with* you. I don't suppose maybe this is the best time to apologize? For everything that's happened?"

"Not really, but you can get started if you want."

Zack inhaled through his nose and let everything out in one breath. "I'm sorry I was a jerk and kept calling you crazy and—"

"Over it," Rosana interrupted. "We're *all* crazy here. Get to the other part."

"That I almost ruined your life along with Crescenzo's, even though I didn't really know what I was doing. I'm really sorry about that."

"How sorry are you?"

"On a scale of one to what?"

"You know I can hear everything you're talking about," Chester said. "And I must say I feel quite uncomfortable."

Rosana could feel the guilt in Zack's expression. "I'm sorry, too. We should have broken you out of the king's tower sooner. Matt said he wanted to keep us safe, but . . . all he saw was my mom. Tell you what, Zack, let's get Crescenzo out of here and make Cornelius pay, and you and I will start off clean, okay?"

"Deal," Zack said, "but I have a question. When you say 'make him pay,' you're not actually thinking about—?"

"Yes," Rosana said, her tone chillingly casual as though she were giving Zack the time of day. "We'll do whatever it takes to protect Crescenzo and get out of here."

Zack tensed up behind her. "Even if that means—"

"Yes. Wanna ask again? Are you with me on this or not?"

"Well, yeah, it's just that—"

"Then be quiet." Rosana shut her eyes and breathed deeply. She knew she was being harsh, but she didn't particularly care.

"I'm only saying this isn't really like you. That's all."

Chester approached the doors of the castle, where the guards lay on the ground with a graveyard of muffin wrappers around them.

Rosana and Zack hopped off the creature's back, took a deep breath, and pushed the door open.

They found the king sitting alone in a large throne at the far side of the ballroom. His expression was smug, as if he'd been waiting.

"Hello, children. How wonderful to see you both again, and that you've come to me of your own volition. I knew we'd have this meeting eventually." Cornelius fixed his gaze on Zack. "Did you enjoy your dance with the shadows, Mr. Volo?"

Zack said nothing.

The king picked up a bottle of green liquid and sipped it without taking his eyes off Zack. "Many people find the power most addicting.

Avoria knows it. I know it. Ha! Even Matthew Hadinger must know it. Nothing else but power gives you that deep euphoria. You should count yourself lucky I handed it over to you. Although, it seems you didn't do what I asked. The daughter of Alice stands before me, and her head sits firmly fixed upon her shoulders. Is this not the opposite of what I asked?"

"I might've had a change of heart." Zack puffed his chest, rolling his shoulders back. "The shadows don't control me. Neither do you."

"Oh? Did you come here expecting to *stop* me, then?" The king chuckled. "I hardly feel worth your time when this city is crumbling, but I do appreciate the chance to eliminate the daughter of Alice myself. A most flattering opportunity."

Rosana stepped forward with her hands in a fist. "Where's Crescenzo?"

"Where is Enzo, the son of Pinocchio, you ask?" The king stroked his chin. "The weakest of your trio by far. When Avoria asked me to break you, I had half a mind to ask why he was even worth my time. You two possess admirable strength and are thus a worthy challenge. The son of Pinocchio doesn't need *me* to break him. You've seen that for yourself. All it takes is one Heart to bring him within an inch of his life. It's a wonder that the mirror predicts your delicate boy to lead an army against Avoria, the most powerful being I've *ever* known. Of course, the mirror *can* lie. I've no idea where Enzo is. I wouldn't be surprised if he lay dead in the square this very instant, an inconsequential smudge on the soles of my boots!"

He's not here? Rosana frowned. *I saw him.*

"So you'd let your army do your dirty work?" Zack challenged. "Doesn't that make you weak?"

"Oh, I hardly depend on them. I merely thrive off the feeling of controlling them. Imagine the power! When you rule so many of the thousand that tried to defy Avoria, you rule everything. Nobody can stand against you, except Avoria herself. That's why nobody else has ever been stupid enough to challenge her. They take example from the Hearts, the brave ones who showed up in my land the day your precious *puppet boy* smashed the mirror."

"I knew it," Rosana said. "I knew those people were here against their will. I won't let you keep them!"

"Tell you what." The king flicked his arm in front of him, and his long, bejeweled mace appeared in his hands. "Why don't you defeat me, and you can take them back home yourself?"

The king didn't waste another moment, and it was like time slowed down as he raised his elbows above his head, his fingers tightly curled around the terrifying mace's handle and his mouth spread in a grin reminiscent of Chester's.

Coldness rushed through Rosana, and alarms sprang up in her brain as the king locked eyes with her.

"*Look out!*" she screamed.

Rosana tossed herself to the ground and slid along the tile, scrambling behind a stone pillar as the king brought his mace down with earth-shattering force. The tile split into dozens of sharp little pieces, and Rosana suspected that her eardrums might do the same. She swallowed and caught her breath in her throat as the king swung around and brought the weapon down a second time. Zack rolled onto his elbows, the mace falling into the space where his knees had been only a second before. The king lifted the mace again and made a backhanded move like a tennis player, and this time he hit his target. Zack went flying five feet through the air and collided back-first into the door. Dust and bits of concrete rained all over him.

"Zack!" Rosana cried.

Zack sat motionless for a while, his head drooping and his feet curled underneath him. Rosana clapped a hand over her mouth and willed herself not to scream as she scrambled across the floor to another one of the stone pillars. When she made it across, she snuck a quick peek at Zack and watched him lift his head again.

"Man . . ." he moaned. "That really hurt."

"You'd do well to stay put, Mr. Volo," the king droned. "Rosana, come out and face me. Stand and prove yourself worthy of your mother's legacy!"

Rosana remained silent behind her column and tried to hatch a plan. *Think, Rosana, think. How do I beat him?* The king stumbled around like a dopey giant, swinging the mace around like a golf club as he scanned the room for signs of Rosana. *He's strong, but he's slow.*

Smash!

The king whirled around and clubbed one of the stone columns with his mace, breaking it into pebbles and dust as a small crack formed in the ceiling. The dust blanketed a corner of the ballroom as the king spun around and continued to search. "Are you behind that one? I'm getting impatient."

When the dust cleared, Rosana saw a small silhouette crouching in the rubble of the stone column. It appeared to be a girl a bit older than her, dark hair streaked with rays of crimson and electric purple. The two locked eyes, and the girl put a finger to her lips before springing out of sight.

Smash! Another column fell to the ground. Only two remained. The crack in the ceiling grew longer and thicker, spilling a thin curtain of dust onto the ground.

Where did that girl go? Rosana wondered. *Who is she?*

Boom!

The door swung open, pushing Zack onto his knees again. He groaned in pain, and a hat drifted through the door like a rogue feather on a winter night. It floated with a certain gracefulness, tumbling in its trajectory and floating up and down without touching the ground. Rosana, Zack, and the king all snapped their gazes in the hat's direction. All was silent as they watched it float through the room.

The king narrowed his eyes and flexed his fingers around his mace. "Matthew," he growled. He swung at the hat like it was a baseball, making a loud *whoosh* sound as the club sliced through the air. The hat, however, remained untouched. It zipped five feet in the air, tipped upside down, and spilled an avalanche of jumbo-sized playing cards on the king's head. They rained on him like a never-ending stream of bats flying out of a bell tower, almost obscuring him from view as he swatted them away and tried to attack the straw hat.

While the king was distracted, the girl with the streaked hair snuck back into view and tapped Rosana on the shoulder. The girl kept a finger to her lips the whole time. "Shh. I'm Tahlia. I'm on your side. Listen. The boy you're looking for? He's safe. He's untying his grandfather in another part of the castle. I don't think the king knows he's here, but he's coming. Don't lose hope, okay?"

Rosana remained silent for a moment, staring at Tahlia in wonder. Rosana nodded, feeling a sort of second wind fill her body.

Crescenzo was okay, at least according to the girl. Rosana had to believe Tahlia was telling the truth, and in the meantime, Rosana and Zack had to stay alive.

Without another thought, Rosana sprinted across the floor, Tahlia protesting behind her, and threw herself in front of Zack with arms spread wide. The king swatted the hat away and looked at Rosana.

Rosana stared back defiantly. "I'm not afraid of you!"

Zack ached all over, but when Rosana threw herself in front of him like a human shield, his strength gradually returned. "What are you doing?" he asked her. "Don't provoke the king!"

"He's not our king!" Rosana snapped. "He's a coward who thinks he can rule by force. I won't let him do this!"

A male voice sounded, "Neither will I."

Zack turned to the side and watched the wilted straw hat float up in the air again, and once it reached six feet, Matthew Hadinger appeared beneath it, his eyes fire red and his hands curled into tight fists. He adjusted the hat and aimed a finger at the King of Hearts. "This is *my* land, Redding. Get out!"

Cornelius grinned devilishly. "Hadn't you just given up, Matthew? You know you don't stand a chance. Not even Alice wanted to stay in your kingdom!"

"*Get out!*" Matt screamed. He rounded on Zack and Rosana. "All of you. Especially you, Cornelius. You're no king! You're a heartless demon!"

"The only reason I'm heartless is because Ms. Trujillo's mother killed the love of my life. Blame her for the way I am today, and turn your aggression toward her friends."

"My mom didn't kill the queen!" Rosana exclaimed. "She was framed."

"Framed? By whom, pray tell?"

"By me," Matt said calmly.

The room fell into a thick silence. Rosana's jaw dropped. The King of Hearts dropped his mace. Zack felt his eyes widen.

"*You*," Cornelius growled.

"*You* framed my mother?" Rosana choked. "How could you? All this time . . ."

"All I wanted was to keep her safe, even if it was in a cage . . . to keep her safe from Avoria and the world beyond Wonderland. Alice was the only friend that ever made me feel sane." His eyes welled up, and his chin quivered. "But she leaves, time and time again, and I'm left here alone to go mad."

"She could have been killed!" Rosana protested. "You didn't really care about her or even about me! You are both such terrible people! You're beyond help."

"Yes we are!" Cornelius dove for his mace, but Rosana was quicker.

Rosana scooped it up, leapt back next to Zack, and waved it in front of her. "Stay back. Both of you."

A smile crept onto Zack's face, and he got his own second wind fueled by Rosana's bravery. He hoisted himself onto his feet and stood beside her.

The King of Hearts frowned. "Insolent teenagers. My quarrel is no longer with you, but if you insist on continuing to challenge me, I'm not so sure I can resist."

"Hey!" Zack looked up to the second floor and saw Tahlia standing on the railing with her bow in her arms. She had a single arrow aimed at Cornelius. *Tahlia!*

Tahlia smiled smugly and drew back her bow. "I'm done working for you, Cornelius. Resist this!"

The king leapt aside as the arrow sailed through the air and collided with another stone column. He caught his breath and gritted his teeth. "*Three* defiant teenagers?"

"There are four of us, Your Evilness." Crescenzo burst through a patch in the wall, where Matt had originally hidden the group during the Evening of Wonder. Enzo spun his knife in his hands.

Geppetto stepped into view behind him.

"And a brilliant old man, too," Crescenzo added.

Cornelius snickered to himself. "Poor little Carver boy. You think you can fight me yourself?"

"Enzo!" Rosana cried. "Be careful!"

"I'll fight anybody who threatens my friends. I'll fight you, and I'll fight *you* if I have to!" Crescenzo pointed at Matt.

"Stay out of this," Matt snarled. He pointed a finger at the other king. "This is *our* battle."

The King of Hearts spun around and swatted Matt's top hat off his head, sending it flying into a torch on the wall. The hat shriveled up in a ghostly wisp of dark smoke, the glowing embers flickering out of existence while Matt stared in horror. "It's hardly a battle if you don't have a weapon."

Matt delivered a right hook to Cornelius's jaw, reached into his jacket, and produced the black dagger he'd stolen from Zack. Upon seeing the dagger, Zack flinched. "You make one stupid assumption, Your Highness," Matt said. "I do have a weapon."

Geppetto laid a hand on Zack's shoulder and leaned closer to Rosana. "Maybe you should go. These two will keep going at it until this land turns into dust. None of you are strong enough to stop them, not even together."

Rosana shook her head. "I'm not leaving."

As Rosana spoke, Matt slashed at the air with the black dagger, and a large rift opened in the space between Matt and Cornelius. At that same moment, Tahlia fired another arrow at Cornelius, but it strayed from its course and soared into the hole in the air.

The King of Hearts held an arm out to his side, and without taking his eye of Matt, he said, "I require my mace."

The mace flew out of Rosana's hands and returned to the king's grasp. He brandished it, swung it in front of him, and knocked Matt onto his back before the rip closed in the air.

"Rosana," Zack said, "we're powerless against these guys. We haven't trained enough."

Cornelius plucked the knife out of Matt's hand and wound it over his shoulder, preparing to throw it across the room.

"Really," Geppetto insisted. "You *must* take my grandson and get out of here. You've seen what that knife can do. If he throws that dagger, this is not going to end well."

As if he'd heard Geppetto, Cornelius loosened his grip and launched the blade in the air.

CHAPTER THIRTY-SIX

THE OLD WORLD: EN ROUTE TO FLORINDALE PRISON

Liam experienced the full range of emotions on his ride to Florindale Prison. First, there was something like freedom. He felt *everything* when he was frozen solid. He felt every fly land on his face. He felt every itch that crawled up his ankles. He felt every extreme temperature. But his body remained locked in place. It was a bit like being bound in wraps, dipped in wax, and then left in a blizzard. So when he got to stretch his muscles again, there was almost no better feeling. His heels and ankles held no restraint when he spurred the horse, and his fingers were in a constant state of flex.

Excitement was another prevalent emotion. He was finally going to see Snow White again soon, and this time, nobody was going to take her away.

Beneath the excitement, fear tickled his soul. What if he *couldn't* make it to her in time? Or maybe he'd get hurt along the way? What if something happened to Alicia and Gretel? Every few hundred feet, he'd toss his gaze over his shoulder and check to make sure they were still behind him. They'd taken a separate horse, and it was the strangest thing because Alicia had chosen to wear her hood along the way, concealing her from all points of sight. As a result, it looked like Gretel was steering the horse without really doing anything at all except wrapping her arms around some invisible force.

To see Alicia alive was also a boost of morale for Liam. He'd played a role in saving her. There was hope. The Ivory Queen was not infallible. And if that were the case, Lord Bellamy certainly wouldn't be, either. Liam thought of his master being cooped in some cage in the center of the prison, and he heaved a breath of hot air through his nose. He would save her, too. He'd make Mulan proud. He'd make *everybody* proud. He'd finally get the chance to prove himself as a prince. As a hero.

He slowed the horse to a stop when Florindale Prison came into view at the bottom of a dry, lifeless valley. The building wasn't particularly large. In fact, he'd been invited to dance in ballrooms that had been so much grander than the grungy, moss-coated prison. Liam supposed it made sense that the prison was so small. He hadn't seen much crime in the Old World. A disgruntled painter once defaced Clocher de Pierre by drawing lewd images all over the gargoyles. That bought him some jail time, but he was released after a fairly short period. There was also the occasional runaway who stole bread and milk from the markets. When Liam really thought about it, he didn't know what happened to any of those runaways. They tended to disappear shortly after their crimes.

All of my friends in that one little space, Liam thought. *I'll get you out of there!*

"State your business!" a high-pitched voice barked. A guard jumped out of the nearest tree and landed smoothly on his feet, as if he were part cat. He aimed a spear at Liam, whose hands flew up in a defensive stance.

"Whoa, chum! I mean no harm." He took a deep breath. "I intend to reason with the king tonight."

"About what?" The spear came closer to Liam's heart. "Who are you?"

"I'm Prince William Chandler Arrington, and I'm going to vanquish the Ivory Queen. But I cannot do it alone."

The guard's lips curled up in hatred. "You'll unleash her on this whole damn realm! I must not let you pass!"

The guard charged as Liam unsheathed his blade, but Liam didn't need it. The guard tripped and fell flat on his face. Liam watched

Alicia's head appear in mid-air as she smiled, plucked the spear out of the guard's hand, and knocked him unconscious with the butt of the weapon. She removed her cloak and beamed. Liam took a knee and inspected the man's feet. The laces of the guard's boots were woven together, creating a single, intricate knot.

"This is diabolical!" Liam exclaimed. "Where did you master such trickery?"

Alicia winked. "New York."

"Quite clever."

"Thank you, your majesty. Shall we proceed?" Alicia wrapped her cloak around Gretel, and the girl vanished in the shadows. "You're the only one without a weapon right now, so you need this. I want you to stay close by. And don't take it off until I tell you it's okay. Do you understand?"

The air was silent while Alicia waited for the little girl to answer.

"Gretel, are you nodding your head?"

More silence.

"I can't see you. Say yes."

"Yes."

"Good. Here we go."

So the three started down the valley and approached the outside of the prison, taking slow and calculated steps to make sure they weren't stepping on anything that would give away their presence.

"I don't see anyone standing watch outside," Alicia said. "This should be really easy."

"Don't let your guard down," Liam said. "Keep watching. Stay alert. And be ready for anything."

Alicia and Liam looked at each other, nodded once, and made a run for the door with Gretel close behind.

Fifty yards away, Violet's eyes snapped open, her mind crisp and alert. Something had changed in the atmosphere. There were more people. Friendly faces. Determined souls, none of which had come in shackles.

Could it be?

"They're coming." Violet smiled. "Somebody's here to rescue us."

When Pino heard the commotion one floor up, a thin smile spread across his face.

"Carla," he whispered. "I think we're getting out of here"

Carla huddled close to Pino and whispered back, "What's going on?"

"Shh." Pino put a finger to his lips and then pointed to the ceiling. "Listen."

What Florindale Prison lacked in size, it made up in complexity. The main entrance, frayed, gray, and covered in cobwebs, split into two corridors, each with its own intricacies, stairways, and rooms. Everything seemed to be made of cold stone, making Liam feel like one of the most luminous and colorful entities in every direction. *Where are all the guards?*

"I have a bad feeling," Liam said. "We stay close together. Mr. Bellamy and the guards could be anywhere."

"We're splitting up," Alicia decided. "This place is way too big for us to cover together. Let's cut the time in half and meet back here when everyone's free."

"But if we have to fight—"

"Then we'll fight," Alicia said, disappearing into the left corridor. Liam heard the sound of shuffling feet behind her, indicating that Gretel had followed.

Liam trudged into the right corridor, pouting and muttering to himself.

He pushed a creaky wooden door open and descended into a dark stairwell, only dimly lit with wall torches set into gnarled stone hands. His bootheels sounded like gunshots when they echoed through the space, prompting him to step more slowly and carefully. He brandished his dagger in one hand and used the other to pry a torch out of the wall. To Liam's surprise and horror, the stone hand tried to scratch him once the torch was free, and then it melted into the brick and disappeared. Liam found himself wondering if the torches were also a security measure and that the hand was about to blow his cover.

When he reached the bottom of the stairwell, he waved the torch in front of him, trying to discern what he'd just descended into. It seemed to be another long corridor, only this one was lined with bars and doors of steel. His heart jumped. Had he found the place where his friends were being held? He didn't dare call their names and attract the attention of any guards who might be lurking in the dark.

Instead, they called him. A familiar voice hissed at him. "Pssst! Hey! Hey Liam!"

Stars, I'd know that voice anywhere. Liam turned to his right and pressed his face to the bars in the wall. He squinted until a masculine face appeared in the dark. It seemed to have lost a small touch of youth since Liam had last seen Pietro. The blond stubble had become unruly and added another five years to the man. Liam smiled. "Pietro, it's good to see you again, chum. How the devil did *you* find yourself in this rat hole? Can't you fly?"

"Goodtoseeyoutoo," Pietro said in one breath. "Listen, do you mind, uh, getting us out of here? I'm *so* bored. I miss the sun. I miss

Starbucks. I miss things that used to bore me to no end like rocks and waiting for the microwave to beep and *Game of Thrones* and—"

"Shh." Liam squinted and peered deeper into the cell. "Who's in here with you? How did you know it was me? I can hardly see any of you."

"Wanna know something? It's because you smell good," Pietro said. "Mr. Bellamy smells like a fish in a dirty sock. Soaked in death. Anyway, my wife is with me too. So are Zid and Chann."

"Shall I call for our ride?" Zid piped up.

"Ride?" Chann grumbled. "Why aren't we calling for food?"

Wendy rushed to the cage. "Sir, um, Your Majesty, can you get us out of here?"

"Right . . ." Suddenly, it occurred to Liam that he had no ideas on how he was going to break everyone out of their cells. Here he was inside the prison, standing on one side of the bars while his friends stood on the other. He shined his torch at the bars, looking for something to pick the large padlock on the wall. He had no explosives, nothing to cut the locks, nothing to pull the bars apart. All he had was—

The dagger, he thought. He pulled it out of his pocket, spun it through his fingers, and jammed it into the lock.

Click.

The lock split apart like a wishbone and clattered to the ground, to Liam's great surprise. *Stars.* By the obscured look on Pietro's face, he was in shock as well. "Really? It was that easy?"

"Of course it's easy, idiots," a new man droned, sending a cold nail through Liam's spine. "But will it be easy for you to run? To escape with your lives? You were safer behind the bars."

Liam threw the cage open and pulled Pietro out by his elbow. "Run!" Liam shouted. "*Exit's one floor up!*"

As Pietro scrambled out of his cage with his cellmates behind him, Liam spun around in time to parry a blow from a silver-bladed sword, leveled and aimed with the intent of piercing Liam's neck. The two blades clashed in midair until Liam managed to duck, swoop under the knight's armpit, and situate himself behind the knight. A quick upward thrust popped the knight's helmet off, and Liam held his blade against the man's neck. "You are on the wrong side, chum," he said softly. "I am not a confrontational man by nature, but I will not hesitate to end a man who stands in the way of my friends' safety. Where is Mr. Bellamy?"

The knight smiled maniacally. "He's waiting for you to let your guard down. Perhaps he's watching you right now, taking every measure to make sure you never reach Tower Nuprazel."

Liam wrinkled his face. "Tower Nuprazel?"

"I'll say no more to you," the guard said. "I'll let you die here first, along with your wife."

Liam pressed the knife more firmly against the guard's neck before jerking the blade away and aiming it into his back. *Snow.* "Take me to her! I order you!"

The sounds of heavy footsteps filled the hall as several more guards approached Liam from behind and the helmetless knight laughed maniacally. *Oh no. It's over.*

But from the darkness of the hallway, Pietro yelled, "*Now!*" and emerged from the shadows with Wendy, Zid, and Chann behind him. Liam had to move out of the way when Pietro rammed into the knight and sent him clattering into the troop behind. "Run, Liam!" Pietro cried. "Go save the others! We've got your back!"

Liam didn't protest. Warning his friends to be careful, he ran down the hall.

When Alicia made it up the stairs, she turned around and smiled. "Are you still there, Gretel?"

Only the silence answered.

"Gretel? I told you to stop nodding your head."

Silence.

"*Gretel!*"

"Shhh!"

Alicia whipped around to identify the source of the hissing, but she was only able to make out faint blobs in the dark.

"You should keep your voice down, dear." The voice was barely above a whisper, but Alicia perceived it clear as day. She followed the whisper and approached a hole in the wall, sealed by thick metal bars and a padlock as big as her head. She wrapped her fingers around the bars, and an old woman approached her from the other side. She patted Alicia's hands and smiled wanly. "Thank you for coming back for us."

A jolly masculine voice sounded from deeper within the cell. "See, Augustine, I knew she would come! I predicted this long before I lost the gift of foresight. Young Alice has returned to free us from this hell! James, you need to wake up, boy-o!"

Alicia swallowed and tried to steady her heart. "Are you the Order of the Bell?"

"Live and in the flesh," said a furry, husky man in the corner of the room. "Though one hardly feels alive after all we've been through recently. First we lose our souls, then the minute we return, we're locked away in a humid, stinking prison. When's the last time I ate?"

"Jacob, do be more polite to our guest. She's here to free us!"

"Right," Alicia said. "Um, how am I to free you?"

Augustine sighed. "Oh, dear. You don't know? Well, that may present a slight obstacle."

"I'm sorry," Alicia said. "I didn't really think this through."

"It's simple, dear girl!" Merlin said. "Find us the key, and open the lock. We'll do the rest. We'll fight our way out of here!"

"Key," Alicia repeated. "Right. I'll be right back, okay?"

And while I'm at it, where the hell is Gretel?

CHAPTER THIRTY-SEVEN

THE OLD WORLD

"Do you understand the course I've described to you, Hansel? Can you repeat the steps to me?" Hansel's father was on one knee, the way he always was when he spoke to him or his sister. Hansel appreciated that. His father always made the effort to meet him face-to-face.

"Yes, father," Hansel said dutifully. "Over the river and through the woods, and when I get to the docks, I should pay the ferryman four gold pieces instead of the two he charges on the sign. He'll know what it means."

"Yes, my son!" His father grabbed Hansel's hand and dropped the four gold pieces into it, one at a time. "One, two, three, four. Now don't stop anywhere else, and please avoid the bandits at all costs. If you get robbed, the ferryman won't take you where you need to go."

"But what if we get hungry?" Gretel asked, munching on a cherry tart she found on the table.

"I'll send you with some bread, but you need to make sure that you don't eat it all at once. The people of Neverland should send you home with plenty of food, but whatever you do, don't come home without the most important thing. Do you remember what that is?"

Gretel nodded.

"Repeat it back to me."

"Mother's medicine," Hansel said.

"Correct. Good boy, Hansel."

"But, Father, if Gretel is destined to be a healer, why does Mother still need the medicine?"

"I've told you, Son, I don't want you talking to Esmeralda. She's a fraud. Just because she says Gretel has these abilities doesn't mean she's correct. Gretel's been hurt plenty of times, and I've yet to see her heal. We need medicine to cure your mother, and you know that I cannot get it myself because grown-ups are forbidden in Neverland. And Hansel"—his father widened his eyes so Hansel would know he was serious—"you'd better care for your sister."

Hansel jolted back to life in his prison cell, his face sweaty and his back groaning with pain. Snow sat curled in the corner with her eyes half open.

"One of your nightmares?" she asked.

Hansel caught his breath before he acknowledged Snow's question with a single nod.

"Which one?"

Hansel sat up and rubbed his forehead. "It's the same one every time I close my eyes."

Snow smiled weakly. "I get those, too."

"Now you know why I never sleep," Hansel said. "When I lie down to rest, the ghosts wake up."

Hansel lifted his head and stared through the bars. What he saw made him wonder if his mind was playing tricks on him or if he'd evoked some sort of spirit with his words. He rubbed his eyes with his knuckles and tried to blink away the small shape on the other side of his prison cell. *Am I still dreaming?*

All was dead quiet and suspended in a dreamlike haze. The only evidence Hansel had that time hadn't frozen was that Snow continued to move her head. She looked to the bars, then back at Hansel, and back and forth twice more.

Slowly, Hansel pulled himself to his feet, feeling like a bag of mud. He trudged to the bars, where a young girl peered at him from the other side. He expected her to disappear, but she remained firmly in place with a red cloak dripping from her fingers. *If this is a hallucination, I swear.*

Hansel tucked a knee under him, the way his father used to do, and he met the young girl's gaze. She hadn't aged a day since the last time he saw her, yet she had changed in ways only a brother could understand. Hansel saw everything in her face, behind her green irises and within her rosy cheeks. Every teardrop of the past, every battle, and every time she had to run for her life had been etched into her eyes. She blinked once and extended an arm. A large, gold key ring with three keys hung from her finger.

Hansel ignored the keys and took her other hand, still so small and warm and caked with little crystals she must've gotten from playing in the mud . . . one of her favorite things to do when they used to play together. A knot rose in his throat and choked him from within.

Snow's voice flowed into Hansel's ear from behind. "Hansel," she whispered, "is this . . . ?"

Without a word, Hansel nodded, brought his sister's hand up to his face, and sobbed.

CHAPTER THIRTY-EIGHT

WONDERLAND: WONDERTOWN CASTLE

Rosana dove to the ground as the black dagger sailed through the air and directly over her head. There was an ugly tearing sound as a horrible rift parted in the air, and she watched the world open like a pair of lips revealing a dark, empty mouth.

Ping! The knife clung to the wall between a pair of bricks.

Meanwhile, the King of Hearts roared with laughter and drew closer to Matthew Hadinger with his spiked mace in his hands. The king beat the handle between his palms. "There's nowhere left for you to run, Matthew."

We have to stop this, Rosana thought.

Matt swept his leg out in front of him and knocked Cornelius to the ground and then scurried away, looking for the staircase.

"No!" Cornelius said. He swung his club, knocked down another pillar, and laughed as bits of rubble flew up in the air and into the dark rift. The rift took up over half the room and sucked up as much as it could like a black hole, pulling paintings and tapestries off the walls, jerking arrows out of Tahlia's pouch, and even causing Rosana's hair to frizz out. It was like being caught in a magnetic hurricane, and she worried that if she didn't cling on to something, she'd go flying into the darkness.

With only one column left standing, the ceiling was weaker than ever. Streams of dust spilled out of the widening crack, obscuring Matt

Without another thought, Rosana broke into a sprint, fighting the pull of the rip in the air, and she dove for the ground and yanked Cornelius's ankle out from underneath him. He went down face-first and smacked his chin, deterred only for a moment before he kicked Rosana in the forehead. Stars danced in her vision for a count of three, and when they cleared away, Matt had returned and jumped on top of Cornelius's back, trying to free the mace from Cornelius's grasp. Soon, Cornelius rolled over and the two were engaged in a sort of tug-o-war, each kicking and flailing and refusing to let go of the mace.

Tahlia slid down the banister with her bow drawn, firing arrows all the while. Time after time, the arrow steered from its course and sailed into the dark hole.

"Stop!" Crescenzo told her. "It's not worth it! You're losing them all!"

"Don't distract me, then," she said coldly. She shot another arrow, and it grazed Matt's shoulder.

Matt howled in pain and let go of the mace with one hand. Cornelius overpowered him, tore the weapon away, and struck Matt in the chest, sending him flying into the final column. Cornelius took slow calculated steps toward him.

"This is the end, Matthew," he said. "You took my heart. Now I'll take your head."

Matt stared up lazily, a thin smile spreading across his face as if daring Cornelius to take another swing at him. "Do it," he said. "Take your swing."

The King of Hearts raised his weapon in the air, prepared to strike, and—

"*Oh!*"

Crescenzo and Geppetto tackled the king from the side. Cornelius soared through the air with his mace in his hand, cursing and wheezing the whole way.

Crescenzo stood next to Matt, catching his breath and offering a hand to pull him up.

Matt sneered at Crescenzo, wiped the sweat off his forehead, and reluctantly accepted the hand. Once on his feet, however, Matt broke into a stumbling walk and hobbled over to Cornelius, who was struggling to stand again after landing on his back.

Without a word, Matt threw himself on the king and started pounding on him, and when Cornelius rolled to the side, both of them were lifted off the ground. They continued to struggle and fight in midair, their hair all spread out and spidery from fatigue, and they were carried toward the dark hole in the room, which was rapidly beginning to seal itself from the outside in.

Rosana gasped. There was no stopping what was about to happen. The dark hole's pull had too strong of a hold on them, like gravity, and it pulled them faster and faster toward its depths. The hole terrified Rosana. It was filled with stars and purple clouds and a bright red moon, and she even thought she could make out some planets. She felt as if she were looking out at the universe from somewhere far above, and she had never felt more vulnerable. One wrong step, and she would go soaring into its nothingness.

And that's precisely what happened to the two kings of Wonderland, Cornelius Redding of the Hearts and Matthew Hadinger of the Spades. The pull ripped them away from the castle and into its vast frontier, and they showed no sign that they even noticed. Rosana watched them spin and tumble and whip through the air, fighting each other and struggling the whole way. As they got farther away, the rip repaired itself and closed up like a zipper from both sides, revealing the full ballroom again. The last thing Rosana saw before the hole disappeared completely was the big red moon, staring back at her like a reminder of all the war she'd seen since she'd arrived in Wonderland.

All was deathly still.

Tahlia collapsed against the wall and tried to catch her breath.

Crescenzo and Geppetto hooked their arms around each other and hobbled over to Rosana and Zack.

There was a long moment of everyone simply looking at each other, not quite knowing what to say.

Rosana clawed her fingers through her hair and shook her head, finally breaking the silence. "They're gone."

Zack picked up a slab of rock that had been chiseled out of one of the columns. "They fought until they destroyed themselves. They didn't even realize they were falling away."

"As is the case with every war," Geppetto said. "We'd do well to remember this, boy. Their fate is no different than anybody else who has been consumed by obsession or hatred or revenge. War does not discriminate whom it tears apart. Old friends. Rivals. Lovers." Geppetto peered at Crescenzo over his glasses. "Family."

Crescenzo nodded. "I'm sorry about everything that happened between us," he said. "I'm sorry I didn't stick up for you earlier, Rosana. Zack, I'm sorry we made you feel left out sometimes. Geppetto, I'm sorry for what I said about you and my dad."

"Would you endeavor to call me Grandpa?" Geppetto asked. "'Tis I who should be sorry. For letting my bitterness consume me."

For the first time, Crescenzo hugged the old man, and Rosana followed suit.

"I'm sorry I acted stupid and ran away from you guys," Rosana said. "And for putting all my trust in a man I barely knew. It was, well, crazy."

"I'm sorriest," Zack said. "I started this all when I insulted you, Rosana. We're going to be great friends, you know. I can't wait to get to know you better. And hopefully from now on, I can resist the darkness."

"I'm sure we'll find a way to forgive you," Rosana said. She swung her arms at her sides, and when one of her hands brushed against Crescenzo's, they gave each other a fleeting glance.

Zack crossed his arms. "You two can finally kiss, you know."

Rosana smirked, a hint of red clouding her cheeks. "Actually, you already missed it. I kissed him on the cheek a few days ago."

"But that didn't count," Crescenzo said.

"Oh, brother." Tahlia stepped in and gently pushed on Crescenzo's and Rosana's shoulders, separating them by a few inches. "This is all really tender and cute and everything, but now there are hundreds of soldiers outside wondering what they're supposed to be doing. Are any of you going to address them?"

Rosana promptly turned away. Secretly, her heart was still dancing, but she bottled it up and willed herself to make it a lasting memory. She'd never been kissed before, and she always wanted to remember the first. She smiled to herself, waited for the warmth to fade from her cheeks, and then turned to face her friends again. "Why are you all looking at me?"

"Who else would I—um—who else would *we* be looking at right now?" Crescenzo asked. "You're the obvious choice. Your mom was going to rule this place. I'm pretty sure they'll listen to you if you ask them to come together. Especially because I think they'll *all* want to stop Avoria. She took some of their souls."

Rosana pondered Crescenzo's words, looking at the ground and fidgeting with her sleeves. "Well, you know what would kind of make sense? I think maybe Zack should talk to them."

Zack looked up at her and furrowed his brows. "Me?"

"You understand them," Rosana said. "Avoria took something from you, too, and the King of Hearts used you against this land. You have something in common with them. They can relate to you."

Zack rubbed the back of his neck, and Rosana was proud of the progress she'd made with him. "Yeah," he acknowledged. "But what about Tahlia? She was one of them. They can *really* relate to her. Or even Enzo! He's supposed to lead us all against Avoria. Why not him?"

"Why not all of us?" Crescenzo decided. "Together?"

Geppetto crossed his arms. "Now that's the best idea I've heard the whole damn time I've been stuck here. All of you together."

"Okay." Rosana nodded. "All of us. Together."

Geppetto beamed. "Before you talk to them, there's something you should know." Geppetto pulled out a large map on a sheet of teal parchment and spread it out on the floor. "Remember the rabbit? I've been following him the whole time I was separated from you. He's been running in circles around the land, and I've been charting his path. See how it looks like a giant keyhole? I think I know how to get us out of here."

When they stepped outside, they found Wondertown in a state of mass confusion. Hearts and Spades roamed the streets with spears in arms and bows on their backs, but the Hearts acted as though everyone they saw was a stranger and they had no idea what the weapons were made for. Zack saw a red-suited archer on top of the Starbucks, scratching his head and looking around as if he didn't remember how he got there.

He even saw the man with the muffins drop his platter to the ground and ask the nearest Spade how he'd arrived. The woman with the glass grieves dropped her bow and put her hands in her hair. The man with the blue-tinted skin looked around, rubbing his elbows as if he were cold.

Two Spades stood by a news van—*SPDE Channel 4! News that gets to the point!*—whispering to each other, and when they saw Zack and his friends, they straightened their posture and said, "I'd use caution if I were you. It seems the Hearts are playing a trick. They're acting as though they don't remember why they're fighting, but we should know better." One of the Spades, a short young woman with coral-colored hair, aimed a spear at Tahlia. "Why is this one with you?"

"Listen," Tahlia said. "We have to stop fighting. I don't think any of the Hearts remember who they are. They don't wish to fight anymore."

The pink-haired Spade pressed her spear against Tahlia's shoulder. "So how come you remember who *you* are? Why were you in the castle?"

Zack cocked his head to the side and looked at Tahlia. He'd been wondering the same thing.

She sighed and reached into the neck of her armor, drawing out a jagged white tooth suspended on a thin silver chain. "This is an amulet my grandma gave me when I was little. The tooth comes from a chameleon wolf she hunted a long time ago. It doesn't ward off *every* kind of evil, but it weakens the darkness and its effects on one's mind. I wasn't completely immune to Cornelius's brainwashing, but he didn't have as strong of a hold on me. I think I started to snap out of it when I met Zack."

Zack met Tahlia's eyes and smiled. She shook her head. "Don't get any ideas. That wasn't supposed to be sweet."

"So you remember most of your past? How you got here?"

"Nope. I remember going to battle against Queen Avoria. Then there's a giant hole in my memory, like I was sleeping. Then, here I was, serving the King of Hearts and having to blend in with the shadows every day."

The Spade raised an eyebrow. "So how come these other Hearts are snapping out of it? I don't see any wolf teeth around their necks. Explain *that*."

"The King of Hearts is gone," Rosana said. "He and King Hadinger opened this big hole in space and got sucked away. Now, we can finally stop fighting."

The Spade turned to her friend and whispered in her ear, giving the group the side-eye. Finally, they nodded with sparkly eyes and toothy grins, and the second spade produced a microphone with the Spade logo on it. "Juicy news!" she said. "Would you tell that same story again for the camera?"

A zebra-striped drone hovered down and a thin light popped on in the center, causing Zack to shut his eyes.

The Spade spoke into the microphone, and the town crackled with the sound of her voice. "People, people of Wonderland! Turn your attention to the hover-screens, please! Have we got a late-breaking story for *you*! Youngling, tell the story."

"Right," Zack muttered. He looked into the drone and cleared his throat. "People of Wonderland, for years you've fought each other for reasons you didn't always understand. Some of you rebelled against the Queen of Hearts. Some of you were just angsty. But many of you didn't even have a real reason. You've all been oppressed for far too long by leaders who don't care about your well-being. You haven't had a real chance to think freely. And I know why you haven't been allowed to make that choice for yourselves yet. I know that each of you is missing something very important to you and that you lost it in Florindale Square. My name is Zackary Volo, and I've lost something, too, thanks to Queen Avoria of the Old World."

Murmurs spread through the crowd, first with an air of puzzlement—*"We've lost something?"*—and then one of familiarity—*"Avoria. I remember her."*

Rosana took the microphone. "Exactly. And I've never come face to face with Avoria personally, but you have, and you all paid a price for it that you didn't deserve. So did my mother, Alice. She lost a small part of her soul, and I want to help her get it back. I want to help *all* of you get your souls back! I plan to get out of here and face Avoria with the help of my friends, and I want you to come with me! Come with me, and let's take back everything she took from us." She passed the microphone to Crescenzo.

"Queen Avoria's taken lives, she's taken mothers and fathers, she's taken away our safety and comfort, and she's taken away what makes you unique. If you want to be whole again, follow us back to the New World! Take back what's yours!"

While the crowd started to cheer, Tahlia grabbed the microphone from Crescenzo and shouted, "Start thinking for yourselves! You don't have to come with us if you don't want to, but don't let any other jerks like Matthew Hadinger, Cornelius Redding, or Queen Avoria of Florindale write your stories for you. We are the strong! We are the mighty! We are the rising stars of the three worlds! Citizens of Wonderland! People young and old from the city of Florindale! Heroes of the New World! Let's come together and *stand as one!*"

Even Zack had to clap as the crowd sprang into applause. He watched a Spade reach out to a befuddled Heart and shake his hand.

"I will help you get your soul back, brother. We will help you together!"

Zack stole a glance at Rosana, Crescenzo, Tahlia, and Geppetto, and nodded at them. A happy chill ran down his spine.

Suddenly, the screens crackled with static. Tahlia's image faded away in a grainy haze, and a pale woman replaced her. The woman's eyes were bone cold, and she looked straight into the crowd. She sat on a silver throne with one leg crossed over the other and her fingers firmly planted on the armrests. And her hair was almost blood red with a few streaks of white hanging beside her ears. She was beautiful, but she wasn't somebody Zack would ever want to meet in real life.

"Ahem!" The woman coughed.

The crowd went silent, and a thick tension blanketed Wondertown.

"Am I on?" the woman continued. "Yes. Beautiful speech. Fantastically conveyed, darlings, but I'm afraid I must interrupt this program."

Zack's blood went cold. It was becoming abundantly clear who was talking.

"For those of you who haven't had the pleasure of meeting me yet, I assure you, you will, and I very much look forward to that day. I hope you will, too. I am Queen Avoria of Florindale. I've been on a property venture while you all bumbled around the World Between, and I've finally settled on a ground that I find most fitting. Now my work will begin. I want every one of you to know that you serve *me* now and that resistance will cost you everything. I speak directly to *you*, Carver, and all of your misguided friends. Hello, Crescenzo. We haven't formally met yet, but I think we can skip the introductions. Have you been enjoying your little trip down the rabbit hole?"

Zack's heart jumped into his throat and he stole a glance at Crescenzo, who stood with his arms crossed and his feet spread apart, his gaze drilled directly into the screen.

"Sorry, lady," Crescenzo said. "I was barely listening."

"You will address me as *Queen*, and you will apologize for your insubordination. Henceforth, that is not to be tolerated from anybody until the end of eternity."

"Yeah, whatever." Crescenzo smirked. "When you apologize for everything you did to my parents, maybe we'll have a deal. Until then, fat chance, lady!"

"Ah!" Avoria clutched her chest as if in pain. "You rude, snot-faced little brat! You, your father, and your friends have been thorns in my side for longer than I care to admit. If I were more certain that I didn't need you, I would order the people of Wonderland to terminate you and your friends immediately. I cannot offer the same generosity to Zack, however." She smiled poisonously. "To the person who kills Mr. Volo for me, I shall reward you handsomely."

Rosana and Crescenzo sidestepped and formed a shield in front of Zack. Tahlia bit down on her lip. Zack looked around, his heart thrashing against his chest as he waited for somebody to attack him.

Instead, they dropped their spears on the ground.

Zack's heart soared at the act of defiance.

"Misguided loyalties." Avoria sneered. "I shall make one more offer before I sign off. You are all cordially invited to a formal gathering in the city of New York, one New World year from today. Attendance is mandatory. Do not be late. At this ball, I shall declare my eternal rule over all the realms. Those of you who swear loyalty will get your souls back. You'll get to live forever with no question of money or time. Those of you who challenge me will lose everything, including your life. I can promise you that."

"Nobody will follow you," Rosana said. "You're a witch!"

"That I am, dear. But as you've seen during your stay in the realm of wonder, people are keen to follow whoever has the most power. Oh, and that's me. Forever."

"See, I don't really agree with that," Crescenzo said. "You may be strong now, but you won't be forever. We'll make sure of that."

Avoria smirked. "Then come and get me, Carver. I'll be waiting for you in the New World, and mark my words: Your darkest hours have yet to pass!"

The screen crackled, turned to static, and finally went dark.

CHAPTER THIRTY-NINE

THE OLD WORLD: FLORINDALE PRISON

As Liam continued moving through the halls, he used his dagger to open the locks and free the prisoners. Each time, he was greeted with quick hugs and pats on the back before the captives would spring into action, join the party behind him, and escort him through the fortress while guards came out of the shadows from all angles. He was particularly happy to see Mulan again, one floor down with Pino, Carla, and Garon.

"Master!" he exclaimed with open arms.

Mulan pushed past him without looking. "No hugs. Do your job."

Pino and Carla both expressed their warmest thanks, while Garon seized his shoulder and squeezed. "Mister Liam," he said, "I am forever grateful to you. *Duck!*"

Whoosh!

A rusty axe flew over Liam's head and stuck into the wall. Zid and Chann tackled the guard, tossed him back into Garon's prison cell, and Carla shut the gate. Liam snapped the padlock back over the bars.

"Thanks, chum!" he said to Garon.

Garon did a little hop and plucked the axe out of the wall. "I'll take this." He shared a brief hug with Chann and Zid, while Pietro, Wendy, Carla, and Pino exchanged their own brief reunion.

"It's good to see you again, Peter," Pino said.

"Likewise, buddy." Pietro rubbed his chin. "Nice stubble, by the way."

Liam unlocked the last cage in the hall, and Violet shuffled out of her cell with her wings folded and wilting behind her. "Liam, thank you."

The last of the seven miners followed behind her, beaming with joy at their newfound freedom.

"Ah, I can finally go for a run again!" Bo said. "Or shoot some arrows, launch some pumpkins at unsuspecting serpents, take a swim . . . and Liam is alive and not a gold statue anymore! This is the best day of my life!"

Liam turned away, hoping nobody would see him turn red.

"The day is not over yet," Violet said. "Tell me, Liam, where is everybody else?"

Alice ran into the hall and caught her breath. "Two floors up!" she exclaimed. "I don't know how to get them out. Have you all seen Gretel?"

Liam clawed at his hair. "I thought I heard her run after you!"

"Wait a minute," Pietro said. "Gretel? As in, our friend from when we were kids?"

Alice nodded once. "I have a lot to catch you guys up on."

Snow wasn't sure she'd seen anything more precious in her life. A brother and sister reunited after years of being apart and presuming they'd never see one another again. Hansel and Gretel had come together at last, separated only by a set of thick bars.

Hansel had been unable to stop crying. He sat cross-legged in front of the gate, sniffling and rubbing the corners of his eyes. "I can't possibly explain to you how much I've missed you."

"I missed you, too," Gretel said.

Snow didn't feel that it would be right to listen to the rest of their conversation. What words could possibly fill the gap between loved ones after twenty-five years, and what right did Snow have to listen to them? It wasn't her place to observe. She hadn't even been separated from Liam for a fifth of the time that Hansel and Gretel had been looking for one another. All she knew was that it made her heart smile to see the siblings find each other once more and pick up the pieces without a single comment on how much had changed between the two. Hansel had matured into a grown man, looking for work and love and a means to put food on his table. Gretel hadn't aged a day. She hadn't grown out of the toys and games she used to have in the Old World. If it hadn't been for the Ivory Queen, boredom would have been her biggest concern in the world. Snow knew that boredom could be a luxury in an age of darkness.

Snow kept her head down and her thoughts to herself until she heard the jingling of metal and Hansel fumbling around with three keys on a gold ring. He tried each one in the padlock, turning them over and wiggling them around, but his efforts were in vain.

"They don't work," Hansel said. "Gretel, where did you find these?"

"I stole them from a guard," Gretel said simply.

Hansel smacked his forehead, his face filled with worry. "Gretel, that's so dangerous! What were you thinking?"

"Well, I was invisible." Gretel took the cloak in her hands, draped it over her head, and disappeared from head to toe. "See?" She took it off and dropped it to the ground.

Snow crossed the cell and gently took the keys from Hansel's hand. "Let me try these. It's an honor to meet you, Gretel. My name is Snow White."

She inserted each key into the padlock, jimmied it around a bit, and bit her lip. The keys didn't want to budge.

Gretel's face lit up like a Christmas tree. "Snow White?" she said excitedly. "Are you Mister Liam's girlfriend?"

"Why, I'm his wife," Snow said with a chuckle. She wrinkled her eyebrows, thought about what Gretel had just asked, and her lips parted. "How do you know of Liam?"

"I came here with him," Gretel said simply. "I came here with Alice and Mister Liam."

Snow felt both a firework in her heart and a tug in her brain, each side fighting over whether she should be elated or suspicious. The full gamut of emotions worked its way through her face: a smile, a frown, and finally, a gentle shake of the head. "Gretel, no you didn't, sweetie. Liam isn't . . ." She struggled with the right word to finish the sentence. *Alive? No, that doesn't feel right.* "Liam can't be with us."

"But he did come with me," Gretel insisted. "He's really nice."

"Hardly as nice as the young lass who set me free."

Snow's mouth dropped open as her lost husband stepped into view, jammed his dagger into the padlock, and opened the cage. After he slid the door open, he pocketed the dagger, extended his arm to Snow, and flashed that smile she missed so much. His touch could have set her on fire.

"Hello, my love."

Alicia led the way to the final cell, where two men, a woman, and a beast awaited the group.

Augustine's fingers were curled around the bars and her forehead was pressed against the cage, her expression riddled with boredom. When she saw Alicia and the group, she sighed. "Really, dear, you couldn't have rescued us sooner? We could have done all the fighting for you. We are professionals, after all."

"A little more respect for our heroes, Augustine," Jacob insisted.

"Did she bring rum?" Hook asked.

"When we get out of here, the lady gets a round on us!" Merlin said.

"Hua Mulan, is that you?"

Mulan pushed her way to the front of the group, plucked Liam's dagger out of his hands, and unlocked the cage. "Let's go," she said. "I want out of this fortress."

When they emerged from the prison, the group collapsed onto the ground and Pino stared up at the stars, which seemed to twinkle so much brighter than he remembered. Perhaps he'd been in the dark for too long.

"And so what do we do now?" he asked. "Now that we're all together?"

"We mustn't rest for very long," Violet said, folding her wings behind her. Her lips were tight as she stared up at the sky. Pino got the feeling she wasn't admiring the stars as he was. "Let's not forget that we still have a door to open. This must be our top priority."

"But we hardly know where to go," Alicia said. "Hansel and I have been everywhere looking for leads on what to do."

"It should have been in Frankenstein's book," Violet said. "I remember it clear as day. I believe that door goes to another world, and Frankenstein was doing research on interworldly travel. It was one of his tabs. Where is his book?"

"He took it back," Alicia said, "just before his lab was destroyed. I found it for him, and in exchange, he sent me to Wonderland to rescue Gretel."

"You shouldn't have given it back to him," Violet scolded. "We need it more than he does right now. We need answers!"

"Well, if it's any consolation, I think he's on our side," Alicia said. "He specifically told me that he hopes we'll meet again in the fight against Avoria. Although, you should all know that he's not entirely who he says he is. He's a man of many faces. I . . . I think we may have all met him at some point."

"That doesn't help. It doesn't!"

"If I may," Liam said, "one of the guards let it slip that your father didn't want us to reach Tower Nuprazel. Might that be the location of the door?"

"Tower New Pretzel?" Pietro asked. "Are there finally pretzels in the Old World? Because let me tell you something: You all have been seriously missing out here."

"Nuprazel," Snow repeated. "The name is so familiar to me."

"Great! Now how do we get there?"

Zid cleared his throat. "Allow me!" He puckered his lips, turned his nose to the air, and let out a long whistle that started off high, gradually got lower, and cycled between high and low two more times.

Pino thought of the police sirens he would hear in Virginia. Zid was a good imitation. When he finished whistling, he smiled and folded his hands.

Pino waited for something to happen, but nothing changed.

Wendy narrowed her eyes. "What did you just do?"

Zid smirked, his beard scrunching up like a big Brillo pad on his face. "You'll see."

Garon shook his head and pressed his fists against his hips. "Are you sure that was a good idea?"

"Of course it was. Now all we do is wait for our ride."

"You mean like those horses in the hills over there?" Pietro asked, aiming a finger in the distance. "Check them out! All of this for us?"

When Pino saw what Pietro was pointing at, his heart sank.

Despite Liam's adamant beliefs that his biggest trials would occur inside the prison, he was wrong. He'd managed to free everybody, keep them together, and escort them out of the building with little trouble, but then he looked to the hills and saw a large army closing in on the prison from all sides.

Forty men. Forty horses. Forty sharp spears aimed in Liam's face.

"Stand up, everyone!" Liam said. "Get ready to go!"

The group scrambled to their feet and huddled together, hand in hand and arm in arm. Liam remained in front of them with his dagger firm between his fingers as the knights closed in. The leader, Liam knew too well.

"Hello, everyone," Lord Bellamy said, clucking his tongue in shame. "This is awkward. A morsel of freedom, a triumphant moment of victory, and yet here you are, at the edge of forty blades ready to skewer your dying hopes and dreams. Did you really think it would be this easy to escape from Florindale Prison?"

Liam gritted his teeth and spread his arms beside him, forming a weak shield over the crowd behind him. "Don't mess with my friends. We've come too far to die by your hand!"

"What's going to save you?" Lord Bellamy responded. "Your tiny little blade against forty spears and a hundred and sixty horse hooves? The odds are laughable. Drop the blade, and we'll show you mercy by returning you all to the cells in which you belong."

In a blink, Merlin, Augustine, Mulan, Hook, and Jacob formed a fence in front of Liam, each poised for battle. "This man is our *rightful* future king," Augustine said. "He is not to be touched, unless you'd prefer to feel that spear inside your—"

"Augustine," Jacob said calmly. "Please."

"—nose," Augustine finished defiantly.

Lord Bellamy cleared his throat. "Ms. Rose, just because you are an elderly dame does not mean I will exercise restraint if you press my temper. As King, I have full authority to act as I see fit. Thus, I may issue you all this ultimatum: Go back inside and retreat to your cages or suffer the direst of consequences."

"Father!" Violet cried. "Stop this right now and join us! You don't think we have a chance, but look at us. We stand united, and we're prepared to do anything to vanquish Avoria. If she truly frightens you so, stand up to her!"

"Shut up, foolish girl!" Bellamy glared at his daughter. "You'll be next to be punished for your insubordination."

"Sir," Hook spoke, "do you know who we are? We've confronted chameleon wolves and vicious dragons and the darkest spirits of the Cavern of Ombra. I single-handedly confronted the pirate Bartlebeard and his entire blasted crew when you were just a sniveling squire. We hardly see reason to fear a group of grown men riding into town on a parade of ponies."

The army snapped into a new formation, this time converging on the entire group. Each spear was a hair's breadth away from the tender skin on their necks. Hook began to sweat when the point scraped his stubble-spattered chin. "Okay," he croaked. "You've made your point. Might I invoke parlay?"

"Just keep stalling," Zid whispered. Liam noted that the dwarf's eyes were fixed on the sky. "Keep him talking."

"There is no more talking to be done, silver-tooth. I have made my final offer." Bellamy swung his spear over to Liam, bringing him to a grand total of five weapons against his neck. "William, I'll let you speak for your group. 'Twas you who wished to reason with me tonight, hmm? Surrender, and I'll spare your lives. Refuse, and everyone dies! Now, boy, what do you value more? Your freedom, or your lives?"

Snow screamed. "Liam!"

Liam closed his eyes and swallowed, his Adam's apple sliding up and down as his mind raced. *What do I do?*

Suddenly, Zid jammed his finger into the sky and smiled triumphantly. "My pets!"

The knights looked up, following Zid's finger, and Lord Bellamy screamed, "Retreat!"

Mass chaos erupted as Bellamy and all the knights attempted to steer their horses in a circle at the same time. An enormous shadow blanketed the group, and knights collided into each other and clattered to the ground. Liam swatted the remaining spears away with his dagger, grabbed Snow's elbow, and ducked behind a tree where he could get a closer look at what was happening. As soon as he tilted his head up, fire rained from the sky and annihilated a group of knights. Liam instantly knew what had occurred. A mixture of both frustration and relief coursed through him when Lord Bellamy thundered away on his horse. *He'll pay for threatening my friends.*

A huge shape descended from the clouds, gliding like a ghost ship in the wind with two massive wings instead of sails. There was also a shimmering red tail and a set of pointed, parchment-colored teeth coated in thick saliva. Liam followed the shape with his chin until the massive creature did a nosedive straight for the ground. It was certainly bigger than any ghost ship Liam could've imagined, and much scalier as well. When the creature landed, Zid smiled triumphantly.

"A dragon," Liam breathed. "It had to be a dragon."

Zid smiled. "Yes. Our chariot awaits."

"You're kidding," Pietro said. "We're *all* getting on this thing?"

"Yes. And we're going to Tower Nuprazel. Prepare yourselves."

CHAPTER FORTY

THE OLD WORLD: THE DRAGON'S WINGS

Travel by dragon wasn't a common form of transportation for anyone in the Old World, but the only ones who complained on the ride to Tower Nuprazel were people who had previously been on an airplane. More specifically, Mulan, Pietro, and Liam squirmed with discomfort the whole way. Violet was so uncomfortable she pushed herself off in the middle of the trip and decided to fly beside Draco the rest of the way.

Zid sat on the dragon's neck with a pair of reins in his hands while everyone else managed to squeeze knee-to-knee on the rest of Draco's back. Every time the creature's webbed, leathery wings came back up, they grazed Alicia's heels and actually soothed her. The whole ride made her feel more alive than ever before. A part of her was tempted to unhook the leather belts Zid had installed to keep everyone secure and lean forward to see the rest of the world below.

"And if you look to your left," Zid announced, "you'll see the lush banks of Ranita, where legend tells of Princess Swan having her first encounter and falling deep in love with Prince Nyle III. What a grand history we have from coast to shimmering coast!" The dragon swerved suddenly, and Alicia bumped her nose on Hook's shoulder. Complaints broke out in front of her, but Zid shook his head and waved them off. "And if you look to your right—"

"Zid," Liam chimed in, "I'm starting to worry that you're distracted.

Could you kindly end the tour and direct your full attention to steering your dragon?"

Zid put the reins in his lap and turned all the way around, giving Liam the stink eye. "Do I hear you offering to switch off, mister backseat driver?"

Liam fidgeted with his collar. "Actually, contrary to the princely stereotype, I'm not so good with dragons. Can you just tell us when we're almost there? My stomach yearns for solid ground."

Pietro leaned forward and tapped Liam on the back. "Are you afraid of flying, Liam?"

Liam clutched his stomach and squeezed his eyes shut.

Snow turned around and answered for him. "He's always felt that if we were meant for the skies, we'd have feathers."

Pietro's mouth dropped. "That's the stupidest thing I've ever heard. No offense. Do you like to swim?"

Liam scowled. "That's hardly the same thing. Zid, can we hurry?"

"With all due respect, your royal princeliness, can you put a stopper in it? Have some trust in ol' Zid! We'll be there in a few minutes."

THE NEXT DAY

Liam awoke when the dragon rolled over in midair. Listening to the sleepy grunts behind him, Liam guessed that everybody else had been sleeping as well. Everybody except Mulan, who sat alert and vigilant the whole time, and Violet, whose wings looked like they were about to burst into flame beside him.

Liam had nearly settled his stomach when Draco gave a violent jerk, dropping a very noticeable, scream-inducing six feet before steadying himself again. He thought of Mulan's private jet and its occasional turbulence. At least airplanes were enclosed.

"*Whoa!*" Zid shouted, pulling on the dragon's reins. "Keep it going, Draco! Only just a little more. I promise."

The dragon shook again.

"What's happening?" Mulan asked.

"Poor thing's exhausted from all the circles we flew," Zid explained. "He's ready to drop. I need to put him on the ground *now*." He patted Draco's neck. "Hang in there, big guy! Tower Nuprazel, straight ahead!"

Violet scrunched her face in anger. "Really, Zid, did you not know which way you were going all this time?"

"Oh, I knew," Zid answered. "I just flew us around in circles for a while because I wanted more time with my Draco."

Liam rubbed his temples and shook his head before he fixed his gaze on the landscape ahead. A magnificent white tower three times the height and twice the thickness of Clocher de Pierre popped through the clouds, nestled between two dirt roads that converged behind it and wound into a snow-capped mountain. To the right of the tower, frigid waters slapped a rocky shore, and that's where the dragon descended.

Hook broke the silence. "It rattles my bones to see this place. Reminds me a lot of a girl I once knew. I wager this is where I first met Rapunzel."

"Who?" Garon asked.

"Rapunzel. She was my first love," Hook recalled. "When I sailed out here from Neverland, she was the first beautiful face I ever beheld." He aimed his right arm to the top of the tower. "Up in yonder window . . . the only way to breach this tower."

The dragon landed with a rocky, bone-rattling *whumph,* and everyone disembarked. Violet reached over her shoulders and massaged her wings, rolling her neck.

Zid patted Draco's belly, scratching him like a dog. "Good boy, Draco! Who's a good boy? Go rest up and catch some griffins, okay? I'll whistle if I need you."

In response, Draco threw his head back and coughed a lance of fire into the air, making Liam cringe. The dragon flapped his wings, scooped a fish out of the water, and crawled into the nearby forest, its scaly eyelids drooping with fatigue.

Zid wiped a tear from his eye and blew his nose. "I wish he was still small enough to carry in my elbow."

"Oh, brother," Pietro said. "You're such a sap."

Liam stared up at the top of the tower, scratching his head in disbelief. "How ever did you get inside this thing? There's not a foothold to be found. It's smoother than butter."

Hook raised his good hand, holding up a finger. "Watch this."

He threw his head back and cupped his face, shouting at the top of his lungs.

"Oh, Rapunzel! What say you to dropping anchor with your shimmering locks for jolly ol' Jamesy? For old times' sake!"

The echo threw Hook's voice around a few times, but once it died away, only silence answered him. Liam kept looking up and waiting for something to happen, but the castle stood stone still and silent as a bone.

"There's nobody up there," Violet said. "I can't feel her presence. Princess Rapunzel went to battle with the other nine-hundred ninety-nine that day in Florindale Square, and she never came back here."

A fleeting hint of sadness and disappointment washed over Hook's face. With his nose in the air, he shrugged, turned around, and started to walk away. "Well, looks like we'll never get up there. The mission's over. Sorry, lackeys."

Violet sighed and gritted her teeth. "So done with *everything*," she said. She fluttered her wings, took off in the air, and sailed above the clouds without them.

Liam frowned and sat on the ground. "Well, I feel useless now."

Two minutes later, a rope came down and thumped Liam on the head. He gave it a tug to see if it was secure and then rolled up his sleeves. "I'm going up," he said. "Follow if you'd like, but this won't be pleasant."

For nearly an hour, Liam endured the arm-searing climb, occasionally wishing he still had the dragon. If Zid hadn't flown in endless circles and worn the infernal beast out, Draco could have let him off at the tower's entrance. Liam had to keep willing himself not to look down or think about the burn in his upper body. Every now and then, somebody would scream at him from the bottom. "*You can do it, Mister Liam!*"

As much as Liam appreciated the sentiment, he found the cries distracting and chose to ignore them.

Finally, he approached the tower window. His shoulders screamed when he hooked his fingers over the ledge. At last, it was nearly over. He wondered if he'd even be able to lift a feather tomorrow. His pulse raced as he pried himself up.

But at the top, his heart stopped. A gruff voice sounded from the tower's opening, spewing curses at the heavens.

"Meddling again, and so help me, Violet, I am going to get through to you!"

With a final push of his palms, Liam heaved himself over the wall and tumbled into a large round room lit by torches. In the middle sat Violet, her arms, wings, and legs bound to an iron chair. Her lips appeared to be sealed with a thick layer of putty, and her eyes were angled in defeat.

And behind her stood her father, carrying a torch and casting a fiery gaze in Liam's direction.

Lord Bellamy had beaten them to the top of the tower.

"Sir!" Liam exclaimed. "Mr. Bellamy, what in the stars are you doing?"

Liam would be forever haunted by the malice carved into Bellamy's face, hardening the wrinkles in his forehead and hollowing the skin under his eyes. The old man's expression didn't change when he answered. "I'm correcting our course once and for all."

Liam pulled himself to his feet, the nerves crying out in his upper body. He rolled his shoulders and touched his fingertips to his temples, smearing a layer of sweat on his face. He didn't know what to say. He peered around the vengeful lord, noting the wooden door that stretched dutifully from floor to ceiling behind him.

Bellamy's brows drew together. "For many years, I have stood idly by while my daughter carved a jagged path that I did not approve of. She poked around the labs of Dr. Frankenstein. She assembled a band of dangerous individuals known as the Order of the Bell. She meddled with mirrors and tempted the wrath of my wife. Worst of all, she allowed you to break her out of prison and escort her to this infernal threshold in Tower Nuprazel." The old man paused and reached into his robe with his free hand. "I cannot allow this door to open. William"—Bellamy produced a rusted blade and held it at the base of Violet's glittering left wing—"the path ends here."

"Sir!" Liam's heart jolted back to life. "She's your daughter!"

With a devious grin, Bellamy tilted the dagger and aimed it at Liam's face. "Then perhaps I should start with you. I should have cleaved the rope while you climbed, boy, let you plummet to your demise. Perhaps I'll mar your face instead. And *then* clip off her wings so she can never fly away from me again." He bent over and stared into Violet's eyes. "Violet, would that finally teach you to cease your meddling?"

A burst of anger erupted in Liam's gut. He made a fist and took a step forward, his voice deep and feral. *"Untie your daughter, Mr. Bellamy!"*

With a twist of the hip, Bellamy extended his dagger within an inch of Liam's nose. "Take one more step and I will skewer your heart! And this time, you'll never be able to return."

For a second, Liam stared hesitantly into the flame, not knowing what to do until instinct flooded his veins. He thrust his right arm up with whip-like speed, swatting Bellamy's wrist out of his face. The rusty dagger sailed out of Bellamy's grip and skittered to the edge of the tower. In the same instance, Liam's left arm shot out in front of him and he drove his knuckles into Bellamy's chest, causing the old man to stumble.

As Bellamy caught his balance, he jerked his arm to the side, bent his elbow, and lit the tip of Violet's wing on fire with a menacing grin.

Silver tears sprang to Violet's eyes.

"Look what you made me do!" Bellamy spat.

A startled breath burst from Liam's lips.

Tiny gray curls of smoke ensnared the room, and an indigo flame fanned across the tip of Violet's wing, filling the tower with a sickly aroma.

Liam rushed to Violet's side and attempted to quell the flame with his coat while her tears flowed freely in her lap.

The fire burned half of Violet's wing away before Liam managed to douse the flame. It had stopped only inches from her shoulder blade. Liam wiped the sweat from his forehead and peeled the putty from Violet's lips.

While Liam was busy, Bellamy jammed his torch back into a nook on the wall, raised his knee, and then drove his heel into Liam's side. Electric pain exploded through Liam's bones. While Liam resteadied his footing, Bellamy swooped across the room, his robe billowing in a dark curtain behind him. He stopped and knelt in front of his dagger.

As Bellamy took a knee, anger gripped Liam with a fire he had never known before, and hatred seized his body like a puppet master. Without a conscious thought, his fingers flew to his hip. He scooped up a cold, slender object in his belt and lifted his elbow.

He spun on his heel, twisted his torso, and flung the object in front of him.

It sailed with a momentum propelled by all of Liam's weight and doubled by his fury, carving a clean, straight path through the air.

When Bellamy straightened his back, Liam's dagger hit him squarely in the chest.

Time stopped.

Violet, her lips newly freed, drew in a harsh gasp. "Father . . ."

Liam's shoulders sagged, and he brought a curled fist to his lips. A wave of fear charged through his blood. *Stars, what have I done?*

Bellamy smiled wanly, staring down at the handle of Liam's knife. The old man dropped his own dagger and used both hands to pry the other blade from his heart. When he freed it and let it clatter to the ground, tiny spheres of blood bounced off the metal. Liam imagined he could hear each and every one speckle the floor.

"Sir!" Liam's hands jittered at his sides. He didn't know if it was the fatigue of the tower climb or the raw state of his nerves. "Mr. Bellamy, I didn't intend—"

"To hit me in the heart?" Bellamy wheezed. He chuckled until a sputtering cough burst from his lungs. "Of course you did! Your aim is true. *Hmm*. The white knight has a shadow after all." Another cough. "You'll need that when you're King."

Liam stole a glance at Violet, whose expression was surprisingly flat.

An iron weight pressed on the prince's lungs. *Did* he intend to hit Mr. Bellamy's heart? He wasn't sure. He took a hesitant step forward. "Sir, let me help you."

"Don't." The old man took a step back and shooed Liam away. His other hand rested over his wound. "I knew you and that foolish boy were trouble when you entered my diner and pried me from my happy New World life. I told you you would bring ruin. This is your fault, *murderer!*"

"Don't help him," Violet affirmed, eerily calm. "He's beyond help."

"Everything I've done has been for your protection, Violet," Bellamy wheezed. "You blind, simple, ungrateful heathen! Perhaps it is my path that ends here. But remember me when you stand at the edge of destruction. Remember how I tried to warn you. You are not prepared to face Queen Avoria. You will *never* be prepared!"

Lord Bellamy took another step back, and this time, his boot connected with the edge of the tower, throwing his weight behind him. Liam knew it was too late before he moved.

"*No!*" Liam dashed across the room as Bellamy lost his balance. "*Mr. Bellamy!*"

By the time Liam made it to the ledge, Lord Bellamy had already gone over and begun his descent to the ground below. The prince reached, desperately hoping to grab onto a finger or a fold in the old man's robes, but he was beyond saving. The life had already faded from Bellamy's eyes, leaving them cloudy and cold. His arms hovered above him as if reaching back for the surface.

Liam was certain that a part of himself went over the ledge as well, desperately reaching for something to cling to until it crumpled on the ground.

CHAPTER FORTY-ONE

THE OLD WORLD: TOWER NUPRAZEL

"Hansel?" The innocence in Gretel's voice nearly disintegrated Hansel's heart into dust. "Did you hurt my new friends?"

Hansel turned away so his sister wouldn't see his eyes water. He wondered when she would ask this question, but for years, he wasn't sure she'd ever have the chance to.

"I did what I thought I needed to do to save you," Hansel whispered. "All this time, I just wanted to see you again."

"So you did hurt them?"

"Sometimes, Gretel"—Alicia rushed to Hansel's side and stared into Gretel's eyes—"people do things they're not very proud of. Your brother probably isn't proud that he did some bad things. But he seems like he'd be a pretty good brother. Sometimes good people do not-so-good things."

Gretel didn't answer. She looked at the ground and put her chin in her hands, staring at the grass as if she were very deep in thought.

"Look!" Bo cried. He pointed to the top of the tower. "Someone's about to fall!"

"Who the devil is it?" Garon angled his hand over his forehead and peered upward. Hansel followed the group's gaze and locked his eyes on the dark robe that had approached the window. "That isn't Mister Liam *or* Miss Violet."

Mulan's lips flattened, her expression hard as steel. "Bellamy."

From inside the tower, somebody cried, *"No!"*

In the thick silence that followed, the looming shadow of Lord Bellamy stretched into view on the ground, growing harder, darker, and longer when the old man toppled over.

There were some startled gasps and a few hard winces throughout the group, but Hansel did his best to tame his shock as he scooped his sister into his arms, cupping his palm over her eyes. "Look away, Gretel."

But it was the sound that would truly haunt him.

I've just killed a man.

No matter how many times Liam repeated the thought in his mind, it didn't lose its power to tangle his nerves in stubborn knots and shred them all over again. He sat against the wall with his knees curled up to his chest.

I've just killed a man.

"My father deserved it, Liam." Violet, free of the ropes that had bound her, had begun to pace back and forth in the tower's room, her lips pressed into a hard line. "He deserved what happened to him."

"Did he?" Liam answered, much louder than he intended. Tears stung his eyes. "Did he deserve that?" He sniffled. "Nobody deserves to die in that way."

Violet stopped pacing and clasped her hands behind her back. She now cast an imperfect, asymmetrical silhouette onto the ground. She tilted her chin up and stared down her nose at Liam. "This is not a moment to be remorseful."

"I just killed your father!" Liam said. "You should be throwing me off this tower. Stars, I'm so awfully sorry for what I've done!"

"My father killed *himself* when he interfered with our war against Avoria. He had it coming."

"No," Liam muttered. "No, no, no, this isn't right."

"Straighten up, Liam," Violet said sharply. She knelt in front of the prince and laid her hand on his knee. "This was just another stroke of the carver's knife, Liam. Lady Fortune is shaping you into the man you need to be. You needed to do this before you'd be ready to kill Avoria. Straighten up," she repeated. She picked up Liam's dagger and casually wiped the blood on her gown. "I need you strong."

Pietro and Alicia climbed into the room. Silence thickened the air as they looked back and forth from Violet's damaged wing to Liam's vacant expression.

"What happened?" Alicia asked.

With a turn of the heel, Violet approached the door. "Prince Liam has corrected our course once and for all."

Pietro peered over the ledge, and then looked back at Liam. After a moment's pause, he wrinkled his brows and pointed at the prince. "*You?*"

Liam shut his eyes and nodded slowly, feeling as though his head were made of iron. "Aye."

Alicia frowned. "So we're safe now. We're safe from Mr. Bellamy."

"There will be ramifications," Violet said. "It's only a matter of time before my father's supporters learn about this, and then we'll have to answer for his death. Perhaps one day they'll see the folly in serving my father, and with Lady Fortune's grace, they'll join us in our fight against the Ivory Queen."

Pietro's shoulders wilted.

"And now," Violet said, "we must open this door."

She folded her hands across her waist and studied the door, a strange combination of oak wood and shimmering blond hair. Liam had the impression that it led nowhere. Violet offered the knife back to him, but looking at the weapon chilled his blood.

When Liam didn't accept the knife, Violet turned and held it out to Alicia. "Dearest Alice. Will you do the honor, please?"

Liam watched as Alicia nodded, and then she carefully picked up

Liam's dagger and walked over to the shimmering door.

Alicia tried to turn the doorknob. It didn't budge. So she studied the lock and rubbed it between her fingers. "Are you ready?"

Violet nodded.

"Be careful," Pietro warned.

Liam watched as Alicia ran his blade across the lock. White light burst through its fibers and filled the room. Liam shielded his face, and when he peeled his hand away from his eyes, the door had lost some of its shine.

"Try the doorknob now!" Violet said excitedly.

This time, Alicia rotated the knob in a half circle, but the door didn't budge. She pressed an ear to the wood, concentrating and listening for any indication of what was happening on the other side.

After a minute, Alicia slumped her shoulders, turned around, and shrugged. "I'm sorry, Miss Violet. I'm afraid we haven't done much. This door's locked from *both* sides."

CHAPTER FORTY-TWO

WONDERLAND

Crescenzo's legs had turned to Jell-O about halfway to the lake, but he refused to slow down. For one thing, he couldn't wait to leave Wonderland. Plus, he had over five hundred people walking behind him.

He turned to Rosana powering along beside him. "Know who I feel like right now?"

Rosana shook her head. "Who?"

Crescenzo smirked. "I kinda feel like Moses, leading all these people out of here like this. It's kinda funny, you know."

"It's not that funny," Zack said, his tone flat. "Did Moses lead the Egyptians to do battle with a psycho queen?"

Crescenzo's lips fell into a pout. "Well, no, but—"

"Then no," Rosana said. "Stop trying to be inspirational. None of these people are going to take you seriously if you try to part the Wonderlake with your arms."

Geppetto spoke up. "If you want to inspire these people, Grandson, you have to let it come naturally. You can't force it on them. That's how monarchs fall."

"I'm not trying to be inspirational," Crescenzo said. "I'm just saying—"

A smug smile breached Zack's face. "You've *got* to do something about that nose problem, man."

"What?" Crescenzo brought his hands up to his face, relieved that there hadn't been a change in size. He socked Zack in the shoulder. "C'mon, that's not funny!"

"It's always looked a *little* funny to me," Zack said. "Just kidding."

Tahlia caught up with a couple of long strides and tugged on Geppetto's shoulder. "Hey, are we almost there? People are starting to get impatient."

Geppetto glanced over his shoulder, and Crescenzo followed suit. Everybody was walking peacefully, making polite conversation with new friends and stopping to help one another keep up. "They don't look very impatient."

Tahlia sighed and rolled her eyes. "Okay, maybe *I'm* getting impatient. I'm bored. Can I at least ride the cat so I can take a nap or something?"

Chester faded into view ahead of the group, trampling on mushrooms and grass. "Only if you promise not to kick me like a horse," he said through the bone in his mouth. "Also, I am not liable for any damages if you fall."

Tahlia grabbed a handful of cat fur and hoisted herself on Chester's back without another word. She went out like a light.

"Are you coming with us, Chester?" Zack asked. "We could use more talking invisible cats in the New World."

"No, no, I shall remain here," Chester answered. "As much as I would love to meet a nice otherworldly hound, my place is here in Wonderland, with the white rabbit and the caterpillar and all those poor souls who need to rebuild after the war on Wondertown. Surely you understand?"

"Yeah, I guess," Zack said. "I get it. I couldn't handle a lifetime of allergies anyway."

"You think they'll be all right?" Crescenzo wondered. "All the ones who stayed behind?"

"They'll be all right," Geppetto said. "I spent a lot of time with them. Mark my words. Now that they can think for themselves again,

I'm sure they'll rebuild bigger and better than ever."

Rosana started to drag her feet a bit, obviously deep in thought. "You think we'll ever have a chance to see it? When they rebuild, I mean?"

"I think you'd be wrong to discount anything as impossible," Geppetto said.

That got a quiet nod out of everybody. Crescenzo knew it was true. Life continued to surprise him every day, and it probably wouldn't slow down any time soon.

"Are you afraid?" Rosana asked quietly. "After everything Avoria said to us?"

Crescenzo thought about his answer, rubbing his chin as he walked. He thought about the Ivory Queen and the way her very sight chilled his blood when she showed up on the screen. "Am I afraid?" He thought of his father, and then he shook his head. "A little, but more than anything, I'm just mad. But you know what, guys? I'm *glad* we ended up here together. After everything we've just gone through in Wonderland, I feel like we're stronger. More ready."

Rosana smiled.

"But there is one thing she said that I can't stop thinking about," Crescenzo continued.

"What is it, Enzo?" Zack narrowed his eyes.

"Do you guys have any idea what she meant about it? That one thing she said about . . . not being certain she wouldn't . . . need me?"

Nobody said anything for a while.

When the clouds parted and the stars appeared again, Crescenzo felt a chill. He found that it was almost impossible to look up at the skies without imagining the two warring kings somewhere above him, locked in combat and spinning out of control. Could they even survive like that? Would they ever stop fighting? Could they have made things right if they'd just lowered their weapons for five minutes?

What a strange world we live in.

"Don't let that be you," Geppetto said, slowing his walk after what seemed like hours of travel. His gaze was on the stars, and his lips were pressed into a flat line. "Promise me that one thing, Crescenzo."

Crescenzo looked back at his grandfather in bemusement.

"You know what I mean," Geppetto continued. "You've seen the destructive effects of war now. It's going on around us, in worlds between us, and even up above us. This war against Avoria may be necessary to protect our loved ones, but before you get caught up in hate, I want you to remember what you've seen here. Before you make a single move, remember Wonderland."

Crescenzo chewed on his lip. "I don't think I can ever forget. I can't even look at the stars anymore without seeing them tumbling away like that."

Geppetto laid a hand on Crescenzo's shoulder. "No, no, boy, don't let war obscure the beauty of the stars for you. The sky is the only thing we all get to share." He raised a bony finger and squinted at a twinkling dot up above. "Except *that* star up there. The brightest one. That one's just for me."

"Noted." Crescenzo smirked, focused on the star, and made a wish.

When Crescenzo looked down, he noticed that the ground was tanned and filled with jagged little cracks, like he was walking on a giant jigsaw puzzle. The ground went on like this as far as he could see, and apparently he'd been looking up for so long that he never noted how long he'd been walking on the dry mud.

Geppetto stopped and took a knee, rubbing a big slab of ground shaped like the state of Texas. "I'll have you know that we're in the middle of the lake now," he said. "It's time to carve."

"It's time?" Crescenzo planted his foot and studied the area around him. It tingled with life, buzzing in his toes and the tiny little muscles in his fingers. It was almost as if the land had a heartbeat, tapping at the worn rubber of his shoes. He held up a hand, turned around, and projected as loud as he could. "Hey everyone, stop!"

"Is this the place?" Rosana asked.

Seeing Crescenzo's excited expression, she and Zack both held up their palms and called out for the crowd to stop walking. "We're here!" The five hundred people behind him slowed to a shuffling stop, whispering excitedly as they picked a spot on the dry lake. Some plopped their bottoms on the ground while others chose to lie down, and many others were too excited to sit.

Chester popped into view with Tahlia still dozing on his back, and he stretched so far he reminded Crescenzo of a Slinky.

Geppetto drew his knife and put a palm on the ground. "Yes, this is it," he said. "We just need to find the exact spot. I must confess something, Crescenzo. Up to this point, the largest entity I've ever carved was the tree I used to build your father. I've never actually tried to carve the land before. I'm not sure we'll have the endurance. We could be working at this for days, even if we do it together."

Crescenzo closed his eyes and kneeled, his palm on the handle of his father's knife. He felt an assortment of curious stares seeping into him as he traced a rough crack on the ground. "I think you're wrong, actually. No offense."

Geppetto frowned. "Wrong?"

"Yeah," Crescenzo said. "This isn't going to take long at all. We're in a pretty big area, but the actual design here is really small." He closed his eyes and studied the beat of the land, letting it sync with his pulse. "Can't you feel that? It's not a big carving, it's just . . . a *powerful* one. Something really wants to be set free here."

"You're sure of this?" Geppetto asked. "Because I've been doing this all my life, boy, and I'm telling you there's something *big* under our feet right now. Bigger than this whole group put together. We're going to need some help with this."

"No," Crescenzo insisted. He started walking to his left, staring intently at the ground the whole time and walking heel-to-toe as if tracing a line. "I get what you're feeling, but this really isn't anything big. It's gonna be like shaving a toothpick out of a forest." The crowd parted as Crescenzo walked into the center, and by the time he stopped, his followers had formed an inquisitive circle around him and Geppetto. Crescenzo pointed his chin at the ground and dug into a crack with his heel. In his mind's eye, a misty gold keyhole appeared, no bigger than the circle he could make with his thumb and forefinger. "It's right there. Do you see it?"

Geppetto squinted, peering through and over his glasses to look at the spot from different angles. Finally, he shrugged. "No, but I can still feel all that energy. If you think you see something, go for it."

"I do." Crescenzo got on his knees, wiped the blade with his shirt, and rubbed some of the dirt away from the gold keyhole.

"Wait," Rosana said, putting her hand over the spot where Crescenzo was about to dig. "I feel all that energy, too. It's big."

Excited whispers and confused chatter broke out among the group.

"*Do you think it's a kraken?*"

"*I think it's a goose.*"

"*No, it's clearly going to be a bear.*"

Crescenzo furrowed his brows. "Well, what do you want me to do?"

"I trust you," Rosana said. "But for the rest of us"—she looked around—"I think we should at least stand back. As far back as we can."

Taking the cue, Zack made wide sweeps with his arms and shooed the crowd into a grand circle around him. "Stand back! Put lots of room between you and this spot! Make a big circle along the edge if you can!"

Crescenzo twiddled his thumbs. "Really, Rosana? You think it's that bad?"

"I just think you should be careful, okay?"

"Yeah."

Rosana flashed Crescenzo a smile that warmed his bones, and then she sprang back into the edge of the circle.

Kneeling across from Crescenzo, Geppetto rubbed the side of his blade along his sleeve. "Let's do this one together," he said. "Like I told you, I can't see it, but if you tell me where to carve, I want to be a part of this."

Crescenzo carefully traced the keyhole with his finger and prepared to dig. "You take the circle part," he said. "I'll do the triangle."

"Okay." Geppetto gave his grandson a knowing nod and followed up with a wink. "Let's get out of here, Grandson."

"Right."

And so Crescenzo and Geppetto dug their blades into the ground, each taking an opposite tip of the keyhole and working clockwise. With every millimeter, Crescenzo felt the ground tingle a little more fervently, as if it were a giant stomach gurgling beneath him. He took special care not to stray from the lines, opting for tiny and accurate strokes rather than long and rushed ones. Geppetto did the same, but he finished his circle within two minutes while Crescenzo started on the third side of the triangle.

I'm coming back for you, Mom and Dad, he thought, his breath catching in his throat from all the excitement. *Pietro, when we hang out again, I will personally buy you Starbucks.*

What will I even say to Violet and Mulan, and Prince Liam? Wayde? He couldn't wait to see them all again and tell them about his strange adventures in Wonderland.

"Almost there," Geppetto said, observing Crescenzo's progress.

"Yes." *Closer . . . closer . . . closer . . .*

Done.

The gold keyhole vanished in a white puff of mist.

Before Crescenzo could smile with satisfaction, he felt himself fall as the ground opened up and imploded beneath him. His heart shot into his throat, and the world became a blur of crumbled mud and screaming men and women. Geppetto's cheeks wobbled as he fell along with him, and Crescenzo panicked when he realized his knife wasn't in his hands anymore.

He didn't fall for long before his toes dug into a combination of solid ground and chilled water. He caught his breath, looked around, and realized that the ground had opened into a hollow basin about fifty feet deep at its center, where a tiny keyhole rested by his knee. From the keyhole, a powerful jet of water rocketed into the air and rained upon Crescenzo and his friends. Thankfully, it didn't appear that anybody had been hurt aside from some mild scrapes, but the water was a major source of panic. It spurted like an aquatic Vesuvius, pumping what seemed like a limitless supply of water at a staggering rate. Crescenzo thought of Old Faithful and how it was supposed to be the most powerful geyser in the world. He wondered what geographers would say if they saw this tiny keyhole shooting thick lasers of water into the air at a rate that would put Old Faithful to shame.

Crescenzo was so impressed and terrified by the sight that he didn't feel himself sinking until he was already waist deep in water. The basin was already half-full, and people were scrambling for the steep, rocky walls to let themselves out.

"What did he do?" a terrified woman asked. "I thought he was getting us out of here!"

Crescenzo's heart drummed on his ribcages. *What did I do?* He looked around for Rosana, Zack, or Geppetto. "Rosana!" he called, kicking his legs to stay afloat. "Zack! Grandpa! Tahlia!"

When none of them appeared among the crowd, a terrifying thought crossed Crescenzo's mind.

Zack can't swim.

Crescenzo used to make fun of him for it because it was the *one* physical activity that he could actually do better than Zack. But now that they were in a fifty-foot bowl of water, there was nothing funny about the thought of his best friend drowning.

With that, Crescenzo held his breath and went under. The world became a murky cerulean, fuzzy and blurred. He tried to swim around and get a good view of the people near him, but his pants clung to his calves and his soaked leather shoes suddenly felt bulky. Hoping to increase his mobility, he yanked them off and let them sink to the bottom of the basin. After struggling to peel off his tux jacket, his shirt, and his socks, he kicked his way to the bottom, where the keyhole had finally calmed down. It rested unassumingly between two red shrubs, which swayed mystically in the water.

Above him, four hundred pairs of feet kicked and scraped the walls, but nobody appeared to find the proper footing to get out. Other people swam around him, evidently looking for loved ones or some sort of solution to get out.

A thin object rested at the bottom of the bowl, and Crescenzo kicked his way over to it. He had found his knife again. He jammed it into his belt loop and continued to search.

Just before he felt like he had to come up for air, a body drifted past him from above.

"Zack!" Crescenzo attempted to shout, but he only managed to spit out a mouthful of bubbles.

His friend sank like a feather falling out of the sky, still clad in tons of leather that stuck to him like a rubber glove. Zack's hands were skyward as if reaching for the surface, and his legs were tense. His hair fanned out in leafy spikes, and his eyelids drooped like he'd been in math class all day.

Crescenzo rocketed over like a dolphin and grabbed Zack's collar. He looked up and kicked with all his might, his thighs feeling as though they might burst into flame or break off and sink to the ground. The worst part: He probably wouldn't have been surprised.

He powered upward, his lungs gradually turning to cement with Zack feeling heavier and heavier underneath him. Every other second, he glanced at his friend and looked for any sign that Zack was still conscious . . . a twitch of the eyelid, a jerk of the heel, a bubble trickling from the lips. Zack's stillness only made him panic, and he felt himself rapidly running out of air.

Come on, he thought, *just a little farther. I'm so close!*

So close . . .

So . . . close.

Crescenzo's eyes started to droop, and his kicks slowed to a dull flutter. His fingers remained tightly hooked under Zack's collar, but the rest of his body was shutting down.

As his vision went dark, he felt a firm hand close around his fingers and pull. He was ascending again. *Did I just die? Am I floating up to Heaven?*

Blissfully, his face broke the surface of the water, and it was the best relief to feel the air again. His mouth opened and drew in a deep breath. Midway through, Rosana's mouth was over his. Sparks crackled in his brain. Or perhaps it was the stars he saw when she let go of his wrist and slapped him. "Dammit, puppet boy, you have to stop scaring me like this!"

Rosana kicked a few feet over and hoisted Zack to the surface, shaking his shoulders until he jerked back into consciousness. He sputtered and coughed and writhed in her arms. "We're all wet."

"And *you,*" Rosana said to him, "you can stop freaking me out, too. Do you think you two can do *anything* without almost dying on me?"

Crescenzo hacked up a stream of water. "Might be kind of a stretch." He hugged Rosana and looked around the basin. There seemed to be considerably less people than he had started with. "Where is everyone?"

Zack coughed, swallowed, and raised his hand up. "Can I just say that I'm—?"

Crescenzo didn't pay attention to the rest of his friend's words. What really caught his attention was what happened while Zack was talking. With every word, his voice grew higher and squeakier until he sounded like a chipmunk. Even stranger: He was *shrinking,* and it was happening at an alarmingly fast rate. One minute, he was six-foot-one, and the next, he looked like a leprechaun. Then a dog. Then a puppy. Then a flea, and Crescenzo had to squint to see Zack at all.

Zack went on talking as if nothing had happened, making casual hand motions and bobbing along on the surface of the water.

Crescenzo clapped his forehead. "What the . . . ?"

"Look!" Rosana said, gesturing to the basin walls. "It's happening to other people, too! There's Tahlia!"

Crescenzo turned around and saw his new friend shrink at the same rapid rate, followed by several other people who had followed him here. Some people shrank in and then down. Some got really, really short first before becoming really, really skinny. For many people, it happened all at once. They bobbed their heads under water, came back up, and then compressed into a tiny little speck of themselves a second later.

"Rosana," Crescenzo said, "we have to drink the water. That's what's happening to them. They're drinking the water and it's shrinking them down."

There was a faint gust of wind, and the water began to swirl around them at a slow, steady rate. Rosana shook her head. "But how will we climb out if we're so tiny?"

Crescenzo pointed down below him as the water began to swirl a little faster, pushing them around the basin like Cheerios in a bowl. "See how the water's getting a little lower? We're not supposed to climb out. We're supposed to go *through*. That's why I carved that keyhole. This basin's going to flush us out of here."

Somehow, he found the idea quite fitting.

"Let's drink," Rosana said. "And make sure you go through that keyhole!"

Rosana dunked her face and swallowed a mouthful of basin water.

Crescenzo dipped his head underwater and drew in a deep sip. When he swallowed, he felt the effects immediately. It was like his bones were melting, like he was trying to squeeze his foot in a shoe that was a full size too small, or like a giant pair of hands trying to press him like Play-Doh and pack him in a little tube. While it didn't hurt, it was definitely one of the most uncomfortable sensations he ever experienced, and he never wanted to do it again. As for what he saw, it seemed more like the world around him was growing. The basin expanded by a thousand times, and with all the ripples and waves washing over him, he felt like he was lost at sea.

He also saw one of Zack's aquamantulas pumping eight furry legs that appeared to have gills on them, and Crescenzo decided he would rather fight the King of Hearts all over again than spend five more minutes in the water with an enormous sea spider.

I really hope that thing isn't coming with us.

The water continued swirling, feeling more like a tsunami with Crescenzo so much smaller, and he let himself roll along the surface until he could muster the strength to dive. Sure enough, he saw all his friends and the people of Wonderland attempting to swim for the keyhole at the bottom of the lake. It was strange to look at the hole from his new perspective. When he carved it, it was barely two inches around. Now, he was looking at an opening wider than the tunnels of New York.

His efforts to swim were useless. The current caught him too strongly, hitting him like a wall, and Crescenzo decided there was nothing left to do but let the water do the rest of the work. He imagined an invisible spoon the size of a skyscraper stirring him around the basin.

I'm at a water park, he thought. *I'm in a mad, twisted water park.*

Crescenzo forced himself to smile and enjoy the ride as he spiraled through the water like a bug in a tornado, whizzing around in hundreds of increasingly tiny circles until the whirlpool shot him through the keyhole and into its dark depths.

CHAPTER FORTY-THREE

THE OLD WORLD: TOWER NUPRAZEL

"I don't understand why Violet can't just chuck a big handful of fairy dust at the door," Pietro said. "I mean, what good is magic if it can't even open a stupid door?"

Violet scrunched up her face and made a pair of fists. "Peter, it doesn't work like that. One person's act of magic cannot directly unravel another. You can only go *around* an enchantment. If an act of magic locked this door on both sides, there's no way to unbind the lock on one. We're going to have to accept that we've done everything we can on our side and trust that the other side will open when the time is right."

Pietro rubbed his chin, his eyes fixed on the ceiling. "Hmm, we can only go *around* an act of magic? So then let's chop down the door!" He turned to Garon. "Munchkin, let me borrow your axe." Seeing the dwarf's anger, he quickly turned away and approached Wendy instead. "Or here's an idea! Honey, do you have the credit card? This trick *always* works."

Wendy grimaced, but there was a hint of amusement in her voice. "Peter. Don't be daft."

"Oh! I have it!" Pietro fished a fraying coffee-brown bi-fold from his back pocket and slid one of his cards out of its slot.

Snow crept up behind him and peered at it, along with Augustine and Merlin and several others. Merlin scratched his bald head, and the women leaned in with their hands on their knees as Pietro approached the door. Pietro licked his lip while he slid the card up and down between the door and its frame, jiggling it and sawing at what he supposed was the lock.

Finally, Merlin yawned and walked away from Pietro. "What a dull, slow-acting magic. It hardly even does anything."

Violet gasped. "No, Merlin, don't trust it. I had one in Hollywood. It makes currency disappear."

Hook slumped back with his arms folded and his one heel against the wall, shaking his head. "Poor, poor Peter Pan, desperately trying to make yourself useful."

Pietro's arm froze, and he slowly turned his head to meet Hook's smug gaze.

Hook smirked. "I know you've been trying to ignore me, Peter, but our business remains unfinished. We cannot be ignoring that forever, lad."

"Yes you can," Violet said quickly. She rushed between Pietro and Hook, who had begun to take slow and careful steps toward the door. She spread her arms apart and pressed on Hook's chest. "I was worried about this from the start. I know you two don't like each other, but right now you're on the same side, okay? We all are."

Pietro dropped his credit card, stepped away from the door, and lowered Violet's hand so he could get closer to Hook. He pulled up his sleeves, rolled his shoulders, and met the pirate eye-to-eye. "No we're not. Hook's only on his own side. If we're all trying to save a world here, we can't trust him. If things get crazy, he'd throw us to the crocodiles to save himself first."

Mulan held up a hand. "Peter, I have to ask that you reconsider that statement. Whatever history you have with James, he has a longer history with the Order of the Bell. He's sworn himself to protecting the Old World at any cost. You may have your personal reasons for questioning him, but I've worked beside him for years. For what it's worth, I trust him."

Hook raised an eyebrow, half of his mouth shooting upward in a cheesy grin. At the same time, he scraped the tip of his hook along a scrap of metal in the wall, making a sickening grinding sound.

Pietro stared back, unwavering, his breathing heavy and his fingers twitching. Finally, Wendy scurried over to him and put her hand on his shoulder. Pino followed suit and approached Pietro from the other side. "Peter, let it go."

Pietro sighed, pulled down his sleeves, and pointed his finger in Hook's face. "Just stay out of my way, got it? You do that for me, and I'll do that for you." After a moment's silence, he stuck his tongue out as far as he could and muttered, "Crippled codfish."

As if Pietro had flipped a light switch in the pirate's mood, Hook scowled, lunged forward, and swung his arm toward Pietro. "Why you little—"

Click.

Hook's arm froze mid-swing, and everyone turned to stare at the door. "Did . . . you all hear that?" Pietro asked.

Silence.

Pino craned his neck and squinted while he listened. "It was probably just the wood settling."

As if defying Pino's words, the door flew off its hinges and knocked him on his back. The wood split into pieces, and he heard screams as a barrage of water thundered through the doorframe, flying like a sideways avalanche that knocked everyone down before raining over the ledge and onto the ground below. The only person who managed to avoid the rush of water was Violet, who struggled as she hovered to the ceiling and watched the stream from above. When the rush stopped, the doorframe vanished in a blink. Violet dropped to the floor, caught her breath, and cleared the water away with a wave of her wand.

"The light was with us."

Pino sat up and rubbed his sore forehead. When he took his palm away, there were many new people in the room. Pino only saw two and immediately broke down, for in place of the doorway stood both his father and his son, staring back at him in a mix of triumph and disbelief.

CHAPTER FORTY-FOUR

THE OLD WORLD
ONE HOUR LATER

"Until you have a boy of your own," Pino said, "you are never going to understand how it felt to be apart from you like that and to see you come back to me. You are never going to understand just what I'm going through right now."

Carla had her arm wrapped around Crescenzo's side and leaned on his shoulder. "I thought we'd never see each other again. I thought my life was over, but now I'm feeling like it's just begun. We're all together again. All together at last."

"With no secrets."

Crescenzo stared out at the ocean and let the mist speckle his face. Being in his mother's embrace and hearing his father's voice again warmed the base of the heart beyond any feeling he could've imagined. He used to think about what he would say when he saw them again— what he would do—but at first, all the DiLegnos could do was cry. They cried for the time lost between them and all the pain it brought. They cried for words unspoken before they'd been separated. They cried for everything his mother had just said: they were together at last, and they were a family again.

Crescenzo yawned, groggy from his exhausting trip through the keyhole. "It all just boggles my mind, you know? Everything I thought I knew and the way I thought the world worked . . . none of that was right. And it made me so mad until I saw you guys again. Every night I would tell myself that I was going to find you. That was the only thing I really cared about. I looked *everywhere* for you."

"And look what you found along the way," Pino said. "You'll look back on all this one day and know that you found adventure. You found strength and independence. You found out who you really are. And I'm guessing you found so much more than I could ever know just by imagining it."

"Hey, Enzo!" Rosana approached Crescenzo from behind, her mother at her side. "Are these your parents?"

Crescenzo leapt to his feet and rubbed the back of his neck, his cheeks suddenly feeling warm.

Rosana's mom gave him a knowing gaze out of the sides of her eyes.

"Yeah! Mom, Dad, this is Rosana. She's—"

"Your girlfriend?" Carla said excitedly. She and Pino stood and shook Rosana's hand while Crescenzo looked for some sort of cue on how to answer. He looked at Rosana's face for any sort of signal, and she looked back at him with a smile.

"Yes?" His heart fluttered.

Rosana nodded.

"Yes," Crescenzo repeated, swooping his arm around Rosana and pulling her to his hip. Not caring who was watching, he planted a kiss on her cheek. "She's my girlfriend."

"We're happy to meet you, Rosana," Pino said. "You look a lot like your mother."

"See, that's what *I* was saying!" Pietro called from behind.

Pietro, Wendy, and Zack shuffled over to the shore, arm in arm, and Crescenzo grinned, feeling a bit like he had just woken up to a family holiday. Man, he missed these times.

"Fun fact," Pietro said, "I totally called it before Rosana told me who her mother was. The very *minute* I saw her, I was like 'Are you Alice's daughter?' and I was totally right."

"That's not how I remember it," Crescenzo said. "It's great to see you again, Pietro. Wendy."

"*Enzo,*" Pietro said. "I have *missed* you and our crazy adventures, Kid. Almost as much as I missed *this* punk." He slapped Zack on his shoulder and broke away from him. "Meet me halfway, buddy!"

Pietro hugged Crescenzo, pulled him off the ground, dropped him, and turned around to hug Rosana. "By the way. You two . . . finally? Yes! I'm taking half the credit on this one, because I was kind of the wingman. I expect groomsman status, I expect leftover cake, I expect—"

"Yeah, whatever, Pietro." Crescenzo rolled his eyes, but deep down, he couldn't have been happier.

Pino grabbed Crescenzo's shoulder and gently turned him to face the giant crowd of people mingling by the tower. It was an interesting bunch indeed. A hook-handed pirate conversed with Mulan, Tahlia, an old woman, a slender bearded man in a robe, and a man who barely looked human. Prince Liam sat on the ledge of a wishing well with Violet and a beautiful woman. Wayde stood in a circle with five other men, all of them equally short and stocky. They each held a floppy cap in their hands, and their heads were bowed as if taking a moment of silence. A flame ignited in Crescenzo's stomach when he saw Hansel, but it quickly burned out when Gretel ran out from behind the tower and surprised him. This wasn't the same Hansel who had abducted Enzo's family and worked for the Ivory Queen. This Hansel liked to smile and laugh and play tag with his sister.

"I should introduce you to some people," Pino said. "You have a lot to meet and catch up with."

Far away from everybody else, Geppetto sat on a log and carved at a piece of wood on his knee.

Crescenzo smiled. "So do you, Dad."

"Isn't it nice to finally have some dinner together again, Rose?" Her mother's words gently wove into Rosana's thoughts as she nibbled at one of the best grilled cheese sandwiches she'd ever had. The whole time, she stared out the window of Midas's Pub and straight ahead at the enormous tower presiding over the Old World. "It's wonderful."

Crescenzo swallowed a truckload of pumpkin soup. It was his third bowl of the night. "Thanks for letting me join you, Mrs. T."

"Just call me Alicia. Or . . . you can even call me Alice, if you'd like."

"Got it, Mrs. T."

Rosana's mom chuckled warmly and rested her elbows on the table. After popping a few knuckles, she reached over her pancakes and grasped a dark lock of Rosana's hair. The touch nearly unspooled all the threads within Rosana's soul. How could she feel so much at one time? Exhaustion. Worry. Elation at having her mother back. The euphoric feeling of having Crescenzo by her side. Crescenzo, who had slowly woven his way into her heart like a thick, silent vine. And his hold was only going to grow tighter. Nobody endured the things they'd lived through without trust. Without shared strength. Without a shared *soul*. Without being willing to laugh and fight and be at least a *little* crazy.

"Is something bothering you, sweetie?" her mother asked. "Do you wanna talk, just you and me?"

"I'm fine." Rosana smiled back at her mom. "I'm just admiring the bell tower."

"It's pretty amazing, isn't it? It's a fixture. This world has seen it all, and that tower stands strong. It's like us." Her mom winked at Crescenzo. "No matter where we are or where we make our home . . . Old World . . . New World . . . we stand strong."

Crescenzo put his spoon down. "I heard something," he said. "Violet was talking to my dad. She knows how to get to the New World, and she wants to send people back there. Soon. *Before* we even finish training."

"Well, it sorta makes sense, you know? We need to know what things look like over there. What sort of damage Avoria's done already. What we're dealing with."

"But what if we all just stay here?" Crescenzo asked. "We're together again. That's all *I* ever wanted. Why not stay? Why do we have to fight?"

"It's not just about us," Rosana's mom said. "Avoria waged war on humanity. And we're the best shot against her."

"I wanna go," Rosana said, causing her mother and Crescenzo to turn their heads. "I do. If Violet is sending anyone to go first, I want to be there. I can take the cloak. I can go unseen."

"Absolutely not, Rose. I won't let you do that."

"Me neither," Crescenzo said. "And if you do, I'm coming with you."

"Crescenzo, that's very sweet of you, but this is *not* up for discussion," Rosana's mom said sternly. "We've put you two through enough already. You are not putting yourselves on the frontlines. I forbid it. Leave that to the Order. And assume nothing about Violet's plans until she calls us all together tonight. She's . . . unpredictable."

The more people Crescenzo met, the more he felt like he was at a large family reunion. Everybody seemed to know him already, whether it was through Pino's stories or something Violet, Mulan, or Liam had said already. Similarly, every time he learned who somebody else was, there was a strange sense of the familiarity from hearing their stories as a child. Meeting Snow White, for example, was a bit like meeting a faraway aunt or a third cousin. He'd heard so much about her already and seen illustrations of her, but the fact was that she was still a brand new figure in his life, and it was hard not to be star struck.

Crescenzo found that most people wanted to be known on a first name basis, such as Augustine, who happened to be Tahlia's grandmother. Snow White. Merlin the Wizard. The miners, Garon, Finn, Chann, Bo, and Zid, whose names Crescenzo would probably mix up time and time again.

The only one who insisted on a title was the pirate. After an awkward exchange where Crescenzo extended his right hand and quickly had to withdraw and switch with the left, the man raised an eyebrow. "You'll address me as Captain, understood?"

"Oh, James, do refrain from bullying the boy," Augustine said. "And as I understand it, you're not the captain of anything right now. Violet and Mulan are in charge until further notice."

"Your word may be true," Hook said, "but whoever's sailin' to Neverland with me best be prepared to obey my command. That, or they'll walk the plank."

"Neverland?" Augustine said. "Whatever are you babbling about?"

"So you haven't heard? Violet's sending me to recruit the Lost Boys. I'm to choose a mate to leave with me tomorrow at sundown." Hook swiveled on his hip and looked at Crescenzo. "Care to sail with me, lad?"

Violet flittered over and wrapped her arm around Crescenzo's shoulder. It took him all of two seconds to realize that half of her wing was missing, and a black burn framed what was left of the new jagged edges. He willed himself not to stare. "It is my wish that Crescenzo remain here for this next phase. He'll be more productive in Florindale, where our training shall begin soon. If you're looking for a partner, though, I'm sure I have the perfect candidate in mind."

Before Crescenzo could ask about Violet's wing, she sauntered away, leaving him in Hook's icy presence. Crescenzo caught a nervous glance over the pirate's shoulder, where Liam was shuffling around in the distance, making soft footprints in the grass.

"Liam!" With a smile, Crescenzo caught up to the prince. "Long time no see. Shall we clash fingers?" Crescenzo curled his hand and invited Liam to do a fist bump.

"Not now." Liam clasped his hands behind his back, flashed a weak smile, and drifted away, his gaze drilling into the toes of his boots until he disappeared into the Woodlands.

"What?" Crescenzo said under his breath. "No *hey how are you* or anything?" Crescenzo wasn't sure why the interaction had hurt so much. He dropped his fist.

A few seconds later, Snow White approached Crescenzo from behind. She had been in an obvious hurry, her face red and glittery with sweat, but she stopped and smiled at Crescenzo, patting him on the back as she caught her breath. "Enzo," she heaved. "Did my husband come this way?"

Crescenzo nodded. "He went into the woods. What's wrong with him, Your Majesty?"

"It's *Snow*," she corrected. "Liam is just dealing with some rough stuff right now. We all are, I suppose. How are you holding up? Do you need anything?"

"Well, I'm fine, but—"

"You're a hero to us, Enzo. Thank you. Now I hate to run so quickly, but I need to go catch *my* hero. Stay safe, okay?"

Crescenzo watched the princess run into the woods, and then he turned on his heel.

In the distance, Pietro and Zack lay side-by-side staring up at the stars. Crescenzo watched Pietro turn and scoop a ladybug onto the back of his finger. His elbow was pink and splattered with blades of grass. Crescenzo took a seat next to his friends, mulling over his awkward interaction with the prince. "What's wrong with Liam, Pietro?"

"He had to do a bad thing, Kid." Pietro blew the ladybug off his finger. "It's probably best if he tells you about it himself, when he's ready." He squeezed Crescenzo's shoulder and arched an eyebrow. "Hey, you okay? Wanna talk about anything?"

Crescenzo thought for a minute, his gaze trailing to a garish flash of purple in a nearby tree.

"What happened to Violet's wing?"

"Mr. Bellamy hurt her."

The words buzzed around in Crescenzo's ears, but he couldn't bring himself to process them. "Mr. Bellamy? Did he *burn* her? Where is he?"

"Gone," Pietro said simply.

"Gone?" Crescenzo repeated. "Like, back to the New World gone?"

"No."

The worry in Pietro's face filled in all the blanks. When it clicked, Crescenzo thought he might be sick. He'd never particularly liked the old man, but the idea of his death sent a shiver down his spine. This whole adventure had started with an innocent road trip. Crescenzo never imagined there would be casualties.

Crescenzo spent a few hours chatting with Pietro and Zack, with Alicia and Rosana, and then with his own family. The happiest part of the day was when he got them all to sit in a circle and talk together. They told old tales from three years ago and from thirty years ago. They talked about Florindale. They talked about New York. They didn't talk about Wonderland.

Finally, Violet fired some purple sparks into the air and called for everyone's attention. She turned in circles so that everyone could see her. "Wonderful ladies and gentlemen of the worlds united, I'm so thrilled to see you all together again! Cinderella, live in the flesh! Jack Frost! Benjamin Baker of Drury Lane! Welcome back, everyone!"

After some cheers and a moment where Crescenzo looked around in awe, not having realized that he had led *the* Cinderella and her friends through the keyhole, Violet continued.

"The New World is under attack by the same woman who took most of your souls. I think we know how dangerous that made her. She can fly. She can disappear at will. She can cast her land into eternal winter.

Those are only some of the things we know about her, and there are many more things we probably don't know. We are not yet equipped to beat her."

There was an uncomfortable murmur of agreement in the crowd, and Crescenzo felt a squeeze on his palm. He found Rosana standing next to him, and he pulled her hand next to his side.

"But we must do our part and end her reign of terror, which we can only do now that we've finally come together. Are we going to let Avoria control the New World?"

"*No!*" the crowd shouted.

"No!" Violet repeated. "Are we going to live in fear for the rest of our lives?"

"*No!*"

"No! So let us use this year to band together and train for the war to come. We are the New Order of the Bell, and we will protect our worlds at any cost! It's time to train, to work, to continue expanding our forces, and when Avoria least expects it, we will journey to the New World together and extinguish her!"

Mulan climbed up on a rock and raised her sword in the air. "Our work begins at dawn! Some of you will quest! Some will infiltrate the New World for recon! Most of you will train! If you do not wish to fight, make yourself useful. Help us make armor. Cook food and nurse the wounded. Offer kind words, and keep your morale up. When you're not training, spend time with your loved ones. Savor every bite of every meal, because we must *all* be prepared for the ultimate risks. Nothing about this will be fair or pretty until the Ivory Queen is gone. If you're with us, raise your right hand now!"

Before Crescenzo could do anything, Rosana brought her right arm up, lifting his left into the air. A sea of hands, paws, and hooks went up with them. Crescenzo smiled at Rosana, who had taken Zack's right hand and lifted his above his head as well. The three stood side by side and formed a chain, their arms forming two strong peaks between them. A warm grip took Crescenzo's other hand and joined him in midair. His heart smiled as his mother pressed her palm to his.

"There's my firefly." She rested her head on his shoulder. "I'm so proud of you, Enzo."

On Carla's other side, the chain continued. Pino. Geppetto. Gretel. Hansel. The miners. Crescenzo looked to his left and saw the chain continue next to Zack. Pietro. Wendy. Merlin. Augustine. Tahlia. Jacob. Cinderella. Benjamin Baker. Jack Frost. Hook. And behind him, many, many others had joined hands as well and raised them above their heads.

"For our worlds, for our dignity, and for our people!" Violet shouted.

"Let's eat and celebrate our alliance and the return of our heroes!" Mulan waved her sword in the air. She made eye contact with Crescenzo, and the two shared a brief smile. It was one of the rare times he had ever seen her grin, and it was something he could get used to. The world looked a little brighter when she smiled, or when anyone smiled, for that matter. Especially Rosana. He tried not to think that someday soon, some of that light they all shared might be snuffed out forever.

"Come tomorrow"—Mulan made a fist and held it in front of her face—"we begin."

TO BE CONTINUED

ACKNOWLEDGMENTS

Yes! We're here! Can I tell you how refreshing it is to fill a few paragraphs with positivity and nice, boring thank yous after splashing around in the dark for all that time? Ah, who am I kidding? The shadows are fun!

First of all, writing a sequel was a whole different kind of challenge for me, and if I would have attempted it by myself, I couldn't have pulled it off. From the outside, writing looks like such a solitary life, and yet I'm never alone. When you write a novel, you mix in all these flavors that you can't produce on your own, and you hope your story will soak them in so you can share the ingredients with the world.

My family helped me put the love and soul into the book. From my mom, who remains my biggest cheerleader, to my stepdad, sister, cousins, and new baby niece, my family has been instrumental in helping me navigate mental roadblocks and supercharge my passion for the life of a storyteller. I have to thank them along with countless great friends who added their laughs, encouragement, and wisdom: Silvia and Alicia, who provided wonderful feedback in the early stages of this book; Josh, who was the first to read the opening chapter as it exists today; Maggie and our adventures plus her priceless text commentary while she read The Carver; and friends like Zoe who add daily laughs and moral support when I can't be near my manuscript!

There are also my "muses" who add a healthy balance of

order and whimsy, along with a strong dose of imagination. I especially have to thank Krystal, my editor, for being an amazing book doctor. She's magic, and I've learned so much from her and the rest of my friends at Blaze Publishing. Thank you all for embracing my vision, and for being great pizza/coffee/BLTs/karaoke partners! On another note, I find daily inspiration in music and the arts, which are a universal language that fill us with joy and understanding. The music of Project Destati, Muse, and Lindsey Stirling fire up my ideas, usually without even saying a word. My characters have taken on identities of their own in my head, but I can't type certain names without imagining talented performers like Chris Pratt, Zooey Deschanel, or Brett Dalton, who is also one of the most genuine people I got to meet while this book was in progress. Then there's Mohammed, who creates phenomenal concept art for this series, Michelle, who dreams up these mesmerizing covers, and Eliza, who breathes life into the actual pages. I am forever a fan.

And, of course, I truly want to thank you, because since The Carver was published, my spirit has ballooned from your love and enthusiasm. I think all writers simultaneously love and tremble in fear of the what happens next question, but I'm so thrilled that you asked me to answer it for you. I can't wait to show you how the story ends!

So, let's meet again soon, because it's time to fight for the New World. When you're ready, take the second star to the right. Look for a little gold fairy that looks like a hummingbird, and make a wish.

ABOUT THE AUTHOR

When Jacob Devlin was four years old, he would lounge around in Batman pajamas and make semi-autobiographical picture books about an adventurous python named Jake the Snake. Eventually, he traded his favorite blue crayon for a black pen, and he never put it down. When not reading or writing, Jacob loves practicing his Italian, watching stand-up comedy, going deaf at rock concerts, and geeking out at comic book conventions. He does most of these things in southern Arizona.

You can find out more about Jacob on his website
https://authorjakedevlin.com/

THANK YOU FOR READING

Now that you've finished reading this book, we'd like to ask you to take a moment to leave a review. You never know how a few sentences might help other readers—and the author! And, as always, Blaze Publishing appreciates your time and support. Subscribe to our newsletter and get a free e-book! www.subscribepage.com/BlazePublishing

www.Blazepub.com

MORE FROM BLAZE

Rose Briar claims no responsibility for the act that led to her imprisonment in an asylum. She wants to escape, until terrifying nightmares make her question her sanity and reach out to her doctor. He's understanding and caring in ways her parents never have been, but as her walls tumble down and Rose admits fault, a fellow patient warns her to stop the medications. Phillip believes the doctor is evil and they'll never make it out of the facility alive. Trusting him might be just the thing to save her. Or it might prove the asylum is exactly where she needs to be.

THE
SURRENDERED
CASE | MAYNARD

blaze

After a financial collapse devastates the United States, the new government imposes a tax on the nation's most valuable resource—the children.

Surrendered at age ten—after her parents could no longer afford her exorbitant fees—Vee Delancourt has spent six hard years at the Mills, alongside her twin, Oliver. With just a year to freedom, they do what they can to stay off the Master's radar. But when Vee discovers unspeakable things happening to the younger girls in service, she has no choice but to take a stand—a decision that lands her on the run and outside the fence for the first time since the System robbed her of her liberty.

Vee knows the Master will stop at nothing to prove he holds ultimate authority over the Surrendered. But when he makes a threat that goes beyond what even she considers possible, she accepts the aid of an unlikely group of allies. Problem is, with opposing factions gunning for the one thing that might save them all, Vee must find a way to turn oppression and desperation into hope and determination—or risk failing all the children and the brother she left behind.

CPSIA information can be obtained
at www.ICGtesting.com
Printed in the USA
LVOW03s2029190417
531456LV00002B/2/P